# THE
# SNOW
# GARDEN

*a novel*

Christopher
## RICE

PAN BOOKS

First published 2002 by Talk Miramax Books,
an imprint of Hyperion, New York

This edition published 2003 by Pan Books
an imprint of Pan Macmillan Ltd
Pan Macmillan, 20 New Wharf Road, London N1 9RR
Basingstoke and Oxford
Associated companies throughout the world
www.panmacmillan.com

ISBN 0 330 49253 5

5 7 9 8 6

A CIP catalogue record for this book is available from
the British Library.

Printed and bound in Great Britain by
Mackays of Chatham plc, Chatham, Kent

For Laney
who remembers her dreams
and Josh
who inspired some of mine

# Inverness Creek
## March 1983

GROPING AT THE ICY TREE TRUNKS AND PUSHING BRANCHES FROM HIS face, he followed the sound of water flowing against the ice until it brought him to the edge of Inverness Creek. The haggard elms stood in regiments along the sloping banks of ice-slick mud. Veils of snow danced on contrary gusts of wind before vanishing into ice punctuated by sudden black pools of creek water. The music of Fraternity Green was an eerie, distant suggestion far behind him. Bursts of drunken laughter and the delighted squeals of young women, underscored by the bass thud of a stereo, barely filtered through the thicket of trees to where he stood, steadying himself on a branch, staring down at Pamela Milford.

She was lying facedown on a sheet of ice that bobbed in the struggling current, her blonde hair fanned forward from her head. A few strands draped the side of her face where her cheek puffed against the upward press of the ice, the corner of her mouth open slightly as if she was trying to draw breath. One arm was pinned beneath her chest; the other was frozen in mid-reach for the far bank. Her right leg shot outward at an awkward angle from her body. A miniature geyser erupted around the toe of the boot on her left foot, water spilling over the top of the ice, a puncture that revealed the frailty of the sheet she lay on.

From this distance, the red trail extending out from her neck could easily have been mistaken for blood. He knew better.

With a gloved hand he caressed the branch he held for balance, then yanked it hard. The branch broke free.

As he descended the bank, she was trying in vain to lift her head. It was no use. Each attempt brought her cheek smacking back to the ice, and she let out a groan.

He didn't have time to linger on the details of this image, no matter how much the sight of this broken woman chased the sting of betrayal from his veins. With both feet planted on the bank, he focused his attention on the clawlike branch as he gripped it with both hands, extending it over the ice. Pamela gazed drowsily into the ice and erupted into muffled sobs, coughing weakly with each ice-laced breath.

The twig tickled the back of her neck. She went to bat it away and missed.

When it caught the back of her scarf, his heart thumped and he tightened his grip on the branch, pulling and tugging until the scarf came free. The tails of red cashmere tossed in the wind as he lifted the branch high and out of her reach, retracting it slowly so as not to disturb the scarf's delicate balance on the spidery twig.

When it was close enough, he grabbed it and shoved it into his jacket pocket. He was about to toss the branch aside when Pamela heaved a groan of protest. Startled, he lowered the branch to his side and watched as she found some reserve of strength, rolling herself over onto her back and twisting her broken leg. Her mouth opened in a silent scream. The back of her head slammed back on the ice. She reached for her kneecap and failed.

He waited until she lifted her head once more and peered through the swirling snow with narrowed eyes. Her lips curled into her best attempt at a grimace, and the same arm that hadn't made it to her leg lifted itself from her body and extended a finger toward him. Breaths whistling in her nostrils, she stabbed the air with her finger as if trying to convince *him* that he was really there.

She couldn't hear what he was hearing: voices entered the woods, male. Their words were unintelligible, but their tone lit by obvious urgency. He tossed the branch aside and looked back over his shoulder. The muddy slope rose five feet, almost over his head, concealing their approach.

There was only one way to go. He turned back to the creek.

Keeping his steps light as the ice protested beneath him, he edged his way past Pamela and swiftly hoisted himself up over the opposite bank. His gloved hands grappled with mud for a second before he got a leg up. As he climbed, he heard a sound like a hand gathering tin foil, but he didn't look back.

At the top of the bank, he turned.

Where Pamela had been, shattered ice bobbed on the black current. He scanned the smoky glass of the rest of the creek, searching for a sign of her passage underneath.

Beyond the shattered ice, flashlight beams stabbed the woods.

He drove the crumpled scarf deeper into his pocket, turned from the creek, and accepted the invitation of the darkness on the other side.

# I

# Atherton

## November 2001

*Not slowly wrought, nor treasured for their form*
*In heaven, but by the blind self of the storm*
*Spun off, each driven individual*
*Perfected in the moment of its fall.*

—Howard Nemerov, "Snowflakes"

# CHAPTER ONE

THE NEON YELLOW SIGN ATOP THE YANKEE SAVINGS & TRUST BUILDING flickered to life at just pass three in the afternoon, its light-sensitive timer tripped by the tide of gray clouds advancing off the Atlantic, casting downtown into gloomy winter shade. Since the building's completion in 1984, the "townies" who lived at the base of the hill would joke that the tallest and newest addition in Atherton's meager skyline liked to send everyone home early during winter by announcing nightfall several hours prematurely. By five-thirty, the last of the insurance adjusters and bank tellers made the short walk to the railroad stations where they would board commuter trains that would carry them as far as Boston and Connecticut, leaving behind an empty stage set of art deco entrances and sidewalks blown clean of litter by the increasingly ferocious winds off the bay.

As the city below drained of life, Atherton Hill glowed with a corona of light. An early winter had stripped the hill; naked branches spiderwebbed among Gothic spires and Victorian rooftops and the streets snaked up the hillside toward the university campus, laid bare in winding concrete strips. The water of the bay usually warmed any snowfall into dreary sheets of rain.

By seven o'clock on the evening of November 14, fat flakes filled the halos of the streetlights lining the paved banks of the Atherton River, a black vein curving its way around downtown. The snow fell with rare and determined force, clinging to the pavement and refusing to melt. Shouts erupted across the crown of the hill. Dorm room windows flew open and students burst from the library, heading for the nearest cafeteria to commandeer its piles of trays to use as sleds. By less than an hour later, however, the hill had quieted, the continuing snow blanketing the campus with an eerie hush. At the base of the hill, squealing brakes and shattering glass broke the silence.

Headlights bounced across the whitening Colonial Avenue bridge, dancing across guardrail and then black water. A Volvo station wagon tore through the barrier, arced silently through the air for fifteen feet and vanished.

A small car stuttered to a stop and its driver got out, slipping on the snow as he jogged breathlessly to the torn opening in the guardrail.

Below, the black water of the Atherton River embraced the Volvo's upended taillights amid torn metal and ice. After the shriek of brakes and shattering of glass, the only sound now was the disgusting, rhythmic thump of air billowing out of the broken rear window in cartoonishly large eruptions. As the man watched the car withdraw from sight, he went to brace himself against the guardrail, but retracted his hands like someone wary of leaving his fingerprints on a murder weapon.


Kathryn Parker couldn't move her feet. She looked down and saw they were wedged under the wooden railroad tie of the tracks she had been standing next to only seconds before. She heard the mournful moan of a locomotive's horn, and then the tracks stretching out on either side of her erupted in a concert of metal against wood. She was blinded by the headlight of an approaching train, roaring toward her out of darkness that had been immaterial only seconds before. Her arms went up to stop the inevitable.

She awoke to the theme from *Shaft*.

Strange shapes drifted across the far wall and she sat up, groping for the halogen lamp next to her bed. The torchère sent light to the ceiling, its Styrofoam panels still scarred by the design of the beer bottle caps that she had found embedded in them on the day she moved in three months before. It was just past 8 P.M. Snowflakes were falling past the window, casting their shadows on the cinderblock wall on April's side of the room. Now that the roar of her nightmare had retreated, she was once again aware of the persistent and grating combustion of Stockton Hall, a four-story beehive of disconnected adolescents announcing their new collegiate identities with stereos turned up too loudly, wailing over the difficulty of their first midterm, their conversations ending in punch lines followed by explosions of forced laughter. Next door, the sounds of *Shaft* gave way to the earnest tones of television actors; it was time for the engineering freaks' weekly *Babylon 5* party. April had been the first one to point out that white Jewish boys from outer Boston seemed to have a propensity for all things Superfly. She didn't know how she had managed to sleep through it all.

Randall's story had caused her nightmare. She reached for it on her desk.

> The town of Drywater, Texas, exists because a woman named
> Elena Sanchez was killed by a train.

Randall Stone was her best friend at Atherton—maybe her *only* friend here or at home in San Francisco—and now he had managed to saunter into her dreams thanks to a short story that had chilled her with its detail, and stunned her with its rage.

> Elena's only son, Ricky, didn't find this out until he was
> fifteen.

She dropped the story to her desk, swung her legs to the floor, and padded barefoot across the threadbare rug—to the poor excuse for a vanity set into the wall between the room's two closets.

Since arriving at Atherton University, she had started remembering her dreams. Maybe it was leaving home and the constant effort she spent whiting out the first half of her youth that had shunted her anxieties from her waking life into her sleep. She raked one hand back through her sandy blonde hair, revealing wide eyes, still brown and not *that* bloodshot. Her fingers reflexively traced a path down to where her hair hit just above the shoulder, searching for split ends, fighting the urge to split them further. She caught herself, forcing her hand down to her side, and stared dead-on at a pretty-enough girl who had stopped being called mousy once she'd entered high school, whose breasts had exploded at fifteen before refusing to expand another cup size. She found herself unable to turn away from her own image, and the hands she had forced down earlier traveled back to her throat. Even as she told herself to stop, her fingers were prodding the soft flesh at the top of her neck, trying to find the pliable beads of her lymph nodes. Bigger than yesterday? Bigger than the day before that?

She clasped her hands in front of her face, breathing into them.

Was it the nightmare that had left her this shaken, or was it the recognition that this compulsion might never leave her? How many more test results would have to come back before a mild sore throat could be just that, a fucking sore throat?

The door flew open and she backed away from the vanity as if she had been caught fondling herself. She expected Randall—he had stopped knocking long ago, as if she were a sister whose moods he'd known since birth, and whose nudity could neither frighten nor titillate—but it was April who shoved her way through the door, bundled in her favorite leather jacket with the faux fur collar, her black braids flecked with white flakes. "It's snowing," she announced flatly, letting her book bag slide off one shoulder to the floor with a thud.

"How was the meeting?" Kathryn asked, standing awkwardly as April got down on all fours and dove headfirst into her closet, which was two feet deep and covered with a tattered curtain instead of a door.

"I need a beer."

She tossed a pair of her Gucci boots out behind her. They landed at Kathryn's feet.

"April?"

April rose, shoving the curtain aside on its rod. "Did you know there was a black national anthem?" She tore several hangers from the rack before depositing the pile of shirts onto her extra-long twin.

"No, I didn't," Kathryn answered. April had gone to a meeting of the African American Student Alliance, and from the tone of her voice, it was clear that her worst fears had been confirmed.

"It was like the first day of high school. I walked into the center and the only person that would even talk to me was Marcel. And you want to know what he told me after the meeting? It doesn't matter that his mother's Irish and his father's black. But with me, see, being biracial is a problem because all the *real* black women there think I'm going to steal all the good men. Good black men who would take a half-white woman over them any day. How's that for unity?"

Kathryn gently curved an arm around April's back, and rested her chin on April's shoulder. "So I guess you didn't tell them you were a dyke."

April's laugh was strained. In their first week of being roommates, Kathryn had gone from calling April a "lipstick lesbian" to a "Neiman Marcus lesbian." "Screw them, April," Kathryn said. "You want some reinforcement? Give the GLA a try. Trust me. I went with Randall once. They're hurting for patent leather and side-zip jeans."

"No thanks," April responded. "I don't feel like having a bunch of bull dykes hold me down so they can pierce my nose. It doesn't matter. Politics isn't my calling anyway." April dug into her jacket pocket and handed Kathryn a crumpled pink flyer. Andy Warhol's face stared up at her, superimposed on a wobbly, spiral top that looked like it had been sketched by a third grader.

"Frat parties are your calling?"

"It's Burton House. They don't card. And we're going. So get dressed."

"The literary frat? The losers that march a pledge naked on the green and make him do tequila shots while they dance around in llama costumes, right?"

"Hey, at least they get out of the room! You've been napping since we got here."

Kathryn tossed the invite aside and fell back onto her mattress with a groan. "I've got work."

"Waiting for Randall is not work!" April shot back. "Besides, I think he's going."

"No he isn't," Kathryn responded, sitting up suddenly.

April squinted at her. "Why? Because he didn't clear it with you first?"

Kathryn rolled her eyes, even though she had to admit she didn't know where Randall was going that evening. And she hated the nights he slipped away and left her on her own, unsure of how to negotiate Atherton without her partner in crime. She had dropped by his room earlier, daring to knock even though it might result in a face-to-face encounter with Randall's roommate, Jesse, and whatever completely naïve freshman female he had bagged for the evening. But both Randall and the walking penis he lived with had been out, and their closed door bore an inane sign announcing the names of the room's occupants in bright letters cut out of yellow, neon-colored construction paper. The resident advisor had taped one to the door of every room on the first day of Orientation, to propagate the homey notions that no nervous freshman would be anonymous at Atherton, but most students had removed or disfigured them. Randall and Jesse's sign remained intact, as if to highlight the odd pairing that lived on the other side, the gay Prada fashion plate who went on long walks with his finger in a novel and his Discman pumping synthesized dance music into his ears, and the aloof stud who rarely left his room because he was usually fucking someone in it.

She realized April had been talking for the last minute.

". . . guy looked like Paul Bunyan on crack, but we both took a flyer and Randall said he might be going if they didn't charge for shitty beer." April turned to face her suddenly. Kathryn hoped she didn't look caught, but April must have seen something in her eyes, because she crossed to Kathryn's bed and sank down next to her. "If you don't snap out of this, I'm going to buy those special light bulbs I read about. The ones that simulate sunlight for little West Coast girls like you who turn suicidal during winter."

"I'm from San Francisco. But nice try."

April smiled slightly, pleased that Kathryn was sparring with her again. "April, don't you remember my rule about frat parties?"

"Oh please. It's a *literary* frat, Kathryn!"

"A literary frat—yeah, right. What's next? A triathlon for smokers?"

April rose, shaking her head. Her gaze landed on Kathryn's desk. She picked up Randall's story. "What's this?" she asked. Feeling a strange stab of panic, Kathryn got up from the bed too. "I didn't know Randall wrote stories," April said distantly, scanning the first page. No sooner had she flipped the page than Kathryn tugged the story out of her hands gently. April looked to her with a surprised, slightly offended smirk.

"Sorry. I just don't know how many people he wants reading it."

"So he's a writer now? In addition to being the prince of Park Avenue?" Kathryn met the sound of her disapproval with an icy stare.

April softened. "Can you tell me what it's about?" She could sense Kathryn's protectiveness of Randall's short story.

Kathryn managed a slight laugh. The story was so peculiar it defied easy description. "It's about this kid who grows up in this small town in Texas—"

"And Randall's from New York."

"That's why it's a story. Should I finish?"

April rolled her eyes as if she couldn't care less.

"When he's a little kid, his mom gets killed in this car accident. Her car stalls out at this railroad crossing and she gets hit and dies instantly. Then the county finally decides to put up gates and warning lights because she's like the ninth person to get killed in that spot. So then . . ." April was holding up a collared shirt that looked like it was made out of aluminum to her chest and examining herself in the full-length mirror. "April, are you listening?"

"Uh-huh."

"All right, so when the boy turns fifteen he finds out that this entire town he grew up in exists only because the county put up the gates and people finally thought it was safe to live near the tracks. Basically, his mother had to get killed before anyone would build his home-town. So the kid just . . snaps. And one night, he derails the train."

Startled, April turned. "How?" she asked, her sense of logic offended.

"He saws through some of the railroad ties."

April's eyebrows arched. "If it was that easy to derail a train, wouldn't more fifteen-year-olds be doing it?"

"It's a story, April. And I don't think you're supposed to believe the boy really means to do it."

But even Kathryn wasn't sure. The descriptions of propane tanks lying in the smoldering cavities of tract homes and overturned trailers had been too emphatic, demonstrating a love of fire even as it con-sumed humans, and more than that a kind of rage she had never seen Randall exhibit in daily life. Or had she just missed it? Was there something darker lurking behind his warm-but-knowing smiles and his dreamy silences? In the retelling, the five-page story now had a dizzying effect, and she slid open her desk drawer and deposited it inside. When she turned, April was studying her, as if she understood the strange spell the story had cast over her.

"What's a Warhol party, anyway?" Kathryn asked.

"I don't know." April brightened at Kathryn's first sign of surrender. "Drugs?"

Kathryn winced. "One condition."

"Here we go!"

"If Jesse Lowry shows up, then I'm out of there."

April lifted both hands in a gesture of defeat. "Fine."

Dr. Eric Eberman wasn't sure what had awakened him, the mournful wail of the siren carried by the wind buffeting the walls of the house, or the feel of Randall Stone's teeth gently closing around one of his nipples. The bedroom window was rattling in its frame, and outside, the tree branches jerked in the streetlight's wan halo, their shadows latticing Randall's face, hiding and then revealing his pale blue eyes and slight, electric smile.

"I have to go," Randall whispered.

He bent down as if to give Eric a formal kiss on the cheek, and in response Eric curved an arm around his shoulders and brought the young man's body on top of his. Randall let out a gentle, almost placating laugh before his head came to rest on Eric's chest. As if he had needed only Eric's reticence to release him to reignite their passion, Randall slid one bent knee up between Eric's thighs, applying gentle pressure with his kneecap to Eric's crotch while his tongue traced a path up Eric's sternum, and then up one side of his neck before he withdrew, face level with Eric's. Eric allowed his lids to roll shut, giving Randall silent permission to lean in for a genuine good-bye kiss.

As their mouths met, Eric allowed his eyes to wander down Randall's naked back, fingers traveling leisurely over taut muscle beneath boyishly smooth skin, wondering how long before the first stab of guilt would come, that sudden weight that yanked him down from the delirious high of touching what had previously been prohibited to him.

Randall withdrew, lips lingering slightly, before he cupped Eric's face in his hands, gazing down at him with a sudden, penetrating stare. Randall's full lips and baby fat–padded cheeks could transform from a pout to a smile in a second, but a rigid jawline added years to his face when it tensed in anger, as Eric had seen whenever he came close to denying Randall what he wanted. Which, to Eric's silent delight, was usually himself.

As Randall rested his head against his chest, Eric's fingers touched the first puckered scar on the back of Randall's thigh, and he felt the young man tense, and then think twice, before letting himself go lax.

"Do they hurt?"

"Never," Randall answered.

"They must've at the time."

Randall grunted slightly as if to say he couldn't remember.

"Remind me how . . ."

"My mother was preparing for this big dinner party. I was three and she put me up on the counter so I could watch her cook. Or not get out of her sight. I barely remember. . . ." Randall paused, as if trying to summon the recollection. "I just remember this entire pan going up in flames. It was like this big curtain of fire. I fell and just started running. My mom caught me and put me out before I set the whole apartment on fire."

The first time Eric had asked about the burns covering Randall's legs, his description had been more vivid. The pan had tipped. His mother had screamed when she knocked it over. Three-year-old Randall had fainted the moment he saw his legs on fire.

"I thought you blacked out the second it happened."

Randall lifted himself off Eric's chest.

"I must have." He kissed Eric's forehead firmly. "Because I don't remember any pain. Maybe when you're that young the mind protects you from pain more than it does later in life."

Outside, the first siren was joined by a second.

Randall slid out from Eric's arms and swung his legs to the floor. He reached for his pack of Dunhill Lights on the nightstand and extended one to Eric. Eric didn't need to shake his head. Randall knew he wouldn't smoke. They shared their silent joke—that the man who had just cheated on his wife with one of his male students wouldn't be caught dead with a cigarette in his mouth. Randall lit it and crossed to the bedroom window. Eric saw the snow for the first time, framing Randall as he stood naked in front of the glass, one arm braced against the panes over his head, where a curl of smoke crept from his fingers through the streetlight's frail glow.

It was ironic, Eric thought, the way Randall's sudden departure from the bed constricted his breath, while the young man's pressure on top of him seemed to push blood and oxygen at a vital clip through his veins. Only several feet away, Randall seemed strangely and quickly withdrawn.

"Where are you going?" Eric asked, suddenly aware that the idea of Randall leaving him alone again twisted something tight in his stomach.

"A party."

"So I was just a pit stop?"

Randall turned from the window. "Are you asking me to spend the night?"

"She's not coming back."

"I know." Randall returned his attention to the flakes falling with determined force past the window.

"Sometimes I think she might never come back," Eric added, unnerved by Randall's silence.

"That would be easy, wouldn't it?"

"What do you mean?"

"I mean it would be easier than leaving her."

A bolt of silence struck. Eric fought the urge to ask Randall if that was what he truly wanted—for Eric to leave his wife of almost twenty years. But that question brought on a cascade of others and Randall wouldn't be able to tolerate the answers, despite his adult composure. The result would be the destruction of the private world they had created in this darkened bedroom, a world that allowed Eric to satisfy a thirst that had gone unquenched for two decades.

"You made the rule yourself, Eric. Can't spend the night, remember?"

"We have rules?"

Randall's amused exhalation of breath couldn't qualify as a laugh. "Rules are good," he said. "Rules make me think that this is more real than what it is."

"What do you mean?" Eric asked.

"Something that both of us are too afraid to give a name. A bunch of stolen moments lined up in a row. When this ends, whatever *this* is, both of us will spend the rest of our lives trying to figure out the kindest way to call it a mistake. It's not fair to me, when you think about it."

"Why is that?"

"Because I'll live longer than you."

"What makes you think that?"

Randall turned from the window. He seemed startled, and Eric realized that in his attempt to keep his tone neutral he had put the dark undertone of a threat in his words. "Because you're younger, you mean? That's why you'll live longer."

"I guess," Randall said, sounding distracted.

His shadow moved to the chair draped with his clothes. By the time he heard the rattle of Randall's belt buckle sliding to his waist, Eric was speaking again. "Randall." He could see Randall's head turn. "I'm asking you to stay."

Randall paused, then moved to the foot of the bed and crawled across it on all fours until his mouth was inches from Eric's. Randall was still shirtless, his jeans unbuttoned. His typically gelled and spiked hair was slightly mussed and matted from being twisted against the pillow. He stared at Eric, eyes bright, teeth sinking slowly into his lower lip, and Eric felt his stomach tighten in anticipation. Randall's mischievous grin drew out Eric's original, burning attraction to the preternaturally assured young man. A no-longer-buried desire to have him, shape him, and conquer him; a desire that to his consternation had not gone away after simply taking the boy to bed.

"No," Randall said. "I like you better when you don't get everything you want."

Randall's kiss was brief but firm. His weight left the mattress, and Eric slouched back onto the pillows, rolling over onto one side and listening to the mournful sirens that no longer seemed to be approaching or departing, but had joined together in a consistent, off-key wail, its direction distorted by the wind.

"Want to cut through the Elms?"

"Shut up, April."

"They're a good shortcut if you're not loaded. Or you don't have an overactive imagination."

The snow was driving now, cutting into their bare faces, and they were forced to walk with their shoulders hunched. April had brought her jacket up over her neck. Kathryn could hear sirens coming from the city below the hill. Kathryn shot a glance leftward at the expanse of suggestive shadows. To bypass it, they had to walk through residential streets.

"I don't get it," Kathryn said.

"How much money did they spend to build the Tech Center?"

"Loads probably."

"And they still haven't managed to build on the Elms?"

Up ahead, the four houses fringing Fraternity Green were fishbowls of light. Strobe lights from inside Burton House cut stained-glass shapes across the snowy lawn. "You think they should put a dorm there just because it gives you the creeps?" April asked.

"No. It's just weird that Michael Price can't get his hands on a piece of prime real estate."

"Please. Be grateful. If someone doesn't stop that jerk, he's going to coat the entire campus in chrome!"

Michael Price was one of Atherton's most prominent alumni, featured, it seemed, in every issue of the alumni magazine as well as spreads in everything from *Architectural Digest* to *The New York Times*. Kathryn had studied a photo of him in *Paper* during a Psychology Intro lecture. Swollen and strong boned, he exhibited a brutal, sexualized assurance that repelled her. Captured in freeze frame, he seemed like the kind of man who swaggered, who believed that little was out of his reach. It was that rare quality that might have led him to import cold and sterile modern architecture to his alma mater. From the blinding, plate-glass Technology Center to the massive refurbishment of the fifteen-story Sciences Library, students and faculty alike found Price's additions glaringly inappropriate for a predominantly Gothic campus.

"You know the Pamela Milford story, right?" April asked. Kathryn shook her head. They were steps from Burton House and the bass pounding of disco was already throbbing in their gums. "I think it was the eighties. She wandered out of some party here, drunk off her ass, stumbled into the Elms, and drowned."

"How did she drown?"

"There's some kind of creek, I think."

"All the more reason to raze it."

Kathryn shivered. On the front porch of the house, she looked back to the green. "He might be inside. Can we just go in?"

April tugged on her shoulder.

Inside, they were instantly swallowed by the shoulder-to-shoulder throng clogging the front hallway. The frat's living room had been transformed into a poor man's Studio 54. Half the dancers were wearing neon-colored wigs and a Warhol film was being projected onto the ceiling, shaggy-headed sylphs staggering and jerking across the frame. Kathryn scanned the crowd for Randall.

A rail-thin boy done up in drag shoved a tray of Jell-O shots in their faces. April took one, shot it, and then handed one to Kathryn. "I told you they didn't card!"

"What's in this?" Kathryn asked the drag queen.

"X," he shouted back, before vanishing onto the adjacent dance floor.

April brought one hand to her mouth. "Oh God!"

"He was probably kidding," Kathryn said, as she placed her shot on the stair above her head.

"Whatever. If I'm still awake in four hours, cuddling up against you in bed and stroking your hair, then these freaks are going in front of the Disciplinary Council!"

Kathryn hooked her by the arm. "Let's find Randall!"

The kitchen was as crowded as the rest of the house. What counter space was not covered in empty beer cases and liquor bottles was blocked by drunken couples holding on to each for support as they were rocked onto the balls of their feet by a steady procession toward the open back door. A hand slapped Kathryn's ass. When she turned, she saw April several steps behind her, and whirled to face her offender. Tim Mathis grinned back at her. His dimpled cheeks had the blush of too many drinks. A stranger might have thought the short, stocky, peroxide blond with the bicycle chain around his neck was making an ill-advised pass. Kathryn knew better. Tim threw both arms skyward with a squeal before enfolding Kathryn in a sloppy embrace.

"Have you seen Randall?" Kathryn asked as she pried herself free.

"Nope. No sign of the Ice Queen. But his *roommate* is certainly here, though!" Tim said, exaggerating the words with a sexual suggestiveness that turned Kathryn's stomach. "*He's* out on the dance floor bumping and grinding with some twelve-year-old girl"

"Who?" Kathryn asked, before she could stop herself.

"Someone who doesn't know any better," April cut in, grabbing at Kathryn's shoulders.

"What's the guy's deal, anyway?" Tim squinted at her. "Randall wouldn't give me any of the dirt. Is he a member of the spur posse or something?" Kathryn was being pressed up against Tim's spandexed chest. April's hand gripped her shoulder, ready to pull Kathryn away from a conversation she knew Kathryn wanted to avoid. "I mean, don't get me wrong. Jesse Lowry is a Bruce Weber photo waiting to be *snapped*, but forgive me for thinking that a man who sleeps with that many women doesn't have something to prove!"

"Have you quit smoking yet?" April asked in her ear.

"No."

"Let's go have one. I can't breathe in here."

"No, I wasn't talking. Really," Tim cut in. "And aren't you a med student?"

"Nice try," April replied. "Biomedical ethics. And aren't you a music major?"

"No!"

"Then why don't you try talking without *sing-ing*!"

"You're just pissed at everyone because you're a dyke."

"I'm also black. Which fills me with rage. Kathryn, cigarette!"

"No, no. Not so fast!" Tim grabbed Kathryn's other shoulder. "Seriously, Kathryn, I know how you and Randall are. You two probably did the whole finger-pricking, blood-sharing thing. He picks out your clothes, you set him up on dates with all your non-threatening male friends. It's a strong bond, I know. And I hate to be the first one to tell you, but I think there might be more going down behind that door than you ever—"

"No offense to you or your kind, Tim, but Jesse Lowry is as heterosexual as they come," April cut in

"Bullshit. He's sexual. When are you girls ever going to learn the difference?"

"Maybe you can interview Jesse for your column," Kathryn managed. "A man, his penis, and the doormats he rubs it on."

"I'm sure he does more than rub."

"All right," April growled behind her, patience gone.

"But screw that," Tim continued, unfazed. "I'm about to quit anyway. They think if they make me a news editor then I'll stop trying to rile things up. I mean, do you guys even read the *Atherton Herald*? It's, like, three pages long and the major headline is always something real scintillating like 'Sophomore Plants Tree.'"

Kathryn laughed.

"I am claustrophobic!" April barked.

"Jesus, April. All right. Tim, if you see Randall, tell him I'm looking for him."

"Yeah, right. Like I ever see Randall anymore," Tim muttered, raising his plastic cup in a sarcastic toast

On the patio, smokers shivered in huddles. Trash cans lined the clapboard fence, spilling flattened beer cases. "That was rude," Kathryn finally said.

"Me? No, *he* was rude. The guy's got to know what you think of Jesse, and he was throwing out all the shit just to milk you for info on Randall. He needs to move on. Randall's too intense for that guy anyway. But just in case you were wondering—" April paused for effect, pulling a cigarette free from the pack Kathryn had just removed from her jacket pocket "—Jesse obviously isn't the only guy on this campus who goes through people like a Ginsu knife."

"Tim and Randall dated, April."

April rolled her eyes.

"How's that shot treating you?" Kathryn finally asked. "Are you rolling?"

"Shit. It's Sig."

"God bless you."

"Sigrid," April hissed.

Kathryn followed her roommate's spooked stare to where one of April's previous girlfriends of the moment stood smoking in a corner of the patio, shooting slant-eyed glances at the surrounding crowd, as if any number of the other guests were going to slap an apron on her and force her to cook dinner.

"Is that Abba?"

"I told you not to call her that. You and Randall need to start learning people's real names. You're both sociopaths."

The girl had claimed to be Swedish royalty, so rather than risk embarrassment in attempting to pronounce her name, Kathryn and Randall had nicknamed her after the famous Swedish pop group. "How royal is she, exactly?"

"I have to talk to her."

"Why? You dumped her last month."

"That's why I have to talk to her. It's like noblesse oblige. Wait here."

"For what?"

But April was already crossing the patio. Kathryn turned, scanning the other guests to see if anyone had begun staring at the girl who had just been left standing awkwardly by herself.

Where the hell was Randall?

She shoved her way back inside. There was no sign of Tim in the kitchen, so she edged into the front hallway and stopped in the doorway to the living room, narrowing her eyes against the flashing strobe lights to make out the wild forms on the dance floor. There were plenty of blonde heads, but none of them belonged to Randall.

When her eyes met Jesse Lowry's, her breath came out in a startled hiss.

He was dancing halfway across the living room, and his partner was a stick figure of a brunette who clung to Jesse's broad frame as if she were in a drunken swoon. Their slow, swaying embrace was completely out of synch with the urgent disco. Jesse wore his usual UCLA baseball cap, with the bill shading his eyes from the flashing strobe lights, but Kathryn could make out his slight, suggestive smile, directed now at her. It was a smile that implied Kathryn had been watching Jesse for hours. He wore a tight, cable-knit sweater that accented the swells of his chest. Most girls went weak in the knees—not unlike his current dancing partner and next victim—when Jesse bothered to look their way. Kathryn had trained herself to react to him with a mixture of disgust and suspicion.

They stared icily at each other for several seconds. Kathryn saw that Jesse's other arm was plastered between his body and the girl's, and she realized it wasn't alcohol that had turned the girl into a limp noodle in Jesse's embrace. One of Jesse's hands disappeared into the unbuttoned, distended waistline of the girl's jeans. She was rocking up onto her toes, trying to bring her mouth to Jesse's, before her intended kiss became a defeated gasp against his cheek.

Jesse withdrew his hands from the girl's pants. His eyes locked on Kathryn's, he slid his middle finger between his lips. Kathryn left the doorway.

When he returned home from getting Chinese takeout that evening, it had still been light out. Eric lingered in the dark on the first floor, where the snowy windows glowed brighter than anything inside the house. The parked cars along Victoria Street sat beneath layers of white, and the snowfall had thinned to frail flakes that danced on their descent; the evening's storm had turned into a dusting.

Wearing only his bathrobe, he padded across the living room without hitting a single switch. He turned on the gas fireplace with a flick of his wrist and lit it with the fireplace lighter. The flames caught with a sudden *whoosh* as they punched through the fake charred coals. Weak firelight played across *The Garden of Earthly Delights* and Eric was struck by the flickering image of Hieronymus Bosch's altarpiece. Above the bookcase, Eden, Earth, and Hell were dancing in the frame. He had launched his academic career with a controversial book that claimed that the medieval painter wasn't truly a member of the established church, but a mitigated Cathar who held the heretical belief that the earth was Satan's terrain, and the body a trap from which one must spiritually escape, and whose vile desires must be denied.

Eric stared up at the painting that had once so shaped his worldview. The cluster of wild academic theories it opened up had seemed to speak directly to his own inhibitions and fears. Still fresh with Randall's sweat, he couldn't fight the feeling that the Cathars were wrong. The body wasn't a trap, but a door to sensations he had denied himself for far too long.

Halfway to the kitchen, something hard banged his knee and he stepped back. He had walked into the liquor cabinet door, which Lisa had left standing open. Angrily, he kicked it shut, then had to admit to himself that he was hardly in any position to curse his wife's forgetfulness. Never mind that Lisa had spent the last three years of her life establishing scotch and painkillers as staples of her diet; he could still taste Randall in his mouth.

In the kitchen, he flicked on the overhead light, glancing at the phone. Lisa had left one of her usual notes, cursory and by now unnecessary. "Went to Paula's," they usually said. Or, "Paula had a bad week. Be back Mon. Prob Late." They were as terse and bloodless as their marriage had been almost since its beginning. What more could be expected of a bond Eric had sought as if it were a Ph.D., another credential meant to tether him to a world with established rules? But in the beginning, Lisa hadn't seemed to want much more either. Only too late had Eric realized that his wife required more than a companion, or a weight beside her in the bed. Now, Eric was sure that a part of Lisa was relieved by her sister's cancer, for she could escape Eric every weekend for someone who truly needed her.

When the phone rang, he was propping open the refrigerator with one hip. Startled, he turned and crossed to the phone, the fridge door making a soft thud as it glided shut behind him. His hand almost to the receiver, his eyes landed on the note written on the banana-shaped stationery usually reserved for grocery lists.

*I SAW. I KNOW.*

His breath didn't catch; it simply stopped, and then a painful stab in his chest reminded him to breathe. He realized the phone still summoned him.

"Hello?"

"Is this Eric Eberman?" An unfamiliar female voice, its tone clipped and professional. "Sir, is this . . ."

"Who is this?"

"My name is Pat Kellerman, sir. I'm afraid I have some bad news."

"Lisa?"

"Your wife's been in an accident."

He looked down at the note he held in one hand. The urge to tear it in two struck him with such sudden force that he almost dropped the phone. Instead, he opened the nearest drawer with one hand and slid it inside, shutting it slowly so as not to be heard on the other end. By the time the woman was explaining that a patrol car was on its way to pick him up, Eric remembered the wail of sirens that had stopped only twenty minutes earlier.

• • •

Behind them, Burton House still shook. Tim rested his head in both open palms as Kathryn fished a cigarette for him out of her jacket pocket. Guests were beginning to depart, their shadows vanishing into the darkness of Fraternity Green. Some of them bravely turned left into the Elms, Kathryn noticed, as she handed Tim the cigarette and he took it with a weak smile.

"What was in those goddamn Jell-O shots anyway?" Tim asked with a groan.

"You don't want to know."

Tim exhaled his first drag. "Smoking kills, you know."

"Shit. Why didn't anyone tell me?"

They smoked.

"Sorry about earlier," Tim muttered.

Kathryn feigned ignorance by staying quiet.

"I just wanted to know what's going on with him."

"Jesse?" Kathryn asked.

"No. Randall."

So April was right, and there was someone else at Atherton who had Randall on the brain. The realization made her feel at once less alone and less privileged. She had assumed that Randall's fling with the guy he had referred to as Bob Woodward in spandex was doomed from the start. The guy rarely shut up, and she knew from experience that you had to allow Randall his silences. And he seemed run through by that journalistic belief that a right to privacy was only a cover for a dire secret that required exposure. Randall had many secrets. The only thing that made that truth tolerable was her faith that she would learn most of them in due time.

"Rich parents?"

"I don't know," Kathryn lied. She knew they were loaded.

"Only child, right?" Tim pressed.

"Yeah. I guess that explains a lot," Kathryn said with a note of finality.

"No, the 'rich parents' thing explains a lot more. Makes sense. I kind of have this image of him browsing the racks at Saks, or power lunching with the Kennedys back when the rest of us were hitting the mall on weekends."

"He's never mentioned the Kennedys."

Tim heard the sharpness in her tone and responded with a weak laugh. "Sorry, I just realized we've been out on a few dates and I don't know anything about him."

"I didn't think you guys actually went out on dates."

Tim smiled wryly. "He tells you everything, doesn't he?"

"I don't ask for all the details."

"Aren't you guys best friends?"

Kathryn felt her eyebrows arch and her mouth curl. When she saw Tim's reaction to her evident anger, she wished she had thought twice before letting it get the best of her  The guy was just still smarting from the sting of rejection, but he'd just crossed a line she didn't know she had. However, Randall had moved on because of a lack of interest—unlike Jesse, whose pathological promiscuity left behind a constant string of the confused and spurned.

Behind them, the door to the house popped open and April emerged, tailed by Sigrid and three other lesbians who looked like they were about to go logging. "We're going to the Hole!"

"Gross. Be sure to shower," Tim commented.

"You coming?" April asked her, eyes on Kathryn as she punched her fists into her gloves.

"Some of us don't have fake IDs."

"I can get you in," one of the lesbians offered  Kathryn attempted a grateful smile and shook her head

"No sign of the Ice Queen?" April asked.

"Looks like my nickname stuck!" Tim said proudly.

April shot Kathryn one last disapproving look before turning to her entourage. "Let's head out, girls!"

They shuffled down the steps past Kathryn.

"We might meet you!" Kathryn called after them, and April waved at her over one shoulder.

She stared after them before noticing a shadow striding down the path toward Burton House, its gait familiar. Kathryn rose and descended the front steps of the house. When Randall's eyes left the walkway before his feet, they lit up and met hers  She had almost closed the distance between them, grinning. Lifting her slightly off her feet, he pulled her body into his. They did a half spin and almost lost their footing, but he didn't relinquish his hold on her. His long limbs didn't suggest strength, but they enfolded her tightly.

"You were waiting. I'm an asshole," he whispered into her ear before he kissed her cheek gently.

"No. It's cool."

She heard Tim rise to his feet behind them and turned to see him brushing off the seat of his pants. He gave Randall an acidic smile and Kathryn felt a current of tension pass between both men before Randall returned the smile with a stiff and formal one of his own. "Tim," he said.

"*Randall*," Tim responded mockingly, descending the steps. "All right, Bobbsey Twins. I'll see you guys later." He passed them and Kathryn heard him add, "Maybe," under his breath.

Once he was gone, Randall gave her a sheepish look. "He bugged you, didn't he?"

"You're a heartbreaker."

"I should tell him to leave you alone."

"I think when it comes to him, you've done quite enough. Or nothing at all."

"He'll live. And the only reason he'd say otherwise is to try to get me to sleep with him again." He glanced at the path Tim had taken into the shadows, then returned his attention to her. "What did I miss?"

"Tainted Jell-O shots. A Swedish princess. But you still be might able to watch Jesse reel in tonight's catch."

"I'm sure I'll run into her later."

Randall tugged his silver flask from his inside jacket pocket, uncapped it, and handed it to Kathryn. She took a slug and winced. "Christ, Randall, can't you add soda or something?"

"Lightweight. Come on." He took one of her hands and began leading her off the sidewalk and onto the lawn.

His hand was warm, as if he had been inside all night, but his body was hot, as if he ran on high octane. "Mind if I ask where we're going?" she ventured.

"Madeline's."

Kathryn yanked her hand free. "No, Randall. I hate that place."

"I'll let you change. They'll only card you if you're dressed like you are right now."

His grin told her he was only half serious, but when she hung back he stuck out his lower lip. "Don't even start," Kathryn said, already starting to giggle. Randall furrowed his brow, jutting his lip out farther. His expression had transformed from baby-faced pleading into a monkey scowl; when he went to push his ears forward to complete the effect, Kathryn grabbed one of his wrists. "Fine!" she barked, to choke off her laughter. "Stupid of me to think you could hang out with anyone who doesn't wear Prada."

"I'm wearing Gucci," Randall said in a small voice.

"Don't push it!" Kathryn made a sharp turn, leading them back toward the sidewalk.

"Where are you going?" Randall called after her. She turned and saw Randall gesture toward the Elms. "Oh, you're kidding," she moaned.

"Come on. I'll protect you." He put an arm around her shoulders. Kathryn let out a defeated groan and allowed herself to be led into the dark woods.

To her surprise, the Elms were easily navigated. There was no underbrush and the only obstructions were shoulder-height branches that were hard to make out in the darkness. Randall kept tight against the left side of her chest, pressing her head down and pushing branches out of their way as they went.

"You don't even want to know what I saw your roommate doing tonight."

"Now I do."

Randall came to a sudden halt. Kathryn thudded into him and saw they were standing at the edge of a five-foot drop down into a stream swollen with melting snow.

"Pamela Milford," she muttered.

"What?" Randall asked.

She looked up and saw she had his full attention. "Nothing. April was telling me the story earlier. The woman who drowned."

Randall nodded and his eyes returned to the flow of water below.

"Maybe she drowned," he whispered.

"You know something else?"

"No one really knows what happened. Why do you think everyone here still talks about it like it's some urban legend?"

"Well, she was *real*, wasn't she? That means it's not an urban legend."

His eyes still on the five-foot drop, he curled his mouth into a weak smile, then took her hand and held it tight. "I didn't know it was so wide down here. Come on."

As they traveled up the bank, the trees thinned out, revealing houses beyond. "So? What happened?" Randall asked, seeming to have recovered from the fact that they had come within inches of falling five feet into near-freezing water.

"Your roommate and this girl were on the dance floor. You would have thought he was her ob-gyn."

"Is there any reason you can't refer to him by his first name? He's always 'your roommate' or 'that asshole.'"

"He's both," Kathryn said. They came to a sidewalk with a stone banister, which crossed over the top of a large drainage pipe emitting crystalline black water amid ice extending from the bottom lip of the opening like white teeth. Kathryn's breaths were more steady now that they were on the solid ground of the sidewalk. The halos of Brookline Avenue's streetlights beckoned them.

"I think it's interesting how some people make concessions for the beautiful, but you hold them to a higher standard," Randall remarked.

"He's not beautiful, Randall. He's hot. There's a big difference," Kathryn said, thinking of the magazine ads of shirtless, buff male models Randall used to bridge the gaps between posters on the cinderblock wall of his room. Did all gay men worship perfectly proportioned men who wore inscrutable, distant, facial expressions that suggested they were not just inaccessible but physically indestructible? Men who bore a striking resemblance to Jesse Lowry? She didn't know enough homosexuals to be sure.

"You might want to sleep with him. Just once," Randall said.

"I'm going to pretend you didn't say that."

"Why, Kathryn? It might take away his mystique."

"He doesn't have any mystique."

"That must be why we're talking about him, then."

They had arrived at the stoplight across the street from Madeline's. Brookline Avenue's only hip restaurant had already accomplished its ten o'clock transformation into a nightclub. Its front door trailed a long and impatient line of the university's best dressed, shivering in the cold as they waited to pretend they were in Manhattan.

Randall had turned to face her, still holding one of her hands in his.

"What's next?" he asked gently. "Campuswide outreaches for one-night stands gone wrong? Are you going to go around campus hand-ing out pamphlets listing the names of guys who *don't call back*?" He lifted his hands and fluttered his fingers at the mock horror of it all.

"You've played me his voice mail, Randall."

"For fun, Kathryn. I didn't know you were going to run to the Women's Center with it."

"Every time it's a different one. Half of them end up *begging*. And maybe it wouldn't bother me so much if I didn't think that Jesse probably gets off on those messages more than sleeping with them."

"Let me guess. Someone didn't call you back once. And you were scared for life." He had lowered his voice to a dramatic bass, leaning toward her until their foreheads almost touched. When he saw her glare, he shrank back, abashed. "Kathryn . . ."

She went to step off the curb. "Forget I brought it up."

"Come on, Kathryn. I was kidding." He reached for her shoulder and missed. Her feet hit the street and suddenly a pair of headlights sliced toward her and she was forced back up onto the curb.

"I'm sick of you and April making me out to be this Puritan."

"I didn't say that."

"You have "

"When?" Randall asked, sounding slightly indignant. He was right, she knew; he had never called her that. But it was too late to relent; silence fell and she stuffed her hands inside her pockets.

"It's not about me, all right?" she managed. When she turned to face him, she saw his rapt stare, which was as confused as it was eager for her to continue. "I know better. But there was a time when I didn't. And that's why I don't like it when I see a guy who does nothing but use people."

Randall narrowed his eyes and nodded. "I know better too," he said gently.

It was this knack for cutting straight to a truth they shared, and doing it with care, that had allowed Randall and Kathryn to form such a deep and all-inclusive friendship so quickly. Kathryn only had to do half the work because Randall could intuit the rest. Did this make her lazy? No. There existed between them a suggestion that something that had shaped them before they met had primed them to become something close to soul mates. It was one of those assurances that hinted there was a little more order to the world than you thought, and made it a less lonely place to live in.

She returned his embrace before giving him a surprise slap on the ass. He jerked. They were both startled by a high-pitched whistle.

"Break it up, you two!"

Kathryn steeled herself at the sound of Jesse's too-familiar voice. His date clung to his shoulder like a barnacle and let out a short, barking laugh as they approached down the sidewalk. Kathryn's eyes immediately shot to the girl's crotch to see if her jeans were buttoned.

Candles on wall sconces lit the interior of Madeline's The bar was clogged with Armani- and Gucci-clad students downing shots between boisterous fits of laughter. Anemic, black-uniformed waitresses maneuvered between the cramped tables, carrying trays of drinks their skinny arms could hardly support. A strange mix of acid jazz and trance pumped from unseen speakers, a stark contrast to the flickering images of the local eleven o'clock news Kathryn was watching on the television above the bar.

She sipped her club soda and shot a glance over one shoulder Through the plate-glass windows, cardiganed students could be seen making the walk back to their dorms. Weighted by overloaded book bags, they shot withering glances at the official hangout for Atherton's Euro-trash and designer-drug addicts. Kathryn prayed none of them noticed her, fearful of losing the respect of those who had come to one of the finest universities in the country to do something other than look good

Kathryn didn't bother to look at Jesse as he slid onto the barstool next to hers. "Where's Randall?"

"Bathroom."

"I thought you two were, like, attached at the hip."

Kathryn took a sip of her drink. "What's her name?"

"Don't know yet." Jesse sipped his drink and Kathryn finally made eye contact. He lifted his glass. "Seven Up "

Kathryn nodded, as if impressed

"You?"

"Club soda. I thought you were a Bud man, Jesse."

"Only when it's free. But not when I have to perform."

Kathryn's smile hurt her cheeks. She looked toward the bathroom, praying Randall would emerge. Instead, she saw Jesse's nameless brunette filing out of the women's room with three other girls. The brunette's eyes shot in both directions before she clasped her hands, as if in prayer, using both index fingers to wipe at her nostrils. Kathryn noticed one of the other girls applying a liberal amount of Chapstick. She read the group's behavior in an instant. They hadn't gone to the bathroom together to put on makeup.

Suddenly she was back in San Francisco. Her best friend Kerry was clinging to her pleadingly, lying and telling Kathryn she was just drunk. Lying even more when she said she was just stoned. And Kathryn, knowing only that alcohol didn't dilate your pupils, was too stupid to know more.

"Hey."

Startled out of her memories, Kathryn turned. Jesse leaned toward her with one bent elbow braced on the bar. "Mind if I ask you a question?"

"Never," Kathryn answered.

Jesse laughed, his eyes not leaving hers. "No, believe me, I know you're off-limits. I'd just love to know what it is I do that pisses you off so much."

She held his gaze. "You need to be humbled."

"Meaning?"

"You need to find one girl who won't sleep with you."

Jesse leaned back on his stool and gave her a slight nod, not in agreement, but as if satisfied to have received an explanation for her constant chill around him. "I haven't?" he asked, gesturing down the length of her body with one hand.

She smirked and returned her attention to the television.

"You know, I think it's kind of cool what the two of you have," Jesse said.

She thought she heard a genuine trace of envy in his voice. But maybe she had imagined it. "What do you mean?"

"I just remember the way you guys were during Orientation Week. Everyone else was hanging out in the lounge making bullshit conversation, spouting off those statistics about how 90 percent of married couples meet their other half in college, or going to those stupid ice-cream social things. Not you and Randall. You guys were like running off in taxis to gay bars on the first day."

"I don't exactly recall you bonding with our dorm unit either."

"I didn't," Jesse responded, without pausing. "That's why I think it's cool."

Puzzled, she waited for him to continue.

"Jesus, it's like everyone on our floor, they're all rushing out to join some club, or they're going to do some whacked-out major like April, with a hundred requirements, and they've already gone to three classes by the time I wake up. It's like they're working their asses off to be anything other than what they are."

"What are they?" Kathryn asked.

"Kids. Away from home. But if you ask them, they'll tell you they're a major or a club. 'Hi, I'm premed.' 'Don't bother me, I have to go weave baskets for starving children in Iran.'" Kathryn couldn't suppress a smirk. "Not us though," Jesse continued with sudden gravity. "You, me, Randall. It's like we didn't get taken up into the fold. But everyone else here? They're like Stepford Child freaks mainlining all that bullshit they tried to feed us during Orientation."

"April says I use Randall to avoid making new friends," Kathryn said carefully, reminding herself whom she was talking to. She left out April's other point—that she used Randall to avoid finding a boyfriend as well.

"I don't know," Jesse said, his tone nonchalant. "We've only been here, what? Two months? It's like the two of you have taken vows or something."

She was reminded of Tim's "finger-pricking, blood-sharing" comment.

"So who's he dating, anyway?" Jesse asked.

"Randall? No one."

"That's weird. What happened to the reporter guy?"

"That's over," Kathryn said.

Jesse's eyes narrowed on her.

"What?" she asked.

"It's just that he's been staying out really late."

"No, he hasn't." Kathryn hated the hint of anger in her voice.

"He comes back with you and then leaves again."

"Maybe he's going to the bathroom."

"For three hours? That's impressive. Even if he's jerking off. And he knows I don't have a problem with him jerking off in the room."

Kathryn's mouth opened to protest, but suddenly the brunette had slid between them, perma-smile plastered on her face, pupils dilated. Kathryn was sure the girl was high, and she watched as the brunette leaned into Jesse and whispered into his ear, then withdrew, laughing slightly, but Jesse's face had gone blank. Kathryn was startled to see him cup the girl's chin in one hand and gently push her face back several inches, surveying her.

"What?" the girl asked

Jesse reached up and swabbed at her nostrils with one finger.

"What are you *doing*?" the girl cried.

Jesse returned his attention to his 7 Up as the girl's eyes moved from him to Kathryn. She surveyed Kathryn as if she were a beauty pageant contestant. Kathryn stared back, as if one of the girl's breasts had squeezed its way out of her V-neck. "Asshole!" the girl barked over one shoulder, stalking to the front door. Jesse didn't look up from his glass.

"High as a kite," Kathryn finally said.

Jesse's eyes shot to hers "You have experience?"

"Not me. I had friends in high school whose entire weekend was an eight ball," she said flatly, praying he wouldn't ask about them. Kerry, Michelle, Debbie, Jono. Somehow, thinking of all their names at once kept her memory from summoning a single face.

"But you never touched the stuff?"

"Never," Kathryn answered, warning him off the subject with her tone.

Randall sidled up between them to the bar. "Huh?" he asked as he looked from Jesse to her He bent over the bar, summoning Teddy, his chosen bartender, who enjoyed Randall's flirtatiousness because it meant big tips. "Can I get an apple martini?"

"Randall," Kathryn began "Someday you're going to introduce me to a homosexual who can drink something that doesn't glow in candlelight."

"Wait!" Jesse piped up He grabbed one of Randall's shoulders and turned him, cupped his chin, and examined his eyes.

"Mind if I ask what you're doing?" Randall asked, his words clipped by Jesse's grasp.

"He's clean," Jesse said to Kathryn with a broad grin.

Teddy delivered Randall's drink as Randall fished his money clip from one pocket and peeled off a twenty. Randall dangled the bill over the bar, Teddy puckered his lips and Randall extended the money in one hand. As Kathryn expected, Teddy didn't ask for ID. Randall turned his back on Jesse and leaned in. "What was that about?" he asked Kathryn, voice low.

"Inside joke. You're on the outside. Sorry."

"You two have inside jokes now? I was only in the bathroom for ten minutes."

"I know, and we wanted to know why."

"Are you saying you two actually bonded?"

"Mmmm. No, not really." Kathryn grabbed his chin "But let me see something . . ."

"I don't do drugs."

"Good. Then can we stop coming here?"

"You need some glamour in life, honey, and jugs of eight-dollar wine in the first-floor lounge don't cut it."

Kathryn had lifted one hand as if to slap him when Jesse barked, "Shit! Check that out!"

He pointed to the television above the bar, where Kathryn saw the mauled remains of a Volvo station wagon being hauled from the black water of the Atherton River. Police lights flared on the bridge overhead.

"Turn it up!"

It took Kathryn a second to realize it was Randall who had shouted the command at the bartender, who was occupied on the other side of the bar.

The news cut live to a reporter standing at the rail of the bridge at the exact moment when Kathryn thought the screen would offer them a glimpse of the person behind the Volvo's steering wheel. The volume stripe suddenly appeared at the bottom of the screen. Heads around the bar jerked at the sound of the reporter's voice, now contending with the music. Kathryn turned to see Jesse bent over the bar, holding the remote, watching intently.

". . . trying to chase down the anonymous caller who placed the 911 call reporting the accident, but so far they are short on leads. But what police are also short on is *any* explanation as to why forty-one-year-old Lisa Eberman drove her Volvo station wagon through the guardrail behind me and into the freezing waters of the Atherton River. The obvious answer might be as simple as bad weather."

The reporter cut to footage of paramedics rolling a gurney toward the flaring light of a waiting ambulance, its bridge lights smeared by the curtain of snow.

"As we told you earlier, Eberman was the wife of Atherton art history professor Eric Eberman."

"Dude!" the bartender snapped, yanking the remote out of Jesse's hand. "This isn't a sports bar."

Kathryn turned to find Randall staring raptly at the television. Jesse had noticed too, and their eyes met before they returned their attention to Randall, gripping the stem of his martini glass, his eyes locked on the now-silent flicker of images.

"You're in that guy's course, right?" Jesse asked him.

"Shit," Kathryn whispered. "Did you know her?"

After several more seconds, Randall pulled his eyes from the TV, stared down into his drink glass, and then brought it slowly to his mouth as he shook his head. He slugged it back and caught his breath. "No, I didn't. But . . . he's mentioned her. In class. It's just weird."

Kathryn touched Randall's shoulder lightly and when she did, she caught Jesse staring at her over the bar. When her eyes met his, he broke contact quickly, sliding off his barstool, feet heavily hitting the floor. "Good night all. I've got work to do."

Neither of them said good-bye.

"She's dead, right? They said   . ." Randall whispered.

"Yeah," Kathryn finished gently.

"That's so weird," Randall said again, shaking his head as he took another slug of his drink.

"Sad," Kathryn said, because she couldn't think of anything better.

But it was good enough for Randall, because he nodded vigorously as he set his glass back down onto the bar with too much force.

# CHAPTER TWO

THE WOMAN DETECTIVE STOOD ACROSS FROM ERIC AT THE POCK-marked table, blocking the interrogation room's single window. Her straight brown hair fell to her shoulders, in contrast to her mannish outfit. The undeniable curves of her body looked like they had been squeezed into the starched khaki trousers and white oxford shirt.

Pat. That was her name. He wasn't sure, but he guessed she was the one who had called to break the news. Eric sat slumped, back resting against the metal slats of the chair, feeling—and looking, he guessed—as if he had been punched between the shoulder blades.

He had lost track of time, and he wasn't sure how much longer the detective was going to allow this silence to continue. Did police officers take courses in how to deal with a man who had just identified the body of his wife by way of a black-and-white video monitor? When Pat asked him if he was ready to give a positive identification, he had expected to be led down a long, tiled hallway toward a set of double doors leading into the mortuary. Instead, she ushered him gently into a side room where he was greeted by the sight of Lisa's face on a television screen. Her black hair radiated from her head in matted clumps, and it was impossible to tell whether the blue pallor of her skin was the result of near-freezing water, the tint of the screen, or death. But there had been no denying that her sharp, birdlike features were just lax enough to suggest something beyond sleep.

The detective had touched his shoulder, squeezed gently, and then left her hand there. When he brought his hand to his mouth, it wasn't to fight a sob, but rather to conceal its absence. Maybe because it was the first time in years he had seen his wife without a glazed sheen of panic in her eyes, or a brow intensely furrowed as she realized that her latest medication had turned the task of chopping vegetables into an almost insurmountable project The peace that came with her death made her seem more fully realized; it conjured up images of the first woman he had ever slept with, who had plied him with champagne on New Year's Eve, in 1984, before taking him to bed in her room. As her parents slept down the hall, that young woman had said nothing when he told her it was his first time. Instead, without pausing to laugh or express incredulity, she had guided him gently through the motions. And from then on, she had regarded him as a challenge, as someone she had to draw out. Almost ten years later, all her efforts had failed. Accusations replaced conversation. Empty silences filled the spaces once occupied by the cold comfort of their intellectual companionship.

"When did she start seeing this therapist?" The detective finally broke the silence.

"Two years ago," Eric answered, trying to lift his eyes to hers. "She had been depressed for a while. During the day she could barely get out of bed, and at night she couldn't sleep."

"And the therapist prescribed something?"

A laugh escaped him before he could stop it. "I'm sorry," he said.

"It's funny?"

"It's . . . within two weeks of her first visit, our medicine cabinet was filled with a bunch of drugs. And I could barely pronounce the names of any of them." A *bunch of drugs*. His careless choice of words sent a shiver through him and when he met the detective's gaze, he saw a sudden intensity to her poker face, which indicated that part of the puzzle had fallen into place for her.

"What kind?"

"The perfectly legal kind," Eric answered.

At the note of defensiveness in his voice the detective gave an abrupt nod. She crossed to the chair opposite his and took a seat. "Antidepressants?"

"Yes. And others."

"What were the others for?"

"To help her sleep. A lot of the . . serotonin reuptake inhibitors . . they kept her awake."

"How many did she take?"

"I'm sorry?"

"Any idea how many prescriptions your wife had? Total?"

"I didn't count "

"But enough to fill the medicine cabinet?" Eric didn't respond.

"Dr. Eberman, how often did your wife combine these pills with alcohol?"

"I don't know if she was deliberately combining them  . . I know that she did take them regularly and . . . well, she drank pretty regularly. I warned her, but .   ." He lifted both his hands from his lap, as if to indicate it had all been out of his control. Had it? Pat Kellerman's questions stirred others that fell outside her jurisdiction, which he knew would return each night before sleep for the rest of his life.

*Did you know your wife was a drunk?*

*Of course I did*

*Did you stand back and let the medicines she craved wreak havoc on her brain? Did you say anything when one pill was magic for several months and then it turned on her, sending her back to bed at four in the afternoon, until that drug-pushing quack of a therapist would write out a prescription for a new wonder cure? Did you ever, once, try to put a stop to the cycles you knew were tearing your wife apart?*

*No. Because they made her hate me less. Maybe they didn't make her forget that I had forced her to come to Atherton, applied for a faculty position without even telling her, forced her to give up her doctorate, but she sure stopped bringing any of it up at dinner. Once she became devoted to fighting her own brain, determined to fight one pill with another until she found the perfect balance, I stopped being the enemy, and instead she took on an enemy ten times as formidable—her mind, which I had helped to warp to the point of illness.*

*But the pills did more than spare me her anger. They freed me to open a door I shut years ago, with a man young enough to be my son, not to mention rid myself of a piece of property that held a plague of memory.*

"Mr. Eberman?"

"I'm sorry . . ."

"When was the last time you spoke with your wife?"

Eric clasped and then unclasped his hands in his lap, thinking, *No, not possible.* He combed his memory for some chance encounter he had forgotten, some phone call. Something. Nothing came. Nothing beyond her parting note. She had seen, she knew, secrets that he prayed she had not told.

"Two weeks ago."

Fibrous clouds parted over the roof of the Eberman house, revealing patches of stars. The quiet residential streets just east of campus were a hushed counterpoint to the rowdy matrix of freshman dorms only several blocks away. Randall Stone stood just outside the halo of the streetlight across the street, studying the house from a distance for the first time. The two-story house had a broad, gently sloping roof, and an expansive front porch with fat, unadorned columns. The living-room windows were dark. While the home didn't seem neglected, the paint was weathered without peeling, and the front yard was a dead, brown patch. The house spoke of two owners who had resigned themselves to living in it.

Eric's Toyota Camry sat in the driveway, parked next to the empty spot where Lisa Eberman had kept the Volvo station wagon that Eric had said she'd bought only a month before. Only now did Randall realize that it had been a strange purchase for a woman with nowhere to go except her dying sister's house. As far as Randall knew from Eric, Lisa did little more than use the car to drive her sister to chemo and buy groceries her sister couldn't stomach.

These thoughts distracted him from the disturbing image of a residence turned prison. For him, coming to Atherton had been ripe with the promise of a freedom he had intensely imagined, down to the smallest detail. But sooner than he had planned, his life there had become entangled with a man who haunted the rooms of his own home. Now the house would have a ghost that fit the dictionary's definition, and Randall wasn't sure whether he had the courage to continue if it meant chasing Lisa Eberman from the house's many shadows.

Randall heard the crunch of tires on snow and turned to see headlights rounding the corner. He moved back into the cover of darkness as the Atherton police cruiser halted in front of the house. He held his breath as Eric hoisted himself out of the backseat, shutting the door weakly behind him without any parting words for the driver of the car. Once Eric had reached the front porch, Randall stepped into the streetlight's halo, crunching snow underfoot.

Eric turned.

Randall waited for some small signal to summon him across the street. A sense of duty had brought him to the house, but also a desperate curiosity. Did Lisa's death mean they were free to be together, or was Eric so crushed by guilt that this awkward stand-off across a dark street would end up being good-bye?

He was confident he could be seen, but he couldn't make out the expression on Eric's face. Eric's shadow turned and slammed the front door behind him.

It was too easy for Eric to think he could have prevented it all by not answering the front door. "Who's there?" he had called out that evening, five weeks ago.

Eric had cursed his word choice. "Who is it?" would have sounded much more collected. But the loud series of knocks startled him and he was standing halfway down the stairs. Early October dusk darkened the foyer, and on the other side of the door a shadow was cupping its hands against the glass pane, trying to peer inside.

"Professor Eberman?"

He didn't recognize the voice, but no one called him "Professor Eberman." His colleagues called him "Eric," of course, and so did most of his grad students, who were the closest thing to family he had if only in that they shared the same obsessions. His undergraduates— that mass of nameless students he was forced to lecture three times a week so that the university could proffer unlimited access to tenured professors in all of its propaganda—rarely called him anything.

"Professor Eberman . . ." There was a pleading note in the voice now and it drew Eric down the last few steps. He opened the door; as soon as he saw the boy jerk back, hands falling to his sides, he fought the urge to slam the door shut in his face. His name was Randall Stone; the only reason Eric knew this was because after spotting him in the second row on the first day of lecture, Eric went back to his office and leafed through his copy of that year's freshman face book. A perfectly harmless, private activity, and one he had done many times in the past ten years, in order to put a name to a set of eyes, or the slope of a neck behind the collar of a sweater. With Randall, it had been the glint in his gaze as it followed Eric's paces across the stage, the way he rested the end of his pen in the corner of his mouth, which was curled into the bud of a smile. Such a knowing, sexual look from a young man suggested experience beyond his years—experience that Eric could imagine in fantasies that quickened his pulse and prevented sleep.

But now the boy was standing right there on his front porch, and those several minutes of tracking down his name suddenly seemed like a sin.

"I'm really sorry to bother you but . . . I'm lost."

But he didn't look remotely lost. There was no fear in his eyes, which Eric could tell, because he was staring at him—expectantly, Eric believed. Randall even seemed amused by the rigid way Eric held the door halfway open.

"Can I come in for a second?"

*Christ, No. Stay in the second row of lecture where you belong.*

"Do you want something?" The question came out just the way Eric didn't want it to, but Randall Stone obviously savored the halting sound of his voice, the fear and trepidation. Loved it like a shark smelling blood, because the boy's lips smiled in small triumph and he moved across the threshold without asking twice. For the first time Eric noticed that the boy was wet. He glanced back out the door to see a misting rain swirling over the street. In a month it might be snow.

And now you were supposed to be polite, to remember your age and remember who you are, his teacher, and forget how in lecture he sometimes lets his head roll back on his neck as he stretches out his arms, pulling the hem of his shirt from his jeans and revealing the flat, hairless stomach.

"Can I get you something?" Eric asked, revising his earlier question. "Scotch?"

Randall's eyes met his. He stood in the living-room doorway. "I didn't peg you as a scotch drinker."

"I'm not. My wife is." *She drinks it by the gallon and just minutes ago I called her sister to make sure she hadn't run off the road on the way there.*

Randall removed a silver flask from the inside pocket of his jacket, accidentally or on purpose flashing the Helmut Lang label, uncapped it, and raised it to Eric in a mock toast. Eric felt hugely foolish because he was so nervous that he had just offered one of his students—a freshman—alcohol. And Randall took a slug like a man, without wincing. It was too easy to forget that this boy was eighteen. Eric moved past him into the living room, turning on lamps as he went. Light fell in stages, and when it hit the reproduction of *The Garden of Earthly Delights*, Eric heard a small gasp.

"Bosch."

"Yes," Eric answered, even though Randall wasn't asking.

"I've read your book," he said nonchalantly, his back to Eric as he stared up at the framed print above the bookcase.

"El Jardín de las Delicias," Randall read in surprisingly unaccented Spanish off the bottom of the print, and then looked to Eric for an explanation.

"I bought that print at the Prado. In Madrid."

"I know where the Prado is," Randall said, without sounding offended.

"Are you familiar with Bosch? Because the last time I checked we had barely made it past the Hellenistic." Eric crossed his arms over his chest and felt a tight smirk on his face.

Instead of meeting the challenge head-on, Randall crossed to his reading chair and eased down into it. He let his head roll back a little and his feet slid out in front of him slowly as his expression became distant and dreamy, his voice softened by a memory he seemed to be looking for just above Eric's shoulder. "My parents took me to Madrid when I was twelve. It was a disaster of a trip, really. They didn't have any idea what they wanted to do once they got there, and my mother was so wrecked by jet lag that all she would do is stay in bed and order room service. And by the time we left the hotel everything would be closed for siesta. Anyway, by the fifth day I had had enough. We were staying at the Ritz so I snuck out without asking them and went across the street to the Prado. I was just wandering through the museum when I saw it by accident. . . ."

His gaze traveled from Eric's to the print across the room.

"I bought a print of it too. But when I got back to the hotel, my parents were furious at me for sneaking out, and I remember . . . my father just yanked it out of my hands, took one look at it, and tore it down the center. He said not only had I snuck out without permission, but I had come back with pornography."

Randall turned his head against the back of the chair, and when Eric saw the smile on his face he realized the story was supposed to be funny. He managed a slight laugh. But something about the story had seemed crafted, and it was a challenge feeling sympathy for a boy who stayed at the Ritz when he was twelve, even if his mother never got out of bed when they were there.

"Do you believe him?" Randall looked at him directly.

"I'm sorry."

Randall pushed himself out of the chair and crossed over to the print. "According to you, Bosch was truly a mitigated Cathar, right? Which means that instead of being a believer in the established views of the medieval church, he was a heretic who believed that the earth was the creation of Satan. And that Satan was the ruler of all things physical and corporeal. Including the body . . ."

The boy was basically quoting the prologue to Eric's book.

Randall turned, as if framing himself directly beneath the work in question as he demonstrated his knowledge of it. But now, his voice had a gently prodding tone to it. "To be cursed, to be the ultimate sinner, was to be ensnared in the physical. Was it that easy to be damned? Simply to feel alive in your own body?"

Eric wondered if perhaps this young man had been spending time with his grad students. Randall's hard but expectant stare suggested that Eric's initial suspicion was correct.

"Where do you live?" he asked.

"Stockton Hall."

"That's three blocks from here . . ." Eric's heart was hammering, knowing that he shouldn't press at all, should shut the boy out with silence and then shut the door after him. "How did you know where I live?" he finally asked.

Without guilt or the sudden shame of the caught, Randall answered, "I followed you."

• • •

It was past one and Stockton Hall was winding down from another Friday night, but the glare of the hallway's fluorescent lights seemed profane and Randall kept his head bowed, listening to the slow scrape of his footsteps over the hallway's thin industrial carpet. As he approached the end of the hall, he heard conversations muffled by cinderblock and the distant pounding of a stereo. None of it was loud enough to drown out the memory of the sound of Eric slamming the front door to his house At the end of the hall, he stopped outside Kathryn's room. He had trained himself to endure moments like these, to fight the urge to confess to Kathryn the truth about what had brought him to Atherton. But the urge was stronger than it had ever been. Once Eric slammed the door, Randall had to suffer the weight of his secret alone. No sliver of light came from beneath Kathryn's door, so he turned for his own.

Randall hesitated before he went in, waiting to hear a grunt or a sudden sharp intake of breath. He could only make out Jesse's voice speaking in urgent, hushed tones. It was the voice Jesse used with only one person, his father. Randall gave the door a gentle shove.

Kathryn had once observed that no dorm room in Stockton was more cleanly divided between roommates than his and Jesse's Jesse's side of the room was stark; the only thing adorning the wall beside his bed was a print of Salvador Dalí's *Persistence of Memory*. On the four shelves affixed to the wall above his headboard, his textbooks were meticulously organized by course, each one Atherton's basic introductory gut. Intro to Psych, American History, etc. Across the room, Randall's wall was an eruption of posters, the ceiling of the Sistine Chapel meeting the edge of Frank Lloyd Wright's Fallingwater, competing with anything else he could buy at the student union or tear out of a magazine. Pages detached from the Abercrombie & Fitch catalog—half-naked models, their arms looped with commercialized nonchalance around each other's shoulders—presided over his desk, their prominent placement an attempt to remind Jesse of his roommate's orientation and perhaps deter him from loafing around the room in only a pair of gym shorts or boxers. So far the attempt had failed.

Blue lights from the miniature television flickered across Jesse's torso where he lay on the bed, the portable phone pressed to his ear.

As Randall hung up his jacket, he heard Jesse giving only sporadic grunts of acknowledgment to the person on the other end of the line. The TV sat on top of the miniature, knee-high refrigerator; they both had been jointly rented from the student union, and without protest, Randall had allowed Jesse to keep both on his side of the room.

Randall sank down into his desk chair, turning his back to Jesse. Shut out by Eric and unable to risk Kathryn's disapproval of his sex life, Randall had somehow been left with only his unattainable, half-naked roommate as company. Staring blankly at the computer screen seemed like the only way to cope. He brought his hands to the keyboard, but one landed on the edge of his desk as another curled into a fist against his lap. Anger formed a knot inside his chest. He shut his eyes, drew breath, and was startled by the sound of Jesse setting the portable back into its cradle.

Canned laughter came from the television.

"Who was that?" Randall asked without turning.

Springs creaked as Jesse settled back into his bed. "Kathryn hates me, doesn't she?"

Startled, Randall turned to see Jesse, his eyes on the television, one arm bent between his head and the pillow, revealing a tuft of dark hair in his armpit. "You two seemed pretty tight at Madeline's," Randall said, unbuttoning his shirt as he moved to his closet, which allowed him to avoid looking at Jesse for too long.

"Whatever. It was all an illusion. I'm not surprised, though. The girl's got so many little voices in the back of her head telling her what not to do that she can barely leave her room without asking all of her friends if it's a good move. And now she lives across the hall from a guy who goes after whatever he wants."

"Whoever he wants," Randall corrected, balling up his shirt and tucking it into the laundry hamper.

"What I don't get," Jesse continued, "is how she had such a problem with the fact that I sleep around, but it's perfectly all right for you."

"Since when do I sleep around?" Randall settled back into his desk chair "Drywater, Texas," his first attempt at short fiction, was still an open file, designated by a rectangle on the toolbar at the bottom of his screen. His stomach clenched and in his rush to close it, the file exploded onto the screen. He clicked the mouse several more times than needed.

"Oh, come on All these late nights have been spent at the library?"

Randall bent against the back of his chair. "You know, Jesse, Kathryn has a value system we should all respect. Maybe even aspire to."

Jesse let out a short, barking laugh as he rose from the pillows, swung his legs over the side of the bed, and turned to face Randall. "No fucking way. I travel across the entire country to get here, to be on my own for the first time in my life, and then I've got some prude trying to pile on more rules about what I can and can't do with my body than I had to put up with as a five-year-old."

Randall held Jesse's eyes because it prevented his eyes from wandering down to where the leg of Jesse's boxers yawned open. "I've never heard such a noble excuse for being horny," Randall said. He turned back to the computer.

"Who are you kidding, Randall? Maybe you respect her, but I know you couldn't be her if you tried every day."

Randall rose from the chair and moved to his bed. He had to step over several piles of his books in the process before he sank down onto his mattress and began unlacing his boots. "You need some friends, Jesse. Someone you keep around for a little longer than it takes to get them into bed. Then I might be able to take you seriously when you lecture me on *my* friends."

He managed to keep his tone steady, but when he shot a glance Jesse's way, he saw that Jesse wore a wry, disbelieving smirk. "What are you talking about, Randall? I have you."

Randall kicked one boot to the floor and then started pushing the other one off with his heel.

"Yeah, well, I think I've figured you two out," Jesse said blithely, his bare feet padding to the fridge. He opened a carton of orange juice and slugged it right from the opening. Randall stared at his back, waiting for him to continue but unwilling to urge him on. "For her, you're the phantom boyfriend she doesn't have the courage to go out and get, and for you . . . well, my guess is you don't really feel alive until that Tim guy or whoever has you flat on your back, but then, in the morning, when you start to feel a little dirty, you've got Kathryn and the pedestal she's put you on."

Jesse turned back, grinning slightly as if this were little more than locker-room banter. Randall surveyed him, trying to hide his anger and confusion. Why had Jesse picked tonight of all nights to share his pop-psychology insights? "Who says I ever feel dirty?" Randall asked icily.

Jesse arched his eyebrows and returned the orange juice to the fridge. Randall began removing his socks before he noticed that Jesse had wandered almost to the invisible line dividing their sides of the room, leaning one hip against the edge of the desk. Randall looked up, startled, as Jesse crossed his arms over his bare chest, waiting.

"What?"

"Go ahead."

Randall furrowed his brow.

"You're not going to, are you?" Jesse finally asked.

Now Randall knew what Jesse was waiting for. The next step of his bedtime routine was to slide beneath the comforter and remove his jeans down to his ankles before dropping them in a ball at the foot of the bed.

"Two months of living together and you still can't take your pants off in front of me."

"You never answered my question."

"What question?"

"Who was on the phone?"

Jesse was silent.

"Your father?" Randall asked.

Randall found a petty triumph in the color that rose to Jesse's cheek and the sudden tension in his jaw. "What drug was it this time?" Randall asked.

"Pride," Jesse answered, turning down the comforter. Randall was about to slide under his own when Jesse spoke again. "You know I got home in time for the repeat of the local news. That's some fucked-up shit. The car accident?"

Randall tensed, groping for any memory of what he might have said to Jesse. He had sworn to keep his pursuit of Eric secret. That was vital. But their room had become a private comfort zone, with Jesse giving details of his sexual conquests that Randall guessed he didn't share with anyone else, and which Randall loved hearing because they afforded him a private, intimate glimpse of the guy everyone else on the floor regarded as either an asshole or an enigma, a man he refused to desire. Sometimes he even considered Jesse to be a version of himself, but without the apologies and the secrets.

"Eberman? Isn't that the guy you have a hard-on for?"

Jesse slid under his comforter and reached for the switch on the gooseneck lamp affixed to his headboard. "Maybe now's your chance," Jesse said, before he killed the lamp and rolled over onto one side.

Any hope that he might get the last word was dashed. Randall stood frozen for several seconds. He hadn't told Jesse anything concrete, but he had confessed his attraction for Eric during those first weeks of school as they traded their evaluations of hot students and sexy professors But there was a good chance that somewhere amid all the freshman psych that formed Jesse's worldview, there might be some pretty good intuition.

He heard Jesse's sheets rustle, and through the shadows on his side of the room, Randall could see Jesse had turned his head to find Randall still staring at him. "Good night, Randall."

Kathryn emerged from her room to see Randall coming out of his. She saw his eyes widen and then he gave a slight laugh at her outfit. She'd pulled on unlaced duck boots with a pair of sweat pants, and thrown her heaviest Columbia-brand snow jacket on over her nightshirt. She must have looked like a bag lady who'd gone on a shoplifting spree at the mall.

She held up her pack of Marlboro Lights. "It's cold in the fire stairway," she said, pointing to the exit door to their right. Randall shook his head no and gestured to the boys' communal bathroom down the hall.

"Great," Kathryn said, as she followed him. "All dressed up for nothing."

Private shower stalls with soap scum–stained curtains lined one wall of the bathroom. A window at the far end was propped open, emitting cold gusts of wind that chilled the tiled floor. Whereas the girls on their floor never left their toiletry baskets behind, the boys had no qualms about it, and Kathryn chuckled when she saw Randall's Aveda-stocked basket on the window ledge alongside more plebeian toiletry kits featuring labels like Gillette and Pert Plus. Contact lens solution was wedged between a bottle of Issey Miyake cologne and matching body wash. She was taken aback. Randall wore contacts? So there were some limits on the small life details they had shared. (And even more limits on the larger dramas she had kept from him.)

Kathryn exhaled her first drag with her head tilted back, watching the cloud of smoke crawl toward the fluorescent light. She offered him one, but he held up his toothbrush in response. "You'd think someone would have done some work to make this place look less like a hospital."

Randall was brushing his teeth hard enough to bring white froth to the corners of his mouth. He bent at the waist and spat into the sink. "Try Princeton," he said as he disappeared into a bathroom stall. He emerged, dabbing at his mouth with a compulsively folded triangle of toilet paper. "I hear they have fireplaces in the lounges there."

"Wait-listed," Kathryn responded. Randall was flossing hard enough to draw blood, and she realized for the first time that he seemed on edge. "You?" she asked.

Randall rolled his eyes. "This again?" He was bouncing on his heels.

"I'm just curious," she said, smiling solicitously.

"Let's not play this game."

"Why? You always win."

"Kathryn, you're at the eleventh-ranked school in the country. Why do you need to keep mulling over your rejection letters?"

"Thirteenth," Kathryn corrected. "And who are you to talk? You were five minutes away from going to NYU to be near . . . what's his name? Adolph!"

"Alex," Randall corrected, staring at his reflection, his blue eyes darkening at the mention of the ex-boyfriend Kathryn had heard so much about that he seemed practically mythical. "But I like how you can never remember his name. I'm trying to forget it too."

"You never told me the whole story."

"What's to tell?"

"Here!" she said, handing him a cigarette. He furrowed his brow. "It'll chill you out."

"I don't need to chill out."

Kathryn shoved the cigarette back into the pack. "Come on,

Randall. You have a mad, passionate love affair with a marine five years older than you and he leaves you to go guard an embassy! I can see you running down the pier waving a hankie in the air as his ship pulls out of port."

"Actually, I dropped him off at JFK and asked him not to write."

Randall reached over and removed the cigarette she had offered him only moments ago. "Careful. They're not imported," she said. He popped it into his mouth. "You turned me into a smoker, you know," she added.

"Liar," Randall said

"It's true," Kathryn protested. "Before I met you, I would smoke maybe one or two when I was drinking. But then you made it look so . . . *sexy!*" She squeezed his side and he leaped back, twisting her offending wrist. Kathryn held her grip and Randall, giggling, continued to try to pry it free. They had almost two-stepped into one of the stalls when the bathroom door swung open. Their laughter abruptly ended when they saw Tran staring back at them, a six-foot-two former Atherton Eagle defensive lineman and their resident advisor, who would clearly rather be crushing the skulls of quarterbacks then watching over freshmen. He did it for the free dorm room.

"Are those cigarettes?" Tran asked.

Randall tossed his into the nearest sink.

"They better just be cigarettes," Tran added.

"Sorry. You got us It's crack," Kathryn told him.

"Put it out," Tran ordered.

"Just kidding. It's not crack."

"Out!" Tran barked.

Kathryn nodded and made no move to extinguish the cigarette. "Kathryn!"

"I don't want to clog up the sink."

Randall couldn't contain his laughter. Tran let out a defeated groan and let the bathroom door bang shut behind him.

"Behold the power of steroids," Kathryn muttered, popping the cigarette back into her mouth.

"Has anyone ever told you that you have a problem with authority?"

"Just my parents," Kathryn responded, sucking one last drag and moving to a stall. *And look what happened the last time I kept a secret from them?* she thought, and then tossed the cigarette into the toilet, flushing it with one foot on the handle before she could answer herself. "Speaking of which, have you talked to yours lately?" Kathryn asked

"No. Why?"

"I got an E-mail from my father. About Thanksgiving."

Randall groaned, a little theatrically, Kathryn thought "I think I managed to wiggle my way out of that one," he said.

"It's only two weeks away. God, it's like a cruel trick, making us go home this soon."

"Why don't we go to Boston?" Randall asked.

Kathryn turned, surprised. "Are you serious?"

"Yeah," Randall turned from his reflection to face her. "It's only an hour by train."

"Where will we stay?"

"I'll ask Mummy and Daddy to get us a hotel room."

Kathryn furrowed her brow "Will they?"

"Of course," Randall said defensively. "If I point out how many hours of my childhood were spent in the care of a nanny who didn't speak my language."

Kathryn laughed. The idea was appealing. Thanksgiving had been a vague concern in the back of her mind for several weeks, but after receiving the E-mail from her father it had turned into a nagging worry. The ease with which Randall had offered her a way out made her slightly giddy. "I've only driven through Boston on the way here. What will we do?"

"Whatever we want," Randall said casually.

Kathryn met his gaze. "Poor little rich boy."

Something flickered in Randall's eyes and his smile weakened.

"Sorry, I didn't mean it like that. . It's just like, well, hey, let's go to Boston! I wish everything could be so easy"

"It isn't," Randall said, tone clipped. "Ever."

Brittle silence settled and Kathryn felt a strange mixture of defensiveness tinged with guilt. She knew that Randall's parents and their money was a touchy subject. Randall told tales of being locked in his parents' Park Avenue apartment, shuffled between stuffy private schools and after-school clubs his parents had enrolled him in without his consent and tended to by an endless succession of indifferent nannies and incompetent baby-sitters, but throughout his war stories he employed just enough self-conscious sarcasm so as not to seem arrogant, while painting a picture of his parents' wealth as oppressive, as his mother and father's best tool for keeping him at arm's length. But whenever she made reference to it, the result was an awkward stop in the conversation.

"Do you want to go?" Randall asked, turning from the sink.

"Yeah. Randall, look, I really didn't mean anything."

"Kathryn, forget about it."

Randall was almost to the bathroom door when he realized she wasn't following. He turned.

"I mean, who am I to talk. It's not exactly like I'm on financial aid."

"You don't need to apologize, Kathryn."

The abruptness of his tone belied his statement, and Kathryn found herself staring at him with growing bewilderment. He let out a defeated sigh and slumped back against the door. "I came here to get away from them. And I had to work really hard to do it. Money didn't help me. Not once You have to have more than money to get away from a man who's so used to getting what he wants that there isn't any room for his son . . . or his wife . . . to want anything."

His eyes had wandered away from hers and she stared at his face for several seconds; his expression was plaintive. Obviously he was visualizing the parents he rarely talked about, but whom Kathryn had formed a mental picture of down to the last detail. Mrs. Stone (Randall had never said her first name) was a fading debutante and the beneficiary of several well-performed plastic surgeries, as well as the unwilling recipient of Randall's sharp wit. Her picture of Mr. Stone was more vague, but Randall's description had just augmented it: a taciturn corporate something or other, in sharp contrast to her own father, whose warmth and openness had become more obtrusive as Kathryn had become an increasingly private teenager. She had trouble imagining how this stern, silver-haired caricature reacted as his son began to wear tight, designer clothing that advertised the curves of his ass, outfits that played leather against metal.

"I know it sounds so stupid," Kathryn said falteringly. "But a lot of us here have things . . . and people . . . we would rather leave behind."

His eyes met hers again, and his smile was warm. "Isn't that called 'running'?"

The idea of returning home for Thanksgiving once again stabbed her stomach, and she shook her head. "No," she said. "It's growing up."

Randall had gone from gazing into space to staring at her so intently it disarmed her. "You're so pure, Kathryn"

"Oh, shut up!"

"I'm serious." His face wore a faint but appreciative smile. "I envy it."

The naked compliment made her uncomfortable and she furrowed her brow as she met his stare again. "No one else here has what we have," Randall said softly. "At least that's what I think."

Part of her was stricken by the suddenness of the statement, but another part of her yearned to believe it was true. After only two months of friendship, she couldn't imagine a night at Atherton without at least several hours in his company, and during those hours they had become experts at completing each other's sentences. They had become the pair that went everywhere together, knew more than anyone together. Meeting Randall had suggested that maybe all men her age didn't use their seemingly God-given self-confidence to erect a facade that hid the frightened and careless little boys they really were. Randall may have had confidence that bordered on stupidity, but at least he sometimes used it to show her the little boy he hadn't outgrown yet.

Without thinking, she crossed the tiled floor and rested her head against his chest. He held her. After several seconds, she found herself taking stock of all she hadn't told him, all he had to intuit. Someday, just not today, she would tell him why she needed to know him, because the last man she had cared this deeply for had taken everything she had to offer, and almost given her death in return.

He kissed her on the top of her head. "Time to sleep," he said in a baby voice.

She grunted. "My dreams have been screwed up lately."

"Nightmares?" he asked.

She nodded, one ear rubbing against his T-shirt.

"I'll tuck you in," he said, grabbing her hand and leading her out of the bathroom.

She was grateful he didn't ask her what the nightmares were about, but she remembered her last one by the time they were at the door to her room. "Hey," she whispered. "I read your story"

"And?"

"I loved it."

He nodded as if that were the answer he was expecting. This bothered her. "But it's kind of cruel to leave your reader hanging like that."

"What do you mean?" he asked, his jaw tightening.

"Well, so the boy derails the train. Destroys the entire town. Then what?"

Randall's eyes glazed over slightly, and she guessed she had mildly offended him.

"I don't know," he said "It would be another story."

She kissed him on the cheek. "You should write it," she whispered.

"Maybe I will," he said with a flickering smile, before heading across the hall to this room.


Randall lay awake listening to the steady rattle of the heating vent and to Jesse's breaths lengthening into snores. Condensation blurred the window panes. Stockton Hall was eerily quiet, and Randall fought the urge to look at the digital clock as night turned into a sleepless early morning. In darkness, the cinderblock cell in which he lived seemed to expand slightly, shadow gave more distance to the space between the foot of his bed and the glimpse of Jesse's naked back above the sheet.

He shut his eyes and imagined Kathryn fast asleep across the hall. But for some reason she was suffering from nightmares, so he guessed his image of her sleeping soundly, her mouth hanging slightly open against the pillow like a little girl's, was a little too envious.

He opened his eyes just in time, before the image of Kathryn asleep in her bed could be replaced by the photo of Lisa Eberman he had seen on the desk of Eric's office and memorized. She was standing on the bow of a sailboat, looking back at the camera as if she were annoyed by the lens and drawing her wind-whipped black hair out of her face with one hand, blue water stretching out behind her.

In the beginning it had gone so well. But how could he have planned for this?

• • •

That October afternoon, he had been halfway to the ATM machine on Brookline Avenue when he spotted Eric standing on the corner, so he slowed his steps. When he saw Eric was headed his way, he stopped, made a sharp left, and deftly slid his card into the reader before deliberately punching in the wrong code. The machine beeped loudly. Randall looked into the reflective glass above the machine and saw Eric notice him, his step faltering. Randall angrily punched in another code without even looking at the keypad and the machine beeped again in protest. Randall slapped an open palm against the side.

"Fuck!" he cried, maybe too loudly. He tightened his face into a scowl and ripped the card from the machine, turning and almost walking straight into where he knew Eric was standing.

"It looks like someone's put you on a budget," Eric said, and Randall could tell from the tight expression on his face that he had hooked him the other night, even if he had left without another word after admitting that he had followed Eric home.

Randall let out an exasperated sigh and whipped his wallet from his pocket. "I've got, like, eight hundred pages to read and all I wanted was some coffee, but my parents forgot to . . ." He trailed off, and Eric arched his eyebrows, either wanting him to continue or alarmed by his display.

If only he knew, Randall thought, before returning to his act.

"They forgot to make the deposit. Remembering isn't their thing."

"What is their thing?" Eric asked, amused.

"Drinking," Randall answered flatly, meeting Eric's stare.

Eric's laughter had an edge to it. "I'm sure I can lend you the . . ." Eric's hand barely made it to his back pocket by the time Randall cut in, reaching out and grabbing Eric's wrist firmly. "No. Please. You can't borrow money from a professor. Isn't that some kind of rule?"

The mention of rules and professors lit something in Eric's eyes, and Randall saw it and thought this might end up being easier than he had first thought. A current passed between them, and Randall noticed some small crack in Eric's decorum, revealing more than the man had allowed himself to show in their previous meeting. Randall tried to keep his eyes from wandering the length of Eric's broad frame to where the collar of his shirt was open, free of the tie he probably wore all day, revealing the stubbly terminus of the five o'clock shadow extending down his neck.

"I'm sorry about the other night. I didn't mean to . . ."

Eric shook his head abruptly and looked away. He was either trying to say it was nothing, or simply didn't want Randall to mention it at all. Eric was staring up the street. At what? Randall followed Eric's gaze to where the sun was a bright suggestion, sinking behind stripped tree branches and a canopy of clotted gray autumnal clouds.

"Perhaps you wouldn't have such a problem with it," Eric began deliberately, as if he had answered some question for himself that Randall knew he would answer, "if I told you I could use some coffee myself."

Buying coffee together was harmless, Randall agreed, as they walked briskly down Brookline Avenue, past Moliere's, where students bought rancid espresso from rude skater punks during their boycotts of the corporate coffee chains. By the time they were waiting in line at the new Starbucks, located next to the green, talk had drifted to the monotonous details of Randall's academic schedule and the amount of coursework. By the time they were walking across the desolate green, where evening was turning the rooftops of buildings, on the quad into lengthening shadows across the sidewalks, Randall was seeing what he thought Eric saw, a professor and student discussing a course. Harmless. And Randall didn't like it, so he began to talk faster, dutifully moving the progression forward.

"The birds are my favorite."

"Birds?" Eric asked, and took a sip of coffee, which burned the roof of his mouth. He winced and hissed.

"Small, quick-flying birds which were meant to represent those fallen souls that still had the potential for salvation. If you ask me, I think Bosch was kind of a prankster."

Randall had read Eric's book twice. He had highlighted different lines over the course of both readings. What had begun as a task became more of a labor of something close to love, if not for Eric than for the supposed torments of the painter Bosch, which Randall already suspected were too similar to Eric's own fears.

"A prankster?" Eric asked, with a note of condescension. Randall heard Eric trying to cut him down to size, trying to restore him to his role as the naïve student. And why would Eric have been trying to do that if Randall hadn't become a presence in his life that refused to depart? "Try heretic."

A hand-holding couple moving their way refused to part, and the two men were forced to step aside and allow the couple to pass between them. Within seconds, Randall closed the gap again and they were walking side by side

"You asked me a question the other night," Eric said, and Randall thought, So he *will* mention the other night, when I showed up on his doorstep unannounced and practically forced my way inside his house. "You asked me whether or not I believed—"

"I remember," Randall said softly

Either his tone of voice or the question itself made Eric stop and turn to face him "I used to believe that the history of art was a superior discipline," he began, lasering hard into Randall's eyes "Superior to studying battles between kings or quantifying the physical forces that shape our universe I thought the real truth lay in the evolving nightmares and fantasies of a culture So, there was a time when I might have been susceptible to one artist's vision of the world. But that time is long gone. So the answer is no. I do not believe that Satan is the ruler of the physical world. And I do not believe that to be damned is to feel _ alive in your own body. As you said"

Randall waited a second before correcting him "As *you* said."

Wind rattled the tree branches overhead, shedding curled leaves.

Eric's gaze left his, but now it was obvious Eric was checking to see if anyone was headed toward them. They were alone on the green and it was getting darker, and for a brief second Randall wondered if Eric would see this circumstance as permission to close the remaining foot of distance between them, but instead Eric looked at Randall with fear in his eyes, fear that Randall would close the distance for him One thing was sure; they were no longer simply teacher and student But before Randall could decide whether or not to advance, Eric said, "I'm going to my office"

He was moving off down the sidewalk before Randall realized that he hadn't simply given some stock farewell—"I better be going" or "Nice speaking with you." He had told Randall where he was going.

Randall waited until Eric had almost disappeared behind the student union before he began to follow.

The art history department was housed in a paint-peeling Victorian just outside the gates to the quad, on a street that sloped downhill toward the river. Randall had to hold the rail as he ascended its steep front step; he noticed that the windows of the building were dark at six-thirty in the evening. He expected the front door to be locked, but it was not and he pushed it open. The front foyer was empty. Beside him was a table stacked with course syllabi and a wall of mail slots for professors and their teaching assistants. At the end of the first-floor hallway an office door yawned open and light spilled across the carpet.

Randall moved down the hallway, wondering if he was trying to force everything to fruition too quickly, or if everything was simply happening more quickly than he had anticipated.

When he appeared in the doorway, Eric looked up from a stack of papers. Something that looked like anger tightened his face. He lifted his head fully as if prepared for Randall to do nothing more than give a speech on why he missed class or why he had to turn in a paper later. But when Randall stepped inside, drawing the door shut behind him with his hand on the knob, Eric placed one bent elbow on the edge of the desk and an open palm over his mouth, sucking in a tight breath against the flesh of his hand.

Randall rounded the edge of his desk and sat down next to the paper Eric had been grading. Suddenly Eric turned his chair by kicking lightly on the floor, and Randall was surprised to see the chair pivot to face him instead of in the other direction. But Eric kept his open palm pressed over his mouth, resting his bent elbow on his other arm, which he had braced across his stomach.

He was not ready to be touched: Randall knew this from experience. His own nudity always broke the ice faster than any physical advance. So he reached down and curled the hem of his sweater and his undershirt into both fists. He lifted them both, listening for Eric to make another sound, which he didn't. He had dropped them both on the floor by the time he sank to his knees, and he saw that Eric's arms were now resting on the chair's arms.

Randall held Eric's gaze, and saw confirmation of all he had been told: there was one thing from which this man could not protect himself from, could not hold at bay with the power of his poise and intellect alone. And better yet, Randall saw confirmation that he was about to become that one thing.

Emboldened, and breaking into the next stage of his planned seduction, Randall lifted one leg, foot planted on the floor, raising himself to Eric's eye level as he slid a hand around the man's neck. Eric twisted his head slightly against the back of the chair, the most he could turn away, and Randall released his neck, sinking back to his knees again. Now sure of where he should begin, Randall sent his hand to the buckle of Eric's belt.

Randall jerked his eyes away from the lightening sky when he heard Jesse grunt as if he had been kicked in the stomach.

He lifted his head from the pillow, peering over his shoulder into the darkness on Jesse's side of the room. Jesse lay on his back, mouth hanging slightly open and one arm bent against his forehead. After staring out the window, Randall's eyes couldn't adjust to the darkness quickly enough. He heard the sound of Jesse drawing the sheets back and the familiar twin slaps of his bare feet hitting the floor. Randall went rigid; he guessed that Jesse had no idea he was being watched as he plodded stark naked to his desk and tore several tissues from the box of Kleenex.

"See what happens when I have to go without?" Jesse said into the darkness.

Startled at being addressed, Randall froze. Turning away in response would make it obvious that he had been staring. Pale light through the window fell across Jesse's chest. He swabbed the wad of tissues across his stomach, his laugh low and gnarled by sleep. He threw both arms out, glanced down at the deflating tube of his erection, and then looked back at Randall. The remaining semen was smeared in a band above Jesse's navel. Unsure of whether Jesse could see his face, Randall tightened his expression anyway. Despite the note of playfulness in Jesse's voice, the boyishness with which he displayed his nocturnal emission, he was not playing the little boy expressing pride in what he'd done. Right now, he was the kid on the playground shoving the dead insect in a little girl's face.

Didn't Jesse know him any better?

"It's nothing I haven't seen. And I've seen a lot," Randall mumbled before turning over and burying the side of his face in his pillow.

Satisfied with his response, Randall tried to wipe his mind clean for the sleep that had so far proven elusive. He was somewhat successful. While the images of memory receded, a single thought swung back and forth in his mind like a pendulum, grating louder each time it scraped the ground on its downward arc. Jesse sleeps naked.

# CHAPTER THREE

McKinley Quad was invigorated by the early snow; students moved more briskly between classes, their breath fogging the air in front of them. Canvas banners concealed the Doric columns of the student union's facade, announcing upcoming theater productions and the imminent Gay and Lesbian Alliance Dance. The broad lawns were still dusted white, and the students who usually lounged on them even in cold weather relocated to the steps of the union, watching the passing parade as they sipped their cups of coffee and hot cider. It was one of those bright, frigid days that Kathryn was growing to love; the sky was a dome of blue above the buildings lining the quad, and sunlight reflected off piles of shoveled snow. Cold seemed to cleanse the air on this side of the country, in stark contrast to San Francisco, where chilly temperatures arrived with slow and creeping fog that would turn to soup outside the windows of her parents' house in Sea Cliff.

Her discussion section that Monday morning for Philosophies of Free Speech had been a dud. The teaching assistant, who resembled a young Prince Charles, didn't have the knack for keeping ten freshmen engaged in a discussion of the ACLU's position on the censorship of pornography, probably because his teaching style consisted of delivering lectures to the wall just above the students' heads. Kathryn had grown increasingly repulsed as she realized that during his monologue, the TA was using as evidence for his argument magazines and videos he probably kept stashed under his own bed. She wished she had found another course to fill her philosophy requirement.

As she made her way to the mailroom entrance, she noticed huddles of lacrosse players sitting outside the mailroom shooting annoyed glances at the Environmental Equality League—one of whom was shouting something incomprehensible through a bullhorn—as they paced in front of a table stacked with flyers and displaying a poster demanding that President Bush mend the Kyoto Treaty. Even as the university preached diversity in all its literature, for most people the word conjured up images of tree huggers smoking pot and strumming their guitars. But Kathryn had seen that diversity at Atherton was just that: socialists walked to class alongside debutantes, in-class debates pitted children of the inner city against New England boarding-school graduates. The only great equalizer was Atherton's hefty price tag and the university's reputation for being sparing with need-based financial aid; skin color and political affiliation among the students may have differed, but most kept a sports sedan in his or her parents' garage at home, a car received brand-new as a gift at age seventeen.

Kathryn slowed her steps when she noticed a Channel 2 News van parked outside the gates to the quad; its satellite dish extended, a glossy black–haired reporter addressing her camera  Kathryn walked several steps past the entrance to the mailroom so she could overhear. ". . . But here on campus, students and faculty have returned to their normal schedules this Monday morning, no doubt trying to cope with the revelation that the tragic loss of a professor's wife this past weekend is being blamed not on bad driving conditions, but on a combination of alcohol and prescription medication."

Two hemp-clad potheads rushed into the frame  One of them threw his arms around the reporter's shoulders and gave her a smack on the cheek, while the other took a bow in front of the camera. The reporter's earnestness evaporated. "Can you two morons go drink some coffee so I can shoot this fucking thing already?" Kathryn couldn't help but laugh.

In her mail slot, Kathryn found hand-delivered flyers for student clubs, the campus equivalent of junk mail. She was hurling them into a recycling bin when a hand hooked her shoulder. She turned, feeling a vague sense of recognition when she saw the girl standing in front of her.

"Hey!"

For a second Kathryn was struck dumb. Lauren Raines was almost unrecognizable. Her shoulder-length red hair had been replaced by a pageboy cut, dyed charcoal black. She had surrendered her typical Ralph Lauren ensemble for a tattered cardigan the color of coffee, and her cargo pants bagged around the kneecaps. It was evident that she used to wear a lot of makeup because its absence revealed alabaster-tinted cheeks marred by red blemishes that couldn't be mistaken for blush. The dark circles under her eyes contrasted with her bloodshot pupils.

When Kathryn's jaw dropped, Lauren told her, "I met someone." She smiled triumphantly.

"Really? Not . . ." When she trailed off, Lauren looked confused for a second, then realized Kathryn was referring to Jesse Lowry. "Please. No," Lauren said, her too-broad smile replaced by a grimace of disgust. She shook her head as if to rid herself of Jesse's name. The smile returned with full, unnerving force. "I know. I'm sorry I've been MIA. I should have called or something."

"Did you move too?" Kathryn asked.

Lauren's laugh was strained. "Almost. Maria's got a place off campus, so I've kind of been hanging out there a lot."

Maria? Kathryn blinked and shook her head slightly, and Lauren grinned sheepishly. "I know. It sounds kind of weird "

"No, I just . . ." She couldn't finish. So Lauren's a lesbian now, Kathryn thought, feeling like the only avowed heterosexual left on campus. Chatty, boy-obsessed Lauren, who the first week of school managed to collect every specially designed Starbucks coffee tumbler and bemoaned her lack of dates, now wore the costume of an aspiring anarchist and mentioned her new girlfriend with a defensive forwardness. "This getup is new," Kathryn managed. Lauren's weak smile told her she had stepped over the line. "Do you have class?" Kathryn asked, covering for herself.

"Done for the day. Mondays are light for me."

"Walk with me."

"How's Randall?" Lauren asked once they were outside.

"Fine. Still trying to bring culture and glamour to Stockton Hall. It's not working though. Everything there's pretty much the same. You haven't missed much."

Lauren pondered Stockton for a moment, as if it were a distant hometown she had left years before. "You know, Lauren, when you stopped hanging out on our floor, I thought it might have something to do with Jesse. And I understand. Totally."

Lauren kept their pace brisk, frowning slightly at the sidewalk ahead of them. "You think Jesse turned me into a lesbian?" she asked, amused.

"I didn't say that."

"Maria's what I need right now. No one's lying to anyone."

Those words hit home for Kathryn, and she was reminded of their previous friendship, in spite of Lauren's transformation. The two had met during orientation, and Lauren had been the first engineering major Kathryn encountered who didn't have a social disorder. She hadn't struck Kathryn as a frightened little girl waiting to emerge from her shell or come out of the closet Now, it seemed as if the contours of her body bothered her. Everything about her new appearance smacked not of metamorphosis into true self, but of self-abasement. The twenty-first century version of covering yourself in sackcloth and ashes.

"I was just worried," Kathryn began again, carefully. "You used to hang out on our floor almost every night. Then you and Jesse hooked up, and it was like you wouldn't come within ten feet of his room."

Lauren slowed her steps until they were both standing in the middle of the sidewalk. Students weaved around them. Lauren met Kathryn's stare with a stony glare of her own. "He didn't rape me, if that's what you're implying."

It was Kathryn's turn to be offended. "I wasn't."

"How is that motherfucker, anyway?"

"The same. He manages to land on his feet no matter who he's just rolled off of" It was a deliberately insensitive attempt to strike at Lauren's composure, and Kathryn regretted it, but when Lauren's eyes shot to her feet, she realized it had worked.

"I told Maria about him," she began quietly. "She's helping me."

"With what?"

"At first I wanted to take every memory of him and rip it out of my brain. But it doesn't work like that. The best I can do is cleanse myself slowly. Lock the memories away in a secret part of my brain and purge the rest of myself."

Kathryn took a second to digest this dizzying stream of . . . she really didn't know what. "Were you two that involved?"

"Is anyone ever really *involved* with Jesse Lowry? Of course not It only took two weeks." She shrugged, then rasped and let out a laugh.

"I feel like I should have warned you about him."

"I'm a big girl, Kathryn. I could have handled a one-night stand."

"Then what was it, Lauren?" Kathryn asked, her confusion sharpening her tone.

"Have you slept with him?"

"Um, no. I think I've made it pretty clear that he shouldn't keep me in his sights."

Lauren glanced down at her watch. "Yeah, well, I doubt he would want to piss too close to home. Look, Kathryn, the guy's an—"

"What does that mean?" Kathryn cut her off.

Lauren cocked her head, meeting Kathryn's glare only briefly before shaking her head slowly back and forth. "It's not just sex with him," she finally said, her tone distant but less guarded.

"You want to talk about it?" Kathryn asked. She tried to sound gentle.

"I have," Lauren responded, with a renewed, but faint smile. "To the right people."

Kathryn nodded, trying to indicate that she got the drift. "I'm sorry for . . ."

"Don't be," Lauren said. Kathryn was surprised to feel Lauren's hand on her wrist. "I didn't mean it like that."

Kathryn just nodded and returned her eyes to Lauren's They were glazed, staring through her. "You should come by some time. Meet Maria. She has a knack for putting things in perspective." Lauren released Kathryn's wrist and looked back to her watch. "Gotta run."

And she was off. Kathryn watched her go. Several feet away, she stopped. "Tell Randall I said hi. I'd love to know what he's been up to." She waved, turned, and disappeared into the crowd.

*Nice of her to invite me to meet Maria,* Kathryn thought, *and not bother to tell me where she lives.*

"Oh come on!" April barked.

Kathryn lifted one hand to quiet her. "She didn't say she was a lesbian."

"No. But *you* did."

"It was weird, all right. You remember her, don't you?"

"Jesse might be a total prick. I'll give you that. But he's not capable of turning a woman into a lesbian." April returned to sawing her piece of overcooked chicken. Kathryn slumped back into her chair, her appetite gone. She should have known better than to tell April, the queen of skeptics, about Lauren, her whacked-out psychology, and her maybe-lesbianism.

Starnes Dining Hall was deluged by the lunch rush. The surrounding tables were packed, but the clatter of dishes wouldn't be loud enough to distract other people if she and April decided to really get into it. She noticed April staring at her across the table and realized she was pouting. "Lauren Raines is going through some sort of freshman identity crisis, and I pity this Maria woman who's going to have to weather it with her. A good dyke would know better."

"Why are you so hellbent on defending him?"

"Honestly? Because I think the fact that you're so dead set on slandering him is a little weird." Having finished only half her chicken, April pushed back her tray. "Kathryn, don't turn into one of those women here who thinks you can't have sex without at least one person being a victim. They're boring. No one wants to hang out with them.

Kathryn felt coldness arrowing into her chest. "I'm not allowed to dislike Jesse as a matter of principle?"

"Jesse sleeps with the first person who falls at his feet. And you're obviously waiting for the perfect guy to bump into you at a party and slide a ring on your finger. Neither of those approaches can be qualified as *principles.*"

Kathryn glared at April. "All Jesse Lowry has done since he got here is hurt people. I don't like that. That's principle."

April seemed chastened by the ice in Kathryn's voice, but if

Kathryn knew her own roommate, she wouldn't give up that easily. "Fine," April said softly. "But if Jesse were someone else's roommate, would you really care what he did in bed?"

"Stop trying to convert her, April. We're getting noise complaints!" Randall dropped his tray at the head of the table, slid his Prada bag off one shoulder, and flounced down into the chair. He brushed gelled spikes back from his forehead with one hand as he looked from one glowering girl to the other. "Alrighty, then," he mumbled.

April rose from her chair, scooping her book bag up off the floor by one strap. "I've got a lab," she mumbled, already several feet away from the table by the time she slid the straps over both shoulders.

Randall was respectfully silent as she departed.

"She treats me like I'm her baby sister," Kathryn finally said.

"She's got a chip on her shoulder the size of the Korean peninsula. Don't let yourself be her whipping girl."

"What's she so pissed about?" Kathryn asked.

Randall chewed a bit of salad slowly in thought.

"Maybe she *is* trying to convert you."

"I'll be sure not to tell anyone at the GLA that you said that."

"Please. Why do you think their latest campaign is against Atherton's heterosexist housing policy?"

"Because all gay people end up being attracted to their roommates?" Kathryn retorted.

Randall looked up from his plate. "Well, if their roommate is as fine as you are, how can they help themselves?" He grinned, revealing even, white teeth, remarkable, Kathryn thought, for such a heavy smoker.

Kathryn managed a weak smile, noting the ease and speed with which Randall had ducked the obvious implication of her question. How attracted are you to the studly walking dick you sleep five feet away from every night? she wanted to demand. "Did you talk to your parents?" she asked instead.

"About what?"

"Thanksgiving," Kathryn said. Randall looked up, fork halfway to his mouth. "Boston," she added.

He shook his head. "Not yet. My dad's in Japan right now and whenever he leaves the country my mom kind of . . ." He lifted one cupped hand as if chugging from a bottle.

Kathryn tried a sympathetic grunt. "It's not that big a deal," Randall cut in quickly, as if embarrassed he had laid his drama on her. "It's only when Dad's gone. When he's home he's like . . . her anchor."

"It still kind of sucks," Kathryn said sympathetically, but trying to prod him for more.

Randall's face went blank, his eyes on his plate as he shoveled another forkful of salad into his mouth. Kathryn decided to let it go. Still, she wondered if maybe it was Randall's parents who didn't want him home for Thanksgiving. A style victim of a gay son who disdained them might not be their idea of someone to be thankful for. New York was three hours away and they had never visited, and Kathryn couldn't recall ever coming into Randall's room when he was on the phone with them. She searched for a new conversation topic. Given her spat with April, she thought Lauren Raines's shift in sexuality was taboo, so she dislodged her sliver-thin copy of the *Atherton Herald* from under one corner of her tray and slid it across the table to Randall.

"Check this out," she said. Randall's eyes alighted on the black-and-white photograph of Lisa Eberman. "Friday night Tim was bitching about how he hated writing for the *Herald*, and today he's page one. He even got the headline."

Randall picked up the paper, chewing slowly as he read it. She watched his face go grave. The grim photo of Lisa Eberman had struck her as well, but not as completely as it did Randall; her thought was that they could have at least shown some respect for the woman by running a picture of her smiling. But the candid shot showed a dour-looking woman, disturbed by the camera's intrusion. A barrette held her black hair back on her head in a flat pleat. Crow's-feet framed slanted, dark eyes above pinched lips.

"Are they *kidding* with this?" Randall asked suddenly.

"What?" Kathryn asked, alarmed, but eager to know what had struck him.

"She's holding a drink!" There was outrage in his voice. He turned the paper for her to see.

Yeah, she was holding a drink, Kathryn thought. So what?

"Did you read the article?" Randall persisted.

"I skimmed it "

"She was a drunk," Randall said darkly, turning the paper

Kathryn remembered Randall's mother hitting the sauce while his father was out of town on business, and fell silent.

"Shit," he whispered. "I've got a lecture."

"Bye," Kathryn said, startled.

He patted the top of her head absently as he departed. She would have made fun of this small gesture if she thought he would have heard her call after him

Throughout the lecture hall, conversations among the two hundred students in Foundations of Western Art I were hushed. Randall guessed that most of them were showing respect for their grief-stricken professor, who might come striding down the aisle at any moment. If any of them had managed to catch the local news, they would have learned Eric had flown to Philadelphia, where Lisa would be laid to rest in her family's plot He sat in his usual seat in the second row, from which he had first stared up at Eric's fine-boned face, watching Mitchell Seaver and Maria Klein whispering at the foot of the steps leading up to the stage. No doubt they were debating who should give the lecture in Eric's absence Randall knew them both to be the unspoken leaders of the course's cadre of teaching assistants, and the rest of the group looked bored, slouched in their chairs, regarding the two prima donnas vying for the microphone

Finally, at fifteen minutes past the starting time of lecture, Mitchell mounted the steps to the podium, and Maria returned to her seat. Randall held a quiet dislike for both graduate students. Maria was the leader of his discussion section (which he had only attended twice). Her coffee-colored hair, parted down the center, and the contrast of her gentle facial features with an olive complexion suggested a mixed ethnicity also represented by her first and last names She had looked dressed for winter back in September, rarely appearing in class without a tweed jacket or a scarf On the first day of discussion, Maria had exalted the Venus of Willendorf, with its bloated proportions, to be the true ideal of female physicality, before she went on to dissect the oppressive body ideals forced on women by the fashion magazines of the current era. Rather than hear great works of art periodically dumbed down by campus politics, Randall stopped attending.

Mitchell Seaver adjusted the microphone deliberately, and the metallic squelch brought about instant silence. Randall thought that underneath Mitchell's shaggy pile of sandy hair, and behind the wire-rimmed spectacles he probably didn't need, there was a reasonably attractive guy being lost to academic anemia. Generous brown eyes and a slightly pug nose gave him a boyish attractiveness, but his appeal disappeared as soon as he began speaking in his lightly nasal, flat, affectless voice, which occasionally rose to a shrill pitch as if he were being forced to talk over people only he could hear.

"I'm sure we're all aware of the loss Dr. Eberman suffered this past weekend, and it should come as no surprise that he's decided to take some time off to sort through personal matters," Mitchell announced. "He has requested that in his absence we do our best to follow the syllabus. With the patience and cooperation of all of you, I hope we can do just that."

Mitchell paused. Randall shot a glance at Maria, who had turned slightly in her seat as if expecting students to pop up from their chairs at the prospect of being lectured by TAs. The lecture hall was stone still. Maria turned forward again, gave Mitchell a nod, and it was clear that nothing else would be said about the weekend's events.

As Mitchell began a general introduction of the Byzantine empire, Randall felt an odd sense of injustice, as if a moment of sanctioned silence should have been held. Maybe no one in the class had known Lisa Eberman, but this was, after all, the academic temple her husband dominated three times a week. He tried to distract himself from this feeling of injustice by sliding the *Atherton Herald* out from under his notebook. As he read by the pale light thrown off a screen filled by a succession of emperors laid out in glittering tessarae, his growing sense of pity for Lisa Eberman was only compounded by the fact that Tim Mathis's article made it clear she had died an unknown on a campus that held her husband in high esteem.

Tim began with a pathetic excuse for an obituary, which said little beyond the fact that she was a native of Philadelphia and had met her husband while they were both pursuing doctorate degrees at Duke University. (Tim probably had no way of finding out that when Eric was offered a faculty position at Atherton, his alma mater, he had all but strong-armed Lisa out of finishing her degree. Randall only knew because it had come up in one of Eric's post-sex, too-many-glasses-of-wine-beforehand confessions.)

Randall struggled to read the article patiently, desperate to get to the raw facts of last Friday night in hopes of answering the question plaguing him ever since Eric had slammed the door to his house. What time did the accident occur on Friday night? Before or after Eric had taken Randall to his bed?

According to a source close to the Eberman family, Paula Willis, Lisa Eberman's sister, is suspicious of rumors that Eberman was intoxicated at the time of the accident. Willis, 31, suffers from cancer, and authorities believe that Eberman was on her way to visit her in Worcester when the accident occurred

While toxicology reports confirm that Eberman was driving with a blood alcohol level of 09, the autopsy has left lingering questions that Atherton police have yet to answer. The coroner's report makes it clear that the official cause of death was drowning, but also specifies that due to the amount of time Lisa Eberman's body spent submerged in the near freezing waters of the Atherton River, her exact time of death can only be approximated.

Further complicating matters, according to official sources, is the anonymous 911 call reporting the accident from a downtown phone booth. Police attempts to track down the caller have been unsuccessful. However, suspicions that the caller might have been involved in the accident have been dispelled by preliminary forensic work performed on the victim's Volvo. The station wagon didn't show any signs of collision with anything other than the bridge guardrail.

Randall slid the newspaper back under his notebook, balling his hands into fists on top. He couldn't help shooting a few glances around to see if anyone had noted the frightened intensity with which he'd read the article three times.

Where the hell was Tim Mathis getting such vital information?

The guy worked for a campus newspaper, for Christ's sake And while Tim was almost obsessively persistent in just about everything he did, he seemed to have taken to this story with a particular ferocity; it left Randall frightened, wondering just what it was about Lisa's death had gotten under Tim's skin. Worse, if Tim had gone this far already in one article, how much further would he have to go before he found out what the real dark secret in Eric and Lisa's marriage was, a secret that maybe Lisa Eberman didn't even know?

*Maybe* Lisa Eberman didn't know.

Randall's row had emptied out by the time he realized the lecture was over.


Atherton's West Campus looked like what outsiders pictured when they thought of campus life—what Randall himself had imagined years before, yearning for escape so badly that his chest ached, conjuring up fantasies of a manicured, perfectly tended miniature city lying placidly between ivory towers The reality was that Atherton was not completely beautiful—Michael Price had seen to that—but it was a more cloistered and protected environment than Randall had ever known, and West Campus remained a reminder of childhood dreams Walking to Tim Mathis's dorm, Randall recalled how his late-night visits in September had been a welcome reprieve from the sterility of Stockton Hall. Tim lived in Braddock Hall, one of the smaller and more desirable colonial-style dorms. Cold had already withered the ivy covering its walls into mud-colored tapestries of dead leaves. As Randall approached the entrance, he spotted Sharif, one of Tim's suitemates. Sharif gave him a slight nod, and held the door open for him with one hand, brushing his dreads back off his forehead with the other.

"Here to see Tim?"

Randall nodded, hoping that Sharif wouldn't point out that it had been almost a month since he last stopped by Tim's room. "Is he here?" Randall asked as he squeezed through the open door past Sharif.

"Should be. He's been bitching all morning about the flack he's been getting for that article in the *Herald*. Did you read it?"

"What kind of flack?"

They ascended the stairs to the second floor. "You know Tim. If there's shit within a mile he's gotta stir it."

Sharif opened the door to the suite: three single bedrooms centered around a common room occupied by a tattered sofa and a suggestion of a kitchenette. The door to Tim's bedroom was closed and Randall could hear Tim's high-pitched, intermittently animated voice on the other side. "You want something from the fridge?" Sharif asked, startling him.

Randall shook his head no, and Sharif nodded. Sharif, like Tim's other two suitemates, was straight, but he was the only one who made a show of being "okay with it" by treating every guy Tim brought back to the dorm as if he were the man Tim would marry. Tim was never that for Randall, but he was older, wiser and safe—and now Eric was at most only two of those things.

Randall knocked lightly on Tim's door.

"John, I'm not testifying in front of the housing board. Go away!" Tim shouted back.

Randall noticed that the door was unlatched, so he gave it a gentle shove. It opened halfway to reveal Tim standing next to his desk, phone pressed to his ear, his bleached hair disheveled. He was dressed in only boxers and a T-shirt and his laptop glowed on his desk. Next to it, an ashtray overflowed with stubbed-out butts. "Whatever," Tim said into the phone. He adjusted his glasses, his eyes landing on Randall's and never leaving as he continued. "All right. Fine. This afternoon." He hung up without another word and turned to face Randall, crossing his arms over his chest, a slight smirk lifting his cheeks.

"The housing board?" Randall asked.

"Don't ask."

"I want to know," Randall said with a playful smile, taking his first step across the threshold.

"Last night John was in the bathroom, so Sharif pissed in one of those Nantucket Nectar bottles. He was on his way to put it in the trash when he ran into John in the hallway and he wanted to know why Sharif was throwing away a full bottle of lemonade. So Sharif let him drink it."

Randall shivered. "Tell me you're kidding."

"No. John's trying to petition for a change of residence. But if he doesn't get it, he's going to take a dump in Sharif's bed. This is what I get for living with a bunch of straight guys."

Randall smiled  Tim just looked at him

"You're working," Randall said. It wasn't a question, but rather an attempt to imply a familiarity that Randall feared might have been lost over the past few weeks of phone calls that he had been too preoccupied, and disinterested, to return. He knew that Tim always wrote in a frenzy, usually dressed in underwear, one cigarette burning in the ashtray and another dangling from his lip.

Randall pushed the door open all the way, then kicked it lightly closed. He took a seat on the bed, then rolled over onto his back with a stretch and an exaggerated yawn. Tim's eyes followed him the whole way, his tongue making a lump in his upper lip.

"You're quite the celebrity today, aren't you?" Randall asked.

"You read my article."

Randall nodded.

"Well, the article you didn't read was a lot more interesting." Tim tore a Camel Light from his pack and lit it.

"I thought you were the news editor."

"I'm *one* news editor," Tim practically snapped, exhaling his drag through his nostrils. "And I've got an editor-in-chief over me with a major stick up her ass. She says I turned a professor's personal loss into a tabloid spectacle."

Randall nodded, as if the description might be apt. Tim's eyes narrowed on him. "To what do I owe the honor?" he asked.

"Your article. I thought it was a great piece." Randall knew the best way to pry more information from Tim was to stroke his ego. The guy could bash the *Herald* as much as he wanted; he still considered it *The Washington Post* and had secretly crowned himself its Bob Woodward.

Tim realized his match was still lit and he shook it out with several flicks of his wrist before dropping it into his ashtray. "I didn't know you were a *Herald* reader."

"Only when I see your name in the byline."

Randall sat up, slid his arms out of his jacket, and dropped it onto the floor. He stretched out on Tim's bed again, rolling over onto one side to face him. "What's the matter, Randall?" Tim asked. "Not getting enough action from your roommate?"

"Please," Randall said with a snort.

"When you stopped calling, I thought maybe you were saving it all for him."

"You think too much."

Tim sucked a drag off his cigarette, expression grave. "What else is there to do here?"

Randall smiled to suggest that there was a lot else they could do, right there, right now. He was satisfied to see the same flicker of attraction in Tim's eyes that he noticed when they'd met at the year's first Gay and Lesbian Alliance Dance.

"I have a question for you, Bob Woodward."

Tim said nothing as Randall reached down and pulled the *Herald* out of his satchel. "Now you have to forgive me, because I'm kind of a babe in the woods when it comes to journalism, but why include this claim by her sister when Lisa Eberman's toxicology proves she was driving drunk?"

"That's what happens when an article gets butchered."

"What do you mean?" Randall asked, trying to maintain a tone of mild interest, and fighting the urge to demand Tim just hand over his unedited piece so he could take his first deep breath in several days and get the hell out of Tim's room.

"I conducted a forty-minute interview with Paula Willis and they cut it right before we went to press."

"You talked to her?" Randall asked, dropping the paper to his lap, his tone sharp with a spike of outrage he hadn't done his best to conceal.

"I called her the day after the accident. I expected her to hang up when I told her who I was, but I had been instructed to write a memorial article and that's what I was planning to do. No one on this whole campus knew a goddamn thing about Lisa Eberman, so I had to get some bio from someone. She was listed in the phone book. Well, her doctor must have her on some serious meds because she just went off."

"I'm not surprised," Randall said. "Her sister just died and she's really sick."

"She doesn't sound like it. And she didn't go off on me. She went off on Eric Eberman."

Randall widened his eyes in curiosity, as he fought down the cold knot of fear that had formed inside his chest. "What did she say?"

"She admitted Lisa drank Often. But she wasn't nearly the lush Eric Eberman made her out to be in front of the police. She basically defended Lisa's honor, implying that if she was driving drunk, then Eric had probably given her a pretty good reason to."

Gooseflesh tickled Randall's arms and he sat up, feigning a posture of attentiveness so he could cross his arms over his chest.

"You came all the way across campus to talk about Lisa Eberman?" Tim asked archly. He'd propped one bare foot on the edge of his desk, pushing his chair onto its hind legs.

Randall brushed the paper in his lap. "I just got out of lecture. Technically, I wasn't all the way across campus."

Tim shook his head, eyes moving to the window and its view of dorm-room windows alight like segments in a honeycomb. Randall pushed his back up against the wall. "You want to know the truth?" Randall asked "I've never read anything you've written before. I was impressed. Every time you used to spout off about bringing real journalism to the student newspaper . . . well, I thought it was a little starry-eyed of you."

"*Starry-eyed?*" Tim snorted, letting the chair down onto all four legs. He rose and moved to the window. "Try sleepless and driven."

"Why this story, Tim?"

"What do you mean?"

"You really went the full mile here Toxicology reports. Calling her sister."

Tim's expression hardened as he stared out the window. Randall went silent, sensing he had touched a nerve.

"I had Eberman last year. The guy's a total closet case." Tim popped his cigarette into his mouth and began picking at the frayed edge of a thumbnail. Randall kept his mouth shut, drawing his knees to his chest and wrapping his arms around them. But Tim seemed to shake free of whatever memory he had lapsed into, and he turned and met Randall head-on. "You know, Randall, I have other boys to jerk me around. In every sense of the word."

"Are you trying to make me jealous?" Randall asked, with a smile that said he wasn't the jealous type.

"Christ." Tim let out a short laugh and stubbed out his smoldering butt in the ashtray. "You're a freshman, for Christ's sake. I should know better. My freshman year here, I was like a kid in a candy store."

"You lost me."

"I wish," Tim mumbled under his breath.

"I'm here right now, Tim. What does that say?"

Tim slumped against the window. It looked like his fight might be leaving him. "It says you've always got me to fall back on."

Randall raised the paper in one hand. "Well, now that I've been given a glimpse of your genius, maybe I'll start falling back on you more often."

Tim's face went lax as his last shred of resistance left him. Randall dropped the paper and curled his index finger twice. Tim complied and crossed to the bed. Randall hooked his belt buckle with the same finger he had beckoned with and Tim fell, knees first, to the mattress in front of him.

"You're too damn cute and I don't know any better," Tim whispered.

"You're half right," Randall said, grazing Tim's lips with his first teasing kiss. "You don't know anyone better than me."

Tim groaned in weak protest before Randall pulled him down onto the bed

"That was vocal," Tim said. Next door, Sharif had responded to Randall's groans by cranking up Shaggy to almost full volume "Have you been taking voice lessons or something?"

"Don't flatter yourself," Randall said, even though that was precisely what his overenthusiastic display had been intended to do. As much as Tim seemed to demand intimacy from his sexual partners in daily life, in bed he was all porn-star curses that delayed the execution of the titilating things he so throatily promised to do. After being enveloped by the honest power of Eric's long unrequited passion, Randall felt that sex with Tim seemed no different from the men back in New York, who showed no apparent interest in how Randall's body worked, holding him down so they could do little more than take in the sight of who they were penetrating. Randall draped himself over Tim's legs as he reached down and removed his silver flask from his jacket pocket.

Tim continued packing his bowl with his thumb, cursing the dryness of the weed under his breath. "I assume you don't want any of this."

Randall fell back against his pillow and took a slug from the flask.

"You and that flask. It's very weird."

"Scotch is a gentleman's drink."

"So it's going to turn you into a gentleman?"

"Cute," Randall responded, but he was distracted by how light the flask felt in his hand. He needed a refill, and for that he needed access to Lisa's storehouse of Chivas Regal. The prospect of stealing scotch from a dead woman washed the warm post-sex flush from his veins, proving it had only been a distraction and exposing the silt of dread that still clung to his thoughts.

Tim drew the sheet up over their naked bodies with a single, uncomfortable glance at the burns on Randall's legs. Also no different from the men in New York, Randall thought. Eric had been the first man to ever touch them without fear or disgusted fascination. "How do you know Eberman's a closet case?" he asked.

Tim rolled his eyes and lifted the bowl in one hand, indicating he needed a hit before he got into it. The lighter's flame disappeared into the bowl and then reappeared magically. Tim sank back against his pillow before letting the smoke escape in a drawn-out breath. Randall hated the smell of pot. Once, it had transported him to alleys behind bars in Manhattan's Meat-Packing District; now it seemed to embody the inherent dirtiness and messiness of college life; it conjured up images of stoners he had met who babbled on about burning down Babylon when they were too high to do anything other than shovel peanut butter into their mouths, let alone set fire to the world's major cities

"I took one of his two hundred courses last year." "Two hundred" indicated a course open only to grad students. "I talked my way into it. Well, flirted my way into it, basically," Tim began. "You know Eberman wrote a book? About the works of Hieronymus Bosch? Well, I had read it and I think Bosch is a genius, so I thought I would be perfect for it. I went into his office one day and made this big impassioned speech  That didn't seem to work. So I poured on the charm."

"Charm?" Randall asked, taking a slug

"That didn't seem to work either. Or so I thought. About a week later, I got this E-mail from him explaining that I had demonstrated a keen and emphatic interest in his area of study. . . . Something like that. I thought it was all code because the guy looked at my ass like it was carved out of gold."

"There's your headline," Randall cut in. "Professor Beholds Boy's Gold Ass. Wife Dies!" He kept his voice steady and hearty.

"Can I finish, please? Anyway, I signed up for the course, which was basically a tutorial of his book. Turns out the whole class is a bunch of grad students holding a circle jerk in his honor. But he's paying special attention to me Stopping discussions that are soaring over my head to explain things like the difference between Catharism and the established views of the Medieval church. And the other students are getting totally pissed off and I can tell. Especially this one guy . . ."

"Mitchell Seaver."

"Yeah. How did you know?"

"I guessed. I'm in Foundations One. Mitchell's lecturing while Er . . . Eberman's out of town at the funeral." Randall said, cursing his near slip. "Mitchell's a total prick."

"Tell me about it. You would have thought this loser was teaching the course too. Anyway, Eberman's paying a lot of attention to me. And I'm not going to lie, he's hot."

"If you like older men," Randall mumbled.

"Whatever. Young. Old. He's a good-looking guy."

"If you like older men." Randall repeated.

"All right. Fine. I like older men. Sometimes."

Randall laughed. "Go on."

"So I asked him out to dinner."

Randall lifted his eyebrows in disbelief. Tim reached for his bowl again as he continued. "Okay, I had no clue he was married. None. I'd had like ten conversations with him outside of class and he never mentioned his wife. Not once. And then when I asked him after class if he wanted to get something to eat . . . Christ, I've never seen someone freeze up like that."

Tim took another hit as Randall waited, confused by the strange stab of jealousy he felt upon hearing about all the "attention" Eric had paid to him, realizing how much he had come to love the idea of being Eric's only one. And why had he let the conversation veer away from Lisa? "And?" Randall asked, impatiently.

"He sent me another E-mail. This one said that he thought it would no longer be wise for me to stay on in the course. That I was too far behind the rest of the class, and that if I wanted to I could audit it. I was like, fuck that. I'm not auditing an art history course my sophomore year when I've got, like, a hundred requirements I haven't filled for my own major. I responded much more eloquently than that. He didn't."

"What did he say?"

Tim exhaled  Randall winced at the return of the smoke.

"I'm married. That's all he wrote. Talk about jumping to conclusions."

"But he wasn't."

"Whatever  He sent out the signals. *Strong* signals. And then he panicked when I picked up on them."

Randall weighed this for several seconds as Tim let his eyes flutter shut, fast on his way to being stoned. He felt anything but high. His blood was heavy as lead, as if it were trying to slow itself, depriving his brain of the oxygen it needed to give voice to his next question. "You think this guy killed his wife, don't you?"

Tim squinted slightly and rolled his head against the pillow to face Randall. "No. But I think Paula Willis might be right. He might have given her plenty of reasons to get drunk and go for a drive "

"How far are you willing to take this?" Randall asked, as casually as he could.

"What do you mean?"

"It's an ethical question, I guess." Randall continued carefully. "It's one thing to lie here and tell me what you really think about Lisa's death, but—and no offense—it all sounds like speculation. Would you be willing to pick up your pen and play with this man's reputation just because you think he's gay?" He prayed that his delivery was unlit by the fear burning under his words, and when Tim rolled his head back against the pillow, searching for an answer on the ceiling, Randall felt relief as he watched his bare chest rise and fall.

"I didn't go through half the shit I did coming out to my family and friends—when I was sixteen, I might add—just so I could end up being an ass that gets stared at by some pretentious fuck twice my age who thinks he's somehow superior to me even though he's too much of a fucking coward to face the thing I did when I was in high school." Tim met Randall's eyes. "If I have a mortal enemy, it's men like Eric Eberman. Because the more men there are like him that try to keep what they want a dirty little secret, the more you and I get turned into dirty little secrets" Tim jabbed one finger just above Randall's left nipple to bring home his point. Randall clasped the offending hand in his own and used it to pull himself into a straddle across Tim's chest. He kissed his fingers and then lowered his mouth inches from Tim.

"Thank you for that Queer Nation moment, Timothy." He patted Tim's head.

"I told you not to call me that." He kissed him lightly on the lips before moving off the bed. "No one takes me seriously at this god-damn school," Tim muttered, sluggish and stoned.

Randall dressed hurriedly, eager to get out of a room now crowded with a suffocating mixture of fact and suspicion. "You're a fine journalist, Tim. I take that very seriously" He picked up his copy of the *Herald* off the floor. "One other thing, though. You wrote this article last night, right?"

"Uh-huh."

Randall turned. "Channel 2 said toxicology was released this morning."

Tim grinned at him devilishly. "Contacts, my friend."

"Really?" Randall asked, all innocence

"Guy's name is Richard Miller. He's been with the *Atherton Daily Journal* for like twenty years. I think he kind of likes me."

"How'd you meet him?"

"The Catch House. Where else?"

The Catch House was one of the city's two gay bars and was housed in an abandoned warehouse on the bay front. On a good night, it drew a crowd of about ten fifty-year-old men in suits and ties who huddled around the bar, never daring to set foot on its scrap of dance floor, and shooting furtive glances at one another as if it were still 1970. "Interesting," Randall mumbled. So that's how Tim got all of his vital information, flirting with a crotchety reporter. It made Randall feel a little less guilty for moaning and groaning his way to the information he wanted.

"Want to know something else interesting?" Tim asked. He was obviously trying to keep Randall from leaving. Randall stopped on his way to the door. "Richard's contact with the Atherton PD said that Eric told the detectives that Lisa was addicted to Vicodin. Supposedly she got it for a leg injury. Paula claims Lisa never took a single pill."

Randall tried to make his voice gently parental. "Drug addicts are never very eager to tell their family members about their addictions."

"Lisa Eberman was staying with her sister every weekend. Cooking her meals, driving her to chemo. You really think she was dropping pills?"

"What do I know, Tim? It's your story."

"See you in a month?" Tim called after him.

Randall didn't answer. *You'll see me a lot sooner than that,* he thought.


"April. Please. Answer it!"

The phone rang again. Kathryn's hand halted over the keyboard. She turned just in time to see April pluck the portable from its cradle without lifting her gaze from the frighteningly voluminous textbook open on her lap.

"I know it's her," Kathryn pleaded.

"Not unless you can tell me anything about the loop of Henley."

"It's in the kidney."

"Nice try," April muttered, and continued reading text sandwiched between stomach-churning color photos as the phone rang again in her hand. "This is the third time she's called today, Kathryn."

Kathryn rose from her desk, abandoning her half-written paper on viable methods of regulating hate speech. She tried not to whip the phone from April's hand before she answered it. Her mother didn't bother with a greeting. "This conversation takes five minutes and you don't have time to think of an excuse not to have it—"

"Mom!"

"There's one direct flight between Boston and SFO and it's booked. I went on-line last night and found some others. On one you would have to connect through Cincinnati I've never been there, but it sounds just awful—"

"Mom. Wait."

"For how much longer, Kathryn? In case you've forgotten, Thanksgiving is a family holiday. For *everyone*." Kathryn heard muffled laughter in the background. Since arriving at Atherton, she couldn't remember a single conversation with her mother during which paralegals weren't present.

"Take me off speakerphone, Mom."

There was a click and Marion Parker's voice was clearer when she spoke again. "Option two. Fly some goddamn awful Fokker thing out of Atherton's little airstrip into JFK."

"It's only four days, Mom."

Across the room, April cocked her head at the first sign of an argument. Kathryn rose from her bed and pushed her way out the door. The fire stairway was empty and during the brittle silence that came from the other end of the line, Kathryn fished a cigarette out and lit it. She modified her breathing so that her exhalations of smoke were barely audible on the other end.

"Will the dorm be open?" Marion Parker finally asked.

"Randall and I were thinking about going to Boston."

"What's in Boston?"

"History. Culture."

"I take it Randall isn't going home for Thanksgiving either."

"No," Kathryn answered, as if this were proof of something.

She heard the shuffle of paper in the background and had a clear image of her mother glowering at the desk in front of her as if she were trying to set it on fire. "Kathryn, I need you to fill me in on what's going on here."

"It's like, a six-hour flight, Mom. For only four days."

"I know how long the flight is. What's going on with you?"

It was a shame that Marion Parker was in-house counsel for Wells Fargo and rarely left the boardroom; she would have been perfect in trial. But now that she had spent several weeks trying to force Kathryn into coming home for Thanksgiving, an undertone of defeatism had crept into her mother's voice, and today Kathryn could feel the gulf between her old home and her new one widen by several more miles

"Have you spoken with Kerry?"

"No," Kathryn said quickly, taken aback by the abrupt change of subject.

"She was calling here so much that I went ahead and gave her your number up there."

"Great."

"Kathryn . . ." Her mother hesitated, and during the pause Kathryn realized that her mother considered two seemingly disparate subjects to be related. "With all due respect, I hope you don't think it's any mystery to us why you don't want to come home."

Kathryn sank down onto one of the steps, sucking a long drag off her cigarette and responding with a tense silence meant to indicate to her mother that she had crossed the line. "How is she?" Kathryn finally asked.

"Who?"

"Kerry, Mom."

"She didn't say. She sounded all right." *She didn't sound sick*, was what her mother meant to imply.

"Mom, I promised Randall—"

"You *promised* Randall? Kathryn, you've known this boy for what, three months?"

"Mom." Kathryn sucked in a breath and managed to control her tone, even though her palm holding the phone was greased with sweat. "I don't want to come home. If you can find a way to make me, go ahead—"

"I'm not going to make you, Kathryn," Marion snapped. "But I'm not going to keep quiet and pretend like it's a good idea for you to run away from everything that happened this summer with your tail between your legs. You're stronger than that. I know you are." Her mother took an exhausted breath. "At least, I hope you are."

"It's too soon," Kathryn said in a small voice.

"Will it still be too soon when Christmas rolls around?"

"I don't know." Footsteps echoed down the stairwell and Kathryn cocked her head before she heard the exit door several floors overhead bang shut.

"I have a reserve on the tickets until midnight tomorrow if you change your mind. After that, there's not much I can do."

"I'll think about it."

"I hope you mean that"

Kathryn didn't answer.

"In the meantime, I think you should talk to Kerry."

Kathryn went rigid. "That's something I don't need your input on."

For a second, Kathryn felt the urge to apologize for the venom with which the response had leaped out of her. "Midnight tomorrow," Marion said.

Several seconds later, Kathryn realized her mother had hung up on her.

Colonial Avenue descended the slope of Atherton Hill in an odd mixture of asphalt and strips of cobblestone that ran a path from the front gates of the university and over the thin vein of the Atherton River before beginning its circuitous route through downtown  Standing outside the gates, with his back to the university's postcard-perfect front flank of administrative buildings, Randall could make out the blinking lights on the bridge below, marking the miniature barricade erected around the spot where Lisa Eberman's Volvo had torn through the bridge's rail. Just across the street, a blast of laughter drew Randall's attention to the front steps of Folberg Library. Students on study break talked and smoked in huddles. In contrast, the distant downtown was a warren of shadows beyond the harsh glow of the streetlamps lining the paved riverbanks.

Urban life was not something he needed from this gritty excuse for a city; he had encountered enough of that on the streets of New York. Refuge was more important to him now. Now his new home had been marred by the scene of a crime. But visiting this one meant leaving the protective halo of Atherton's campus.

The sidewalks were poorly lit, so Randall walked in the street alongside the curb  He was almost to the bridge entrance when he noticed the tree, a leafless elm, one of the many that had been planted amid the sidewalks. A four-foot section of its trunk had been torn free, revealing whiter, splintered bark. Randall moved to it, fingering the edge of the massive wound with a gloved hand, and mentally gauging the distance between the tree and the torn opening in the bridge's guardrail several yards ahead of him.

He withdrew his hand slowly, mounted the curb, and took in the sight just across the street. Orange city works barrels had been set up in a U extending out from the gouged-out opening of twisted metal. Under the bridge, the river lay without detectable flow, its surface moved only by the ripples of stronger winds off the nearby bay. Randall surveyed the cold details of the scene, wondering why he had felt so compelled to visit the site. Had he come to obtain a mental picture of the Volvo's final descent into the river? Or worse, to lay his hands on the guardrail and say a silent prayer for a woman whose bedroom he had known better than he knew her?

He could feel a shiver coming on. He yanked his flask from his jacket pocket, uncapped it, and took a hearty swallow. He was still swigging when he heard the sound of tires thudding over the bridge's metal crossbars. He backed up several steps as a Toyota Tercel advanced toward him, headlights illuminating frail flakes of snow he hadn't noticed before. For a second, he was caught in the glare of the lights, the flask in one hand and the cap in the other. He screwed it on the flask and turned on his heel.

"Randall Stone?"

Caught, Randall turned. He didn't recognize the car's driver until Mitchell Seaver gave him a polite, puzzled smile. "A little cold to be out for a walk, isn't it?"

"I'm used to it," Randall offered.

"Walking the streets or being cold?"

"Both," Randall answered.

"Looks like you've got a little warm-up there."

Randall shrugged and held up the flask. No sense in trying to hide it, he thought.

"Headed back to campus? I can give you a lift "

Mitchell was right. It was cold and Randall couldn't think of an immediate excuse not to accept the offer, so he rounded the nose of the car and slid into the passenger seat. Mitchell cranked up the heat. As Randall slid the seat belt over one shoulder, he saw the backseat was loaded with brown paper bags, but instead of groceries the stems of paintbrushes stuck up out of them. "Working on something?" he asked.

"You could say that." Mitchell pressed his foot down on the gas and the Tercel's engine groaned as it mounted the hill "There's an excess of wall space in my new place."

"So you're going to paint it yourself?"

"Sort of. With the help of a slide projector."

"Sounds kind of involved."

"Don't worry. I have some help."

Randall glanced at Mitchell, and saw that his eyes were on the rearview mirror. "Horrible, isn't it?" Mitchell asked, and it took Randall a second to realize he was referring to the blinking lights on the bridge receding from view behind them.

"How is he?" Randall asked.

"Holding together. I spoke to him last night before he flew to Philadelphia for the funeral. I'm glad he isn't around today. Losing your wife and then having half the campus find out she was a drunk is a little much for anyone to handle."

"I can imagine."

"Where do you live?"

"Stockton."

Randall allowed a brief pause before he spoke again. "Was she a drunk?"

Mitchell flicked his eyes toward Randall. "You don't read the papers?"

"The *Herald* sometimes. But I'd hardly consider it one of the *papers.*"

Mitchell laughed in his throat. "It was a poorly kept secret that was bound to get out sometime. I had been studying under Eric for almost half a year before I found out he was married. With all due respect to him . . . and her, I guess . . . he did his best to keep her at home."

"What do you mean?"

"I guess I mean he wasn't very proud of her."

Anger stabbed inside of Randall. *What the hell do you know, you prick?*

"We aren't boring you are we, Randall?"

"I'm sorry . . ."

"Maria said you stopped showing up for discussion sections," Mitchell explained. "Not like it's any of my business, and Maria has a tendency to be—"

"Long-winded and standoffish," Randall finished for him.

Mitchell's smile was tight. "Maybe. But when she mentioned it to me it probably would have gone in one ear and out the other if Eric hadn't mentioned you as well. Apparently you're committed to office hours. Eric says you're one of the few regulars. So I guess it's understandable. Why share your insights with some grad student when you have the ear of the professor?"

Randall shot a glance Mitchell's way, and found Mitchell staring evenly at the street ahead. Earlier that day, he had discovered that Eric had once paid "special attention" to Tim. Was it possible that his close academic relationship with Mitchell Seaver masked a deeper bond between the two?

"I think I've gone to office hours twice since the semester started," Randall retorted.

Mitchell lifted his eyebrows. "Eric must be mistaken, then."

"Stockton's your next right," Randall said. Mitchell made the turn without another word. "The few times I did go to office hours it was to talk about his book."

"We're covering Bosch in depth next semester."

"Couldn't wait," Randall responded, too sharply.

"Nice flask." Mitchell said after a pause. Randall looked down. He'd left the flask in his lap. "Looks like a gift."

"It was," Randall said, carefully tucking it back inside his jacket.

"Who from?"

Randall's hand tensed around the door handle. "My father," he lied.

"Must be liberal."

"No. Just a man's man. And every man needs a flask, right?"

"Even when the man's eighteen?"

Randall leveled his gaze on Mitchell. "I could give you *my dad's* number," Randall said. "Maybe you should call him and share your opinions on alcohol moderation. And men. He might appreciate being enlightened."

Mitchell's eyes shot to Randall's as the Tercel rolled to a halt in front of Stockton.

"What does a man keep in it?" Mitchell asked softly. "Before he's legally a man, that is."

"Scotch. I have my ways."

"I'm sure."

Randall searched Mitchell's half-lit face for some indication of an unrequited attraction to his mentor Nothing physical confirmed the suspicions raised by Mitchell's prying, presumptuous questions. "Be sure to give Eric my very best. And if there's anything I can do .. he just needs to let me know," Randall said and stepped out of the car.

Several steps from the curb, he glanced back and saw Mitchell glaring at him through the windshield Randall gave a small wave and headed for the entrance to the dorm.

When Kathryn thought about returning to San Francisco, she saw China Beach by a bonfire's light, flames dancing over the small crescent of mud-colored sand and up jagged cliff faces curtained by dark pine. She saw Jono, a shadow standing on top of the rock formation at the beach's far edge, framed by the soaring red towers of the Golden Gate Bridge, spotlit above the dark mouth of the Bay

"Jono Come on!" she barked.

But he had found the perfect spot. "Behold!" he shouted, gesturing toward the distant bridge with one arm. From behind them, Kathryn could hear Kerry's high-pitched laughter. It sounded as if one of Jono's friends was giving chase. "Can we go back now, please?" Kathryn called, not sure whether she was demanding or pleading. But even as she shouted, she had made it to the rock, grabbing one of his shoulders to steady herself. Jono was transfixed by the view, but Kathryn found herself casting nervous glances to the glowing windows of houses perched on the cliffs above. Luckily, her own home didn't peer down on this tiny beach and its illegal bonfire surrounded by spidery shadows. Kerry's laughter had stopped; she had obviously been caught and was probably making out madly with one of the college boys she had found to be so intimidating several months before, when Kathryn had first introduced her to her new boyfriend's circle of aspiring musicians and legal, dedicated drinkers.

"Check it out," Jono said in a low, wind-whipped voice.

Paying no attention to the view, she held her balance with one arm around his waist and used the other to trace his strong, stubbled jaw with one finger, all the way to the soft dimple of his prominent chin.

"I have the same view from my room," she whispered, nibbling gently on his earlobe.

"And I've never been in your room," he said, turning and circling her waist with both arms.

"And you know why," she said softly, resting her head on the solid rock of his chest, savoring the sensation of being in the arms of someone older and wiser, someone who had grown intimate with the woman inside her whom everyone else kept missing or ignoring. But her parents knew next to nothing about Jono and she wanted to keep it that way. "Hey!" she said, catching sight out of a tiny light making a determined path into the black Pacific. "Check it out!"

Jono followed her extended arm, and saw the light hovering just above the black surface. "A boat?" he asked.

"No. A submarine. Watch."

And just like that the light began to descend, dissolving into a smear of diffuse light and water before it was gone completely, and they were both awed for a second by the immensity of the Pacific stretching out for miles before it became indistinguishable from the cloudless night sky. "I'm freezing," she said, breaking the moment. In response, Jono brought his hot breath to her neck and—as expected— she went weak in his embrace, digging her hands under his leather jacket and clasping them against the small of his back.

"Don't leave me," he whispered into her ear

"As if."

"You mean it?" He lifted his head so that he was eye to eye with Kathryn, the tips of their noses touching. She peered through shadow into his wide eyes, saw that blend of rugged handsomeness on his face lost to the gradual, but still cruel, punishment of hard drinking mixed with constant brooding  Here it is again, she thought, one of those desperate moments of neediness that suddenly pops up amid his mischief and daring.

"Say it again," he said, pulling his clasped hands into her back in two jerking motions.

"Never."

"Never what?"

"You'll leave me first. How's that?"

If it hadn't been so dark, maybe she would have seen the shadow of something pass over his face. But she felt that shadow in the sudden rigidity of his embrace. Then the moment was gone and his mouth was at her neck again. "This is what they call romance," he said.

"Romance isn't this cold. Let's go. They're waiting."

"Bullshit. Kerry's got enough dick to last her the whole weekend."

"*Jono!*" But his only response was to slide his arms out of his jacket and bring it up over her shoulders. She tightened her embrace on him and realized that she couldn't tell him how afraid of the ocean she was because that fear belonged to the little girl, and Jono knew, slept with, and maybe loved the woman she'd become in the hot glare of his gaze.

"Jono. Come on."

But one hand was crawling under her shirt, fingers playing over her bare stomach and toward the underwire of her bra. She jerked her arm free. The jacket fell off them.

She heard the wet smack of the jacket hitting the rock at their feet, and the next thing she knew Jono had bent down, the pivoting of his butt almost forcing her off the rock. "What?" she shouted.

"Fuck! My jacket!"

He fell into a full crouch, leaving no space for her, and her only choice was to hobble down to the rock one level below, or else be forced into the tide-pool-swollen cracks between them. She barely made it to the slick surface when a wave broke, the wash frothing all around her for a brief terrifying instant. She landed knees first, hands slipping against the stone, and when she looked up he was gone.

"Jono!"

"I need it, Kathryn!" he called back from somewhere between the rocks.

He had scared the shit out of her over a goddamn thrift-store leather jacket.

Another wave hit, this one weaker, but she heard Jono curse from somewhere between the rocks as the afterwash lashed him.

Without a good-bye, Kathryn set her sights on the distant bonfire and carefully made her way off the rocks and back to the sand

• • •

"Hey."

Kathryn cocked her head. She'd expected April, coming to retrieve the phone from the fire stairway, but there was Randall, his cheeks flushed with cold and his blue eyes slightly bloodshot from the frigid wind. He looked fatigued, and his leather jacket slid farther off one shoulder as he slumped down onto the step next to her. She extended the pack of cigarettes. "Where have you been?"

"Library. What's wrong?"

"Nothing. I . . ." She shook her head. "My mother."

Randall grunted and lit the cigarette.

"So, honey, how was your day?" Kathryn asked brightly.

Randall's smile flickered at her. "Uneventful," he muttered.

Her guilt rolled forward to fill the silence between them. After three months of friendship she had not told Randall a single thing about Jono Morton, the guy she had dated for six months. The guy to whom she had given her virginity and almost her life. How could she have gone for so long?

The answer was simple. Because Randall hadn't asked. She had never viewed this as a slight. One of the unspoken tenets of their friendship was that they never discussed home. They could both drop tidbits of information, but their conversation in the men's room Friday night was evidence of what happened if one of them tried to pry for more. Who they had been now took a backseat to the people they thought they were both becoming. She never could have developed this deep a friendship with anyone who poked and prodded at her silences, so maybe it was only fair that Randall greeted her with a deep chill whenever she tried to talk about his parents.

"Remember Lauren Raines?"

Randall was rubbing the back of his head with one hand, too slowly to be scratching an itch, as he stared at the floor. After several seconds of silence, his eyes rose from the steps. "Sorry?"

"Lauren Raines. Third floor. Engineering major."

"What about her?"

"She's a lesbian now."

"You're kidding," Randall said, not interested.

"I ran into her this morning. You wouldn't recognize her."

"What did she say?" Randall asked with a sigh, pushing his butt back on the step and resting the small of his back against the next one.

April had reacted with anger, and Randall was responding with disinterest, so Kathryn guessed this was the last time she'd bother recounting her conversation with Lauren to anyone. "She was kind of cryptic about it, but she's dating some girl who lives off campus, so she's been spending most of her time over there." Kathryn paused.

"Who's the girl?"

"Martha or something. I can't remember."

"Weird," Randall said, more to himself than her. He rose suddenly, stubbed out his half-smoked cigarette under the toe of his boot, and bent down to give her a kiss on the cheek. "I've got class in the morning."

"'Night." He was almost through the exit door when she said, "Give Jesse a big kiss for me."

Startled, his eyes met hers and she watched a flash of anger tighten his features. At least he was paying attention to what I said, she thought. "I don't *kiss* Jesse. Ever," he said with too much force.

"I was joking."

"You on the other hand—"

"Good night, Randall," she said with a dismissive wave.

Back in her room, she saw April was down for the count. Kathryn undressed and slid under the comforter. Her thoughts were distorting at the edges. Faces in places were they shouldn't be indicated the onset of dreams; her mother outside the student union trying to get her to take a flyer, Randall staring at the gaping hole in the chain-link fence that Jono had cut so they could sneak down to China Beach that night.

A door brushing across the carpet in the hall.

But this was real, bringing the succession of images to an abrupt halt. She lifted her head from the pillow, trying to determine if she had imagined it, and then she heard the door shut with a soft thud. A glance at the clock told her it was almost one thirty. Minutes later, she was still trying to determine if it had been Randall's door, remembering Jesse's words to her at Madeline's on Friday night. *Sometimes he leaves after the two of you get back.*

# CHAPTER FOUR

GRIPPING THE STEM OF HIS WINEGLASS WHERE HE HELD IT ON THE arm of his reading chair, Eric watched Randall sit straight-backed on the sofa, staring down at the banana-shaped paper that bore his wife's parting words in block letters. Eric wasn't quite sure just what he wanted to see on the young man's face. Some shame equal to his own, maybe?

"She wrote this?" Randall asked in a surprisingly steady tone. He lifted his gaze from the note to Eric; his eyes were steel, his posture still rigid, as if he were prepared for Eric to deliver a second blow.

Eric nodded and slugged the last of his wine.

"What?"

"Excuse me?" Eric asked.

"What did she see? Randall asked.

Eric slammed the glass back to the chair's arm. Randall didn't flinch. Angered by Randall's defiance, Eric rose from the chair and crossed to the fireplace, taking care to set the empty wineglass down gently on the mantel. On the one hand, the note was general enough to allow for dozens of interpretations, most of which weren't nearly as damning as the one he had accepted. She saw where their marriage was going, she knew that he was incapable of loving her fully. Maybe she had been referring to how close he had become with a certain group of graduate students, the time and attention he had devoted to them.

Eric thought of Mitchell, and found himself speaking in words

Mitchell would use as he held his back to Randall, "I left out some-thing. When you asked me about Catharism, and the belief that our body is a trap we have to escape." Behind him, he heard Randall let out a fatigued breath. It was impossible to tell whether he was annoyed or whether or not the awful weight of the note was beginning to press down on him. Eric continued, unfazed. "There is something about the dualistic view of the universe that's always stuck with me. It's the belief that certain desires should be ignored, not simply because they've been labeled sins and we fear God's punishment if we indulge them; they should be ignored because by their nature they disguise themselves as a calling, when really they can provide nothing permanent beyond destruction."

*How was that, Mitchell?* he thought. *Good enough for your new-found housemates who hang on your every word?*

He turned. Randall sat lax against the sofa. The note rested on his lap, but he had crossed his arms over his stomach. "Why did you show me this?" Randall asked again, the first quaver of anger evident in his voice.

"I don't know."

"I do."

"Really?" Eric asked with bitter sarcasm.

"Would you like to hear it?"

"Since when do you need my permission to share?"

Randall's mouth closed in a thin angry line. The only sound in the living room was the steady hiss of the gas fireplace. Eric finally lifted one arm, gesturing for Randall to continue, but Randall didn't move or speak. Half a bottle of wine had given Eric a strange, wry energy. "I'm very tired, Randall. Please forgive me if I'm not showing you the respect you think you deserve."

Randall got up from the sofa. "I'm not getting down on my knees and praying for forgiveness with you, Eric."

"Who asked you to?"

"You did!" Randall held the note up. "Showing me this! What . . ." Randall looked to the note again as if his next line were written on it. "Who do I owe an apology to? She's dead. And you? I gave you all you deserved every weekend for the past month."

Did he want Randall to repent? No. That day, playing the role of grieving husband, but with his guilt beating like a second and stronger heartbeat inside his chest, his hell had been a private one, yet he hadn't committed his crimes alone. Of course, Randall, all of eighteen and without a wife to hurt, didn't share the same burden as Eric, but the fact remained that Lisa had probably seen two people in bed together in the minutes before driving to her death, and by sharing that disturbing truth with Randall, Eric had made his hell seem less private. It eased the sense of total isolation he had felt that morning in Philadelphia as his wife's body had been rolled down the aisle of her girlhood church. And God forbid, if Mitchell, once his shining pupil and now his neglected stepson, ever found out—he couldn't think of facing that level of disdain alone.

"Blame yourself all you want, Eric. Not me. You were waiting for me."

"How did I ever get along without you?"

"You're drunk," Randall muttered. He dropped the note on the coffee table. Eric saw evidence of the pain the note had caused. Randall, usually so infuriatingly poised, had no idea what to do with his arms and they hung limply at his sides, one hand bunching the pocket of his jeans. He brought one hand to his mouth and his breath made a whistling sound against his palm. Watching, Eric felt a small tinge of remorse that was instantly subsumed by memories of the day.

"Men like you, men who try all their lives to kill a desire that won't die. You are the ones who destroy. Trust me. I know."

More startled than offended, Eric turned from the fireplace. "If you and I went upstairs right now and did the same thing we've done every time she left Atherton, can you tell me honestly that you won't see her, Randall? Because I don't know. Maybe because I don't know how she ever saw us. Maybe she was hiding in the bathroom or—"

Randall whipped his jacket off the back of the chair.

"It's not a difficult question, Randall."

"I don't even know what she looks like."

Eric knew he was lying, but he played along anyway. "Oh. Well, we can fix that."

"Eric!"

But he was already in the dining room. The last time he'd checked, there had a been a wedding portrait of Lisa and him on top of the liquor cabinet, but in its place he found a framed shot of Lisa that had been taken on vacation in Florida. How had one replaced the other? He picked it up and returned to the living room to find Randall uneasy in the doorway, his coat still draped over one arm.

"This is her," he said, holding up the picture in front of him as he approached.

Randall's eyes held Eric's stare and Eric shook the picture slightly. "Look!"

Randall shut his eyes.

"It's just a question, Randall. I'm not judging you. I'm not *judging* either one of us. Just tell me if we went upstairs and had sex, would you—"

Randall grabbed the photograph and hurled it against the wall. It shattered and slid to the baseboard.

Eric crossed to the picture frame, bent down, and picked it up. Lisa's face was still held inside the frame, slivers of glass radiating from her wan smile. He shook the frame and they fell to the floor. Then he saw Randall had crumpled the note in one fist and crouched down in front of the fireplace.

Some instinct, something not entirely blotted out by the wine and the exhaustion that follows grief, leaped inside of him, and Eric crossed the room in no time, seizing Randall's wrist in one hand.

"No!" Randall yelled. As he tried to twist his arm free, he lost his balance and pitched forward into the gas flame. Eric heard Randall's cry, a wail blocked by clenched teeth before he thudded to the floor.

He looked down to see Randall sitting at his feet, clutching one hand to his chest. "*Fucker!*" Randall growled, clamping one hand over the one held tight to his chest. Tears sprouted from his eyes "Fucker!" he groaned. His choice of curses was childish, and the way his lower lip quivered completed the image of a young man instantly reduced to a little boy. Eric felt a shard of Randall's history stab him in the gut. Eric crouched next to him, half expecting Randall to crawl away from him, but Randall didn't move as Eric gently pried his hand away from his chest.

The blistered strips of skin looked like the imprints of fingers on Randall's palm.

"This needs ice."

"Say it's over and I'll leave."

Eric met Randall's gaze, wary behind his tear-stained eyes. For an instant, he sought to dig deep and come up with an answer he knew he should give. But he couldn't find it.

"This needs ice," he said again, releasing Randall's burned hand and getting to his feet.

Randall blinked as he tried to focus on Eric rooting through kitchen drawers in search of some first-aid kit that Randall suspected he didn't even own  The black spots that had crowded his vision the minute his hand hit the fireplace were finally dissipating, but Randall kept his lips sealed so Eric wouldn't hear him struggle to regulate his breaths. He kept his burned hand resting on the kitchen table. It trembled slightly at the wrist. Only one thing would blunt the tensing of the fiery pinpricks across his palm, drown out the searing flash of memory the burn had sparked. Randall brought the flask to his mouth. He almost emptied it.

Eric shot him a glance. He still looked chastised, convinced that he knew full well exactly what memory this accident had sparked. Rather than tell him otherwise, Randall drained the flask and shot a glance into the dining room.

In the beginning, Randall had been skeptical of Eric's stories of his wife's alcoholism, and presumed that Eric embellished them in a warped attempt to justify his urge for Randall, which is what Randall had hoped for from the start. Then Randall had discovered the virtual warehouse of Chivas Regal in the liquor cabinet. That, and the fact that he had never seen Eric drink anything stronger than wine, convinced Randall that Lisa Eberman belonged to a special category of high-end drunk. Now, his palm still burning, he prayed that Eric hadn't emptied out the liquor cabinet in some attempt to purge Lisa's ghost from the house.

"Here." Eric took a seat across from him, setting a role of Ace bandages on the table. Eric cradled his hand. "I don't have anything to treat it with."

"It's not bad. Trust me. I know."

Eric met his eyes. "But this time you didn't have the luxury of blacking out."

"Is that supposed to be funny?" Randall demanded.

Eric's gaze shot back to Randall's burned hand. He wrapped the bandages around his palm so slowly and methodically that it was obvious he had no clue what he was doing. The intensity of the act left Randall strangely moved. He began to realize that Eric's dogged, if drunken, attempt to get Randall to face his own guilt was the type of reaction he had been hoping for during the long walk from Stockton Hall that night. But he had expected to find Eric cocooning into his own guilt and despair, shutting Randall out. Instead, fully aware that he didn't have the strength to end what they had started, Eric had been dead set on driving their mutual guilt to the surface, forcing the two of them to face it before they landed in bed together again.

Eric rose, leaving the mess of bandages shrouding Randall's hand. He pulled a roll of Scotch tape from a drawer and returned to the table, tore off a piece of tape, and took Randall's hand in his own.

"What are you doing, Eric?"

"I have to tape it . . ."

Randall shook his hand and the wad of bandages fell to the table. When he turned sideways in his chair, away from Eric, the scotch pulsed in his temples and he sucked in a breath to prevent dizziness. Groping for some thought to bring him back to more solid ground, Randall remembered the strange car ride he had received earlier that night.

"Mitchell Seaver has a thing for you," he said as gently as possible.

When he glanced at Eric, he saw his face stitched with angry bewilderment. Too angry, Randall thought. The confusing jealousy, which he had only started to feel that day, returned as he wondered whether Mitchell's feelings weren't unrequited. Eric pushed himself up from the chair carefully, turning his back on Randall as he moved to the sink. "I wasn't aware that you and Mitchell were friends," he finally said.

Randall turned forward again. "We aren't "

"Then what would make you say something so preposterous?"

"Why is it so preposterous that someone could have feelings for you?"

Eric snorted and began arranging dirty dishes in the sink. "Not only is Mitchell not a homosexual, he's barely even what you would call sexual."

"Right. Like all those elderly male choir teachers who return home to their cats and a case of child pornography."

Eric turned, abandoning his dish sculpture. "You're off the mark, Randall."

"He's strange," Randall said, being deliberately coy and hoping to anger Eric further.

"I guess you're young enough to find academics like Mitchell to be *strange*."

"That isn't what I meant."

"What did you mean?"

*New tactic*, Randall thought. "Forget I asked," he said, drawing his burned hand to his lap and staring down at it as it suddenly held him in thrall. A brief silence passed before Eric spoke again, "Are you jealous of him?"

"Excuse me?" Randall asked, stricken.

"My relationship with Mitchell is a close one, but it's purely . . . academic. Maybe the fact that he and I don't need to hide bothers you."

Eric's words stung, and it must have been evident because Eric let out a fatigued breath. "I didn't say you were fucking him," Randall muttered. "I said maybe he was in love with you."

"And I asked you what gave you—"

"He gave me a ride today," Randall cut in. "Maria Klein ratted me out because I stopped going to discussion sections."

"And Mitchell wanted to talk to you about it?"

"It seemed like an excuse to . . . I don't know. Belittle me."

"For what?" Eric asked.

Randall surveyed the fear in Eric's eyes before continuing. "I don't know. You know him a lot better than I do."

Eric leaned against the edge of the sink, eyes wandering lazily past Randall as if in search of some subject to derail the topic "The attention I've paid to Mitchell has never been sexual. But it might have been too much. His head has swollen. He fancies himself my colleague rather than my student and occasionally he steps over the line."

"Does he know about us?"

Eric crossed to the table with renewed vigor and picked up the Scotch tape and Ace bandages. "Of course not," he muttered under his breath.

"So I'm the only student you've ever slept with?" Randall asked.

Eric's manic laugh was not the response Randall had hoped for. "Yes," he answered when he caught his breath.

"The first man?" Randall asked.

Eric threw up both hands as if to shield himself from a blow, then brought them to his temples as he turned away from the sink. He let them fall to his sides before he responded, "Let's see. What do I say to that? I could try pointing out that it's none of your business, but I'm sure that will only encourage you to dig deeper. Or I could say that it was a very long time ago, but that would imply that you're too young to understand, which I happen to know from experience is the equivalent of throwing ice water in your face and expecting you not to fight back."

"What was his name?"

Eric shook his head as if in disbelief that Randall had the nerve to ask. "It was a very long time ago. Which is why you shouldn't even care. How's that?"

"How did you go for so long?"

"Appetite wanes as you grow older. You'll see."

"Come on, Eric. If it was just *appetite*, you could sign onto America Online and meet hundreds of eighteen-year-old boys all over New England who want nothing more than a forty-one-year-old to fulfill their daddy fantasy. But instead you're here with me."

"Yes. Enduring questions you already know the answers to."

Some desperate urge that he had been so good at fighting up until that moment, that had been stirred and prodded by the events of the past few days, forced him to ask a question he had promised himself he wouldn't. "Why me?"

"I looked. You were the first one to look back."

Randall thought of Tim Mathis's dinner invitation. Maybe the subject of Mitchell Seaver had pitched Eric into a state of evasiveness. "Wow," he whispered. "I feel so special."

"Maybe you should. Trust me, everything about you is an exception."

Randall took a moment to gauge Eric's sincerity and found it to be strong. "You and me, Eric. The two of us. I didn't do any of this on my own." He let this sit and then got up from the table. In the kitchen door-way, he turned to see Eric watching his every move. "Should I . . ." he gestured down the hall to the front door. "Or . . ."

Eric's face may have been a mask of resolve, but Randall could sense the collision of desire and dignity inside him.

"I'll be up in a minute," Eric muttered, his eyes falling from Randall's.

Next to him, Eric slept.

Randall sat up in bed, knees drawn to his chest. The bathroom door yawned open and Randall stared at the rectangle of deeper dark-ness and tried to summon an image of Lisa Eberman staring back out at them. Nothing came.

The clock on the nightstand read two forty-five.

Randall rolled over onto one side and watched Eric sleeping. Strangely peaceful, given the events of the day. Watching Eric's bare chest lifting the sheets in drawn-out breaths, Randall felt a swell of emotion that he easily could have mistaken for love if he didn't know better; rather, he felt the intoxicating sensation of owning some-one completely, a fulfillment so great that he would have trouble acknowledging it in daylight. But the elation left him quickly as he realized that the heart beating in Eric's chest now belonged to a wid-ower, no longer to an almost unattainable conquest. The game of seduction had begun to bleed to an unexpected death.

He managed to dress without waking Eric, and then descended the stairs carefully with his empty flask in one hand. Once he was in front of the liquor cabinet, he stopped. In the darkness of the dining room, a vision of Lisa Eberman struck him with such force that he couldn't suppress a bitter laugh.

Look for her in the shadows and she's nowhere to be found, he thought, but when I'm least expecting it, I'll see every hair on her head, just the way the wind is blowing it in that goddamn photo.

He told the vision to pass, and using the powers of imagination that had so often lifted him outside himself in the interest of getting through, he envisioned the note dissolving into the fireplace.

He filled his flask without spilling a drop.

• • •

Whispering was permitted in the first-floor reading room of Folberg Library, which made it the most popular place for students to study and escape their books at the same time. But Kathryn arrived early enough to get a table all to herself. For the last twenty minutes, she had been trying to finish a poli sci reading, but in her mind she kept hearing the scrape of Randall's door over the hallway carpet. Her concentration broken, she leaned back in her chair just in time to spot Jesse emerging from the periodical racks. He didn't see her, and as she moved down the aisle toward the photocopying room, she spotted the hardcover book he was carrying under one arm.

Jesse was the only one in the copy room. Unnoticed, she sidled up to his machine before he brought the lid down on the spread book. "Writing a paper on plane crashes?" she asked when she saw the title.

Startled, Jesse looked up, managed a polite smile, and then closed the lid over *Transportation Disasters Volume IV.* "Just a little project I'm working on," he responded, feeding quarters into the machine.

"Jesse, I was wondering . . ."

"Have you had lunch?"

Kathryn narrowed her eyes. "I had breakfast."

"You aren't one of those career anorexics, are you?"

"Do I look like one?"

"Good. I'll meet you out front as soon as I finish this," Jesse said to the machine.

She turned, took a few steps, and then stopped. "Do I even have to tell you this isn't a date?"

"Please. Who takes their dates to the Ivory?" he asked.

She nodded.

"I'll be right out," he said, one finger poised on the copy button.

Ten minutes and two cigarettes later, he met her in front of the library, and as they descended the steps, Kathryn realized she was shooting glances in every direction to see what familiar faces they might come upon. Jesse noticed too and let out a throaty laugh.

"What?"

"You don't want to be seen with me, do you?"

"With all due respect—"

"Hey, I'm actually *due* respect from you! You should have told me awhile ago."

Kathryn continued, unfazed. "Most of the girls spotted with you end up being the butt of a joke."

"Yeah, well, you obviously have something to ask me, or otherwise you wouldn't risk it."

The Ivory was the rundown snack bar in the Union where students could use their leftover meal plan points to buy undercooked pizza and greasy piles of French fries. Kathryn waited for Jesse to obtain his lunch, drumming her fingers on the table. Students around her feigned studying, their books spread open on tables as they conducted conversations over the backs of their chairs.

"Sure I can't get you anything?" Jesse set his slice of pizza down between them.

"No. Thanks."

He nodded and slid one arm out of his navy pea coat. His bright red corduroy shirt was unbuttoned from the top just enough to reveal a teasing glimpse of smooth chest. "Nice jacket," she said.

"Thanks. I bought it here." He slung it over the back of his chair and took a seat. "The minute I got here I realized I've never owned a winter coat, so . . ."

"I don't even know where you're from."

Jesse's eyes met hers. "I'm not telling you."

As he took his first bite of pizza, Kathryn realized he was trying to be funny. "Why?"

"Because you hate me enough already."

"Quite the mind reader."

"Beverly Hills."

She couldn't contain her laughter. "Where's your cell phone?" she asked.

"Don't have one yet. But don't worry, I'm getting one. I don't want to pose a threat to your image of me as the Mercedes-driving, spoiled brat." He chewed his pizza deliberately and then swabbed at his lips with the napkin in a manner she found oddly prissy. *Vain*, she corrected herself. But there was no doubt that Jesse was acting unusually in her presence. His posture was more relaxed, his tone less suggestive than usual. After a few seconds, she realized she was seeing a Jesse free from the insipid, posturing charm he poured on his sexual conquests.

"It sounded pretty bad the other night." He saw her furrowed brow and continued, "The fire stairway isn't exactly soundproof. You were on the phone."

"I was hardly yelling."

"Spend all your time in the dorm and you learn how to listen. Kind of like how a blind man develops excellent hearing. You sense when someone's not playing their TV at the usual time. Or when someone slams a door too hard." He made this comment with his eyes on hers. "It's kind of cool," he added before taking another careful bite.

"Stockton drives me nuts. I have to go on a walk just to clear my head."

"I like it."

"Why?"

"It makes me feel safe. Like being in the womb. Knowing there's constant activity above and below me." He paused to chew. "When I was little I couldn't go to sleep unless my parents were awake downstairs. If the house was quiet, I'd lie there with my eyes open. So . . ." He used the napkin to wipe his hands, and Kathryn wondered if Jesse, who familiarized himself with a new person's private parts every weekend, was a closet germ freak. "Who were you talking to?" Jesse asked, with a bright smile that indicated he didn't expect her to answer.

She decided to answer indirectly. "Are you going home for Thanksgiving?"

She caught a flicker of something in his eyes, but it vanished before she could figure out whether it was anger. "No," he answered.

"And how are *your* parents handling that decision?"

"My mom's dead."

Kathryn was startled into silence. There wasn't any gravity in Jesse's voice, and the abruptness of this revelation prohibited her from coming up with any response. "Oh . ."

"She died when I was four and left me to take care of my father."

"Is he sick?"

Jesse's eyes moved past her as he nodded slightly. "You could say that." He met her curious stare as he continued, "He has an illness specific to people with Type-A personalities. He's a man who knows how to make things happen. Too many things sometimes. He's got incredible talent, but sometimes his talent gets bigger than him. Kind of like a fire that he has to douse."

"He drinks?"

Jesse nodded.

"It's really none of my business. I'm sorry if—"

"Don't be," Jesse cut her off. "And who the hell made up that rule that people can only ask about stuff that's their business? How are we supposed to learn anything that way?"

*Clever*, Kathryn thought, *but you didn't answer the question.* "Is he an actor?"

"He was for about five minutes. Right before I was born, he was on this cop show that got yanked mid-season. After that, he couldn't find anymore acting jobs, so instead of heading back to USC Law, he became a producer."

"Have I seen anything he's done?"

"Not unless you have a penchant for slasher flicks that get shipped straight to Asia. They love seeing blonde-headed Americans get sliced and diced over there." Jesse finished his pizza, swabbed at his mouth again and folded his napkin before dropping it onto his plate. "Five more minutes of this, Kathryn, and I might think you're hitting on me."

"You know better," she told him, smiling. "Do you miss him?"

"Who?"

"Your father."

Without planning to, she had cornered him. If he said yes, that would seem odd in light of the fact that he wasn't going home for the coming break. But instead of looking caught, Jesse cocked his head, lips pursed in thought, as if the topic of his father required him to summon the patience of a caretaker. "It was time to go. For me. And for him. He's just having a little trouble realizing it."

"You sure went far."

"You're one to talk. Kathryn Parker, Presidio Public, San Francisco, California," he responded, quoting the information listed below her picture in the freshman face book. "What? Not a fan of the higher education in our home state?"

"I wanted to see snow."

Jesse grinned, clearly appreciating the fact that her answer lacked even the pretense of honesty. Kathryn felt a strange tightening in her chest at the thought that he might be flirting But Jesse's relaxed behavior hadn't altered. She had witnessed a great many of his seductions and they had all been brief, carnal, and crude, like fingering a girl in the middle of a dance floor. Romance might be a foreign concept to him, and this interplay of smart aleck comment, gentle smiles, and awkward pauses was not his usual prelude to the sex act Now Jesse was studying her intently, and without lust.

"Kathryn, I don't know where Randall's going every night. But if he's going to tell anyone, I would think it would be you "

She shifted in her seat and clasped her hands in her lap. "We don't tell each other everything, Jesse."

"Could have fooled me."

She squinted at him, and from his curious expression she could tell she wasn't the only one bothered by whatever Randall was up to, and that comforted her. "Do you know what time he came home last night?"

"Now we sound like his parents."

"If Randall is seeing someone and not telling me about it," Kathryn began, "it's probably because he thinks that for some reason I wouldn't approve—"

"Maybe you wouldn't," Jesse cut in.

"That's ridiculous. Why wouldn't I?"

"Well, let's just say he's perfectly aware of what you think of *my* sex life. Maybe he'd like to spare himself the same disapproval."

"Jesse, I'm not here to discuss your weekend activities."

"Why do you hate me, Kathryn?"

"I don't hate you, Jesse."

"Kathryn, come on. I thought we already established this. In your own words, please."

Thrown, she took several seconds to gauge his sincerity as well as compose herself in the face of his sudden candor. "I think you hurt people," she said, surprised to find herself speaking, her voice slightly hushed as if to soften the force of her words. "I think you use and then discard women in the name of feeding your ego. And I think it's wrong."

Jesse's face went lax. He bent one elbow against the table and rested his chin on one fist. "And if I told you that I learn more about a person during the two hours I spend in bed with her, as opposed to three weeks of hearing her talk about her father, or where she came from, you wouldn't believe me?"

"Not for a second. I think if you believe you're actually getting to know any of them, then you're deluding yourself. Specifically, so you can keep doing it without feeling any guilt."

Jesse tapped his fingers against one cheek as he considered this. "Kathryn, I don't want to gross you out with any of the details, but I don't really *hurt* any of them. They want what I have. I give it to them. And in a way, they walk away healed"

The only thing worse than witnessing Jesse's hormones in action was hearing the emotionless, paper-thin rationalizations he used to defend them. "Jesse, what are we talking about here?" she asked, sitting forward.

"You have a particular attitude toward sex."

"Who doesn't?"

"Whatever. The point is that your attitude might be different from Randall's. And that's why he isn't telling you where he's going." Jesse leaned back against his chair. "He got home at three, since you asked."

He may have been free of posturing charm, but Jesse still had some ulterior motive. There was something suspicious about the confidence with which he discussed Randall, considering that Randall barely discussed Jesse at all. Maybe he was trying to demonstrate a superior knowledge of her closest friend; that thought frightened her more than being labeled a prude. "And just what is my attitude toward sex, Jesse?"

"Maybe I've gotten off the subject . . ."

"Yeah, well, you brought it up. So, shoot, Freud!"

"You're afraid of it," Jesse declared.

"Because I won't sleep with you, I'm afraid of sex."

"I don't recall *asking* you to sleep with me," Jesse said with mock indignation. "I'm just saying that to an outside observer it looks like—"

"Jesse, maybe that's just it. You're an outside observer, okay?"

"Is Randall?"

The thought that Randall was sharing insights about her with Jesse, of all people, made her feel both naked and isolated. "You're saying that I've done something to make Randall afraid to be honest with me?"

Jesse took a long pause to consider this. "You're his best friend, Kathryn. And I live with him, whether you like it or not. Are you telling me that you never get the sense that there's a large part of Randall that he keeps just out of everyone's reach?"

Of course she did, but she wouldn't tell him. This whole conversation had come about because Randall had left the dorm late at night without telling his roommate or his best friend where he was going. Whenever he and Kathryn met up he was usually late and his excuse was that he was usually someplace by himself; the library or the bookstore. But even though Kathryn was aware of these chunks of missing time, they had never bothered her because Randall always seemed to have spent the time alone, pushing away the social clamor of campus life, and most important, not granting anyone else more access than he gave her.

"Maybe," she answered weakly.

"Listen to him, Kathryn. The guy's not just a private person. He's a borderline loner. And good luck to the person who tries to get him to talk about his home life. The first few times he threw down that whole act about being uncomfortable with his parents' wealth, I believed it. But now, it's like he's just trying to throw up a big roadblock. Personally, I'm surprised he's gotten as close to you as he has."

"And you?"

"What do you mean?"

"Just how close are the two of you?"

Jesse's eyes widened at the implication and his mouth curled into an amused grin, as if he was taking pleasure in the fact that she had the nerve to suggest it at all. His only response was a laugh that shook his chest. "Now, there's something that you *really* wouldn't like, would you?" He got up from his chair, slung his coat over one arm, and picked up his empty tray. "Randall left out that you have an incredible imagination."

She glowered at the table in front of her and fought an urge to shoot him the bird. He'd been so confident and smug throughout their conversation that she had to think of a way to disarm him, prove that she wasn't just a tortured little prude clinging desperately to her only friend. "Jesse?"

He dropped his tray on top of a trash can and turned back to her.

"Can you tell me something?"

Jesse shrugged.

"Why won't Lauren Raines set foot on our floor?"

Jesse's smile vanished. "Have you asked her?"

"She wouldn't say."

Jesse approached the table with his head bowed. "I hope she didn't say that what happened wasn't consensual," he said in a low, firm voice.

"No. She didn't," she said. Jesse nodded. "What happened?"

"She didn't like what she wanted."

Kathryn's hands, clasped on the table in front of her, went white. She tried to read Jesse's icy glare. "And you knew what she wanted better than she did?"

"Unfortunately, I did."

Kathryn met his gaze. "It's a damn good thing she made it clear it wasn't rape."

Jesse narrowed his eyes. "You're wrong. I do get to know people by sleeping with them. You want to know how you do it?"

"No."

"Make sure they aren't afraid to ask for what they want, at the same time you're making them feel as good as you can. You'll be shocked what you find out."

"Hideous, isn't it?"

Startled, Kathryn turned, an unlit cigarette still clasped between her gloved fingers. She had no idea how long the guy had been sitting on the bench a few feet away. He had a slightly upturned nose and a mess of sandy blonde hair. His scarf was bunched just under the high collar of his trench coat, and despite his boyish appearance, his wire-rimmed spectacles suggested that he was older then she. He lifted a hand, gesturing vaguely.

Overhead, giant crossbars of steel swept from the entrance of the Technology & Science Center to the first floor of the thirteen-story sciences library. The Tech Center was a four-story pile of plate glass attached to exposed I beams; its main staircase formed a rotunda at one end of the building, encased in white concrete punctuated by box windows. If the sun had been out, the Tech Center's walls of plate glass would have blinded her

Kathryn continued to survey the Price Courtyard. She had only been passing through when she paused to light a much-needed smoke, but now a stranger's comment had drawn her attention to the polished steel of the benches and lampposts, which blossomed into mushroom-shaped heads resembling giant metal lampshades. Underfoot, the names of generous alumni had been etched into each brick.

"It probably looked better on paper," she offered.

"You have to wonder if the administration really thinks Michael Price is a genius, or if they're just smitten with the fact that he's regularly written up in *The New York Times* Or maybe he's got something on them. It must be kind of satisfying, though, coming back years later, to leave footprints on the campus of your alma mater entirely in plate glass and steel."

"I don't get the sculptures," Kathryn said.

The guy surveyed the off-white sculpture sharing the bench with him. It was a naked human form, sitting with one leg crossed over the other, but what struck her most about it was that the body was perfectly proportioned and looked baby-skin smooth, while the face was a mess of clotted wax. Three more ghostly figures were caught in mid-descent on the steps leading to the sciences library, their frozen poses lifelike, their bodies detailed down to the folds of the skin, but their lack of any facial features made them eerie What did they signify? Not science or technology "My guess would be that when you're an egomaniac like Price, you become convinced that you can master more than one art form. I bet no gallery in all of the Northeast would agree to exhibit his sculptures, but thanks to some hefty checks to the Alumni Foundation, he gets to plop them all over campus with abandon."

"I'm Kathryn," she finally said, approaching the bench with an arm extended.

He gave her a hard, polite shake. "I won't ask where you're from."

"Why?"

"Because I'm sure freshmen get tired of that question by the second week."

"I look that wide-eyed and lost?"

"Hardly."

"Then I must have 'freshman' tattooed across my forehead."

"Not at all. You just haven't learned how to properly hate Michael Price yet. That's usually an act most people get down by their sophomore year."

"Do you smoke . . . ?" She gestured for his name

"Mitchell. No. Thank you."

Kathryn withdrew her hand holding the pack, noting that there wasn't much reason for this attractive guy to be sitting on a bench in the freezing cold unless he was a smoker (or wanted to talk to her). "I noticed you standing here," he said, "and I just thought I would stop to tell you that modern architecture was a failed movement before it was subsumed by contemporary architecture, which is barely a movement at all. Just a collection of styles and volumes without any of the driving utopian philosophies that made modern architecture worthy of inquiry, but a popular failure."

Kathryn burst out laughing. Mitchell's smile let her know he didn't take himself too seriously. "You looked like you might be debating the question," he added. She took a seat between him and ghost man.

"Is this your field?" she asked.

"This. No. This is . . . a little boy playing with steel and construction equipment."

"You seem to know your stuff."

"I'm a second-year master's student in art history As of right now, I'm supposed to know a little about a lot. Unfortunately, certain artists have more of a draw than others. Certain artists who have a worldview that's entirely their own Not"—he gave the entire courtyard a dismissive wave—"shiny gimmicks and eye-popping tricks of gravity."

Kathryn scanned the patio again, trying to see it entirely in his terms.

"And you?" he asked.

"Pre-law," she answered flatly.

"Interesting. With all due respect, I don't think pre-law is really a major."

"Why do you think I picked it?" she retorted. Mitchell smiled. She groped for a more genuine response. "No, um, I'm kind of biding my time until I have to pick one next year."

"Sounds like a plan. What brought you here?"

She gave him a puzzled look.

"To Atherton," he added.

She rolled her eyes and blew out a drag. "You want the answer I gave on my essay?"

"I don't know. Do I?"

"Yale waitlisted me and Claremont was too close to home," she said. Mitchell grunted approvingly at her candor, so she continued, "Seriously, it was shallow. I didn't apply anywhere early, so I got all of my acceptances and rejections in April, and when I did, I popped open my handy copy of *US News and World Report*, and Atherton was at the top. And when I visited last year, I don't know, it just looked the way I thought a college should look, I guess. Don't get me wrong. On all of my essay questions I went on at length about how I was going to save the world. I think I told Brown I wanted to be a lawyer who would save the children of tomorrow. . . ."

Mitchell's smile was a half grimace.

"I know. Shoot me, please. Anyway, now I'm here, and I'm surrounded by scholars and activists and all these people who have such passion. And I'm here because of the brochure." Maybe her conversation with Jesse had put her in a funk, but depression settled with a sudden weight on her back and she found herself staring vacantly at the expanse of etched brick. "This wasn't the answer you were expecting," she said, trying to snap out of it.

Mitchell, she saw, was observing her carefully. "I'm pleasantly surprised by your honesty. But I can't say I was expecting any specific type of answer."

"Good," she said, with a nervous laugh. "So. You?"

"Me?"

"What are you doing here?"

"Dr. Eberman brought me here."

"Eric Eberman," she said. "The guy . . ."

"Yes. That one."

Kathryn just nodded her head out of respect for a dead woman she didn't know. Mitchell's eyes were downcast, his lips pursed as if they both needed time to let the mention of Lisa Eberman pass like a gust of wind. "He's a brilliant man. I read his book when I was an undergraduate at Middlebury."

"So you're a TA?"

"Yes. Against my will. Foundations One. Otherwise known as Slides One."

"My friend's in that course."

"Who's your friend?"

"Randall Stone."

Mitchell's stare was blank, and she assumed he didn't know him. "Sorry, I know there must be like a hundred—"

"Your friend Randall's kind of a character."

"Is that a polite way of saying he bothers you?"

"No. Not at all. You're right, there are almost a hundred students in the class, but Randall seems to stand out. He walks taller than your average wide-eyed freshman."

She smiled at the reference to her own line. "I guess New York forces you to walk tall at an early age."

"That's where he's from?"

The mention of Randall seemed to have distracted Mitchell; his eyes had wandered past her and his brow was creased in thought. Several seconds of silence passed, during which the suspicion that Mitchell might begin to fish for information on Randall rushed to the front of her brain and made her consider switching schools.

"Mitchell, can I ask you something?"

"No."

"I'm sorry . . ."

"No. I know what you're going to ask and the answer's no. That isn't why I find Randall to be interesting."

Kathryn breathed in, then out. "You have to forgive me. It's the curse of being a gay man's best friend If a girl's not playing his pimp, she's consoling the guy he's run through like a knife through butter" She smiled so as not to seem bitter, and Mitchell returned a weak smile of sympathy for her petty plight.

"I knew he was gay"

"What was it? The Prada everything?"

"No." Mitchell met her eyes. "Tell any of our resident activists I said this and there will be punishment involved."

"Uh-oh"

"Randall Stone has gay eyes."

She waited for an addendum to this bizarre statement, but Mitchell said nothing.

"I'm sorry. *Eyes?*"

"They have this perpetual, self-aware glint to them. They're always rapidly alternating between surveying everyone around them and then pretending to be distant at the moment when they know they're being surveyed. I don't know. Maybe it's a more evolved form of insecurity or paranoia. But I think it's fascinating, and I don't mean it to be a slight to your good friend."

Kathryn nodded. "That's pretty strange, Mitchell."

"Pay close attention to them. You'll see what I mean."

"Deal," she said.

He lowered his bent leg and reached around his back for his satchel. Kathryn watched uneasily as he removed a notebook from his pad, began writing on the bottom of a piece of paper, and then tore it off and handed it to her. Hesitantly, she took it, for a brief second expecting it to be some sort of message that he didn't have the courage to voice.

Instead, she saw his phone number. When she looked up, he was already on his feet. He gestured to the paper in her hand. "I think it's pretty barbaric that the university doesn't allow freshmen to have cars on campus. If you ever feel the need to get off the hill, I know a pretty good seafood place down on the bayfront."

"Thanks."

"I have to go lead a discussion section. Forgive me "

She only had time to nod. She was about to slide the paper into her book bag when she noticed Mitchell had stopped several yards away, his head turned toward her.

"Forgive me if this comes off as presumptuous," he called back, "but even though the things that brought you here might seem shallow, you haven't been here long enough to know why you're here." He gave her his weakest smile yet, and it warmed her when she realized that these words had taken up most of his nerve.

She smiled and held up the paper in one hand.

He must have thought the gesture to be a little too direct, because he bowed his head slightly as he left the courtyard.

• • •

"Philadelphia?"

Eric turned from the window and its view of students processing into Folberg Library across the street. "I'm sorry?"

John Hawthorne swiveled his Herman Miller desk chair to face him. "The funeral was in Philadelphia, so I'm assuming Lisa was from there."

"Yes," Eric said.

The two men had been classmates, and Hawthorne took this as license to address Eric like an old friend. Never mind that, two years ago when he had assumed the role of the university's publicist, John had to remind Eric that the two of them had graduated together.

Eric eyed him as he returned his attention to several copies of the *Atherton Daily Journal* spread out on his desk. As usual, Hawthorne's salt-and-pepper hair looked as if it had been plastered on his head with shellac, concealing any natural part. Eric assumed the man would have been more at home in a New York advertising firm, baring his teeth over the speakerphone and pitting journalists against one another. Two years of being forced to keep his tone gentle and conciliatory seemed to have worn away at the man's patrician features.

Clearly Eric wasn't going to make small talk, so Hawthorne folded his hands on his desk and cleared his throat. "This is a small town, Eric. That's why I asked you here. Sometimes I wonder why a city of Atherton's size even has a local news station. But that being said, it should come as no surprise to either one of us that the local news media would attempt to . . . exploit the sensational details of your wife's death."

"You'll have to tell me what they've written. I haven't read any of it."

"Unfortunately, one of the most egregious articles happened to run in our student newspaper here on campus. Which makes it more manageable."

"What exactly do you need to manage, John?" Eric's tone was stiff enough to raise Hawthorne's eyebrows.

"*Manage* is probably the wrong word to describe my role here. It's my job to stand by you during all of this."

"Protect me?"

"Maybe."

"From what?"

"Opportunistic journalists," Hawthorne answered flatly. "The reporter covering Lisa's death for the *Journal* is a pretty well-known staff writer. Richard Miller. The guy has a reputation for being a muckraker. I don't know if you remember the river refurbishment scandal. Scandal that wasn't, I should say. Miller was going to run an article on how the city was trying to lowball the contractors when their estimates didn't fit the budget. He had quotes from a bunch of John Does, so the paper wouldn't let him run it. He got his revenge by leaking it to Channel 2, and Channel 2 got theirs when it turned out the quotes were all from contractors who didn't get the bid. Sending camera crews to city council members' houses without any cause."

Hawthorne sounded as if he was recounting the massacre of children by terrorists.

"At the end of the day, Channel 2 takes the fall. And Miller gets the satisfaction of watching the tempest in a teapot he's created without having to endure any of the fallout."

"You think he'll do the same with Lisa."

"I think the man's unethical, and he's covering the death of your wife." Hawthorne scrutinized him, and Eric realized he wasn't finished. "Your wife's death is no longer being considered a homicide."

"I wasn't aware it ever was."

"Patricia Kellerman is a homicide detective. She questioned you the night of the accident."

Hawthorne took the surprise on Eric's face as an adequate response. "In any instance of sudden death, suspicion is always cast on the spouse. The next of kin, even. That's not the issue, Eric. Your wife's death was considered a possible vehicular homicide for the last three days. However, the lack of any evidence of a collision with anything other than . . ." Hawthorne stammered and stopped.

"She went into the river, John."

Hawthorne's eyes shot to his. "I appreciate this might not be the time . . ." He shook his head. "You're tired. This is draining, I know. Let me cut to the point. There's a reason I'm being overly cautious here. Richard Miller also covered Pamela Milford's death. Back in eighty-three "

Eric worked to draw in a breath.

"Two deaths you have been involved in. Both were covered by the same reporter. I have to have a contingency plan in case this guy tries to draw some inane connection so he can write something that will land himself on *Dateline*."

"You do?" Eric asked. "Or I do?"

"I know it's unfair, Eric. But live with caution right now. Until this dies down. Which will be soon enough. But just in case, if there's anything Richard Miller could find on you if he looked hard enough, I'd like to know about it before he does."

The urge to get out of Hawthorne's office was so strong that his lie came easily. "My closets are empty."

"That's good to hear," Hawthorne said.

Eric turned and saw the skepticism on his face. Of course the man had no way of knowing it was a lie, but perhaps it was the abruptness of Eric's declaration that had made him suspicious. Eric bid him good-bye as quickly as possible before fatigue let anything else slip.


His palms sweaty and the sound of his pulse beating in his ears, Eric first noticed the furtive glances sent his way when he fell in with the afternoon throng moving up Brookline Avenue: the girl waiting at the stoplight who had pivoted her head on her neck when Eric looked at her, the group of students who went silent as he passed, their whispers audible in his wake. By the time his walk turned into a labored shuffle in front of the campus bookstore, real and imagined stares were igniting the hairs on the back of his neck.

Seeking some sort of refuge, he entered the bookstore. The first floor resembled a Barnes & Noble, with potential best-sellers stacked on display tables. He had never been a lover of fiction, so the front sections of bookstores always seemed foreign to him. Lisa had been the reader of novels. She devoured several mysteries a week. When Eric had picked up the paperbacks off the nightstand, he had discovered, to his surprise, that his wife's tastes ran to hard-boiled Los

Angeles detectives and corpses baking in the Southern California sun

He wandered down one of the aisles, feeling dizzy and short of breath. Confident he was hidden, he reached out for the edge of a magazine rack, drawing a few deep and labored breaths. He felt the oxygen return to his brain. Composing himself, he looked up to find one word leaping out at him from the row of glossy covers. PRICELESS!

The name of the magazine was *Blunt*, and it was ludicrously thick for what its cover claimed it contained. A glossy, high-fashion tome, its cover featured some nymphet of a rising film star holding a lollipop inside her mouth so that it made a suggestive lump against one cheek. But it was the headline that had caught his attention. *FROM SOHO TO SEATTLE, MICHAEL PRICE LIKES THEM BIG!*

His suspicion confirmed, he flipped pages until he found a table of contents. The profile of Michael Price began on page 222. He pondered flipping to it and then glanced around, feeling strangely like a kid perusing porn. Buying it in public would be enough of a chore. Reading it was something he would have to do in private.


Kathryn turned Randall's burned hand over in hers. "Jesus," she hissed

"The moral of the story is, Don't touch the heating vent."

Kathryn released his hand so he could take his first bite from his gyro. "Mine doesn't get that hot," she said, turning away from the sight of the long blister extending between his thumb and forefinger.

"Maybe ours is broken," Randall said between chews.

"Randall?"

He swallowed. "Yeah."

"You have gay eyes."

Randall's gyro stopped halfway to his mouth. "Are you stoned?"

"No. It's just something I noticed."

Randall nodded and went back to eating.

"All right. Spill it," she demanded.

White sauce Kathryn didn't know the name of had squirted from her pita onto her fingers and she wiped her hands with a napkin, waiting for Randall to snap out of his funk. They were the only customers in Lance's Gyros.

"Huh?"

"Who's the lucky guy?"

Randall briefly looked as if he smelled something foul, and then his face went blank. Kathryn folded her arms on the counter, hoping that her expression struck Randall as playful and not demanding.

"Where did this line of questioning come from?" Randall asked.

"From you getting home last night at three."

"Jesse . . ." Randall muttered under his breath before taking a bite.

"I heard you leave."

"And you waited up until I got back? How sweet." His smile was tight and forced, and Kathryn felt herself buying Jesse's theory that Randall was keeping his late-night rendezvous secret for a reason.

"Fine. Jesse told me what time you got home."

"Just told you out of the blue?"

"Randall!"

"All right already. But if I tell you about it you have to promise not to get mad." Randall turned his stool to face hers, waiting for her to agree. She gave him a weak nod. "Tim and I are giving it another shot," he said and then sagged as if a shotgun had been removed from his back.

"You're kidding."

"I said you weren't allowed to get mad," he warned in a singsong voice.

"I'm not mad. I'm just . . . How? Has he agreed to stop talking?"

"I know how to keep him in line," he said. She must have looked floored, because his eyes shot to hers. "Are you mad?"

"No. It's just weird. I thought you weren't interested."

"So did I. But Tim has ways of arguing his case, if you will."

"You mean he gives good blow jobs."

"Unfortunately, that burden usually falls on my shoulders."

"You mean tonsils."

Randall dropped his half-eaten gyro. "All right. You're pissed."

"I'm not."

"Kathryn, when you break with character and mention sex acts, that means you're pissed."

All she could do was roll her eyes. It wasn't that she felt lied to, or even that she disapproved of Tim. They just didn't seem like a match, and she had enough respect for Randall that she didn't want to see him settle.

"Okay, I'll admit it." Randall went on. "I didn't think you would approve. That's why I didn't tell you. But you'd better think twice before you listen to what Jesse says."

"Why is that?"

"Because the guy's a borderline sociopath. He's got no friends, so he sees what you and I have and it makes him sick. No wonder he's trying to mess with it."

"I think that's a little extreme. And what happened to being Jesse's biggest sympathizer?"

"Kathryn, why would he go to you and tell you what time I was coming home if he didn't—"

"I asked him."

Randall's blue eyes met hers, widening slightly with some mixture of indignation and fear before his teeth sank into his lower lip. He was fighting anger.

"Look, Randall, he asked me this weekend if you were seeing someone because you'd been leaving the dorm late at night. . . ."

"Exactly. He just told you this—"

"Wait. All right. Jesus, chill, it's not that big a deal. . . ."

"Kathryn, you thinking less of me because of what someone else said is a big deal. Especially someone who doesn't even know us."

"All right, you know what? I'm sorry I brought it up. Because you're freaking out over nothing."

Randall took a deep breath, turning his gaze to the window and Brookline Avenue's deepening evening shadow. "He's jealous of us, Kathryn," he said after a long pause.

"Randall, please, let's just move on."

"Why would he tell you any of those things? To imply that he knows me better than you do," Randall said, "That's why. And he doesn't."

"I think you're being paranoid. And I don't think less of you."

Whatever she'd said had worked its magic, because he bowed his head in what looked like shame, then took a breath that raised his shoulders. Despite his anger, she could sense how much he valued her opinion of him. But this defensiveness on his part suggested that maintaining her positive perception of him might be more important to him than their friendship occurring at the expense of honesty. Jesse's words returned to her. Did she feel that there was always a part of Randall that he kept just out of reach? Sadly, she couldn't have come up with a better way to phrase it herself.

"I should have told you," Randall finally said, looking out at the foot traffic on Brookline.

"Yeah. It would have been nice."

"I'm sorry"

"Don't be," she said, grabbing him by the shoulder as she slid off her stool. "Hey, there's an upside for me here. Now that he's getting the goods, Tim will stop harassing me at parties for info on you."

Randall's short laugh was strained, as if he didn't believe her sudden good humor was sincere.

They walked back to Stockton without speaking, without Kathryn groping for a good conversation topic. "Hey, I have some news too," she finally said.

"Share."

"I got a guy's phone number today."

"What did you have to do for it?" Randall asked teasingly.

"Just a minor discussion on the evils of Michael Price. I think you might know him."

"What?" Randall asked sharply.

Kathryn turned to see Randall had stopped, his eyebrows pinched. "Sorry. What did you . . "

"His name's Mitchell." Kathryn said.

"Mitchell *Seaver*?"

She felt herself bristle at his disdain. "Yeah. Why?"

"Nothing. I . . ."

"You don't like him?"

"I barely know him ".

"Then why do you look like you're passing gas right now?"

"Kathryn, I don't want to rain on your parade," he told her, dismissive and parental as he moved to walk past her.

"We had one conversation. I wouldn't call it a parade," she called after him.

He stopped and turned, lips pursed as if he was trying to hold his words in. But it didn't work. "I don't know him that well. But he's managed to rub me the wrong way a few times."

"I'll take that into account." Her words were icy with sarcasm.

Randall groaned in defeat and approached her, curling an arm around her waist. "You don't have to take *anything* into account. He's just not my type."

"Good! Cause he didn't give *you* his phone number."

"That's right, babe." He kissed her forehead. "I'm jealous."

He released her waist and she followed him to the entrance door. He slid his ID card through the reader and held the door open for her.

She hesitated. "You know maybe it might be healthy for *both* of us to start coming home at three in the morning." Halfway through the door, she caught his wrist before he managed to slap her on the behind.

Michael Price stared down into a lens that was angled so that the twenty-five story Bowery Tower seemed to be sprouting from his back. His black flattop of hair was riddled with gray. His cartoonish bulk had to be the result of steroids; his chest was too tweaked, his jawline too statuesque. It was Michael's face, though, narrow slits for eyes, a lip-less mouth that looked like a thin slash above his jutting chin.

"Rise to it or get the hell out of bed," the quote exclaimed, running down the margin of the photo in enlarged text. "If my dreams can't fill the room, I leave."

The article, called "The Price of Everything," was what Eric had expected, general ass kissing tempered by occasional flashes of sarcasm directed not at the cooperating subject, but at his critics, complete with a photo spread of Michael's penthouse atop the Bowery Tower.

> Three years ago, all of Manhattan's city-makers had marshaled forces against architect Michael Price. His design for the 25-story Bowery Tower drew the ire of politicians and preservationists alike. "A dagger impaled in the heart of downtown," *The New York Times* called it. Others were less kind, dubbing Price's erection "the work of the devil" and

Price "the Donald Trump of the visual arts." And when the building's construction was abruptly approved, rumors flared about behind-closed-door dealing at City Hall. Op Ed columns decried the sudden elasticity of zoning ordinances bent to accommodate the advance of high-rise architecture in a neighborhood made up primarily of tenements, artists' studios and warehouses.

Who would have guessed that three years later, the controversial amalgamation of plate glass and steel would become one of Manhattan's hottest new residential complexes thanks to a design that one critic called "the first 21st-century architectural masterpiece." The man who stood at the epicenter of controversy has ended up living at the very top, literally, of New York's art scene

Michael's penthouse was a vast, loftlike space decorated without discernible color. Absent walls, the living spaces were marked off by metal-framed furniture arranged along axes. A massive chandelier hung from the vaulted ceiling, which the photo blurb described as "a Gaudi-inspired amalgamation of wrought iron and ceramic, paying tribute to various forms of sea life." *Mutated octopus* would have been a better description. The soaring plate-glass windows commanded the downtown Manhattan skyline, and the expansive terrace took up the remaining roof of the building. Eric wasn't surprised to see that Michael had crowded the terrace with his ghostly white, wax sculptures; a strange carnival of dancing figures that looked naked beneath the sun's glare.

Eric fought the flutter of panic he felt every time he was forced to recognize that Michael hadn't ceased to exist—even though Eric hadn't spoken to him in twenty years—and continued reading.

Price grins when asked about the now infamous *Village Voice* cover, a cartoon rendering of the dashingly outfitted, barrel-chested architect straddling lower Manhattan with the Bowery Tower extending from his groin like a missile. Anyone familiar with the architect's pedigree knows he has reason to smile  . . and straddle. At the age of twenty-seven,

Price was a relative unknown. What name he had managed to make for himself was due to a handful of John Lautner–inspired residential projects throughout the Northeast His critics accused him of importing the most superficial elements of Southern California Modern to the opposite coast. But it was his bold proposal for the Seattle Aviation Museum that earned him overnight status as the enfant terrible of the contemporary architecture set, vaulting him into the ranks of Frank Gehry and Gwathmey Siegel. The young Manhattan architect beat out several prestigious West Coast firms for the Seattle commission, and seized his sudden celebrity status as a chance to both shape and create trends in a movement considered stale and lacking surprise.

For all Price's swagger and courting of controversy, his critics might be surprised to learn that despite his celebrity, the architect still pines for his college days at prestigious Atherton University. He's completed three commissions for his alma mater at half his normal fee, further inciting critics to speculate on whether or not Price is in it for the art or the glory. Price's explanation of his nostalgia is brief, almost terse: "I had a tremendous experience there. Why wouldn't I want to give something back?" While his private life is generally off-limits to journalists—Price adamantly claims he is a workaholic with little of interest to discuss beyond his work—the architect did reveal one of his more personal pursuits. One room of his Manhattan penthouse has been turned into a studio so that he can pursue his under-celebrated talent: sculpture. One can't help but wonder if the wax sculptures populating his expansive terrace are the only company such a driven public figure can afford.

Eric flipped the magazine shut and tossed it onto the sofa
Under-celebrated? Michael's sculptures were crap. They always had been.
When the two men met during their sophomore year at Atherton, it had been in an introductory sculpture class called The Kinetics of Form. Michael had mastered the technical aspects in no time flat, so

the other ten students in the class decided to take out their frustration on him when he presented his finished pieces. Michael had defended his perfectly proportioned, physically accurate representations of the human form with a passion that turned into self-righteousness, all of it made more intolerable by his always-coiffed movie-star good looks matched with an excess of charisma, which, Eric guessed, had charmed everyone except his fellow sculptors.

Represent something intangible or spiritual? Michael had practically sneered at the idea.

"My genius is for making people," he had announced. "I deal in the real."

Eric held his tongue as the war dragged on for a semester, watching Michael put up a fight and feeling anger and a measure of envy toward his arrogance, until the cabal of art students at Atherton banished Michael with their silent disapproval, which led Michael to shift majors. To Eric that seemed like a desperate move, but Michael had ended up laying the foundation for a career that was as impossible to avoid as Atherton's Tech Center. But the fact remained that Michael was not an artist. Eric found all of his projects to be towering amalgamations that, for all their flash and their defiance of gravity, dazzled, clashed with themselves, and then died of asphyxiation.

Perhaps that was why Eric had forced himself to read the article. So that he could make sure that, after all these years, Michael was still a collector and manipulator of styles, one whose ego made up for his absence of vision. He needed to know that the man he had lived with, the first man he had ever felt something close to love for, still had the same fault lines running through his soul.

Still, when he shut his eyes, he saw Michael descending the front steps of the house they had shared together for almost a year. "Eric, you study art because you're envious of people who can actually create. Because you can't. Because when you try, all your hear is the scraping of your fingers against the wall of your empty soul."

The phone rang. "Hello," Eric answered, sounding drugged.

"Can't make it tonight." Randall's voice was low and slightly hushed. Maybe he was trying not to be overheard by his roommate.

"How is it?"

"What?" Randall asked.

"Your hand."

"Better."

He thought of Michael Price, who had narcotized him and led him where he promised he would never go again. Pamela Milford's dead eyes rose up from the ice to accuse him. But whoever else he was, the fact remained that Randall Stone was not Michael Price. He had to remember that.

"Randall?"

"Yeah."

"We need to be careful."

In the ensuing silence, Eric anticipated anger, but all Randall said was, "Aren't we?" Eric heard a door open on the other end of the line, and before he could say anything else, Randall hung up.

# CHAPTER FIVE

THE MCKINLEY BALLROOM WAS USUALLY RESERVED FOR THE MOST exclusive of alumni fund-raisers, but for one Friday night it had been transformed into a gay club. "Absolution" was the theme of the second Gay and Lesbian Alliance Dance of the year. The word was written in string lights on the wall. Crepe paper hung between the brass chandeliers, and strobe lights flickered over the plush burgundy draperies. The dances were some of the most popular on campus, regardless of sexual orientation of the clubgoers, and as Randall pulled her onto the dance floor, Kathryn found herself searching the gyrating crowd for Mitchell Seaver.

She still hadn't spotted him by the time Randall fell into rhythm beside her, dancing with restricted hip motions, his neck rigid as he scoped out the crowd around them; he exercised just enough movement to look into it, but not so much that it distracted from his perpetual search for the next hottie. Or maybe he was just looking for Tim, considering that the two of them were giving it "another shot," whatever that meant. She felt the first familiar seizure of awkwardness and found the best that she could manage was shifting her weight from foot to foot while she held both fists in front of her chest, as if to protect herself from the flailing arms on either side of her.

Across the dance floor, Tim Mathis spotted her and gave her a wave with his glow stick. Most dancers were wearing them around their necks, but Tim had unfastened his and was waving it through the air like a wand. She shouted into Randall's ear, "Tim's right there!" and stopped dancing.

"Nobody likes a quitter!"

"I can't keep up tonight, Riverdance. Go mingle with your own kind!"

She gave him a slap on the ass as she left. April and her date for the evening were sitting on the burgundy upholstered chairs that had been shoved to the wall. Kathryn had barely exchanged a word with April's new squeeze, mainly because she'd been so whispery she was difficult to hear on the way to the dance and was now unintelligible over the music. She thought her name was Kelly, but didn't want to risk saying it out loud. She flounced down into the empty chair next to April; it barely gave under her weight and she pitied the alum who had to sit through entire dinners in it.

On the dance floor, Randall had fallen in with Tim and his circle of bopping, tank-top wearing boys, all of whom had exerted considerable effort to look like twelve-year-old white supremacists. Their buzz cuts were all the same color, a flat shade of gel, and their limbs extended, lanky and shaved smooth, from their sleeveless shirts. Tim, clad in a two-sizes-too-small T-shirt that screamed out *Porn Star* in red letters and black pants made out of some material that reflected the disco lights above, inched closer to Randall before hooking one arm around his waist and bringing his crotch to Randall's rear end in a pose that might have ended in their murder anywhere off the hill.

Randall let his head roll forward, eyes shut. He was either enjoying the pressure of Tim's groin so intensely that she shouldn't be watching, or he was enduring it without protest. Kathryn couldn't decide which. In contrast to the rest of the group, Randall seemed strangely adult, moving in rhythm but without the excessive arms-in-the-air antics of the surrounding dancers. All the other gay boys took to the dance floor with a newcomer's enthusiasm enlivened by a sense of newfound liberation. Randall shared neither their joy nor their acrobatics.

"I don't get it!" April shouted, and Kathryn anticipated a remark that was intended more for Kelly's amusement than hers. "Fags take all these perfectly good songs and then mix in a bunch of pots and pans falling down stairs while some disco diva groans out half a lyric over and over. The only way I could dance to this shit is if you set me on fire!"

Kelly said something inaudible, and April took it as an excuse to laugh and slide her arm around her shoulders. "Hey Kathryn! Why don't you go back to the dorm and call your boyfriend so you don't bring the rest of us down?"

"He's not my boyfriend," Kathryn shouted back. "We haven't been on a date."

"Talk to someone at Atherton for longer than fifteen minutes and it's a date."

"He lives off campus."

"What?"

"I said he lives off campus!"

"So what?"

"I looked him up in the directory and he wasn't listed."

"Kathryn, you *have* his phone number!" April shouted.

"He's probably thirty."

She wasn't about to tell April that Randall's dislike of Mitchell had wormed its way under her skin, forming a perfect excuse not to make a potentially awkward call every time she reached for the phone. Never mind that Mitchell had been one of the first people to whom she'd expressed her feeling of listlessness and repression and in return received flashes of wit, a phone number, and an abrupt departure. She was listed too. Kathryn knew this was all bullshit, but April would probably point that out soon enough.

"Fine. Don't call him," April barked. She threw one arm out toward the dance floor. "And welcome to the rest of your college career."

On the third floor of the Student Union, the ballroom's terrace offered an expansive view of the quad below and the campus beyond, which ambled over the hill in a sea of sloping rooftops that looked stark and semi-nude without leafy branches to bridge the gaps among them. Smokers crowded between the ballroom's floor-to-ceiling windows and the waist-high stone banister, which Randall rested his butt against as he held Tim around the waist. Both of them puffed cigarettes and watched Tim's gel-haired, tank-top-clad circle crouch around a guy named Taylor, who had curled into a ball, his arms clamped around knees that were weakly bent against his chest.

"X?" Randall asked.

"I wish I knew," Tim said. "He's a cute kid."

Randall grunted, wondering if Tim's entourage of activists and scholars-by-day, muscle-hungry whores by night, would have been paying as much attention to a party foul if it didn't involve a stocky, corn-fed boy with dimpled cheeks and pouty lips. "Now looks like your time to score," Randall said.

Taylor's caretakers had begun vigorously massaging his shoulders and back.

"You're sick, you know that, Randall? He's from Tennessee."

"What? That puts him out of your league?"

"Parents are also total Bible thumpers and he's thinking of letting them in on a little secret over Thanksgiving." Taylor's head rolled forward and a weak groan fought to escape his chest. His masseurs exchanged worried looks and struggled to keep his shoulders upright.

"Someone needs to call Health Services," Randall said gravely.

Obviously not wanting to leave Randall's embrace, Tim barked, "Ethan! Call Health Services!"

The guy Randall assumed was Ethan shot Tim a withering look to thank him for his input as he and several others hoisted Taylor to his rubbery feet. Taylor's athletic arms, covered in a sheen of sweat, and his shoulders, taut against the tight-fitting club gear he had probably been outfitted in by his caretakers, bore too much of a resemblance to Jesse's for Randall, so he downed a slug of scotch while Taylor was carted out of sight. The flask was full. It had been a Catch-22 in his jacket pocket for the last three days; each time he thought about how he had filled it he wanted to take a drink to sand the edge off his guilt, and each time he brought it to his lips he saw Lisa Eberman's face.

He clamped his eyes shut, wiped his brain clear, and swallowed more. The slug had a stringent bite to it. It burned as it went down and Randall sucked in a breath to cool the inside of his mouth. Just then, Tim let out a small cry when he saw Randall's blistered hand wrapped around the flask. "What's that from? Intro to Juggling Flaming Batons?" he asked.

"Close," Randall answered. "Where are they taking him?"

Confused, Tim followed Randall's gesture toward the window where Taylor had been. "Don't know," Tim answered, glancing again at the blister. "Maybe Health Services. Thank God it doesn't go on your record. The guy's got enough shit to go through with his parents as it is." Tim clasped the flask, trying to pull it from Randall's hand. Randall pulled back. "Shouldn't you have something *on* that?"

"Everyone's a doctor," Randall mumbled.

Tim threw up both palms and took an exaggerated step backward. "'Scuse me!"

Randall drew him back in with one arm around his waist. Tim went taut for a second before giving in fully to Randall's halfhearted embrace. "I'm so glad I came out to my parents when I did."

"Were *they*?" Randall asked

"They were all right. They didn't exactly throw a parade. What about yours?"

Silence, Randall knew, only encouraged Tim the journalist to dig further. So Randall summoned his rehearsed lines and took a moment to stud them with sordid detail that might scare Tim off the topic. "If I walked into my mother's room one day and told her I was gay, she would drown herself in a bathtub of Glenlivet. The woman's like a hairsbreadth away from being a character in a Jackie Susann novel. I would rather old age push her over the edge before I even have the chance."

"You shouldn't talk about her like that."

"Clean up enough vomit and I earn the right."

Tim winced and lifted his head from Randall's chest. "It's that bad?"

Randall managed a half smile at the sympathy in Tim's question, but which he hoped sent the message that he could handle his domestic traumas if everyone just gave him some space and stopped asking questions. "Sorry," Tim muttered. "What about your father?"

*No such luck*, Randall thought. "I think he knows. And he'll be fine as long as we never talk about it." Randall heard the impatience in his tone, and brought the flask back to his mouth.

"You will, someday."

Tim's declaration ignited anger in his chest, which didn't mix well with the stinging wash down his throat. The result was a series of hacking coughs that turned Randall rigid against the banister, and forced Tim off his chest. Tim slapped him on the back several times until the coughing subsided. He must have seen the anger in Randall's eyes, but he misread it. "Your sordid family life makes you all the more mysterious and alluring—you know that, don't you?"

"Sure," Randall answered, voice thin. He turned to the banister and the view of the quad beyond—anything to distract him from Tim's prying questions and presumptions.

"I thought you said scotch was going to turn you into a gentleman."

Back to Tim, Randall shut his eyes and drew a breath, trying to forget the certainty in Tim's words, *You will, someday*. Feeling like he had stepped back into the spotlight, he turned and gave Tim a broad grin. "Maybe I need some more," he announced, and brought the flask to his mouth. This time the slug exploded in his throat and the result was another coughing fit. Tim didn't touch him this time, just backed up a step, and through smarting eyes, Randall could see his wrinkled expression of concern. "This stuff is rancid," Randall finally managed.

"Where'd you get it?"

"The liquor store," Randall got out. "Where else?"

"Right. The one that sells scotch to eighteen-year-olds."

"Which would be everyone on Brookline. How the hell else are they going to make their money?" Still coughing, Randall capped the flask and tucked it back inside his jacket. Gooseflesh crawled up the back of his neck; his entire body shivered. "So . . ." He swabbed his mouth with the back of his hand. "Any big break in your story?"

"Not really. I did have another meeting with my contact."

"Richard? The guy at the *Journal*?"

"Yeah. He told me something kind of interesting, but not earth-shattering."

"What?"

"I don't know if I should tell you."

Randall seized one cheek of Tim's ass and brought their crotches together. He squeezed. Tim would tell him.

"Yikes. All right. How gentlemanly. Let me put it this way. Lisa Eberman is not the first woman the good professor's been involved with to end up drowning."

"Who's the other one?" Randall asked.

"You ever heard of Pamela Milford?"

"That was years ago, wasn't it?" Randall tried not to sound interested. His body felt as if it were easing free from his brain.

"Eighty-three. She was dating Eric Eberman. Hey . . . Randall?"

Black spots clotted in Randall's vision. Tim's hand clamped his shoulder. Randall blinked, and he saw that he was staring up at the roof of the Union. Tim let out an alarmed cry and Randall felt the stone banister dig into the small of his back; he had pitched backward and suddenly Tim was holding him by both shoulders, staring at him as if he had to peer through several layers of gauze.

Nausea boiled Randall's stomach and he batted Tim's arms away.

"I'm fine . . . I'll be back in a second." His voice came out reedy. The only lucid thought he could pluck from his brain was that he should get the hell out of there. Away from anyone who might see him vomit up his entire stomach.

He heard Tim calling out his name from a great distance and suddenly realized that his feet had landed on the hardwood floor inside the ballroom. The disco lights painted slow, thick swaths across his vision, streaks that blinded him briefly before fading into pinpricks of light and vanishing completely. Dancing bodies seemed to slide past him, a few rocking him back on his heels and almost throwing him off balance. The exit sign was a rectangle of light and he moved toward it as darkness began to crowd his vision.


"Bullshit!" Kathryn cried.

Neither April nor Kelley considered Randall's sudden departure from the dance to be an emergency, and Kathryn had been angrily striding paces ahead of them since they had left the ballroom. She slid her ID card into the slot at the Stockton entrance, flung the door open, and bounded up the stairs to the first-floor hallway.

Randall's door was shut and she tried the knob. Locked. She knocked and got no answer.

April and Kelly shuffled up behind her.

"He might still be there, Kathryn. We didn't look everywhere."

"Tim did." She turned to face them. "He checked the bathrooms. He checked outside—"

She heard the door crack open, and saw April's eyes widen with a flicker of shock before she quickly bowed her head. Kathryn spun around to see Jesse holding the door open several inches, just enough to reveal that he was wearing only a pair of white briefs. Her eyes shot down his half-naked body, the dunes of his chest and abdomen, but she stopped herself before she hit the bulge in his crotch. Oddly enough, he seemed the most exposed because he wasn't wearing his baseball cap, and she was surprised to see that his tousled black hair had a slight curl to it.

"Is the dorm on fire?" Jesse asked.

"Is he here?"

Jesse nodded.

"That's our cue," April mumbled behind her, and Kathryn heard their footsteps departing over the carpet.

"How is he?" When her palm braced the door, Kathryn was shocked to feel Jesse holding it firmly in place with one hand curled around its edge. He had never prevented her from entering the room. She let her arm falter to her side.

"Where have you been?" Jesse asked.

"At the dance. With *him*."

"He got back over an hour ago."

"Are you going to let me in or not?"

Jesse shrugged and sighed, stepping away from the door without bothering to open it any further.

Randall lay cocooned in his comforter, curled into the fetal position with his back to her. She sat down on the edge of the bed and brought a hand to his forehead. His breaths were slow and even and his temperature seemed normal. "Tim says he got sick," she said to Jesse, who didn't respond. Kathryn risked a glance at him. He sat perched on the edge of his bed, his eyes locked on Randall. Kathryn began to withdraw her arm. "Was he here when you got back or did you . . ." Her elbow disturbed the comforter, which slid off of Randall's shoulder, revealing his bare chest. She picked it up and pulled it back, stopping when she knew she should have seen the waistband of Randall's underwear. Instead she saw just naked flesh and hip bone.

"He was pretty drunk," Jesse finally said.

"He didn't have time to get drunk. He left after only twenty minutes." She saw she had curled the comforter into one of her fists.

Jesse was giving her nothing—just like Tim, who hadn't offered to help search for Randall if it meant leaving the dance. And if they were giving it another shot, why had Randall gone to the dance with her instead of Tim, who was already there with his entourage when they showed up? Questions swirled in her head, none of which Jesse could answer, so she smoothed the comforter back over Randall's shoulder.

"It looks like you took pretty good care of him, Jesse." She rose from the bed.

"I'm his roommate. That's my job."

That same suggestive, teasing tone, which he'd manage to delete from their conversation three days earlier, now returned to his voice. It stopped her halfway to the door. He had his old smug smile on his face "Can I ask you something, Jesse?"

"Always."

"How would you get rid of him when you're done?"

Jesse narrowed his eyes on her, as if the implication of her words were written in tiny letters across her forehead.

"Never mind the fact that he's not as stupid as the little girls you always bring through here. But he's your roommate. It's not like you could just not call him back."

"I'm not even sure what you're accusing me of."

"I'm not accusing you of anything. But I've always known that you can't resist anyone who worships you enough. I'm just asking you to think twice about this one."

She managed to shut the door behind her without slamming it.

Kathryn realized that it all boiled down to small omissions, little things Randall hadn't told her. But after she left his room, she realized that being confronted with secrets of any kind returned her to the night on China Beach when Jono's secret scattered to the rocks at the mouth of the Pacific. She tried to sleep and instead found herself in a speeding car. Kerry was gunning the Miata out of the China Beach parking lot. After only a few weekends spent with Jono and his friends, the Kerry who had once been wary and suspicions of college kids now worshiped them as one would a patron saint.

"Are you sure we should just leave him there?" Kerry asked, her voice tense.

"He'll get a ride with Peter."

They were approaching the edge of Golden Gate Park, on their way to the late-night party at Kerry's house in Noe Valley, which had been vacated by her parents for the weekend. Kathryn could hear the Miata's tiny engine protesting as Kerry kicked at the gas and hiccupped across two lanes of traffic. "Damn, how'd he piss you off so much?" Kerry asked.

"We were out on the rocks and he started pawing me and—"

"Oh, and you so hate it when he paws you, right?"

"Can I finish, please?"

Kerry shook her head, once, twice, each time faster. There was something wrong with the way her head kept jerking on her neck, almost like a plastic, windup doll. Then, with one palm on the steering wheel, Kerry brought a hand to her nose, swabbing at her nostrils and then raking her fingers back through her hair. Kathryn wondered if she was trying to plaster her bangs with her snot.

"So he's acting like an idiot and then he drops his jacket into the surf and I can't find him . . ."

"His jacket? He lost his *jacket*?" Kerry's voice ratcheted upward in alarm. She glanced fiercely at Kathryn, not seeing what Kathryn saw—the car was barreling toward a stoplight at fifty miles an hour.

"*Kerry!*"

Kerry slammed on the brakes and Kathryn's arm went out, her hand smacking into the glove compartment. Stunned, Kathryn lifted her head to see the stoplight had gone green, but Kerry still had her foot on the brake and the car was halted in moving traffic.

"We need to go back, Kathryn!"

Kerry twisted against her seat belt, and in the wan green halo of the stoplight, she saw that Kerry's eyes were wild, her pupils dilated. "What's *wrong* with you?" she demanded.

"Nothing. We just can't *leave* him back there. I mean, without his jacket. He's probably freezing his ass off."

"He got a ride with Peter. I'm sure! Kerry, the light's green!"

"No, seriously, Kathryn. We need to go back and get him."

"*Kerry!*"

But before Kathryn could protest further, the Miata lurched left and Kerry tore out in a wide, stomach-wringing U-turn across the intersection. In disbelief, Kathryn heard the sound of peeling rubber beneath the car's shuddering wheels, and when they almost collided with the curb, Kerry let out a cry that was more infuriated than afraid.

Kerry, brow furrowed slightly in concentration, gazed fixedly ahead, got into her lane and accelerated. Once again, her hand swabbed at her nose.

"Pull over," Kathryn said.

"Chill, Kathryn, it'll only take a—"

"Pull over!"

Kerry let out an annoyed grunt and the Miata bounced to the curb. Once the car came to a stop, Kerry released the steering wheel, threw up her hands, and stared at her friend as if she had sprouted devil's horns.

"What are you on?" Kathryn asked.

"Excuse me?"

"You're high on something. Not drunk. Not stoned. You're fucking high."

She saw protest flicker and then fade in Kerry's eyes before her face became a tight mask of indignation. "Like you don't know," she muttered.

"Don't know what?" Kathryn barked. Afraid that Kerry's foot would hit the gas again, she curled her fingers around the door handle, ready to make a quick escape.

"He's your boyfriend, Kathryn. Shouldn't you know?" Kerry saw the confusion on her face and added, "Please! You've seen his apartment? You think he paid for all the stuff with work-study?"

Kathryn's hand slipped off the door handle. The questions hit her rapid fire. How did Jono, the bartender and struggling college student, afford the matrix of electronics equipment in his apartment? Did she ever really believe the story about how he had a friend who got it for him wholesale? A friend she had never met? Where did he go after the sudden phone calls and abrupt departures from his apartment, when he assured her that he was not going to see another girl, and that he would be back in time to drive her home from Berkeley to Sea Cliff before her curfew? Suddenly all the unanswered questions, which had in the beginning given her boyfriend his enigmatic appeal and sense of mystery, solidified into the obvious conclusion; she should have figured it out during the many nights she'd spent alone in his apartment, waiting for him to come back.

"He had it in his jacket, didn't he?"

Kerry sighed. "It's not that big a deal."

Kathryn slumped against the passenger seat, feeling as if the wind had been pummeled out of her.

"Kathryn, if you're going to be his girlfriend, you need to grow up a little bit."

"Grow up? You're so fucking high you almost got us killed, and you want *me* to grow up!"

"Yeah. And you're really bad at playing dumb," Kerry said, all sobriety now.

Once she got out of the car at her house, after a ten-minute ride in abashed silence, Kathryn slammed the car door as hard as she could, because *dumb* didn't even come close to describing how she felt.


Floating somewhere between sleep and waking, Randall was afraid to turn over for fear that any change in position would further twist his gnarled stomach. After several minutes of indecision, he managed to roll onto his back, and when he did he realized he was naked. He saw Jesse sitting cross-legged on the foot of his bed. His legs, the etchings of his past he carried with him always, had been laid bare before Jesse's eyes.

He groped for memory and saw only Tim Mathis staring at him as he held him by both shoulders, and then a mad jump cut of flickering lights on the dance floor. "What time is it?" he asked groggily.

"Almost six."

"What happened?"

"I found you out front. You were passed out "

Alarm snapped Randall totally awake, and he tried to sit up. The comforter tumbled down his bare chest. He managed to catch it in his burned hand. Jesse hadn't moved. "Why am I naked?" Randall asked, taking a breath between each word.

"You were out of it. Kind of awake but totally incoherent. Not like I haven't had experience with that kind of thing . . . But anyway, you kept saying you were burning up. I opened the window and that wasn't good enough so I—"

"Where's my jacket?'

Gray light teased the edges of the window shade, and Randall could make out Jesse moving to his closet, dressed in only his underwear. He reached in and pulled Randall's leather jacket from a hanger. "It needs to be cleaned," Jesse said, displaying the spill of caked vomit down one of the flaps.

Randall jerked one hand impatiently, and Jesse handed the jacket to him. He felt for the hard lump of the flask in the inside pocket, and, to his relief, found it. Jesse stood over the bed, watching intently as Randall removed the flask and uncapped it. It was more than half full.

"You must have hit the scotch pretty hard," Jesse said.

No, I didn't, Randall thought. I've hit a lot of goddamn things pretty hard, and never fallen so fast.

"Jesse, did I . . ." He couldn't finish and let out a frustrated sigh.

"What?" Jesse asked, a smile in his voice.

"I didn't . . . *try* anything, did I?" He brought one hand to his aching forehead.

Jesse spoke, mouth inches from his ear. "No you didn't. And I was very hurt." Jesse tousled Randall's hair before crossing to his side of the room.

Randall tried to prop himself up on both his elbows and his stomach yowled. He landed on the pillows with a groan. Three deep breaths and the cramping in his abdomen abated. This was not a hangover. This was something worse. Had the scotch truly been rancid? Could scotch even go bad? He had no idea.

Something else had been in the scotch.

He froze, eyes on the ceiling. The realization quickened his pulse, flushing his veins, sending blood to his brain and clarifying his thoughts.

Jesse's voice startled him. "Your hand looks like your legs. Only newer."

Randall let his eyes fall to Jesse, who was leaning against the edge of the window. "Different," was all Randall could manage.

"I figured." Jesse seemed to lose interest in the subject, his eyes narrowing on the crack between the shade and the window. "Remember the phone call last Friday?"

Randall grunted no.

"The one you asked about."

"Yeah?"

"It wasn't my father. It was his lawyer."

"Jesse, I didn't mean to . . . piss you off about it."

"Yes, you did," Jesse retorted calmly. "My dad's a pretty good addict, if there is such a thing. I mean, I remember him showing up at school functions, acting all the gentleman, when I knew he'd sucked down a few lines in the limo on the way there. Well, a few weeks ago he kind of lost control. He was having some big party at the house and he and a few guests ended up in the neighbor's pool. Considering this is the third time this year Dad's got the two pools confused, the neighbors decided to file a trespassing charge. I'm sure it didn't help that he refused to get out of their hot tub even when the police showed up."

Pale light around the shade had brightened into a beam that sliced across Jesse's chest.

"Anyway. He's looking at twenty-eight days."

"Prison."

"No. Rehab."

"That sucks," Randall said, his voice wary. "So you're not going home for the break?"

"I was never going home for the break," Jesse said, his eyes on Randall's.

Quickly Jesse lifted the shade. Even the pale light of dawn forced Randall to squint, and at first he didn't see the flakes tumbling past the window, which seemed to hold Jesse in sudden thrall. "People like snow because they think it unifies everything," Jesse said in a low voice. "They think it draws all these disparate elements into one landscape. Like how a layer of white over everything draws your attention to things you didn't notice before. The telephone pole, the wires overhead, the rooftops." Jesse paused, his eyes glazed and distant as they stared through the glass at the silent snowfall. "Bullshit," he whispered. "Too much of it is suffocating. It robs each thing of what it really is."

Randall realized he had been gazing at Jesse for longer than he usually allowed himself to, for fear of feeling that familiar hot flicker of panic that told him looking too long would make him want too much. But given what Jesse had just shared, it would be too rude just to curl up into a ball. For the first time, Randall felt Jesse's solitude like a crushing weight; here he was at Atherton, friendless and having run across country to escape the nightmare of his only living parent. But the longer he watched Jesse gaze out the window, the more Randall could feel Jesse's hunger for his companionship. It was too loaded an invitation for Randall to accept.

"Well." Jesse broke the silence, turning to his bed. "Since you don't look like you're about to choke on your own vomit, I'm going to get some sleep, okay?" He slid beneath his comforter and rolled to face the wall.

Randall couldn't say anything in response. He couldn't tell Jesse that he knew his solitude, knew the damage that resulted from turning yourself into an orphan.

He reached down and shoved the flask under his bed.

In the driveway, Eric's Camry sat alone in a bed of deepening shadow as late Saturday afternoon turned into an evening of darkening pewter sky. Randall's hangover slowed his steps, even though he was invigorated by a strange blend of purpose and fear. By the time he reached the front steps, he had managed to convince himself that the bottle hadn't been poisoned and that his mind was running wild with guilt-fueled fantasies. He'd skipped dinner the night before. Could drinking on an empty stomach drop you to your knees?

With one hand on the banister, he realized there was still only one way to quiet the racket of accusing voices in his head. Get the bottle.

He'd taken several steps when he heard the unmistakable sound of voices raised in argument in the living room, and while he couldn't make out the words, Randall could hear Eric arguing, and another male voice trying to trump his volume.

Randall squeezed himself between the Camry and the side wall of the house, moving slowly toward the gate to the backyard, illuminated by the bright halo of a security light. At first, instinct had driven him into the alley. He hadn't called to say he was coming over, maybe hoping to catch Eric off guard, but that meant running the risk of being seen. Now, as he listened to footsteps and saw a shadow pass over the wall of the neighboring house, curiosity led him to eavesdrop.

Eric and his guest moved into the kitchen.

Randall shut his eyes, hoping it would help him concentrate on the muffled voices inside. The sudden song of water through pipes told him Eric was standing at the sink beneath the window. "How many times do I have to ask to be kept in the dark?" The other voice gave an inaudible response, and when Eric spoke again, he had obviously turned from the sink because he was harder to hear. "I don't see why it's so important to you . . ." Nothing, and then Eric again. "Just a look? That's all? Even when you know you don't have my approval?"

They left the kitchen and the conversation was lost within the house. Next, Randall heard footsteps plodding down the front hallway. When he heard the front door open, he held himself flat against the side wall.

Mitchell Seaver strode past the entrance to the driveway, tossing his head back and brushing his bangs off his forehead before he disappeared. Randall moved swiftly down the driveway and caught a glimpse of Mitchell a block away before he made a sudden right, heading away from campus.

Randall managed to wait almost a minute before mounting the front steps.

Eric threw the front door open with such force that Randall guessed he had been expecting Mitchell to return. "Did you call first?" he asked.

"No. Sorry."

Eric nodded, his eyes flitting past Randall, probably checking to see if Mitchell was still in the street.

"Can I come in?"

Eric shrugged and let out a grunt. "Good to see you too," Randall muttered as he brushed past Eric through the doorway.

The dining-room light was on and Randall's eyes flew to a stack of stapled student papers on the usually empty dining-room table. Eric crossed briskly out from behind him, and Randall watched as Eric began to leaf through them with feigned nonchalance. "You should really call," Eric said absently, holding his back to him.

No mention of Mitchell, Randall thought. Eric turned at his silence

"You look horrible."

"Thanks."

"I didn't mean it like that," Eric returned his attention to the stack as if Randall were too bright to look at. His altercation with Mitchell had agitated him, and Randall, woozy and squinting at the brightness of the dining-room chandelier, waited to see what Eric would say next. "Seems Mitchell couldn't make it through all of these while I was gone."

*How many times do I have to ask to be kept in the dark?*

Was Eric just averse to grading his own students' papers? Randall doubted the imposition alone would lead to a shouting match. At the bottom of the pile, Randall noticed the label tag of a manila file folder. But then Eric lifted the stack with both hands and carried it to his satchel, which rested on top of the liquor cabinet.

"More emphatically written treatises on why the Greeks removed the arms from all their statues?" Randall asked, summoning an old joke between them. Eric didn't laugh, just took extra care to shove the cumbersome pile of papers into the straining confines of the leather bag. Once done, he turned, letting out a fatigued breath of accomplishment.

"I think she dropped the course," Eric sighed.

Randall averted his eyes from the liquor cabinet that Eric blocked with his body. "I hope you didn't fail her," he said. "Her stuff had entertainment value at least."

Eric couldn't manage a laugh and his eyes fell to Randall's feet. Randall could barely focus on Eric, feeling the distance grow between him and the scotch bottle that contained something other than scotch.

"Rough night last night?" Eric asked.

"You could say that." Randall hesitated and drew breath, but the light was blinding him and he was surprised when the room went dark.

"Better?" Eric asked through the sudden shadows.

Randall grunted. "I was thinking . . . Maybe tonight I could sleep here."

His eyes hadn't adjusted to the darkness when Eric answered. "I don't see why not."

• • •

Jean Pierre's was all white linens and muted conversation. A lobster tank gurgled next to the host stand, and the other diners seemed to be locals Kathryn had never laid eyes on, or else professors in need of a refuge from the concentrated collegiate hustle of Brookline Avenue. Through the plate-glass windows, Atherton Bay lay in darkness pierced by the beacon lights of small ships making their way toward the Atlantic. Beyond the far bend in the coastline, Kathryn could make out the dark rise of the hill and the campus glowing atop its crown. It warmed her to be disengaged from the campus, if only for an evening.

"Thanks," she said.

Mitchell looked up from his menu, gave her a swift smile, and raised his water glass. She toasted it with her own. When he had picked her up, she had been relieved that he had dressed for the occasion; khaki trousers, a starched white oxford, and a loose-fitting blazer. But the fact that he had traded his glasses for contacts was what struck her the most. All of it made her feel less self-conscious in the form-fitting black cocktail dress she had borrowed from April without asking. Despite the more formal attire, he seemed more relaxed, and less eager to get a laugh out of her.

"What are we toasting?" Mitchell asked.

"Bosch?"

Mitchell arched his eyebrows, surprised that she had picked up a conversation thread they had left behind in the car.

"I don't know his stuff very well," Kathryn said. "But what is it about him that turns you on so much?"

"He was a heretic," Mitchell said, closing his menu. "There's pretty sufficient evidence that Hieronymus Bosch was not a true member of the medieval church, even though he was painting for them. His works are filled with all these little symbols, and over the years scholars started figuring out that they were the codings of heresy, basically."

"What do they mean?"

"We'd better order before we get into this."

The waitress rattled off a million specials, none of which sounded as appetizing as the lobster. "You're paying, right?" Kathryn asked as she ordered it.

"I guess so. But how subtle." He smiled briefly and averted his eyes from hers. Feeling like a forward woman if not an independent one, she smoothed her napkin over her lap.

"I'll make this as simple as possible," he began again.

"Don't," Kathryn said, resting her elbows on the table as she sat forward. "Confuse me. Please."

"Well, then." Mitchell picked up his fork and began running the tines along the edge of the tablecloth. "The established medieval church held the view that the world was the mirror of God—that our creator basically poured himself into his work and he presided over it with a kind of constant, fatherly diligence. This was the conventional Christianity that Bosch supposedly believed in. But his work tells another story entirely."

Kathryn tried to pay attention to his words and not to the little flecks of yellow she had noticed in his brown eyes.

"Many scholars—Dr. Eberman included—believe that Bosch was what you would call a dualist. Now that would put him directly at odds with the established church doctrine, because dualists believed that the earth was nothing more than God's castoff—that God didn't really take great pride in it, that in fact, he abandoned it. God presided over a higher, and more spiritual realm. Meanwhile, Satan moved in and made earth, our earth, his terrain."

"What happened to hell?"

"It was still there. And you went there when you enjoyed your time on earth too much." Mitchell smiled, then let his smile lapse.

"Which sounds exactly like Christianity."

"No. Christians never claimed that our earth belonged to the devil. But that was Bosch's worldview. All of his depictions of earth are of an inherently unsound and even sinister world. He couldn't paint a plant without covering it in clawlike spikes. Storm clouds always hover on the horizon. Masses of humans collide in acts of war. Earth was chaos to him. It's hardly the mirror of God."

Mitchell sighed "And that's where Christianity and dualism part ways. As a dualist, and entrenched in the belief that the earth is Satan's terrain, you must believe that everything about the physical world is not just a temptation, but also a trap. To free yourself from Satan and the chaotic terrain over which he presides, you must devote your entire life to separating yourself physically, and, more important, mentally from your body."

His words had quickened and grown more urgent. He took a delicate sip of water. "So, to answer your question, not only am I obsessed with Bosch because I admire the fact that he was a rebel who managed to work for the establishment, I also believe that he secretly obeyed a religious doctrine that even the most dedicated Roman Catholic would have trouble aspiring to: the complete disavowal of one's physical self," Mitchell said, his voice verging on exclamation. "Not to mention the horrifying thought that God, the supposed heavenly father, presides not over our lives, but over some distant spiritual plane that can be accessed only by learning not to trust the very flesh we've been imprisoned in. Not just by loving your fellow man, or showing up at Sunday mass."

Mitchell's passions struck her hard, and for a second, she thought she shouldn't risk responding. "It doesn't sound possible."

"What do you mean?"

"Disavowing your physical self."

"I guess it would involve convincing yourself that your body is something to be overcome. Not obeyed."

"And sex?"

Mitchell's eyes met hers. "Out of the question."

Kathryn grinned involuntarily, then tried to bring one hand casually to her mouth, wondering if Mitchell had just given a forecast for how the evening would proceed. When she looked up, Mitchell was gazing out the window distantly. His words reverberated in the aftermath of his monologue. Even before Jono had sidled into her life, she had often felt sexual desire to be a kind of poison, infusing the body with urges beyond reason, driving fantasy and reality together in a potentially fatal equation.

"I'm boring you," Mitchell said suddenly.

"No."

The waitress delivered their salads, and Kathryn stabbed the leaves with her fork, trying to fend off the memory of walking Castro Street with Kerry back when they were little girls and slowing their steps at the sight of a thirty-year-old man walking with the support of a cane, both of them silently wondering how such a devastating disease could come from an act so cloaked in adult magic.

"I didn't mean to upset you either."

She looked up to see Mitchell leaning forward, his yellow-flecked gaze intent and a slight, sympathetic smile on his face. Between April's condescending lectures and Randall's recent evasiveness and perpetual distraction, she found herself relishing someone else's attentiveness to her moods.

"What you're saying, it reminded me of someone . . ." She trailed off, realizing that if she continued this would be the first time she had ever discussed Jono Morton with a single person at Atherton.

"How so?" Mitchell asked, gently.

"My boyfriend, senior year of high school . . ." She faltered. This shouldn't be this hard, she thought.

"Your boyfriend was a dualist?" Mitchell asked.

Kathryn laughed too fast. "No," she said. "He was a drug dealer."

Now she was laughing by herself. Mitchell's mouth had assembled itself into something that was both grimace and smile. His expression obviously wouldn't go away unless she kept talking.

"I'm sorry," she went on. "I was reminded of him because I think if I hadn't been so attracted to him, I might have been able to see who he really was a lot sooner than I did. Too many times with him I let my body do the talking."

Mitchell nodded. "I take it you two are no longer together."

"He's dead."

Her eyes shot to Mitchell's, waiting for the obligatory apology for a death in which the speaker had played no part, an apology that Jono Morton didn't deserve. But instead Mitchell seemed to be diagnosing her emotions around her revelation. "Drugs?" he finally asked.

"Oh, no. You could say he was smart in that respect. He knew better than to do them himself." She regretted her response instantly, realizing that Mitchell would probably ask how he had died.

If he did, she would lie. "We'd been together for about a month when I found out he'd been giving coke to my best friend, Kerry. She was kind of my partner in crime when it came to hanging out with older guys. Her brother was a bouncer at this hot new club down in So Ma—sorry, South of Market—anyway, he used to let Kerry and me in all the time if we promised not to drink. But of course, we found a bartender who would serve us."

"Your boyfriend," Mitchell interjected gently.

She nodded quickly, and continued. "Anyway, Kerry and I used to get drunk all the time, but drugs? Never. So when I found out that she'd been . . . getting coke from Jono, I lost it. And confronted him about it. Of course, he claimed he had only given it to her a few times. Claimed he wasn't a dealer. And I made the mistake of believing him."

"Sounds like it ended up being a bad mistake," Mitchell said almost tonelessly.

"Maybe," she said, looking over his shoulder out the window. She told herself to stop, but kept talking. "What makes it worse is that the things about him that made me look the other way were so superficial. We didn't have great talks late into the night or share our deepest secrets. He was just this good-looking, brooding college guy I made the mistake of thinking was superior to me. After all, I was just a spoiled senior in high school who'd never even touched weed."

The voice in the back of her head telling her to shut up had grown less loud. Even though she felt a frightened, fluttery sensation in her chest as she continued, her breaths were coming easier. "I guess in some screwed-up way I thought he was going to teach me how to be an adult. As if just being with him gave me access to this world of independence that all the other girls in my class were missing out on."

"If only we could all learn so much from our mistakes, Kathryn."

She met his eyes again. Of course he had no way of knowing she just told him barely half of all that had happened. But given her inability to tell Randall or even April, bringing it up at all seemed like a victory. Mitchell seemed gratified if not moved by her honesty, and somehow fully aware of how difficult it had been for her. She realized that her small triumph was not totally her own. Mitchell Seaver had an uncanny ability to put her at ease.

"I imagine you're looking forward to Thanksgiving." Mitchell turned the Tercel out of the rambling neighborhood of mostly abandoned wharves and decrepit warehouses. This seemingly benign comment crushed the giddy buzz Kathryn had felt since leaving the restaurant.

"Fuck," she whispered. "Do the dorms stay open?" she asked.

"They might. I wouldn't know. Not going home?"

"It's only four days," Kathryn muttered, trying to recall the last mention Randall had made of their trip to Boston. "I thought I had plans . . ."

Last night, she had suspected that a drunken Randall and Jesse might have taken their roommate relationship to another level, and while that disappointed her, she had been prepared to suck it up. Then, when Randall made no attempt to track her down or speak to her the entire day, she had felt left out and offended, cut off by his silence.

"Plans with Randall?" Mitchell asked.

"I'd love to get through one day without talking about him."

"Deal." Mitchell smiled into the black windshield.

Kathryn was startled by the metallic clatter of the Tercel's tires passing over the steel girders of the bridge, and when she looked up she saw the blinking lights of the barricade surrounding the torn opening in the bridge's rail. "Oh God," she groaned.

"I know. I wish they would just hurry up and repair it."

"How is he?" Kathryn asked.

"I'm sorry?"

"Dr. Eberman. How is he handling everything?"

The blinking lights flew past the driver's side window, and Mitchell glanced at her as if still unsure of what she had asked. "I think he's handling it in his own way," he said dryly.

Kathryn sensed she had touched a sore spot, so she kept quiet. Maybe mentor had withdrawn from pupil in the wake of tragedy.

They crested the hill, the university's front flank rising behind the gates to the quad.

"Break starts Wednesday afternoon, right?" Kathryn finally asked.

Mitchell nodded. "Where were you and Randall planning on going?"

"Boston."

"Why?"

"It was close," Kathryn said, her voice tight with anger: she was going to have to eat crow in front of her mother, and possibly to no avail, because it was probably too late to get a ticket. The midnight hour had long since come and gone. "It was Randall's idea," she added weakly.

Mitchell slowed the Tercel to a halt next to the curb in front of Stockton, but Kathryn didn't rush to get out. He released the steering wheel and turned a little to face her, his clasped hands folded on one leg. He hadn't bothered to put the car in park.

"Again?" he asked.

Kathryn laughed at the brevity of his question. "Sure."

"Good."

Kathryn prepared her body for the inevitable lean-in of a man's mouth to hers. Mitchell didn't move. "So I guess it's decided, then?" she said, sarcasm tinging her tone.

"Seems like it. Yes." Mitchell turned back to face the steering wheel.

Kathryn breathed once, twice, then brought her hand to the door handle. "Good night, Mitchell."

Halfway up the front walk, she glanced over her shoulder to see that Mitchell hadn't pulled away from the curb  She gave him a weak wave over one shoulder.

*Great*, she thought, *A goddamn gentleman.*


Randall lay on one side, just outside the tug of Eric's weight against the mattress, watching the digital clock on the nightstand. At a little past ten thirty, Eric's weight lifted slightly and Randall went rigid, anticipating the sweaty slide of Eric's arm across his chest. But instead, he heard Eric's bare feet moving to the bathroom, the whine in the old shower pipes and then the splatter of water against tile.

Eric's satchel was on top of the liquor cabinet.

It was the file that had bothered Randall, and something about the awkward haste in which Eric had bothered to conceal it. His fingers found the label tag, jutting out from the other papers, and he gave it a gentle yank. A handwritten note was clipped to it.

*I have confidence in this one—M*

Only two items were inside the folder; the first a stapled essay, four pages long and double spaced, the second, a small, square, computer printout, which in the darkness of the dining room was a jumble of letters so small they could just have been chemical symbols. Upstairs, the shower continued in a dull rush.

Milky light from the streetlights outside fell across the living-room sofa; Randall sank down onto it. The printout bore the letterhead of Bayfront Medical Partners. Still, he could barely make out the dot-matrix–printed letters. Frustrated, he turned his attention to the essay. There was no title or header offering up the name of its author. Randall folded the printout and tucked it into the pocket of his jacket, still slung on the back of Eric's reading chair.

> Alan Raines is my father's brother, but I stopped calling him my uncle a long time ago.
> After his wife left him, he came to live with us. I was nine years old My mom ended up clearing out her office so that he could have a room—a room that was right next to mine.

To the best of Randall's knowledge, Eric didn't teach a single course that required students to submit personal essays. But that was exactly what this was. Dumbfounded, he continued reading.

> I always knew something was wrong with Alan. My parents never told me outright, but after he came to live with us I realized he was a drunk. That was why he lost his job, and that was why he was in our house.

Upstairs, the shower halted and Randall looked up at the ceiling as he folded the essay in half. He got up from the sofa and stuffed the essay into his jacket pocket, debating whether he should get a glass of water from the kitchen to give some pretense to his excursion downstairs. He heard the wood creaking on the front porch. He peered out the front windows; the porch looked empty but the sound had been unmistakable. He knelt on the sofa, his face pressed to the glass, hands braced on the window sill, trying to see down the length of the porch.

Two palms slapped the other side of the glass and a dark shape rose up, blocking out the streetlights. Jesse's eyes were level with his He had reared up from his hiding place beneath the window, his mouth a leering, triumphant grin. Randall let out a sound between a shout and a cry, and lurched back, his knees sliding off the sofa and slamming into the floor, the back of his head slamming against the edge of the coffee table.

"Randall!" Eric's shout echoed down the stairs

Stuck in his absurd position, Randall stared up at the window to see Jesse backing away slowly, pressing the tip of one trigger finger against the glass. *"Found you,"* Jesse clearly mouthed before withdrawing his hand from the window and receding into shadow.

# CHAPTER SIX

RANDALL KICKED OPEN THE DOOR TO HIS ROOM SO HARD THAT IT slammed into the side of his closet. But Jesse was not waiting for him, perched on the edge of his bed, a triumphant smile on his face. Jesse's bed was made so tightly Randall could have bounced a quarter on the tasteless plaid comforter. There was no Jesse to look up from his laptop, startled, before managing to form some barbed question like, "Get much sleep last night?"

Randall's breaths were nasal and rapid, and he had bunched his hands into fists against his sides. All semblances of a self-righteous speech left him. He took care to shut the door more gently than he had opened it.

Lisa's bottle of Chivas Regal, the one he had used to fill his flask and the only one open in the liquor cabinet, was a hard lump against his thigh where he had wedged its bottom half into the inside pocket of his jacket. It made a ludicrous lump inside his coat. After another hour of fitful sleep, he had managed to dress without waking Eric before swiping the bottle. Returning to Stockton, with dawn's first feeble light crawling over the rooftops of east campus, Randall had walked with his arms held in front of him, wrists meeting just above his crotch. He hid the bottle under his bed, right next to his flask.

He sat down on his bed to catch his breath and glared at Jesse's side of the room. Clothes dangled like ghosts in the closet, and without Jesse it seemed bare. Was it a testament to Jesse's refusal to put down roots in his new home? Did he have nothing to put down? Or did the guy just travel light, keeping his commitments few while he accumulated sexual accomplishments?

Randall crossed the invisible dividing line. In the bottom-most file drawer of the desk, he found file folders labeled with course names. He flipped through them; they were copies of submitted papers and graded ones. In accordance with the textbooks on the shelves above the headboard, every course was your basic introductory gut.

Examining Jesse's living space, he saw no evidence of any driving passion that determined the flow of his roommate's life. There was none of Randall's strange marriage of buff models and fine art, none of Kathryn's clutter of textbooks devoted to courses ruled by logic and analytical thinking. Anyone who knew Jesse would say his outstanding quality was vanity. But there was not a single photograph of himself or anyone else on his side of the room. Nothing to indicate the self-love that his swaggering evoked.

But what bothered Randall the most was that there was no secret buried in his drawers, nothing Randall could use to his advantage. There were only two material things Jesse showed consistent affection for; his navy pea coat and his laptop computer, both of which were with Jesse at that very moment.

A dream and a dire obligation had brought Randall Stone to Atherton University.

But what had brought Jesse? What was now driving this warped All-American guy to turn Randall into a conquest?

"Is this a date?" Tim took a seat across from Randall, his eyes deliberately downcast as he lowered his satchel off one shoulder. Outside, Sunday hushed Brookline Avenue. Hangovers and homework kept most students indoors. Randall and Tim sat at one of three occupied tables at Madeline's.

"I'm sorry about the other night," Randall said neutrally.

"I was worried about you," Tim said, sounding as if he were ashamed to admit it. He clasped his hands on the table in front of him, evidently waiting for Randall to explain the purpose of their lunch.

Randall took a sip of his club soda. "You want to order something?"

"I'm not hungry."

"Tim, just order something, okay? This is going to take awhile."

Tim furrowed his brow, obviously puzzled. "Look, Randall, I'm sorry I didn't try to find you Friday night but . . . I think it goes without saying that I shouldn't have any illusions here, all right? It's not like I'm planning our commitment ceremony."

The waitress appeared and set a cocktail napkin down in front of him. His eyes darted from Randall to the hovering waitress before he ordered a glass of water. "We have fun together," he continued. "I mean, I don't exactly want to use the term *fuck*—"

"I need you to help me with something," Randall cut in. When Tim got on one of his rolls there was only one way to stop him.

"All right."

"Friday night. I don't remember much, but—"

"You were pretty sloshed. Of course, I'm not anyone to point fingers. Last year, I got so totaled my roommate called Health Services and I had to spend the entire night in the Health Center so some med student could check my pulse every hour."

"Stop talking, Tim."

Tim's eyes widened and he crossed his arms over his chest, and slouched back in his chair. "What's going on?"

"Friday night, before I got sick, you were telling me something about Dr. Eberman."

"I don't remember what—"

"About how you had a meeting with your friend Richard at the *Atherton Journal* and he told you . . ."

"Oh! Pamela Milford. What about her?"

The waitress delivered Tim's water and he nervously drank it, almost emptying his glass. "Back in eighty-three, she's the girl who wandered into the—"

"I know who she was. Every students here does. But was there anything else?"

"Her parents were very wealthy. Thanks to them, that's probably why everyone remembers her so well. She vanished without a trace one night in March and her parents swept into town talking to reporters left and right, holding press conferences and accusing the university of somehow being at fault. She had been missing for one day and suddenly they posted this huge reward, which got the Atherton PD flooded with a bunch of crank calls from crackpots and psychics. The next morning, their daughter turned up in a drainage canal that empties out the north side of the hill into the bay."

"And she was dating Eric?"

Tim cocked his head as if he'd heard a strange sound but couldn't pinpoint it. "She was romantically involved with *Eberman*, yes. He was the one who reported her missing."

"But there were no signs of foul play?"

"No. The police concluded that she got drunk at a party in the Chi Kap house on Fraternity Green, wandered into the Elms, and fell into Inverness Creek, which isn't really a creek but a drainage canal. The reason the Elms are even there is because the city won't lend Atherton the money to reinforce the canal with concrete, so they can't exactly start pile driving next to it." Tim looked at him hard. "I'm sorry. Did you call him *Eric*?"

It hadn't been a slip, but Randall's small attempt to break the ice in preparation of all he was about to reveal. Randall kept calm as he watched the first indications of suspicion coming to life in the back of Tim's brain. But it wasn't clear how many connections he was making and how fast. Randall was relieved Tim wouldn't force the question. Obviously, he had enough of a reporter's finesse to know when he might frighten his fish away from the spear. And Randall had enough at stake to know that in what he hoped to do, he would never allow himself to be bait or prey.

But in the silence that settled over the table, Randall saw Tim realize that Randall's sudden reentry into his life last week had a clear explanation. Animosity swelled within him. Randall allowed Tim his moment, draining his club soda before he spoke again. "Your friend Richard usually gives you scoops, right?"

Tim nodded curtly.

"And he'd probably give you more, if you could return the favor. In a big way."

"Wait a minute. Richard doesn't work for the AP. The stuff he usually gives me is town versus gown stuff. Hardly sexy. But he did have a lot of high hopes riding on the Lisa Eberman thing. He thought the police were going to turn up evidence of a marital squabble at least."

"And no doubt you shared your take on Dr. Eberman."

"Yeah, I may have planted the seed. But Richard couldn't find anything to back it up."

"But he looked, right?"

"Of course he did. The coroner's office conducted what's called a medical legal autopsy. It's standard in all cases of sudden death and all the findings are collected in a manner that would make them presentable in a court of law. I got the one-up on Richard by telling him about my conversation with Lisa's sister, Paula." Tim looked sour. "He was giddy He managed to convince himself that Lisa hadn't been drunk. Tox reports came back and she was point oh nine. That's drunk."

"Anything else?"

"What do you mean?"

"Toxicology. Did it turn up anything weird?"

"Traces of stuff she had prescriptions for. Why?"

Randall took a deep breath and brought a hand to his forehead. He saw disco lights panting swaths across his vision instead of flickering. In his stomach, he felt the churning of rancid scotch. He imagined the same things happening to a woman behind the wheel of a car. "Randall?" Tim seemed to call from a distance.

He jerked his head up. "Eric Eberman's your mortal enemy, right?"

Tim, who had bent forward over the table, sat back in his chair as if the force of Randall's sudden question had hit him in the chest. "I think the guy's a closet case. As a rule, I don't like closet cases."

"Be honest, Tim. Why were you and your reporter friend panting to pin Lisa's death on Eric if you didn't think it was a way to prove he was as queer as a three-dollar bill?"

"I made the connection. Yes." Tim sounded defensive.

"But it didn't work."

"No," Tim said, as if a great personal failure of his had been pointed out. "The car went into the river in perfect condition. She was good and numb, and she was driving. End of story."

"Does Richard Miller agree?"

"No. Richard wants to know how a man who has been involved with the deaths of two different women had managed to slide through both investigations with less than twenty minutes spent in the interrogating room. And I'd like to know too."

"Wouldn't you be halfway there if you could prove Eberman was gay?"

"Maybe."

"And how could you do that?" Randall asked. "Write an editorial in the *Herald* about how he threw you out of his course after you hit on him? See if maybe he's been brave enough to make advances toward some male students."

"That wouldn't be good enough. We're not talking about a government official with a history of condoning anti-gay policy here. If somebody like that makes an advance, his entire career is founded on hypocrisy, and that's a story. But with a professor at a private university—well, the story wouldn't carry any weight unless it entailed something like what he did to me but with some wandering hands involved and some proof that a student was penalized for not accepting his advances."

Randall lifted his eyes to Tim's. "And if a student did?"

"Did what?" Tim asked, even though it was clear he already knew.

"Accepted his advances?"

"You son of a bitch, Randall." Tim's eyes shot away from Randall's as his upper lip curled in disgust

"Chill out, drama queen, I haven't confessed to anything."

"Are you going to?"

"I need you to help me with something first."

Tim gave a slow, exaggerated nod of his head. "Do you ever!"

"I'm not coming forward tomorrow. And you're not running to your friend Richard until I tell you it's okay."

Tim was silent. His shock was giving way to disapproval. And perhaps a healthy portion of jealousy he would never admit to.

"Tim!"

"It sounds like you're giving me orders."

Randall felt his face tighten as he bent forward, clasping his hands around his glass to anchor himself. If he took a deep breath it might force him to think twice, so instead he dropped his voice several volumes. "Depending on how badly you want to ruin Eric Eberman, maybe I am."

"Since when do I want to *ruin*—"

"Don't bullshit me, Tim." Randall fought to maintain his steady volume and won.

"Maybe I'm just returning the favor, Randall You think I didn't wonder why you suddenly waltzed back into my life after not returning a single phone call for a month? You wanted to know if anyone had a clue you were sleeping with him, didn't you?"

"I wanted to know if he killed her," Randall said as flatly as he could. The coldness of the statement obviously struck Tim, because he shook his head and scanned the empty tables around them. Emboldened, Randall continued, "And I need you to help me find out."

Tim drew a deep breath, and Randall could see what was contending inside him—whether or not to believe Randall in the face of the realization that their renewed affair had been little more than an information-gathering mission, and the fact that a man he knew might have killed his own wife. "I'm listening," Tim said finally.

Randall looked to his water glass and summoned the nerve required to articulate his role in the narrative. "Lisa Eberman drank only scotch. She kept bottles of it stored in her liquor cabinet. You want to know how I've been filling my flask, Tim? You're right, I haven't found a liquor store that's been sold on my fake ID. And since Lisa always seemed to have extra, I started borrowing from her. I filled my flask from the last open bottle three nights after she died. After three slugs of whatever was in that bottle, I threw up my entire stomach and couldn't remember a thing the next day. Whatever was in that bottle, Tim, it wasn't just scotch."

Feeling like he had just confessed a crime of his own, Randall worked to lock his eyes on Tim's. Tim's expression was fixed, intense.

"You think he slipped her some of her own meds."

"That's what I want you to help me find out."

"This is out of my league, Randall."

"This is exactly the story you were hoping for."

"And you?"

"What do you mean?"

"What do you get out of this?"

"Nothing. This is about Lisa."

Tim smirked. "Nice try."

Randall fought his ingrained reflex against telling anything about himself that someone could read as motive. "I was in bed with him the night of the accident," he finally answered, sounding as reedy as he had after a slug of poisoned scotch. "She left him a note."

"What did it say?"

"That she knew about us. That she had seen us that night. Eric tried to make me believe that I was the reason she was driving like a maniac." That was all Tim needed to know, Randall told himself, and even that admission felt like a giant one. Tim would serve a specific purpose and therefore require only specific information.

"I see you're not very good at feeling guilty."

"For what?" Randall snapped. "The fact that Eric killed his wife?"

"You have to prove it first."

"We will."

"I haven't agreed to anything yet."

Randall summoned his most acidic smile. "Sorry, I forgot. You're way too busy covering the latest student outcry against the administration's policy of not letting freshmen keep cars on campus."

Tim rolled his eyes. "It's not like this isn't tempting."

Randall waited for Tim to continue, and when he didn't, Randall bent forward, one hand almost touching Tim's across the table. "I don't expect you to help me with this just so I can sleep better. And I'm not defending the fact that I had a thing with a married man. But Lisa Eberman's death should not be on my back, Tim. And that's exactly where Eric tried to put it."

"Go to the police," Tim responded promptly. "Tell them you were in bed with him the night she died. That's all they would need to take a second look. Unless . . ." Tim bent forward, mimicking Randall's posture and bringing their faces within inches of each other. "Maybe you think if the two of us start playing detective we might prove your little conclusion wrong. Clearing the way for you and the good professor to live happily ever after."

Randall felt his jaw clenching, his top teeth grating against his lower ones. How desperate was he to put himself in this situation — enduring sermons from Tim? Tim Mathis had that undeniably gay male quality of being great at self-righteous indignation and all too eager to abandon his lofty principles when it came time to get on all fours. Randall had witnessed this sweaty, split-second disappearance of integrity in Tim and many men before him — too many to remember all at once. Randall coated the sting of honesty in Tim's statement by reminding himself that a year earlier, if Eric had accepted Tim's dinner invitation, the inconvenience of a drunken wife might have faded into the background for Tim as well. Randall clung to these thoughts as he spoke again. They gave him fragile moral ground and kept the full force of his anger from his words.

"I'm done arguing my case, Tim. You either want this story or not."

Tim seemed disappointed that the sparring was over with. "I'm not going to tell you this isn't tempting. But if I agree, my number-one priority would be Lisa Eberman. Not your conscience and not Eric's reputation. That said, we should go to Richard now—"

"No!"

"Randall, look—"

"Tim, there's one thing that you would have that Richard and the police don't."

"What would that be?"

"Me. The guy Eric lets into his house every weekend." Tim's eyes brightened and Randall felt a tinge of relief as he realized he'd hooked him. "And I've already got something to show you."

"These are test results," Tim said.

The file Randall had stolen from Eric's satchel was open on Tim's desk. On the other side of his locked door, Sharif and John were arguing over who had ignored the prominently placed note inside their fridge and drunk all of John's Japanese beer. Tim had slid the essay aside and gone straight for the medical printout. "What kind of tests?" Randall asked, rising from the bed.

"Christ, this is the five-hundred-dollar test."

"What's that?"

"A guy I used to date back in Chicago called it the third-date test. It's a full STD panel. It's everything. HIV, gonorrhea, herpes . . ." Tim lifted the sheet from his desk as Randall sidled up behind him, reading over his shoulder. "Lauren Raines. Fit as a fiddle. You know her?"

Randall straightened. "Yeah. She lives in my dorm. Kathryn used to hang out with her."

"Does Kathryn know?"

Instead of answering, Randall removed the test results from Tim's grip.

"Wow. So there *is* something you guys don't tell each other," Tim said.

Randall was done thinking of comebacks to Tim's jibes, finding refuge in an obsessive focus as he picked up the essay. "Alan Raines was my father's brother," he read off the first page. "Lauren wrote this."

Tim furrowed his brow as he examined the essay. "You found this in Eric's house?" he asked as he flipped pages.

"Yeah."

A strange glint in his eyes, Tim looked up at Randall. "You haven't read it?"

Randall shook his head. He felt a surge of anger when Tim smiled slightly, sensing Randall's need for a partner's complicity. As Tim skimmed the first page, Randall turned to the window. "It's about her uncle. He's a drunk. He comes to live with her family . . ." Tim's words trailed off and Randall turned to see his face had gone lax. "Lord," Tim whispered.

"What?"

Tim took a deep breath and began reading aloud. "The details of what my uncle did to me are of no real importance now. How was a nine-year-old supposed to know that something that felt so good, something that was not accompanied by violence, was wrong? At the time, it was not clear that my uncle's affections came from an adult world that could potentially render me—a nine-year-old girl with no knowledge of her sexuality—powerless."

Tim glanced up at Randall as if checking to make sure he could handle it. Randall gave a weak nod, praying that his face didn't betray the sudden clenching in his chest, the strobing memories of wandering hands and prying fingers. Not nine, *fifteen*, he told himself, And I was never powerless. I knew *exactly* what I was doing. But as Tim continued reading, Randall found his own words hollow as Lauren's words jabbed at the parting in a curtain he had dropped between Atherton and the past.

"I have wondered whether or not that at the age of nine, I had any sexuality to speak of at all. Now, I believe that I did, but that it was dormant, lying in wait for the right moment to emerge. My uncle's hands brought it to life before it had a chance to be properly born. As a result, my sexuality is the equivalent of a premature baby with a permanent birth defect. It can grow all it wants, but it was brought to life with only poison as nourishment, and no amount of growth can bridge the hole in its heart." Tim's voice had gone from detached sarcasm to toneless shock. "Uh . . . God," he grunted.

"Keep reading," Randall commanded.

Tim shot him a wary glance. "Please tell me what this has to do with anything," he said. But his eyes had returned to the paper in front of him, like a motorist unable to look away from a roadside accident.

"What the hell was it doing in Eric's house?"

Tim just shook his head, reading silently for a second. He sat forward suddenly, staring down at the paper as if the text had blurred. "What?" Randall asked sharply.

"I do not hate my uncle," Tim read. "I believe he was diseased. And such a diseased man usually ends up infecting others. By the time I came to Atherton, I believed I had come to terms with what he had done to me. Then I met Jesse Lowry."

Randall froze, standing over Tim. After a moment, he removed the essay from Tim's hands.

"Jesus. If she slept with Jesse no wonder she got tested for every STD under the sun," Tim said.

"Jesse uses condoms," Randall told him. Tim arched his eyebrows. "I've seen *the box*," Randall added.

"I thought you might be working double — Sorry, make that triple time." Tim crossed to his fridge and pulled out a beer.

Randall sank down onto the bed, reading.

"Randall, maybe you shouldn't be . . ."

Randall ignored him, and Tim drank from his beer.

After arriving at Atherton, Lauren Raines had found it almost impossible to sleep, plagued as she was by nightmares. She went to a guidance counselor seeking prescription sleeping pills. But the counselors at the health center weren't even licensed to give out aspirin and were reluctant to make referrals, believing most student problems had to do with too much raw independence, too much stress, or just too much drinking. But the counselor was a "sweet guy" and after several sessions, Lauren told him about her molestation. Further sessions were devoted to coming up with ways to exorcise her memories. According to the counselor, whom Lauren didn't name, the more she tried to repress the memories, the more likely they would spring up when she tried to sleep.

Randall thought the counselor's final solution was insane. He continued reading with increasing disbelief.

> One of my favorite classes is Workshop in Creative Writing I. It is also one of the hardest. Everyone is very tough on each other's work. Most students don't like reading aloud. Me included. But I believed that by placing my story in a fictional context and forcing myself to read it aloud to the entire class, I would experience what my counselor called a catharsis.

The story was called "Hands," and Lauren worked on it for weeks, altering all the major details. "Hands" was a success, but she speculated on whether or not the story's subject prevented the other students from hissing their usual poison. The story's reading was followed by a sober class discussion on the nature of molestation. Lauren noted that the class's conclusion was the same as her own: while molestation was essentially about manipulation and control, the real sin inflicted upon the child involved was the period of disillusion during which the child believes that the actions of their molester are a new and valid form of showing love.

One student didn't contribute to the discussion. Jesse Lowry.

At first, Lauren thought the guy was silently revolted by the proceedings, but as soon as the class let out, Jesse approached her, showering her with praise. By the time he asked her out to dinner, Lauren had convinced herself that her reward for facing her demons was the sudden attentions of the strikingly handsome classmate she had secretly been ogling for weeks. As self-conscious as Lauren's essay was, even she went into a kind of swoon when she described Jesse, with his "proportioned athletic body in which every muscle moved in fluid union" and "All-American good looks with a flash of boyish playfulness lighting up his smile and his perceptive eyes."

"Give me a fucking break," Randall muttered.

"Huh?" Tim asked.

"Nothing," Randall answered and continued reading.

Lauren's opinion of Jesse was unchanged after their first date. Jesse was charming, honest, and most important, didn't make a move after dinner. This struck Randall as especially odd; he didn't remember Jesse going on a single date. Usually, he either didn't need to, or didn't care enough to devote even that amount of time to a potential sexual conquest. To Randall, Jesse had only mentioned Lauren in passing, as he had the many girls who stumbled out of their room in various states of undress.

> I decided I was ready to make love to him. I was the one who took the initiative. After making sure my roommate would be out for the evening, I invited him up to my room. I wasn't exactly subtle about it, but that didn't seem to be a problem. He started performing oral sex on me. He was very good at it.

Lauren's cold frankness in describing the sexual act drove home the fact that Randall was eavesdropping on a private pain. But a potent blend of horror and curiosity drove him to keep reading. He hoped it wasn't the voyeuristic pleasure of hearing what Jesse was actually like in bed.

"Are you done yet?" Tim asked.

Randall shook his head. "In a second."

> I've never been so ready for someone to enter me before. He was gentle, he was affectionate, and as soon as he was inside me he whispered in my ear, "Just like your uncle, Lauren." I experienced an immediate orgasm I could not prevent.

"Jesus!" Randall tossed the essay aside and rose from the bed.

Tim shot out of his desk chair and retrieved the essay off the bed.

It took him a few minutes to finish, and when he did, he dropped it to his lap and looked to Randall, who was staring out the window. "How well do you really know Jesse?"

"I'm starting to think Kathryn might know him better."

"Huh?"

"She wouldn't be surprised by a single word of this. She's always thought Jesse was some kind of . . . predator. I always thought he was just a big hornball and that she was just attracted to him and had to take out her frustrations on him, but that's not it. She always sensed that he was using his body, using how attractive he is to . . . undo people."

"Very *Dynasty*," Tim commented wryly.

Randall ignored him. "It's almost like Jesse thinks the only honest thing in his life is his body and the pleasure it can give him. And he's always trying to convince everyone else. I can see him . . . I can *hear* him saying that to Lauren. And believing it."

"I repeat," Tim said, retrieving his beer off his desk. "It has nothing to do with what we're looking for."

"What was it doing in Eric's house?"

"You said you thought Mitchell Seaver dropped it off. Maybe he left it with the paper he hadn't graded by mistake. Maybe Lauren is friends with him. I don't know, Randall, but you asked me to help find out if he killed his wife, and this shit is not helping." Tim took a slug of beer. "Better luck next time."

"I have the bottle," Randall said, turning from the window.

Tim nodded. "That's a start."

"Maybe. We can't exactly take it to the medical examiner's office and ask them to run a few tests without telling anyone except us what they find."

"I could take it to Richard. He's covered the police beat here for twenty years. Maybe he'll know some doctor who can run tests or something."

"That's ridiculous, Tim. He's a reporter. You don't think he's going to want to know why you're bringing it to him?"

"Look, we're fairly limited in what we can do here, all right? Now unless you think you can dig around the house again and find some diary or something, then you might start considering my suggestions."

"I've got a suggestion of my own," Randall said. "Her sister."

"What about her?"

"Lisa was spending every weekend with her. I'll bet she wasn't bothering to pack a suitcase. Anything she wanted to keep from her husband, she would keep there."

"The woman's got cancer, Randall."

"That didn't stop you the first time."

Tim flounced down onto his bed, holding his beer against his chest and draping an arm over his forehead to indicate a splitting headache. Randall knew what was coming, more poking and prodding at his real motive. Maybe he hadn't given a good enough performance the first time. He inhaled deeply and took a seat next to Tim on the mattress. Tim opened his eyes when he felt Randall's weight on the bed, and Randall met his gaze, infusing his voice with the necessary gravity.

"You want to know the truth, Tim? I would love to go the police tomorrow morning. And then I'd go straight to Richard Miller and tell him everything I know about Eric. But if I did that, I would be out of here faster than you can blink."

"Why?"

"My parents don't even know I'm gay, Tim. If they find out that I've been sleeping with one of my male, married professors they would yank me out of Atherton the next day."

"And back to Park Avenue where they'd lock you up in a room padded with Frette couture and throw away the key. Poor baby."

"So I'm a baby. No one's arguing with you on that." Forced self-pity had brought a slight quaver to his voice. The sound of it emboldened him, and he continued, "But that's not the point. If I'm locked up in their apartment, there's no way I can find out who killed Lisa Eberman."

Tim propped his back against the wall and stared at his bent knees as he gave consideration to Randall's suggestion. "I'll call Paula Willis. Tell her I'm doing a follow-up on Atherton's continued grief. She'll like that—the idea that the whole town's still mourning her sister's death."

Randall nodded, collecting the contents of Lauren Raines's file.

"It's weird," Tim continued distantly. "She talks so fast, it's like she's trying to get everything out before she goes."

"Call me if something works out," he said, heading for the door.

"Randall."

He turned around. Tim looked older, drawn. "If she grants me another interview, you're going with me." Randall was silent. "To see her," Tim added. Realizing that Tim was also going to play both judge and jury, Randall managed a curt nod before he shut the door.

Someone had opened his window to share the sound of Moby with all of West Campus. Randall slowed his steps as he followed one of the winding pathways through the labyrinth of redbrick walls. He found an empty bench just off the pathway and lit by the blue light on top of one of the campus emergency phones.

He flipped to the last page of Lauren's essay.

> I did not hit him, I slugged him. It was like hitting a brick wall.
> "So it wasn't just a story?" he asked me.
> He was so calm. So unfazed by the fact that I was coming apart right in front of him. I was practically sobbing by the time he got his clothes on. And the whole time all he kept saying was that it wasn't wrong of me to enjoy what my uncle did to me. He told me that my uncle hadn't been the one to fill me with poison—that job had been accomplished by the therapists who had to tell me it was wrong after the fact.

Lauren's story all but proved Kathryn's suspicion that there was some darker motive beneath all of Jesse's sexual maneuverings. But Randall had resisted the idea for so long not because he liked Jesse and wanted to believe of him better than that. Randall's path to Atherton had been paved with the sexual secrets of men. He had learned them and exploited them to the best of his advantage. But he had done it to survive. For Jesse, it was like a game. No, a pursuit, Randall thought. But why?

Why was Jesse so desperate to show Lauren that the memory of her molestation would result in an orgasm?

He continued reading in hopes of finding something that might spark an answer.

I can't claim to know Jesse Lowry. All I know is that I allowed him to violate me. I was lulled into a state of complacency by the lust I felt for him, and that lust comes from the same place my uncle poisoned. The sad reality is that Jesse might be half-right. How can I embrace my sexuality when all it wants to do is sink its teeth into me? My fate has been predetermined. I will never be someone capable of making love.

As for Jesse, I'm only left to wonder what incident in his past would give him the conviction to attempt insight into mine. I can only speculate.

So can I, Randall thought, lifting his head from the essay, wondering if he had just found the secret he had searched for on Jesse's side of the room that morning.

# CHAPTER SEVEN

SUNDAY AFTERNOON HAD TURNED INTO SUNDAY EVENING, AND Kathryn had rewritten the E-mail twice already. Only one sentence had survived: "I know it's probably too late to get a ticket." It was not an E-mail she wanted to write or a trip she wanted to make, but after two days of not speaking to him, she assumed Randall had forgotten their trip to Boston. She had just started Rewrite Number Three when a knock on her door startled her. Randall ducked his head in. Before her face could betray her anger, she forced a weak smile and returned her attention to the computer, hoping the sight of her back communicated the anger she didn't have the energy to voice.

"Friday night," Randall said. She waited for him to continue. He didn't.

"Yeah?" she asked without turning.

"Is something wrong?"

"Friday night?" she repeated, her tone clipped.

"I was gone. I'm sorry. I skipped dinner and then once I got to the dance I realized I was trashed." She nodded to the computer screen, not believing a word of it. She returned her hands to the keyboard before she realized her focus was shot. "Working?" he asked.

"I have to write my mother an E-mail."

"Have you seen Jesse?" Randall asked, apparently not having gotten what she just said.

She turned against the chair, one arm braced over the back. "No. I haven't."

Startled, Randall turned from April's bookshelf, where he'd been running a finger along the spines of her text books. "Kathryn?" he asked, sounding wounded by the sharpness in her tone.

"Yes?"

His blue eyes were glazed and distant, stricken by her anger and suspicious of its source. He took a seat on the edge of April's bed. "Don't lie to me. What's going on?"

"I'm writing an E-mail because I have to get down on my knees and beg her to try to find me a plane ticket for Thanksgiving."

"Oh shit." Randall's exhalation sounded almost relieved. He got up from the bed, but she turned back to the computer. He squeezed her shoulders with both hands. "Kathryn, I'm sorry. I forgot to tell you. I talked to my parents and they pulled the plug."

Your parents who never call, she thought, the parents you never want to talk about, and suddenly they want you home for Thanksgiving. "What did they say?"

"Same old shit."

She laughed. The expression meant nothing in reference to Mr. and Mrs. Stone, whose *shit* Randall discussed in the most roundabout way possible.

"I'm really sorry."

"Good," she said, refusing to soften. "I'm not about to spend four days alone here in this tenement!" She rose and his hands slid weakly off her shoulders. "And from the looks of it, the only way I'm going to be able to get home is on a fucking Greyhound, which would take four days anyway so . . ." She had left the chair without any clear idea of where she was going to go. The room seemed five times smaller than usual. They stood an awkward few feet apart. Randall bowed his head, nervous breaths puffing his cheeks.

"I said I was sorry."

"Say it again."

"How about something new? Like, it's all my fault."

She nodded curtly as if the answer were acceptable. Which it wasn't.

"The last time I saw Jesse he was leaving the dorm," she began, icily. "That was about an hour ago." She studied Randall for a response that would give some clear indication of what had happened on Friday night. Nothing; he was just a pouting child looking for forgiveness.

"I stopped by last night."

"I had a date."

"With who?"

"Mitchell Seaver."

Randall just nodded as if accepting the inevitable. "How was it?" he asked tightly.

"Nice," she said, sounding like her mother. "Why were you look-ing for Jesse?"

"Because I had to ask him something."

"About Friday night?"

Randall hissed and lifted his hands to either side of his head, as if Kathryn's continued anger was making his head swell. "*What* is going on?"

"Are you pretending for my sake?"

Randall's face fell, his mouth curling open slightly and his eyes narrowing on her. Sudden fear added breath to his voice. "Did Jesse say . . . something to you?"

"He shouldn't have to "

Randall looked like he had been punched in the stomach. He turned away from her, grabbing the back of her chair with one hand to steady himself. "Fuck," he whispered. "He told you."

"Of course he didn't tell me. But he certainly wanted me to believe that something happened. He shows up at the door wearing nothing but his underwear and he won't let me in the room. And then you're out cold, stark naked—"

Randall pivoted to face her again, and now his face wrinkled with confusion. "*What?*"

"Randall, you said you knew better."

"Oh my God. I didn't sleep with *Jesse!*"

Ardor and disgust met in his words with convincing force. Kathryn felt confused as well as foolish. "Well . . . who did you sleep with?"

"Friday night? No one. I was gone! I told you. The scotch . . ." He stopped.

"Oh my God," she groaned, and flounced back onto her mattress. Randall crawled onto the bed next to her, his arm around her stomach bunching part of her shirt in his fist. Still a child trying to apologize, now with a sudden burst of physical tenderness. She tried to bury her head in the pillows.

"You really thought I . . ."

"Yes!" She groaned. "It was so weird. I walk in and I realize you don't have any clothes on and Jesse's just kind of sitting there smiling and . . ." Her words collapsed into another groan.

"What did you say?"

"I'm not telling you. It's stupid."

"Come on, I'm sure it's entertaining."

She rolled over, resting her head on the pillow with Randall's face inches away. "I said he couldn't get rid of you the way he did everyone else. I said you weren't that stupid."

Pain flashed over Randall's face so quickly she almost missed it, a slight wince while he kept his eyes locked on hers. Then his smile seemed uncomfortable, but it gained warmth and lifted his features. For several seconds, he stared at her, then brought a hand to the side of her face. She hadn't expected her words to move him. His mouth opened. Nothing came out, so he tried again. "I'm very glad you were there to defend my honor," he said, sounding slightly winded.

She must have seemed stricken by his sudden gravity, because his eyes left hers and he slid down into the bed, resting her head in his armpit. For several seconds, the only sounds in the room were the thud of footsteps one floor above and muffled but animated conversation from the engineering freaks next door.

"He didn't try to kiss me," Kathryn finally said.

"Mitchell?"

"Is that weird?"

"Maybe it's a good thing," Randall said, too fast.

"One small peck on the cheek would have been nice."

"Right. And then he would have gone for the knockers!" Randall's hand started to follow suit before she caught it. "And the thigh!" His other hand sunk into her thigh. They were both wrestling and giggling like six-year-olds. "And then he would have slobbered all over you in that gross way that only grad students slobber."

She was laughing now. "I don't think he slobbers. He's way too composed for that." One of her legs was pried between both of Randall's, and she was sliding it free when April walked in, tailed by the girl from the dance, whom April had angrily informed her was named *Karen*.

"Are we interrupting something?"

"Kathryn had a date last night," Randall announced.

"I know. She told me. How did it go?"

"He slobbered all over her!"

"Thanks, *Kathryn*. How did it go?"

Randall turned to Kathryn and kissed her on the cheek. "There's your peck."

When he got up and went to squeeze past Karen, the girl jerked as if a shotgun had gone off and Randall shot an amused look at Kathryn. Once he was out of sight, Kathryn recognized April's too-familiar look of parental condescension; her tongue was a lump under her upper lip and one eyebrow had gone up. "Let me guess. Randall doesn't like him."

Behind April, Karen let out a slight laugh, which lifted her shoulders.

"Can you excuse us please, Karen?" Kathryn asked.

Offended, Karen looked from Kathryn to April, as if April had veto power. "Just a second," April muttered to her. Karen didn't restrain her pout as she shuffled into the hallway.

"Knock it off."

"Excuse me?" April barked.

"I said knock it off. I'm not your baby sister and I'm not your pet project. You want to make your five-minute girlfriend laugh, learn some jokes."

Resignation replaced anger on April's face, as if Kathryn was now a lost cause. Kathryn left the room.

Kathryn assumed the only reason Randall had come with her to Folberg was to avoid returning to his room and confronting Jesse about the *Melrose Place* mind game he'd tried to pull on her. When he got up and left the table, Kathryn was relieved. He had been jittery ever since they'd sat down—twirling his highlighter in one hand, slouching back in his chair and extending his legs until his feet knocked hers. Once he was out of sight, Kathryn reached over and flipped his textbook to its cover. Geology. Randall had admitted to her that he only signed up for the Geology of Natural Disasters, nicknamed "Quakes for Flakes," because the course was packed with hot lacrosse players. On the first day of class, he told her, the professor began his lecture with a slide show. "What's this?" he asked the class after displaying a slide of a more-than-familiar blue planet. "*Earth!*" several enthusiastic jocks responded.

A hand landed on her shoulder and she looked up to see Lauren Raines. "Hey." Lauren's smile was bright, but Kathryn's soon disappeared when she remembered their last meeting.

Kathryn stood with one hand falteringly on the back of her chair, and Lauren bowed her head, as if marginally amused by Kathryn's sudden discomfort. "How are you?" Kathryn asked. The question came out all wrong—condescending enough to imply that Lauren's flirtation with lesbianism was like a bad flu she couldn't seem to shake.

"Come meet Maria," Lauren whispered.

At their last encounter, when Lauren first told Kathryn about her new girlfriend, Kathryn had formed an immediate mental image of a purple-haired student activist. But Lauren led her across the room toward a black-haired, fine-boned beauty bent over what looked like a schematic grid. Maria lifted her head as they approached, her generous dark eyes surveying Kathryn without any skepticism or wariness.

"So you're the one that stole Lauren from us?" Kathryn whispered as genially as she could. Maria's smile was as soft as her handshake, and she gestured for Kathryn to take the empty chair at the head of the table.

Once she sat and they offered their pleasantries, Kathryn noticed that Lauren's eyes were moving steadily between her and Maria. She looked proud, but Kathryn couldn't determine whether Lauren thought she was showing off her graceful girlfriend, or proving that her former close friend had no apparent problems with her new sexual orientation.

"I meant to apologize—" Kathryn began.

"For what?" Lauren asked.

"I didn't mean to get on your case last time about—"

"Oh," Lauren said, and then to Maria. "Jesse."

Kathryn was surprised when Maria nodded her head in recognition and then returned her attention to her work, which Kathryn realized was a color photocopy of a painting. Maria was dividing it into an evenly proportioned grid of squares. Kathryn knew the technique from a high-school art project that involved creating an enlarged cardboard replica of a Snickers bar. To accurately reproduce the label, she had been required to draw the same type of grid, in one scale on the label itself, and then five times as big on the cardboard, before reproducing the image square by square. She wondered if Maria actually was going to reproduce the incredibly detailed image onto a larger surface.

"I just wanted to apologize," Kathryn repeated, pulling her attention away from Maria's work before she was able to recognize the painting.

"That's really sweet," Lauren said. "How's Randall?"

Had Kathryn imagined the ripple of tension that passed over the table? "Fine. We were just talking about you the other day."

The statement felt stupid once it was out of her mouth, and she jumped at the sound of Maria's pencil hitting the table. She turned to see the girl had merely traded writing implements, and was starting to retrace her pencil lines with a Sharpie. "He just asked how you were doing," Kathryn added in a quick whisper. Wasn't that a lie? Randall hadn't even noticed Lauren's absence.

"Did you tell him I'm a woman reborn?" Lauren asked her. Kathryn was taken aback by the broadness of Lauren's smile before she noticed that Maria had jerked her head up from her work.

"How was dinner?" Maria's voice was almost caressing.

"I'm sorry?"

"Mitchell says he took you to Jean Pierre's. He considers the place one of his better kept secrets, so you should consider it an honor. He's also quite fond of showing people new things." Maria looked back down at her grid, and Kathryn wondered if she expected an answer.

"It was fine. . . ."

As if sensing she had caught Kathryn off guard, Maria lifted her head again and surveyed Kathryn. "Mitchell and I are in the masters program together. There aren't that many of us, and few of us have the time for exciting weekends. So when someone has even the most casual Saturday-night outing, it usually ends up becoming fodder for the rest of us. Don't worry. We're not gossips. Just observant."

"I'll remember that," Kathryn said. Maria smiled and returned to her work. "Be sure to spread the word that I was very impressed with Mitchell," she said. "But I'm still trying to wrap my head around the idea that the earth is Satan's terrain."

Maria lifted her eyes to Kathryn's again and looked pleased. She nearly chuckled, as if shocked as well as impressed. Lauren wore the expression of a thirteen-year-old whose parents are getting along famously with her new beau.

*Good note to end on*, Kathryn thought, and rose from her chair. "Nice meeting you," she said to Maria, who only nodded and smiled. She gripped Lauren's shoulder as she passed her chair.

"Have a good break," Lauren whispered.

"Don't hold your breath."

As she sat back down at her table, Kathryn realized that nothing about the two girls' behavior toward each other indicated a romantic relationship. And hadn't there been the slightest edge in her voice when she mentioned Mitchell?

She looked over to see that across the other students bent low and whispering across their tables or with their heads buried in their books, Maria's eyes were locked on her. When she didn't avert her eyes from Kathryn's, she felt caught, forced into either smiling or looking away, both of which would embarrass her.

Then Maria smiled, her face even warmer and more genuine than ever before. Kathryn was so caught off guard she smiled back, genuinely. Maria gave a small nod, as if a positive assumption, as opposed to a suspicion, had been confirmed for her by their brief meeting. She returned her attention to the painting in front of her.

After abandoning Kathryn downstairs, Randall stepped off the elevator to the science section on the third floor and found himself facing shelves stretching the entire building. Half of the fluorescent lights were out, turning the aisles between the racks into heavily shadowed passageways. Many times in his life libraries had been his refuge, and his first step into them seemed like an embrace. But now he was looking for something specific, and he wondered why a school that taught courses on everything from the history of bookbinding to how to plan your own urban metropolis didn't have a course on how to find what you wanted in the goddamn library.

Downstairs, he had typed "psychotropic medication" in the computer directory and the result had been a dizzying surplus of results. He had jotted down the name of several desk references that sounded easy to use and which he hoped would include general information, including solubility. Namely, exactly what drugs could be mixed in with a bottle of scotch.

Before Atherton, he'd spent most of his time in public libraries and had familiarized himself with the Dewey decimal system. The Library of Congress system was about to drive him over the edge when he spotted April standing at the far end of the aisle. He approached slowly, and she looked up from the thick book spread open against one arm.

"Hey," he said.

Her smile was weak.

"I need help, Doc."

"Uh-huh."

"I'm looking for general information on psychotropic drugs."

"Don't bother. Ecstasy isn't a psychotropic drug."

"I don't do X. But maybe later you can teach me some Indigo Girls songs on the guitar?"

April's eyes fell to her book. "Before this gets to be too much fun, why don't you tell me what you're looking for specifically?"

"General information. Solubility. Stuff like that." When he saw her puzzled expression, he quickly added, "It's for a story I'm writing."

"Another one? Sounds like you've been hit by the writing bug." She must have seen him pale. "Sorry. Kathryn told me about the last one you wrote."

"Told you?" he asked tightly.

"Of course, she wouldn't let me read it. Yanked it out of my hands actually. She's very protective of you. But I think you know that."

Relief flooded him, but April's hard stare didn't waver. "I sense a *point* here," he said after a strained pause.

April responded by shoving her book back onto the rack. "This guy Mitchell makes her happy. Let her have that."

"Uh-huh."

April grimaced at his lack of sincerity, but rolled her eyes instead of pressing the point. "Three aisles over. You're on the border between chemistry and chemical dependency. They're very clever here at Folberg." She turned on her heel and moved off down the aisle.

Randall watched her go, cursing the nakedness of his reaction when she'd mentioned "Drywater, Texas."

"April?"

She turned.

"You can read it if you want."

Her brow furrowed.

"My story."

"Thanks. I'm not a big fiction fan."

Thank God, Randall thought. I don't need another amateur detective on my tail.

Several minutes later, he was flipping pages through a general desk reference, his shoulder leaning against the rack, as the dying fluorescent light overhead threatened to blur the microscopic text. He heard a scraping of chairs on the other side of the rack followed by hushed whispers. Eric had never referred to one of Lisa's medications by name. During those rare moments of less than romantic pillow talk, when Eric laid on Randall his fear for the fate that awaited the wife he had just cheated on, Eric referred to the mass of medications in the liquor cabinet as nothing more than "the drugs." But Tim had mentioned Vicodin. And supposedly, Eric had mentioned it to the police.

Every book he consulted was in agreement. Vicodin and alcohol didn't mix.

But could they *be* mixed? But that was what Randall needed to know. Water soluble was one thing; alcohol soluble another. And obviously, the authors of prescription medication desk references didn't think their patients should be grinding up pills into their nightly cocktails. He slapped the book shut against his arm, suddenly overcome by the immensity of the task he and Tim had undertaken. Earlier that day, panic had prevented him from seeing the complexity it entailed. He and Tim—who had yet to throw himself into their investigation with his usual tenacity—would have to become interrogators, investigators, and, God forbid, chemists. He slid the book back onto the rack shelf, braced himself against the rack, bowed his head, and took a breath.

When he heard Jesse's low, throaty laughter, it sounded as if it was coming from some faraway place, but after a moment, Randall could pinpoint the location: only several feet away and on the other side of the rack. He remembered the scraping chairs he'd heard seconds before.

He kept his steps almost silent over the sticky linoleum floor until the low voices of Jesse and another male were intelligible. While the center of the floor was taken up entirely by shelves, the outer wall was lined with private study carrels reserved for seniors working on their honors theses. Randall plucked a book from a shelf and glimpsed Jesse sitting across from a guy Randall didn't recognize. The guy had Jesse's build, with broad shoulders, dimpled cheeks, and pouty lips.

Tyler? No, Taylor, Randall remembered, the Tennessee boy with Bible-thumper parents. His clothes today were a far cry from the sleeveless club gear he had been outfitted in for the GLA dance. His hair had been tamed from a wild bed of spikes into a rigid side part. He wore khaki trousers. The collar of an oxford poked above the V-neck of his sweater. And his eyes were fixed on Jesse with awe and desire. It turned Randall's stomach.

Taylor's voice had a low, gentle drawl to it, and he spoke timidly. His statements had the intonation of questions. " . . . so I'm practically racing all the way home and as soon as I get there I hide my entire backpack under the bed? I mean I never get to take it out."

"*Hustler*? You bought *Hustler* and they didn't ask how old you were?" Jesse asked.

Taylor grinned proudly and nodded. "Uh-huh. So anyway, that night Daddy calls us—"

"*Daddy*." Jesse's imitation was just gentle enough so as not to mock.

Taylor bowed his head slightly and then shook it with embarrassment. "Sorry."

"Don't be."

Their eyes met for a second before Taylor snapped himself back into his story. "So he calls us down for dinner and Mom's in the kitchen and I sit down at my place and she comes waltzing out with two plates. One for my daddy and one for me. Sets his down in front of him. And sets mine in front of me. And guess what was on it?"

"*Hustler!*"

After a moment, they realized how loudly they were laughing, and Taylor threw nervous glances in every direction. Randall's breath caught as the guy's eyes looked his way. He was witnessing one of Jesse's seductions, this one with what he guessed was a new twist.

"What did you say?" Jesse asked, bending toward Taylor, his elbows braced on the table.

"Oh, I denied it to kingdom come. Didn't make any difference, though. Dad . . . my dad, he could tell just by the way I came in the house that I was up to something no good. And there wasn't much I could do. It *was* in my backpack."

"Shame you never got to look at it," Jesse said, eyes bright as if suggesting the untold pleasures of pornography.

Taylor just shook his head and pulled an open book across the desk until it rested protectively against his chest. "I've done plenty of looking since."

"At *Hustler?*" Jesse asked with a crooked smile.

Taylor lifted his head halfway, as if debating whether to meet a challenge.

"They have guys in *Hustler?*" Jesse asked.

In the heavy silence that passed between the two of them, Randall realized that Taylor hadn't told Jesse he was gay. Of course, Jesse knew. Had known before he moved in on him the same way he knew Lauren's story was anything but fiction.

"Who says I . . ."

"I do." Jesse cut him off gently, leaning back against his chair.

"*Do* you?" Taylor asked with a smirk.

Jesse smiled and shrugged. Randall recognized the shrug. It was Jesse's silent way of saying anything's a possibility when you're me. The sight of it now, directed at sweet little Taylor, with Bible-thumper parents and now, Randall believed, a very good chance of being fucked in the head, just like Lauren Raines, filled Randall with cold, useless anger.

"Your father? How did he punish you?" Jesse asked. His eyes were intent, but slightly glazed. It was a look Randall didn't recognize at all.

"You mean for the magazine?" Taylor asked.

"Yeah."

"He made me burn it."

"That's a shame."

Taylor let out a short, choked laugh. "What? You think he and I should have sat down and read it together?"

Jesse's smile was slight, teasing the corners of his mouth. To Randall, it seemed slightly pained.

"Why?" Taylor asked. "What would your daddy do?"

"It sounds like we have very different *daddies*. My *daddy*," Jesse began, rising out of his chair as Taylor's eyes widened slightly, "taught me that the majority of evil crap in this world comes from people who are afraid of what their bodies are capable of "

Taylor's mouth opened in what looked like shock. With his crotch pressed against the edge of the table, Jesse lowered his face inches from Taylor's dumbfounded stare. "It's kind of amazing what you can do when you stop being afraid of yourself."

Randall slammed the book back onto the shelf so hard the spine collided with the rack's crossbar, producing a deep metallic twang. He moved off down the aisle, wondering if he should track down Lauren Raines and tell her she could stop speculating.

When she heard Randall's hurried footsteps, Kathryn looked up abruptly from her book. "I have to go," he said tersely.

"Where?" She looked startled, and mildly annoyed.

"I was supposed to call my mom an hour ago," he lied. He whipped his bookbag off his chair, picking up his geology text with his other hand. "I totally forgot."

"Do you want me to come?"

"No. It's cool."

"All right, good, 'cause I really need to finish."

He grazed her shoulder affectionately with one hand to reassure her he wasn't blowing her off.

"I'll stop by when I get back," he heard her call after him.

Randall's hip slammed into the exit turnstile before he found the sense to reach down and give it a shove. It rotated with a thud and a clatter and he passed through it. By the time he was descending the front steps of Folberg, he heard footsteps behind him, matching his own pace.

"Randall!"

Jesse. The fucker was following him everywhere, stalking him practically. And for what? Breaking into a run was out of the question, but he didn't dare look back as he crossed the street and passed through the gates to the quad, keeping his steps even on the salted sidewalks and his gaze fixed on the spotlit regiment of administrative buildings up ahead. When Jesse's hand landed on his shoulder, he whirled around. "Do you know what a psychopath is?" he spat out.

Jesse hadn't even bothered to put on his prized pea coat. His eyes flared at the anger in Randall's voice, but the faint smile hadn't faded from his face. "Enlighten me," he muttered.

"A psychopath only uses people they need—"

"Really? I thought they just ate people."

Randall continued, voice growing shrill. "They don't have friends. They don't have anyone they love. They don't really know anyone. That's what you are. No one is really even a person to you, are they, Jesse? Just a big secret you have to figure out. And now you know mine. So move on!"

The look of anger was so unfamiliar on Jesse's face that at first Randall didn't recognize it. When Jesse opened his mouth again, Randall turned and stalked away When Randall reached the dark passageway between the Admissions Center and the Alumni Building, Jesse hooked one of his shoulders with surprising, violent force, spinning him so suddenly that Randall's bag went sliding off his shoulder, the strap landing in the crook of his arm.

"And just who's feeding me this bullshit?" Jesse growled. "The same person who tells just the right lies to everyone he knows so he can keep them right where he wants them! What do you tell Kathryn? That what you two have is *special*. That you're soul mates. Anything to keep her from figuring out who you really are!"

"Let go of me," Randall whined, instantly hating the childish tone in his voice because it betrayed his realization that Jesse wasn't just flaunting secret knowledge of Randall. He was implying they were one and the same, and that knifed him.

Jesse released Randall's shoulder with a shove that almost threw him off balance. "And your professor? What do you tell him? Did you cry about your parents who haven't called you since you got here? Did you tell him you need rescuing? Anything to make him think your feelings for him are noble! When really, you're no different from me. You can't resist the challenge of it. You have to see if you're good enough to break him down!" Jesse's brow darkened more. "But the one thing I can't figure about you, is where do I fit in?"

"You don't!"

"Wrong. I'm the only one here who knows who you really are. And I'm the only one you know who won't be disgusted by it. You are who you are when you're with me." Jesse shook his head as if in disbelief that Randall hadn't already figured this all out. He sucked in a labored breath. "I've never judged you. *Never*. I've done better. I've known you. I've understood you when Kathryn put you on a pedestal and—"

"Lauren Raines."

Jesse's eyes shot to his, went numb with shock.

"Her story. The one about her uncle. The *drunk*. Why did it bother you so much?"

Jesse's mouth shut and his eyes narrowed, as if trying to fathom the lengths Randall would go to fight him off.

"Every word reminded you of your father, didn't it?"

For a second, Randall thought Jesse would punch him in the face. But Jesse's expression was almost plaintive amusement. Randall searched for a hint of lunacy in the sudden smile curling his features. "You sound just like every other fucking victim on this campus," Jesse said. "They scream about what they hate with so much passion that you can tell they love it. And you're so disgusted by what my father did to me that I can tell it turns you on."

"No. It doesn't. Sorry." Randall grunted in disgust. "It makes me sick. But the sad thing is that it explains you perfectly. Someone had to convince you that you needed to steal part of someone. And that's what you think it is, isn't it? That's why it's never the same girl twice. And that's why you think that little boy in there is the best way to finally get to me. Because you always need someone new. Because you're so fucking warped that you think you're always walking away from every fuck with something different. You walk away with nothing, Jesse. It's why you're so alone."

Randall turned on one heel and strode into the passageway.

"I didn't ask for this, Randall!" Jesse called after him. "At first, I thought it was a privilege, knowing you so well. Too bad you can't return the favor."

Randall turned around to see Jesse standing in the wintry halo of light at the mouth of the alley. "I just did!" Randall shouted.

Jesse approached, walking slowly and deliberately and without fear that Randall might bolt, which Randall was telling himself to do. His footsteps echoed between the two buildings. Jesse was several feet away when he spoke again. "How about we try a little experiment? Since I've made it clear that you can't cast the same spell on me as you do on everyone else, I'm going to ask you about those burns all over your legs. And you're going to try not to lie."

"You need help, Jesse."

"Okay, that was a strike. Why don't I ask you about your parents? The ones who've never visited you. The ones who never call. The ones who might not even be *alive*."

Randall lunged. His loose fist hit Jesse's stomach, but Jesse clamped his wrist and after several dizzying seconds of scuffling through darkness, Randall felt his back slam against the stone wall and his feet lift off the ground. Jesse's breath was against his neck, his arm braced across Randall's chest and pinning him against the wall.

"You want to know my secret?" Randall fought to get his body under control. "I will never be a notch on your belt. Your fag room-mate knows better."

Jesse released Randall's fist. His nose grazed Randall's cheek, and Randall felt Jesse's hand probe the erection straining against his jeans. Jesse's laugh barely made it past his lips. "Randall, face it. You just don't know how to lie to me."

Randall slumped back against the wall. His head rolled forward, his nose brushing Jesse's shoulder. Jesse's hand left his crotch; it gripped the back of his neck.

"Who burned you, Randall?" Jesse whispered.

Randall gasped in a breath that didn't make it past his throat

"*Jesse!*"

Neither of them moved until they heard the high-pitched call echo down the alleyway a second time.

"I have to go," Jesse said.

When Jesse departed it felt like he carried a tide of air with him.

Randall kept his gaze on the darkness at his feet, listening to the sound of Jesse's footsteps heading toward Taylor's voice, which continued to call after him with increasing alarm.

He shut his eyes and heard inside his head a screeching of metal, slowly turning into a roar.

Kathryn was heading down the hall, bound for Randall's room, when she recognized the ringing phone as her own. She dashed into her room. "Hello?"

"Did I interrupt something?" Mitchell asked.

"Yeah, I was just trying to work feng shui on my room, but I can't move my desk without opening up a portal to hell."

Mitchell's laughter seemed genuine. "I was calling to see if you came to a decision," he said.

"About the desk?"

She sat down onto the edge of her bed and began unlacing her boots as she held the phone to her ear with one shoulder.

"No. Thanksgiving."

"My parents won. Now they just have to see if they can find me a ticket."

"I think that might be a good thing."

Like not kissing me, she thought, and then stifled the thought because it made her feel fifteen. "Well," she said. "Four days alone here in Stockton Hall would probably have me cowering in a corner and eating insects by the time everyone got back."

April entered, pushing through the door Kathryn hadn't bothered to shut all the way. Kathryn watched her to see if she was in the mood to manage a greeting, but she wasn't, and she sat down in front of her desk, snapping her computer out of idle with a mouse click.

"But after the way I went on at dinner the other night, my guess is you probably think I'm pretty close to losing it anyway," Kathryn said in a lower voice.

"Please."

"Seriously. The only thing missing was the violin I could have played for myself." And the kiss at the end of the date, which even though she didn't like to admit it, would have been some small confirmation that the silent magnetic pull between them that she'd felt for the entire evening hadn't been her own fantasy, her desires outstripping her mind.

"Well, I also have something to apologize for."

She transferred the phone from her shoulder to her hand as she waited.

"I enjoyed dinner and it was rude of me not to say so."

Had she really gone on a date with Mr. Belvedere? "Thanks." Her tone was dry as a bone and she could feel her patience wearing thin.

"And I would like to do it again. I said that, didn't I?"

"Yes. You did. When?"

Mitchell's breathy laugh made her curse her eagerness.

"I imagine you're kind of swamped this week."

"Not really."

"Well . . . *I'm* kind of swamped this week. How about after you get back?"

"If I get back. It's four whole days with my parents."

Mitchell laughed again. Kathryn didn't. "When are you planning on returning?" he asked.

"Don't know yet. No tickets, remember?"

"Well, that kind of complicates things . . ."

You're doing a fine job of that on your own, buddy, she thought.

"Why don't you give me a call when you get back?" he asked, with a note of finality that tensed her hand around the portable.

"Sure thing."

"Good-bye, Kathryn."

"Hey!" During the ensuing silence she cursed the sharpness in her tone.

"Still here," he said.

"I ran into a friend of yours. Maria?"

"Did you?"

"She's dating a friend of mine."

"I'm sorry?"

"Lauren Raines?"

Mitchell answered with a laugh that sounded strangely relieved. "Lauren, yes."

"You know her?"

"Absolutely."

"I knew her when she was straight."

Mitchell exhaled loudly. "It all seems to be about choices here, doesn't it?"

"You could say that."

After they said good-bye for the second time, Kathryn brought the phone in front of her and punched *end* with too much force. April shot her a glance and then returned to her E-mail. Several silent seconds passed, during which Kathryn wondered if she had frightened Mitchell off.

"What?" April finally asked, as if someone had poked her in the ribs.

"He's not interested."

"And you know this how?"

"He doesn't sound excited to see me again and he talks to me like I'm five."

"He's not excited to see you again, or he can't see you tomorrow? Oh!" April lifted both hands as if to shield herself. "Sorry, sis."

Kathryn set the phone down in the cradle.

"How much longer are we going to do this?" April asked.

"Hey. It's only been a few hours. I can go another day at least."

She crossed the hallway. One firm knock on the door to Randall's room, and nothing. She had spent two more hours reading in the library that evening after he had left so abruptly. She knocked again. She stepped back and bent down. No sliver of light came from beneath the door.

Back in her room, April's fingers were dancing over the keyboard. Kathryn felt aimless, her eyes would smart if she read anymore, and she had already opened her E-mail: "Still searching. Don't give up hope. We'll get you home yet. Love, Dad." She flopped down on her mattress.

"Did I ever tell you about my friend Sara?" April asked.

April's attention was fixed on her computer. "This is freshman year in high school. And it's Dover, Massachusetts, we're talking about, so I'm like the only remotely black girl in my entire class. So I pretty much had the act down. Teacher's pet, my parent's pet, everyone's nice, agreeable, half-black girl. Then all this lesbian shit came up, and I thought, well now I have two strikes against me. There's only so much a fourteen-year-old girl can try to make up for."

Kathryn lifted herself up on both elbows. If nothing else, April's lack of cynicism held her rapt.

"And then Sara comes along. Beautiful, but in this edgy kind of way. The kind of look that gets to everyone whether they admit it or not. You could tell the male teachers were afraid she was going to get raped, and all the female teachers were afraid she was going to enjoy it. And me, well, I knew I just had to make her my best friend. Because there was, like, this aura that surrounded her wherever she went, and I thought, If I can get inside that, then who gives a shit what I really am."

April closed out whatever file she'd been working on, but her hands remained on the desk beside the keyboard, her head bowed and brow furrowed.

"Pretty soon I'm doing shit you wouldn't believe. Just 'cause it was Sara's idea. We start by toilet-papering this teacher's house. Then we decide to burn a few bags of dog shit on people's porches. Next comes getting plastered at her parents' house every weekend. And for the big finish, shoplifting. Christ." April let out a snort. "When I think back on some of the shit I did with her, just 'cause she was Sara . . ."

She trailed off, finally looking up to where Kathryn lay uncertain on the bed, without any clue where April was headed with this.

"Funny thing is, I never made a move on her. That wasn't what I wanted from her. It was just, when I was with her, and when I had her approval, I felt protected."

Kathryn let a few seconds pass, if nothing more than to be polite in the wake of this rare glimpse into April's past. "I missed it," she finally said, as politely as she could.

"My point is that Randall and Jesse living in the same room . . . Well, let's just say it bothers me just as much as it does you."

"So Randall is you and Jesse is Sara?" Kathryn's tone was sharpening faster than she could control it.

"You don't have to take it that literally."

"Then how should I take it?"

April let out a deep breath, as if even she wasn't sure, before she turned to face Kathryn. "Beauty does fucked-up things to gay people, Kathryn. It's like this all-powerful wonder drug that erases that feeling of difference. These feminists and media studies people can take all their babble about body ideals and codes of aesthetics and shove it. We all know beauty when we see it. And when gay people see it they have to fight with everything they have to keep from heading straight for it and letting everything else fall away."

And everyone, Kathryn thought, but April had said as much.

"Randall's been fighting how bad he wants Jesse since the first day he got here, Kathryn. Please, I don't think of you as my pet project or my baby sister But that boy's not just a free spirit. He's untethered. And it scares me to see how hard you're holding on to him."

Kathryn felt a swell of anger lacking words. April rose and left the room, and Kathryn wondered if her own voicelessness was a product of Randall's growing silences.

Randall pulled off the old trick of hanging back and letting a student slide his card through the reader and then grabbing the door before it shut all the way behind him. Inside Braddock Hall, Randall rushed up to the second floor, feeling like an intruder, and found the door to Tim's suite standing open. He pushed it open and took one step into the common room, trying to feel his feet on the floor.

Sharif and John were playing poker. A mess of textbooks and notes lay strewn around an open pizza box and its half-eaten contents. Obviously, John had set aside his hard feelings about being conned into drinking Sharif's urine out of a Nantucket Nectar bottle. Not to mention the Japanese beer drama.

"Yeah, he's here," Sharif said, arranging pairs in his hand.

John stared at Randall so intently over his hand that it looked as if someone had long ago convinced him that upon entering a room all gay men break into song and dance. Of course, it could have been that Randall's eyes were still bloodshot and he looked like the wind had been knocked out of him, thanks to Jesse's assault, which had left him rattled and raw.

Tim cracked the door to his room after one knock, and Randall recognized a wary tightness around his eyes. "Did something happen?"

"I need a beer"

"I've got work. My *own* work"

"One beer," Randall said, holding up his finger, and Tim registered that he was coming down from the throes of near panic. Tim pulled the door all the way open. As Randall took a seat on the bed, Tim removed a Corona from the fridge and punched the cap off against his desk. Randall managed a weak thanks before he downed the first third. Tim took a seat at his desk. "If you keep hating me," Randall declared, "we'll never be able to do this."

"I don't hate you," Tim responded evenly. "But that doesn't mean I think we can do this. And I don't think you should stay, if that's what you're asking."

"Jesse's fucking someone right now and I don't think I'll get any sleep at Eric's."

Tim just shook his head in disbelief at Randall's nerve

For several tense minutes, Randall lay on the bed, waiting for the beer to flush memories both recent and distant. Tim feigned studying. When he realized that his concentration wasn't going to return, he let out a sigh, dropped his pencil and met Randall's gaze. Randall returned it, trying to escape himself for one minute, trying to see what Tim saw: a home wrecker, a stupid little boy trapped in the middle of something spinning out of his control. If there was one thing Randall was still sure of it was that he had a gift for seeing himself through other people's eyes. Before, that had helped him survive; now it was a curse, and of absolutely zero use amid murder

"You want another?" Tim asked, shutting his book with one hand.

Randall handed Tim the empty bottle.

"You know, back in Chicago, I saw guys my age dating older men all the time," Tim began, tossing the empty bottle into the recycling tub and pulling out a fresh one. "It was always the same dynamic. Young guy, just out of the closet, new to the whole scene. Older, usually rich, father-type figure takes him under his wing. Fucks him silly. Gets rid of him once he's twenty." He handed Randall the bottle. "There's nothing new about you, Randall."

Randall twisted his head against the pillow. "Do you think it's possible that I might not fit into one of your equations, Tim?"

Tim sat down carefully, his butt resting inches from Randall's head, but with his hands folded across his lap. "You can't convince me that Eric Eberman, married closet case, maybe even a murderer . . . that a man like that could never have made you feel safe."

"No one's ever made me feel safe," Randall said to the ceiling.

Tim let out a dismissive snort, leaning back against the headboard and staring forward. "At least you're not trying to justify it, I guess."

Randall could sense the prodding reporter beneath Tim's questions, and he steeled himself, worrying that the confrontation—could he even call it that?—with Jesse had loosened a valve that might start leaking memories.

"What I'm about to say might sound like flattery, but it isn't. Trust me." Tim looked down at Randall before continuing. "When I saw you at the first GLA dance, you want to know what drew me to you?"

"Maybe."

"You looked like you couldn't care less that anyone else was in the room with you."

"A bunch of fags with glow sticks and straight boys wearing Dr. Seuss caps. Maybe I didn't."

"No." Tim shook his head, obviously in no mood for sarcasm. "You were magnetic because you were so indifferent. You were a challenge. So I had to talk to you."

"Do you regret it?"

Tim lowered his eyes to his. "Yes. I do."

*I'll be sure to sand your notch off my belt*, Randall thought, and stifled a smile.

"I just want to know if you went after Eberman for the same reason," Tim said.

Randall lifted himself to down more beer. "What? Because he was a challenge?"

"Maybe. Or because he had a wife."

Randall lowered the bottle "Whatever was in my head, it didn't kill Lisa Eberman. *I* didn't kill Lisa Eberman. So what I was thinking or feeling really isn't relevant. It's also none of your business"

Tim wasn't deterred, rather he seemed encouraged by Randall's flash of anger. "Maybe not. But you'd better decide just what you feel for this man. Because there's a very good chance that we might ruin his life."

"And mine," Randall answered.

"Oh, come on, Randall. The scale isn't even tipped that way and you know it. If word gets out that he was in bed with you that night, his face will be on the front of every newspaper, and you'll probably be a blue bubble, almost as good as a rape victim."

"Bullshit. I'm eighteen. I'm old enough to be the whore."

"And his career will be ruined, or he'll be in jail for murdering his wife," Tim retorted. "Or are you just desperate to prove that something else happened that night? Something other than Lisa seeing the two of you in bed."

The casual use of her first name chilled Randall and he tensed his hands around the beer bottle.

"Do you believe he killed her?" Tim asked.

"Yes," Randall answered, feeling as if the answer had been pressed out of him.

"Do you believe that you were his motive?"

Randall's eyes shot to his. "Yes."

Tim sucked in his bottom lip, averting his eyes before he asked the next question. "Do you *like* being his motive?"

For several seconds, Randall massaged the bridge of his nose between thumb and forefinger. "Part of me does, yes. The same part that loved being the one who could somehow make a forty-one-year-old man cheat on his wife of ten years. Yeah, the part of me I'm trying to make shut up loves it. Anyone would love having that kind of power." His eyes left Tim's, and when he spoke again, he sounded in need of breath. "But most of me wonders what Kathryn would think if she knew about any of this."

Tim's eyes widened.

"Eric showed me this picture of Lisa, and afterward I kept seeing her face every night when I tried to go to sleep. Now I see Kathryn's face. I see what it would look like if she knew." Randall's eyes filled with what felt like a year's worth of tears.

"No one ever listened to me the way she did. No one ever thought what I had to say was so important. I wanted so badly to be who she saw when she looked at me. And I probably won't ever be. But if I find out what really happened to Lisa Eberman, maybe I've done what I can. And maybe, once she finds out, I won't have lost all of her respect. Even though I probably never deserved it in the first place."

Randall swabbed tears from his cheek with two quick motions of his hand. In the silence that followed, he realized his words had been meant more for Jesse than for Tim. But Tim seemed moved, the skepticism gone from his face.

Tim took a deep breath. "I spoke to Paula Willis earlier tonight. We're supposed to see her on Wednesday."

Randall brought his eyes to Tim's, managing to blink them clear. Tim bowed his head. "I need to keep working," he said. "Try to get some sleep."

Tim took a seat at the desk while Randall stripped down to his underwear and T-shirt  His scars revealed, he ventured a glance at Tim, to see him gazing stoically down at his book.

Once in bed, Randall rolled over so that his back was to the desk lamp.

It was a strange feeling, knowing that he had finally won Tim over by being honest to him for the first time since they had met.

# CHAPTER EIGHT

"Wuhr chester?" Randall asked.

"It's pronounced Wooster."

Once Atherton's compact gathering of downtown buildings had disappeared from the rearview mirror of Tim's Cherokee, Randall felt a tug of relief that belied the nature of their destination. Draining the last lukewarm sips from his Starbucks cup, he flipped through Tim's notes from his first interview with Paula Willis. The dynamic between the sisters caught Randall by surprise. For some reason, he had always assumed Lisa was born into money, but apparently that wasn't the case. In Paula's tone there was the jealous edge of lingering sisterly competition, fading into a mild bitterness now that one sister was in the grave.

Tim broke the silence. "When my grandmother died, it took my mother months before she could go through her things. I guess you either want to get rid of all evidence of them, or you just can't bring yourself to start throwing their stuff away. Paula's in my mother's camp." Tim flicked his eyes to Randall. "She says she hasn't been able to touch anything in the guest bedroom. That's where Lisa was staying."

"What about the police?"

"Return to earth, please, where you and I are the only ones who think she might have been murdered. The police don't root through the belongings of a drunk driver."

The Cherokee was flying past the industrial landscape of outer

Boston. Once they had crossed the Massachusetts state line, the sloping hills gave way to seemingly endless car dealerships, their flag banners battered by frigid winds. Now smokestacks, crumbling and intact, were giant sequoias emerging from a landscape of warehouse roofs. Plowed, mud-stained snow lined the freeway. A bleak landscape, but for Randall a welcome reprieve from Atherton. And from the prospect of seeing Jesse, who had returned to the room the last two nights after Randall was tucked into bed, facing the wall and feigning deep sleep.

Tim slowed the Jeep as they approached the Worcester exit, and within minutes they were traveling down streets lined with two-story, multifamily, clapboard houses, their small scraps of lawn fenced in by chain link. Preemptive Christmas lights in the few windows weren't sufficient to give warmth to Paula Willis's neighborhood. The few snowmen on the block weren't being maintained with the same effort that had gone into building them, and Randall felt the eerie sensation that they were traveling into a neighborhood that had been suddenly abandoned by its residents.

Paula Willis answered the door after one knock. Dressed in sweats, she shivered at the blast of cold air and gestured wordlessly for them to enter. Her short, reddish brown hair had a shine to it. Randall wondered if it was just a matter of time before she lost it all again to more chemo.

"I have tea," she said in greeting, leading them into the cramped living room. "Couple upstairs brought down a basket. It's got all the regular stuff, then it has all these fruit teas. The names don't even make sense to me."

She had Lisa's angular features, but on her rounded, chubby face, they seemed more girlish and less sharp. She moved to her recliner and offered them a seat with a gesture of her arm toward the sofa. "Mrs. Willis. This is my intern, Luther."

Luther? Randall stifled a grimace, but this was the story they had agreed to do on the way there, despite Randall's objection that he was about three feet taller than Tim and might appear too old to be his assistant. But Paula Willis just nodded, grunting as she yanked the footrest out of her La-Z-Boy. They shouldn't have even bothered, Randall thought; the woman couldn't give a shit. Randall thought her curtness was one step short of rudeness, yet he acknowledged she was a woman without the time for pleasantries and bullshit.

"We're going to talk about Lisa, right?" Paula asked.

When Randall looked up, startled, he saw that Paula was winded by the walk across the room, and her question was nothing more than an attempt to keep track by a woman whose daily schedule had become bloated with medicinal tasks and doctor's appointments.

"If you feel up to it," Tim said.

"Sure." Paula sighed.

Tim went over some of his old queries and as Randall waited for the right moment to excuse himself, he tried not to take in the details of the room. He failed. Paula Willis and her husband had surrounded themselves with humble tokens of domesticity. Behind the La-Z-Boy, the wall was adorned only with a framed print of a sailboat tossed on a wind-whipped sea, a distinctly New England lighthouse rising in the background. The print would have seemed more at home in a room at the Ramada. Inside a ceramic, heart-shaped frame on the end table beside him, a wheelchair-bound Paula fed seagulls on a seashore. She wore a baseball cap to conceal her bald head. No wig, Randall noted, sensing the woman's pride and lack of pretense. So she had already lost her hair. And grown it all back.

Contrasting pictures of two different sisters were emerging for Randall. Lisa, the professor's wife, who lived in surroundings of academic prestige, every room of her house a library. Paula, working class, thought any decoration that took up much table space was pretentious.

"As I said on the phone," Tim was saying, "the loss of your sister has had a pretty profound effect on the city, as well as the entire campus. So the *Atherton Herald* would like to . . . highlight Lisa's contributions to the community, as well as present a clear picture of her life before she came to Atherton." Tim sat uneasily on the sofa, legs crossed and a notepad resting on one knee. Randall fought the urge to point out that he wasn't holding a pen. He looked at Paula and was surprised to see that her eyes hadn't left his.

The fixed expression on her face, the slight furrow to her upper lips and her narrow eyes, set off a blast of nerves in Randall's stomach. "You don't want to sit?"

"Actually, if I could just use your bathroom?"

"Down the hall to the left. Right across from the guest bedroom."

Randall managed a smile before he turned. Halfway down the hall, he found himself between the opposite doors to the bathroom and guest bedroom. When he looked over his shoulder, he only had a half view of Tim, bent forward over his pad, nodding as Lisa spoke.

The guest bedroom had a mirrored closet with sliding doors that took up an entire wall. Slowly, with enough care to make almost no sound, Randall pushed the middle door open.

Lisa Eberman had brought enough clothes to her sister's house to last her a month without ever doing laundry. Sweaters were piled on the shelf. Randall thumbed through them in growing disbelief. Dry-cleaned shirts too small to belong to Paula hung in arrangement by color. On the floor of the closet, an open suitcase spilled folded pairs of panties. Randall scanned the closet again for anything personal.

Against the far corner of the shelf, he spotted a row of paperback books. He slid the middle door shut and then opened the left one.

Paperback mysteries extended from the wall to the first stack of sweaters. Randall removed one; its pages were still crisp. He checked several more and saw that they were unread. He recognized a few of the authors' names, Jonathan Kellerman and Patricia Cornwell. Gruesome murders and heroes placed at odds with the world as they tried to solve them—twenty books in all, and they were alphabetized by author, and then subsequently by title. Lisa had her future reading list laid out and ready.

Randall slid the door shut and turned to the bed. Several more paperbacks sat on the nightstand. The one closest to the bed had a bookmark. It gave him a chill. The books on the nightstand had been read, the edges of pages darkened from contact with fingertips, the spines run through by white cracks indicating where they had been bent open. All mysteries. Not a single romance novel in the bunch. The one-time doctorate student and scholar had been reduced to finding her escape in murder, violence, and, most important, Randall thought, solvable mysteries. While he knew it was trite, he couldn't help but wonder if Lisa's affinity for seeing the killer caught in handcuffs by the final page gave her a satisfaction she couldn't find in the mystery that was her husband.

Steeling himself, he went for the dresser drawers, which held no surprises. They were stuffed with more clothes, and nothing was buried beneath any of them. No note saying, "My husband did it." Feeling foolish, and fighting the hot flicker that warned of the onset of panic, Randall returned to the nightstand and opened the single drawer. Inside was a daunting mess of papers. Sheets torn from the notepad on the nightstand contained phone numbers jotted down in spidery print.

How long did it take to go to the bathroom? Randall shoved the contents of the drawer into the pockets of his coat. He scanned the room to see if he had missed anything, half expecting Paula Willis to come bursting into the room, one fist raised as she demanded what right he had to go poking through her sister's things.

When he saw the wedding photo, he froze.

Eric had a copy that he used to keep on the shelf above the liquor cabinet, but Randall had noticed it was missing when he went to swipe the bottle earlier that week. This photo had the exact same frame of varnished wood. But was it Paula's copy?

He rounded the foot of the bed and moved to it. Lisa Eberman wasn't a blushing bride; she was an ecstatic bride. Her head was tossed back in laughter. Eric held her around the waist with one arm, gazing right into the lens with a wan half smile.

He turned away from the photo and the stinging sight of Eric the groom, distracting himself with the undeniable fact that for some reason Lisa Eberman had brought the majority of her clothing to her sister's house, an hour away from Atherton.


"When we were teenagers, she talked so much about getting out of Philly that I guess she was the one who ended up putting the idea in my head. Who knows? I might never have left."

Randall gave Tim a barely perceptible nod when he appeared in the living-room doorway. He was relieved to see that Tim had finally taken out a pen.

"Find everything?" Paula asked him. Randall tried a smile that froze on his face

"Mrs. Willis, do you mind if Luther listens in on—"

"Sure." Paula gestured to the spot on the sofa right next to Tim, and Randall crossed to it, taking a seat directly across from the woman, where she reclined in the La-Z-Boy. When Randall looked up, he was startled to see a cigarette burning in the ashtray on the chair's side table. Paula continued, proving Tim's assessment to be dead on; she spoke with the speed of a woman trying to get everything out before her time was up.

But she didn't look that sick. And why was she smoking?

"I guess that was really what all her phases were about when we were younger. Getting out. Kind of distancing herself from the rest of us I remember"—Paula lowered her eyes to fiddle with the drawstring of her sweat pants as a muffled laugh shook her frame—"when she was thirteen, she went around in one of our dad's tweed jackets with a pipe stuck in her mouth. She brought home all these Greek plays from the library and stayed up late reading. I remember I couldn't even pronounce the names of the guys who wrote them. It pissed me off when I was little, but later I realized . . . the smarter she got, the more her chances of getting out."

Randall averted his eyes from Paula to hide how much her last words hit home.

Tim broke the silence. "You said Lisa met Eric while she was pursuing her Ph.D. What was she studying?"

Paula lifted her gaze from her fidgeting hands and fixed Tim with a tight stare. "You mean the Ph.D. she never got? Eric didn't even tell her when he applied for a position at Atherton. She had another year to go. I remember she was . . ." She trailed off, sucked a drag off her cigarette, and turned her head slightly so she wouldn't blow the smoke directly into their faces. "I can crack the window if you . . ."

"I'm fine," Randall said.

"I remember the first time she came back from Duke after she met him. I had just dropped out of Syracuse and was living back home. I guess it was Thanksgiving. Gosh . . ." Her eyes went distant for a second "Almost eighteen years ago to the date." She took time to honor this anniversary silently before continuing. "She said he was a perfect gentleman, but he was obsessed with gargoyles and medieval stuff. That's what she told our parents, at least. Later, she told me that he was a *challenge*."

She pulled on her cigarette, set it down in the ashtray, and then pushed herself out of the chair. Tim kept silent as she crossed to the window and cracked it. "How's that?" she asked, back still turned as she steadied herself with both hands on the windowsill. "A challenge," she whispered angrily.

Randall looked at Tim to see if he was going to press, but Tim gazed fixedly at Paula's back.

"How often did you visit Lisa at Atherton?" Tim asked.

"We stopped," Paula said to the window. "Mainly 'cause Eric always rubbed Clark the wrong way. We used to do holidays there, especially Christmas. I don't know—the holidays seemed more *right* up there on the hill, with everyone's lights up. But on the drive home Clark would always complain that every time he tried to talk to Eric about real-life things he would just get this faraway look."

On the console table behind the La-Z-Boy, Randall saw an exact replica of the wedding photo hanging in the bedroom. This one in a different frame. He was silently shocked. "You talked about her reading the classics at a very young age. Do you think it's safe to say that your sister was kind of a prodigy?" Obvious flattery intended to lull Paula out of the funk she'd slipped into.

"Prodigy?" She braced herself against the top window with both hands before pushing it shut. "Know-it-all, maybe." She heard the echo of her own words. She whispered to herself, "That's not fair. She wasn't like that. Sometimes she even seemed sorry for being so much smarter than me. For being so . . . brilliant." Paula shook her head slightly. When she spoke again, her voice sounded as if the wind had been knocked out of her. "She could have been so many things other than that man's wife. So many."

Randall looked at Tim, trying to ask silently how much longer they had to endure this.

"But I guess you're not going to print something like that, are you?"

Tim sat forward. "What would you like us to print, Mrs. Willis?"

Paula turned her head from the window. At first, Randall saw skepticism on her face, but as she surveyed Tim, who sat with pen poised over his pad, the look was replaced by one of confused gratitude, the look of a woman who had been led to believe her words carried little importance. "Say she was strong."

She turned to face the window again. "Maybe she drank. Does it matter? Does it change the fact that she was strong enough to stay with a man who didn't care she existed? I *know* it doesn't change the fact that she came here every weekend to take care of me, when all I had done most of her life was say stupid, mean things to her because I was so jealous."

Randall touched one of Tim's knees gently, hoping the gesture said what he couldn't. Enough. Lisa's real now. A lesson has been learned, so can we please get the hell out of here? In response, Tim cleared his throat and closed his pad.

"How are you feeling now, Mrs. Willis?" Tim asked as mildly as he could.

"All right, I guess. I should be." She managed a smile. "I've been cancer-free for almost half a year now."


It was almost three o'clock and the Cherokee was doing seventy-five south on 95, away from Paula Willis's double-edged guilt and grief and the photo of Eric and Lisa as bride and groom.

"She was moving out, Tim!"

"Randall, all you found was a bunch of clothes."

"Enough clothes to last her until spring. And she lied to Eric and told him Paula was still sick when she's been in remission for almost six months. And the wedding photo—"

"Which proves nothing! Start moving out on your husband and you take a symbol of your failed marriage as a souvenir. Kind of ironic, isn't it? And why didn't she tell Paula? You heard the way she talked about Eric. It's not like she wouldn't have been supportive."

"Maybe Lisa was doing it gradually. Eric had been the bread-winner for their entire marriage, so maybe she thought if she just told him she was leaving, he would have thrown her out without any-thing. Who knows. And you heard what Paula said? Lisa was the smart one, the know-it-all. Maybe she didn't tell her baby sister about her failed marriage because she didn't want Paula yelling 'I told you so!'"

"It's weak, Randall."

Twenty miles outside of Atherton, the landscape had evolved from suburbs to rolling hills and the dark suggestions of the Atlantic beyond. Randall started digging into his pockets. Tim glanced over as he started dumping the mess of papers into the coin holder under the stereo panel. "What's that?"

"Probably nothing. Phone numbers. Grocery lists. There was all kinds of shit in the nightstand."

"And you just took it?"

"I didn't exactly have time to go through it."

"Anything else besides clothes?" Tim asked. "Boxes?"

"Books. Some read, most of them new. Paperback mysteries. And that's all."

"She was obviously a reader."

"She was obviously planning on doing a lot of reading. There. With a sister who's been cancer-free for half a year." Randall started sorting the papers.

"All right. I'm not saying there isn't evidence that she was leaving her husband. But do you think Eric would kill Lisa because she was leaving him? Why bother, when he's spending every weekend with *you*? There's another possibility that you haven't even considered—"

"I know what you're about to say, and don't bother, because it's bullshit."

"She left a *note*, Randall!"

"It's too messy for a suicide."

"Maybe she liked the drama of it. Plunging to her death in the middle of town."

"Really? Is that why she rented herself a storage locker in her name in October? Because she was planning on killing herself?" Randall held up the receipt from Bayfront Storage. Tim looked back to the road before grabbing it out of Randall's hand, flattening it against the steering wheel with one hand.

"It's in her name," Tim finally said.

"And her name only."

Tim furrowed his brow at the highway ahead before handing back the receipt. "The police might have already been there."

"Then why do we have the receipt right now?"

"That's a carbon."

"So? You said yourself the police don't go poking around the belongings of a dead, drunk driver." He checked the address on the receipt. "Jesus Christ, Tim. This place is on Walker Street. Do you know where that is?"

"The bayfront?"

"How many storage facilities are there within spitting distance of the freeway and she goes into the worst neighborhood in town?"

"Maybe it's cheap."

"Yeah, and maybe whatever's inside it is a secret."

"Like what?"

"Like the majority of her belongings."

"Find the key," was all Tim said.

"How am I supposed to do that?"

"Randall, breaking and entering is not going on my résumé. If Bayfront Storage is in Atherton, maybe she kept the key in Atherton."

"Yeah. On her *key ring*, which is either at the bottom of the river or in an evidence bag somewhere."

"What are Eric's Thanksgiving plans?" Tim asked.

"I didn't ask."

"Does he have family nearby?"

"His parents are dead. His brother lives in Seattle."

"What are you doing for Thanksgiving? Painting your nails with Kathryn?"

"Jesus," Randall whispered.

"Hey, if I remember correctly, this was our only advantage over the police—who have much more experience with stuff like this than us, by the way . . ."

"Fine."

Automatic headlights were blinking on beneath a tide of bloated clouds threatening snow. "I'm flying out tonight," Tim finally said. "It's supposed to snow like a bitch too. I get back Sunday. Can you wait till then before you decide to break into any storage facilities?"

"If there's a key in that house, I'm going to find it."

"That isn't all you should be looking for. See how much stuff of hers is still there. Maybe Eric got rid of some of it, but you should still be able to get some sense of whether or not she was really leaving him."

A memory struck Randall with surprising force. He tensed his hand around the door handle. Tim saw it. "What?" he asked.

"Something he said the night of the accident."

"Uh-huh," Tim said impatiently.

Downtown Atherton came into view through the windshield.

"He wanted me to spend the night. It was the first time he ever asked. And I wouldn't. So he said he thought she wasn't coming back. At all, he must have meant."

"He thought she wasn't coming back. Or he knew?"


"I have to connect twice?" Kathryn asked her father.

"Yes. Once in Chicago. Then Denver. You get in at midnight our time, but East Coast time it will be . . . well, you'll be really tired."

Over the phone, Philip Parker always adopted a placating and solicitous tone with his daughter, as if it were his goal to repair any damage her mother, Marion, might have caused in the conversation prior. "Your mom's going to meet you at the airport because I've got a meeting with our new service provider pretty early."

"Gotta keep those doctors on line, bitching about their HMOs, right?"

"My website provides an invaluable service for doctors around the world to provide much-needed medical advice. But I have a feeling you already know that, because I've told you a hundred times."

"You don't ride around your office on a scooter now, do you?"

"Why do I have to defend the dot-com generation to my tech-savvy daughter?"

"Just don't go bust yet, okay? 'Cause I kind of like it here."

"Your mother could support us quite nicely, but you might end up working in the cafeteria."

Kathryn grunted. The cab would be outside Stockton in two hours, ready to take her to Logan. She looked down at the carry-on she'd hoisted onto her bed. The flap was open. It was empty.

"Hellish as it is, there is a bright side," her father added.

"I'm waiting."

"Coach was full on your flights, so . . ."

"Cocktails before takeoff. Woo-hoo!"

"You are expected to behave like an eighteen-year-old flying first class, Kathryn." But there was a hint of a smile in her father's voice, so she didn't bother telling him that save for a few swallows of scotch from Randall's flask, she hadn't touched a drop of alcohol since arriving at Atherton. Jono Morton had mixed the last drink she had ever consumed. Now intoxication didn't mean relaxation or fun, it meant weakness, having your common sense smeared, and your guard lowered before you noticed it was down.

"I know it sucks, Kat. Just get some magazines or a good book or something."

"I'm like three hundred pages behind in poli sci and I have to familiarize myself with just about everything the ACLU has ever said about anything, so I think I'm set."

She pushed her suitcase back to make a seat for herself on the bed. On the other side of the room, April's duffle bag was packed and ready to go. She'd be taking the Metro Line North, leaving a couple hours after Kathryn. As Wednesday afternoon had turned into evening, the boisterous music of Stockton Hall had intensified with prebreak excitement. Now an eerie hush had fallen over the first floor as students departed or made final preparations.

"One more thing. . . ." Her father hesitated. When he began again rather abruptly, Kathryn had the eerie feeling that he had changed his mind about what he'd planned to say. "I don't want you to worry, but I've been watching the Weather Channel and there's a big nor'easter headed your way. It might cause some delays."

Kathryn didn't tell her father that as Thanksgiving had approached, the thought of her plane being grounded in Boston had grown more appealing. "Don't get your hopes up," Philip added. "You're coming home if you have to stuff yourself inside a FedEx package."

"Then I miss the cocktails."

Her father managed a short laugh. Kathryn's eyes shot to the door. Randall had been off gallivanting with Tim for the afternoon, probably sharing sweat for one last time before the break. He had an hour to come tell her good-bye before she got pissed.

"Kathryn . . ."

She perked up, thinking her father was about to tell her what he couldn't a moment earlier, when he'd decided to discuss the weather. "Yeah."

"If I say I know how hard this is for you, you're not going to believe me, right? You're just going to think I'm saying whatever it takes to get you to come home."

Even though she knew her answer, she waited a polite amount of time before giving it. "Yeah."

"Oh. Let me say this, then. After all the trouble your mother and I went through to try to make this trip happen, we're *trying* to understand. Trying harder than we were before, which, with all due respect, was pretty damn hard." Kathryn brought one hand to her forehead because it felt necessary to hold it in place. "I know you still look at us as figures of authority more than anything else," her father went on. "But if that means you can't discuss things openly with us, well . . . let me know what I can do to change that."

"I'll think about it."

"Okay"

Kathryn just breathed for a few seconds. "Dad?"

"Yes."

"Just tell Mom that I'll call Kerry when I'm ready."

She could picture her father's expression; his wide-set, generous eyes staring straight ahead into space, the tip of a pen held against the corner of his mouth. "I will."

"Love you."

"Me too," he said.

As she hung up, the stereo roared to life in the room next door. She rose from the bed, tossing the phone to the mattress instead of setting it back in the cradle. She left the room, bound for the fresh air and quiet that would be in short supply over the next few days.

She would call Kerry when she was ready. But being ready meant summoning the willingness to bridge the gap between the present and the last time she had seen Kerry, seven months earlier.

Kerry's mother had called her because Kathryn was the only one she could think of with the power to lure Kerry out of her bedroom. Driving her mother's Lincoln Navigator along Castro Street, Kathryn was buoyed by the thought of being the one who could exonerate Kerry, free the girl of her guilt and draw her back into the land of the living. Kathryn didn't doubt that Kerry still felt guilty about her coked-up driving, so it was only natural that her apology was next in line behind Jono's. Kathryn had forced him to endure four unreturned phone calls, after which he had driven to her house after midnight, angled his Mustang uphill toward her house on Sea Cliff Drive, and persistently flashed his headlights on her bedroom window. And even after she had snuck out and met him in the street, she'd forced him to exhaust every possible plea. Jono had to call himself stupid, thoughtless, and a liar before she slid into the passenger seat and asked him point-blank if he was dealing.

"You think I would do something so stupid as deal the shit? Do you think I would do anything to ruin what you and I have?" he'd told her desperately, breathlessly, with a fear she needed to see.

With Jono humbled and her authority over him affirmed, Kathryn accepted his apology.

Now it was Kerry's turn to get down on her knees.

Brightly painted Victorians flanked the hillside on Kerry's street. When she and Kerry were younger, the paint jobs on most of them were peeling because the houses' owners were either dead or dying. But things were better now in Kerry's neighborhood, and Kathryn sure felt better, holding fast to her power to grant forgiveness as she ascended the steep set of steps to Kerry's front door.

Inside, Navajo art decorated the walls. For Kathryn, Kerry's house was a place of refuge from the sterility of Sea Cliff and her stucco house overlooking the ocean. Kerry's parents were former members of the hippie generation that had spread out over San Francisco and found various teaching positions. They allowed dinnertime conversation her own parents would never sanction. They treated Kathryn as if she were a bud in danger of being strangled by the vines of her parents' trappings of upper-middle-class wealth.

Debbie, Kerry's mother, led Kathryn upstairs, her head bowed, the exertions of spending three days trying to get Kerry to come out of her room slowing her steps. Kathryn felt like the doctor in hold of a miracle cure, on her way to the patient for whom everyone had lost hope.

"Hon, Kathryn's here. Open up, okay?"

No sound from the other side of the door. Debbie tried the knob. It wasn't locked. She pushed the door open and let Kathryn do the rest.

Kerry's room was a mess. Three days' worth of dirty laundry littered the floor. She'd taken down the photo collage from above her four-poster canopy bed and leaned it facing against the wall. Weeks earlier she had made Kathryn an exact replica; a sliced-up mélange of photos of the events they had shared, everything from their fifth birthday party, which their parents had organized together, to softball camp, and right up to bonfires on beaches with Jono and his friends from Cal.

The toilet flushed and Kerry emerged, dressed in a gym shirt that hung almost to her knees, the Presidio Public logo looking out of place given her disheveled blonde hair, poorly squeezed into a ponytail. Her eyes were bloodshot.

"Hey," Kathryn managed with a smile meant to put Kerry at ease.

"Not you," Kerry said. She sounded numb. "Shit. Why did she call you?"

Kathryn felt her grand plans being thwarted, so she pushed the door shut all the way behind her to make it clear that they were speaking in confidence. Kerry sat down on the foot of her bed so hard it looked as if someone had shoved her there. "Look, Kerry, the other night, I freaked out," Kathryn began. "All right, you scared me. But I talked to Jono . . . Just don't do it again, okay? It's all bad. And he's agreed to stop giving it to you. He just got it from a friend of his. . . ."

Kerry lifted her gaze to Kathryn, the first sign of a sneer on her face. "I don't give a fat fuck what he told you," she whispered.

"Well, from the look of things right now, you don't give a fuck about much, do you?"

Kerry's eyes glazed over and Kathryn felt as if they were staring through her. Kerry slowly rose from the foot of the bed and went to her vanity. She pulled open the center drawer and removed a slip of paper. She turned, crossing the room halfway, then extended the paper to Kathryn. She took it.

"Remember when I gave blood?"

The world narrowed into the printed words before her. Kathryn was reading that a test performed on Kerry's donated blood had turned up antibodies for HIV. The results of this test are confidential, it said. The recipient of these test results should seek the professional care of a health provider immediately.

"They're wrong!"

"Kathryn, don't—"

"Kerry, they're just wrong! I mean, come on. You don't even sleep around."

"Kathryn, *please!*"

"What?" Kathryn asked, lowering the paper in front of her. "What do you think?"

Kerry was shaking her head, slowly. She turned away from Kathryn, and Kathryn took her by one shoulder. Kerry broke into convulsing sobs that racked her chest and bent her at the waist. "So what?" Kathryn said in a cold panic. "So what, Kerry? It's not anywhere near as bad as it used to be. They have all these new drugs and they can almost cure it now."

It took Kathryn a second to realize Kerry was fighting her embrace. She had wedged both fists between their chests, bowing her head in an attempt to slide out from under Kathryn's arms curving around her back. "You don't get it!" Kerry cried.

Kathryn backed away only because it was what she thought Kerry wanted.

"Kathryn, you have to get tested."


"And I thought this was my secret spot!" It was Jesse's voice that broke the hold of her memory, and for the first time ever, she was relieved to hear it.

His footsteps crunched over the snow-covered lawn. The snow had started up, halfway through Kathryn's aimless walk through the residential streets just east of Stockton, and now flakes fell vertically on Overlook Park. She'd heard of the place and its view, but had not meant to come here. In fact, as Jesse approached, his hands buried in the front pockets of his pea coat, his eyes looking fatigued under the bill of his baseball cap, Kathryn had finally come to the conclusion that she was lost.

"I found it by accident," she said, reticent to express any affection for any place Jesse considered his.

She turned her attention back to the view as Jesse sidled up next to her. Like her, he gripped the spokes of the waist-high, cast-iron fence with gloved hands. Beyond them was a twenty-foot drop down the hillside and then the spread of the city, sweeping toward the churning bay. Beneath the sickly gray light of afternoon snow clouds, the city had a strange glow.

"A good view of a shithole," Jesse remarked.

Kathryn shot him an annoyed glance. Something seemed odd about him. He was panting slightly, trying to catch his breath, and he scanned the view with impatient, short bursts of his head. Had he followed her? "I don't think it's that ugly," Kathryn finally said.

"From up here? It looks like some kid's dirty little toy city."

"So why is this your secret spot?"

"Everybody's gotta have one, I guess."

"Well, don't let me intrude," she said, turning to cross the lawn.

"Have fun in Boston!"

"We're not going."

"I know."

Kathryn stopped and turned to see Jesse holding his back to her where he stood. It's not worth it, she told herself. But she didn't listen. "You know, Jesse, the health center provides psychological counseling free of charge. Actually, it's included in our health packages. . . ."

Jesse turned, his crooked smile indicating, as usual, that he found her very attempt at humor more amusing than any joke she might make. "You headed home tonight?"

"Yeah. You?"

Jesse shook his head. She realized she was standing awkwardly in the middle of the lawn. "You're lost, aren't you?" he asked her.

She just glared at him.

"Come on." He crossed the lawn toward her, one hand gently taking her by the shoulder. "I'll show you the way back."

She removed his hand. "Why don't you just tell me?"

He huffed and began moving across the lawn with snow punching steps. By the time he hit the sidewalk, she found herself following him. She kept deliberately behind as they passed beyond the nicer area of houses, with their views of the city below. He was ten feet ahead of her as they moved down Victoria Street and her intuition told her they were headed in the wrong direction.

"Jesse?"

He didn't stop walking

"Where are you going?"

"The dorm," he called back without turning.

Wondering what cruel fate had temporarily placed her at Jesse's mercy, she whipped snow out of her eyes with one glove and followed him across the street. He continued walking down Victoria. She fell into step next to him halfway down the next block. "You know, I might be the one who's lost and all, but why are we headed straight for the Elms?"

Jesse stopped and turned around, one eyebrow arched. "You don't trust me?"

"I think that goes without saying."

"Fine." He shrugged. "You don't believe me, then go knock on that door and ask Tim Mathis how to get back to campus" He gestured to a house across the street with a Toyota Camry in its driveway.

She looked from the house to him, waiting for the punch line.

"What?" he asked.

"Tim Mathis doesn't live there."

"Are you sure?"

"Yeah. Only seniors can live off campus. And Tim lives in Braddock."

When Jesse furrowed his brow again theatrically, she realized that he was fucking with her. He turned to face the house, scratching the top of his cap absently. "But Randall and Tim are giving it another shot right? Isn't that what he told you?"

Kathryn said nothing

"Funny," Jesse said, pointing toward the house behind her. " 'Cause I could swear, that's where Randall's going every night."

When he saw the anger on her face, he abandoned his act. "You want to get back to campus. Go up to Inverness and take a left" He turned and began walking in the opposite direction from where they had come.

She didn't move until he rounded the corner

Afternoon was turning into evening and pale light illuminated the front windows of the house Jesse had pointed to. Before she could think twice, she had stepped off the curb and crossed the street.


"Your parents aren't expecting you?" Eric asked flatly.

Randall held the phone to his ear with one hand, punching a ballpoint pen open and shut with his other. "I'll see them tonight and come back here in the morning," he told Eric.

"Odd," Eric said.

"Do you want me to come over or not?"

"I wasn't planning on going anywhere."

"Well, the idea of you being alone on Thanksgiving was kind of getting to me," Randall declared.

Unreadable silence came from the other end before he heard Eric clear his throat. "That's very sensitive. Christmas will be worse. But thank you." Randall didn't have the energy to draw out this performance much longer.

"I'll cook something," Eric added absently

"Okay."

"Can you hold on a second? Someone's at the door."

"Fine," Randall said.

He popped open his notebook and removed the folded-up receipt for Bayfront Storage from his pocket, jotted down the address, and then opened the Atherton Map Search page on his computer. By the time he had typed in the address, enlarged the neighborhood, and printed out detailed directions from the hill, he realized how long Eric had been away from the phone. He moved the mouse to the print icon and by the time the pages came out in a hum, he could hear Eric's footsteps moving back to the phone with speed.

"Who was that?" Eric barked.

"What?"

"Who just came to *my* house asking for *you*?" Eric's panic and anger turned the last word into a snarl.

Randall didn't realize he had shot up out of his chair until he was gripping the back of it.

"What?"

"It was a girl. She wanted to know if Randall Stone was here. *Goddamnit*, Randall! How could you—"

Breathless, Randall spun to face Jesse's side of the room. When he hurled the phone, it slammed into the miniature television, knocking it from its perch on top of the refrigerator. It hit the floor on one side, and the screen cracked.


"Kathryn?" She didn't turn at the sound of Randall's voice, just kept kneading the sweater back into her suitcase. She was trying not to see

Dr. Eberman's face when she had said Randall's full name, or the way his eyes had remained locked on hers, even as his head rocked from side to side in a tired attempt at denial. He had managed only a weak, "He's not here."

She yanked the zipper on the suitcase and it caught again.

At first, she had been struck by how handsome he was. It had become almost reflexive since she had become Randall's best friend to wonder whether or not Randall would find a certain man attractive. As she stood on the front porch, the question had started to form in her mind: Would Randall agree that this fine-boned man, with his hard jawline, stubbled chin, and expressive, dark eyes, was classically handsome? She must have looked like an idiot, wide-eyed and numb with shock, her voice sounding the way it did when she was twelve.

"Kathryn. Come on—"

"How long?" she asked, lowering the suitcase to the floor.

"Please. Not because of something Jesse did—"

"Jesse didn't have to *do* anything." She turned around. Randall was holding the edge of the open door, his eyes wide and pleading, his mouth hanging open, shaking his head and generally looking like a kid about to get grounded for a month. "How long have you been going to that man's house at one in the morning?"

Randall screwed his eyes shut, grimacing.

"When did you start? Before or after his wife died?"

"Kathryn, I understand why—"

"What do you understand? 'Cause let me tell you what I'm feeling. Let me you tell *all* I'm feeling. I'm in awe, Randall. I'm in awe of the number of lies you had to tell to keep this a secret "

He moved for her and she grabbed the handle of the suitcase. She made it past him, but the wheels caught on one of his feet and she gave it a yank. She hit the hallway in full stride.

"Kathryn! Stop!"

She didn't. There was no way she was going to wait for the elevator, so she lifted the handle and headed down the stairs.

"Kathryn!"

In the foyer, she could see her own reflection as she approached the glass door. Through it, the headlights of the waiting cab cut twin swaths through the falling snow. She heard Randall barreling down the stairs behind her. She popped the door open with one arm and tried to roll the suitcase through ahead of her. The wheels caught on the threshold and she gave the suitcase a kick. It lurched in front of her and landed on the sidewalk outside.

"Kathryn, I was going to tell you."

She had one foot through the door when his hand seized her shoulder. She turned, the door resting against her back "What made you think I would ever want to know?" She turned, grabbed the edge of the door with her hand and slammed it behind her.

The door shut behind her with a loud thud instead of a bang.

She whirled. Randall had vanished on the other side. In his place was a thin dark smudge across the glass. Backlit by the foyer, it looked black. Kathryn knew it was red. Then, behind the glass, Randall straightened up, one open hand covering his mouth. Blood stained the spaces between his fingers, and above them his eyes were wide with shock.

He removed his hand, revealing the smear of blood at the corner of his mouth and surveyed his palm. When his eyes met hers through the glass, his shock was replaced by pained resignation and a shame she needed to see. Blood spilled from his mouth. When his eyes swelled with the first sign of tears, he turned, bringing his hand back to his mouth. He disappeared into the stairwell.

Once her breath returned, she realized she had been holding one hand extending toward the door handle for the past few seconds. Behind her, the cab driver honked the horn. Her arm fell to her side.

As the cab pulled away from the curb, fat flakes pelted the windshield. "What time's your flight?" the driver asked.

"Six," Kathryn answered, watching Stockton Hall disappear from the window

"Traffic might be pretty bad, but we should get there in time. Sure hope this blow doesn't ground yah. Funny, last winter we barely saw a flake."

Headlights from an approaching car blinded her and she blinked. The driver's eyes met hers in the rearview mirror.

"Oh, hey, it's nothing to cry about. Takes a lot more than this to shut down Logan."

• • •

Running water sent his blood swirling down the drain of the bathroom sink. Randall spit again, bracing himself with both hands on either side of the basin. He tongued the tattered, salty-tasting flesh where his teeth had torn the inside of his cheek Laughter echoed down the hallway, followed by the squeak of snow boots over carpet. Randall's knuckles whitened against the basin as he brought his face closer to his reflection, seeing not himself, but Kathryn's empty gaze through the glass door.

Outside, Jesse spoke in a low, conspiratorial tone as he passed the bathroom door. Another male's laughter followed, growing softer as they moved down the hallway. Randall ran more water over his face. He got some toilet paper from one of the stalls and methodically dabbed at the corners of his mouth, hoping to pick up any stray dried blood. He had hoped the menial task would distract him, but when he glanced around at the bathroom, everything about it seemed suddenly foreign and alien. Rejected by Kathryn, Randall suddenly felt like a lone intruder in the dorm he had lived in for months.

Quiet had settled over Stockton Hall. Most of its residents had departed. Wind drummed along the walls. It hissed and howled around the edges of windows in empty rooms. At the door to his own room, Randall couldn't bring more than three fingers to the knob, letting them rest there.

"Hey."

He spun around. April was shouldering her duffle bag out the door, then pulling it shut. "Is she gone?"

Randall nodded. April's eyes shot up and down his body. On instinct, he brought his fingers to his mouth. No blood. From his room came a high-pitched whine followed by a sharp, gasping intake of breath. April flinched. "Good-bye, Randall," she muttered

Randall waited until he could no longer hear her footsteps brushing over the carpet.

He opened the door. Snow fell past the window with heavy, determined force. The gooseneck lamp spilled light over Taylor's naked back. His head was pinned to the pillow by Jesse's hand. His mouth was open in a silent scream. Jesse was a dark shadow above him, hips pistoning.

Randall gently pushed the door closed behind him.

Silently, he crossed to his desk chair and turned it around, its legs scraping slightly across the linoleum floor. Taylor's eyes shot open and met Randall's. At first, his smile looked like a leer. As Randall sank down into his chair, Jesse's hips didn't stop their shadowed rise and fall. As Randall watched, his eyes adjusting to the darkness, the only sounds in the room came from the wind battering the window, the steady rattle of the heater, and Jesse's breaths, swelling and draining his chest.

Even as he refused to rise from the chair, Randall realized that Jesse had won. Once Kathryn realized that Randall had shown her only the elements of himself he was willing to reveal, she had reacted with revulsion and horror. And now, the girl who had provided both escape and some hope for a better self had left Atherton carrying a newfound knowledge of him. Hatred would follow, he knew that. It always did.

Jesse saw him for who he was and had returned him to the person he had run from, ever since the day he had arrived at Atherton: a practiced whore. And Jesse was the first man to realize this and extend kinship rather than desire.

When Jesse released his grip on the back of Taylor's neck and extended his arm toward Randall, the gesture summoned not only lust in him but fear—fear of returning to the solitude that had blackened his life before Atherton. Randall rose and crossed the invisible dividing line that had once separated their sides of the room.

# II

# Thanksgiving

*Long before morning glories perched upon opening day,*
*I left yesterday under a worn goose mattress*
*The cotton tapestry still had creases*
*from my nocturnal lullabies of dreams long past.*

—SALIH MICHAEL FISHER, "Hometown"

# CHAPTER NINE

RISING SUNLIGHT PEELED FOG FROM THE TOWERS OF THE BAY BRIDGE.

Kathryn shut her eyes. Landing at SFO could rattle the most seasoned of flyers. Winds off the bay rocked the plane as it made a determined descent toward the fog-shrouded water. At the last, precious second, the runway appeared, a ribbon of concrete, and Kathryn felt the wheels hit earth with a shudder in her spine.

The guy sitting next to her awoke with a snort. He had drifted off right after they took off from Denver, three hours late, and Kathryn had been envious of his simple sleep. It was dawn on the West Coast and she didn't have the energy to calculate what time her body thought it was.

Despite their fatigue, passengers leaped from their seats as soon as the plane rolled to a halt, heaving their bags out of the overhead compartments. She was pleasantly taken aback when sleepyhead dropped her suitcase on the empty seat; she tried a grateful half smile that died as an intention.

The terminal was almost empty. Kathryn was jarred by the transition. In all the hours of flights and delays, the drone of jet engines had been a numbing white noise, but the terminal was hushed save for the staccato of footsteps as passengers crossed the gate area and proceeded down the central walkway.

Kathryn stopped when she spotted her mother. Marion Parker had dozed off in her chair, a hardcover novel closed on her lap. In the early morning light, she looked like a passed-out drunk. Having expected to meet Kathryn's flight six hours earlier, she had dressed up in a beige pants suit and matching pumps. Now, her silk blouse had been rumpled up over her breasts, displacing her pearl and silver necklace. Her black hair, usually a neat, shoulder-length bob, had been flattened by the back of the chair, and her glasses rested precariously on the bridge of her nose. The portrait of diligence, Kathryn thought. After hounding her to return, Marion Parker was determined to be there the second the plane landed.

"Mom?"

Nothing. Kathryn reached out and gave her mother's limp wrist a tug.

Marion started awake, one hand shoving her glasses into place, eyes darting past Kathryn to the file of departing passengers before she recognized her own daughter before her

"Oh, honey." Her half-groan told Kathryn that her mother was bemoaning her own fatigue. "These idiots," she said, stuffing the book into her purse "They couldn't tell me what time you were going to get in. First it was two, then four." She hoisted her purse onto one shoulder and got to her feet. "I couldn't have you just . . . arrive alone."

Marion put her arm around her daughter's back and began leading Kathryn and her rolling suitcase through the terminal. As they walked, her mother leaned in slightly, squeezing Kathryn's opposite shoulder, the warmest greeting Marion was going to give. "You made it out just in time. These TVs they have everywhere have been going on about the Thanksgiving Blow. Boston got something like twelve inches in one hour."

"I didn't check anything. Can we just go?"

"Sure," Marion said with a yawn.

When they got outside, Kathryn dug in her pocket for the pack of Camels she'd picked up at Chicago O'Hare. She was exhaling her first drag when her mother looked up and saw her. Kathryn managed a sheepish grin and a shrug. "We'll walk slow," was all Marion said. "You can't smoke in the car."

In the parking lot, Kathryn was still searching for the Navigator when her mother stopped next to a gleaming new BMW X5. She unlocked it with her remote. "What happened to the Navigator?" Kathryn asked.

"Too much space," her mother told her, ducking inside the driver's side door to unlock the cargo door.

On the ride home, Kathryn drifted off, not waking until her mother slowed the BMW as she angled her way into Sea Cliff. Ocean-view houses fought for space on the tiny lots that lined the winding streets. The Golden Gate's towers rose over the red tiled roofs and dense pine. Squat and finished in stucco, the Parker residence would have looked better beneath Southern California sun.

Kathryn was lulled out of her stupor when the garage door slammed shut behind them. She and her mother sat in the darkness for several seconds before Marion shook her head and popped open the door. Kathryn didn't make a move to get out of the car until she heard the wheels of her suitcase being dragged over the garage floor.

She guessed her father was still in bed. She trudged upstairs.

Her room was exactly as she had left it.

Kerry's photo collage, "The Best of Times," was still on the wall above Kathryn's old bed, with its metal frame of curlicues, feminine enough to please her mother, but just restrained enough to give her the illusion of maturity Kathryn had desired as a high-school student. Through her picture window, the fog parted in tendrils, revealing the rolling hills of Marin and morning traffic filling the Golden Gate Bridge.

When she was a little girl, the black mouth of the bay's entrance had terrified her, conjuring up images of sharks swimming through its depths. Now the view from her window struck her as strangely flat, a painting with a color palette of only grays and faded greens. Not real.

Kathryn sat on the foot of her bed, and soon found herself rolling onto her back, eyes lazily scanning her old and now unfamiliar sur-roundings. Her old desk from Ikea looked tiny and inadequate, pushed to the far wall and piled with mail that couldn't be that impor-tant, because whoever sent it all obviously didn't know she had left for college. The TV set on top of her bookshelf gave her pause; she and April had decided against one and she hadn't caught more than five minutes of a *Friends* rerun since she went away to school.

She reached for the phone on the nightstand and her palm landed on empty table space. She started. The phone was on the other side of the bed. Holding it against her chest, she counted four hours ahead. Had Randall gone to New York?

Has he gone to Dr. Eberman's?

She replaced the phone, brought one bent arm to her forehead.

*It's just four days*, she told herself for the hundredth time.

Before she could repeat the words to herself again, she fell into a deep sleep permeated by dreams of submarines descending into the black depths of the Pacific, and waves breaking around rocks too small for her to balance on.


"Honey?"

Kathryn's bedside lamp fell palely across Philip Parker, sitting on the edge of her bed. Her room was dark and she glanced at the digital clock on the nightstand: almost 5 P.M. She had slept for almost ten full hours. Her dad was dressed in a pale blue oxford and dark trousers. His salt-and-pepper hair was slicked back from his high forehead, his wide-set chestnut eyes staring at her expectantly from behind his invisible-frame glasses.

She managed a smile, and he leaned in and kissed her on the cheek.

"I'll get ready," she mumbled, propping herself on her elbows.

"Don't worry. Linda and Dale won't be here for another hour."

When she saw her mother, her arms crossed over her chest, her top lip covering her lower one as if standing in Kathryn's doorway had become too time consuming, Kathryn felt a stab of dread. Her parents' positions and posture reminded her of another moment, months earlier, when they had awakened her with news she didn't want to hear.

"We didn't want to hit you with this right away," Philip began.

"You're getting divorced."

Marion's laugh didn't make it much past her throat. She recrossed her arms and leaned her hip against the doorframe. Her father bowed his head with a slight, forced smile. "I got a phone call at the office a few days ago," Philip tried again. "Have you ever seen that show, *Cover Story*? It's sort of a news-type show. Kind of like *Dateline* but—"

"It's trash," Marion said from the doorway.

Philip's face tightened, but he kept his eyes on his daughter. "A producer from the show called me. Apparently, they want to interview you for a story they're doing."

"About Jono?" Kathryn asked. Her voice sounded deflated and dead.

"Frankly, I'm surprised the media didn't pick up on the whole thing earlier," Philip said.

"There was an article in the *Chronicle*, if I remember correctly," Marion cut in, her tone implying that her memory rarely failed her. Kathryn took bitter note of the fact that Marion still acted as if she had shouldered the bulk of the trauma Kathryn had been through.

"The woman's name is Heidi Morse." Philip continued. "And the only reason she called me is because she was looking for your phone number at Atherton. The school refuses to give out student phone numbers, but from what she said, it's only a matter of time before she gets her hands on a copy of the directory. Now, we have several options here—"

"Your father's leaving out that this show is repugnant. It's paternity suits and white trash in trailer parks."

Philip grimaced at his wife, who wasn't deterred by her husband's anger. At least some things don't change, Kathryn thought. She pushed herself off the bed and went to the window, looking for solace from the dark gulf of the Golden Gate passing under the spotlit towers of the bridge.

"This *woman* may have told your father that they're determined to do a balanced piece, which is what your father is about to tell you. But it doesn't change the fact that the show is lurid, sensational, and cheap, and you should distance yourself from all of this as much as possible"

"This is exactly what we agreed not to do, Marion."

"This isn't about what *we* do," Marion retorted.

"This is your mother's roundabout way of saying it's your decision."

Her parents' gazes were both on her, her father's slightly pleading and distressed, showing the wear and tear of having to bring steadiness and composure to a situation that had threatened to tear away at his only child's mental fabric, her mother's etched by the irritated impatience that had been her sole defense against the specter of losing her daughter ever since she had first learned of Jono Morton's existence that previous May.

"No doubt this producer woman's tried to get in touch with all the girls. It's probably why Kerry's been calling so much," Philip explained.

"Kerry's calling because she wants to know if I'm sick." Kathryn was surprised by the steadiness of her voice.

Her mother's eyes dropped to the floor. She shook her head. Philip shut his eyes briefly as if to say, Perish the thought. Seeing how her words had bruised them, Kathryn regretted opening her mouth.

"I'll be downstairs," Marion finally muttered, leaving the doorway.

Kathryn and Philip listened to her heavy footsteps on the stairs.

"What do you think, Dad?"

"I think I'll get shouted out of this house if I say what I really think," Philip told her, rubbing his forehead gently with open palms.

"She's downstairs," Kathryn said.

Philip lifted his gaze to her, smiling slightly at the prospect of being coconspirators against the woman responsible for the clatter of dishes in the kitchen.

"You have to talk to someone about it," he said. "Obviously, it's not going to be us."

"I don't need any more counselors asking me why I'm so angry. After listening to what happened, how can anyone honestly ask me why I'm still angry?"

"Of course, but you only went to a psychologist. Not a psychiatrist. Not a real doctor—"

"What would be the point? Ritalin?"

"Kathryn. Please," Philip chided, without anger. "I'm not saying you need therapy, or that you have to make your pain public with this TV show. I'm saying that you have to find some way to let this out of you"

Kathryn considered this as she examined the carpet. "Do you have this woman's phone number?" she finally asked.

Philip got up from her bed and disappeared into the hallway. He returned and handed her a piece of paper, then left. Heidi Morse. Kathryn read the number as she crossed to her old desk. Eight one eight was an area code she didn't recognize. She opened the desk drawer and pulled out *The Chronicle* article from the pages of an old notebook.

**BAY AREA DRUG DEALER**
**INFECTS TEN WOMEN WITH HIV**

She set Heidi Morse's phone number on top and closed the drawer on them both.


"Is this turkey?"

Marion looked at her younger sister's husband as if he had just hawked a loogie onto the dinner table. "Duck."

Kathryn watched her uncle shovel a forkful of creamed spinach into his mouth. "Did you shoot it yourself?" he asked, between chews, then guffawed.

"I don't shoot things," Marion told him, sinking back into her chair after fifteen exhausting minutes of sawing meat from the bird.

As a little girl, Kathryn had suffered from a powerful crush on Dale, her aunt's husband. A former Stanford linebacker turned corporate real estate agent, he had first earned her adoration by deeming her worthy of learning the intricacies of that time-honored backyard game that males around the country treat with a reverence that only adds to its allure: catch. By the time she turned fifteen, sexual experimentation with her boyfriends had added a creepy dimension to her previously innocent crush, and she had set about snuffing it out. Now Kathryn saw her uncle for what he was, a blowhard who laughed at his own bad jokes.

Next to her, Kathryn's Aunt Linda had barely said a word since they had sat down to eat, but whenever her husband's mouth opened, her head snapped to attention as if she expected a shotgun to go off. Linda's career had always been her excuse for not having children. Kathryn guessed the real reason was that Dale would be their father.

The meal had gotten off to a start with a discussion of Linda's good friends, victims of the dot-com fallout who had just been forced to sell their two-million-dollar home for seven hundred thousand. Then the conversation had bottomed out into silences punctuated by long looks at Kathryn from every side of the table.

"Someone just ask me how school is so we can get it out of the way," Kathryn said.

"How's school?" Dale asked, with the bravado of a third grader shouting out the right answer.

"Great!"

"Have you picked a major yet?" Linda asked, her eyes on her plate in front of her.

"Animal husbandry," Kathryn answered.

Philip laughed into his napkin.

"We've decided to leave Kathryn alone on that front," Marion spoke up. "I'm sure she'll steer clear of whatever we suggest, so we're actually improving our chances by keeping quiet and hoping she doesn't pick something preposterous." Marion's note of wry humor had deteriorated steadily as she spoke.

"It's been months since someone's talked about me like I'm not in the room," Kathryn remarked to a forkful of duck she didn't have the stomach for. She ate it anyway.

"I read an article on Atherton the other day. Well, skimmed it really," Linda said. "I didn't know Michael Price went there."

Kathryn groaned. Linda continued, "The guy's like one of the most popular architects in the world and he's done three projects for Atherton at half off. He must have loved the place."

"I thought you said you skimmed it," Dale said.

"Well, I just picked it up in the waiting room . . ." Linda trailed off.

"The waiting room of what?" Marion asked in her best big-sister voice.

"The doctor."

"She missed her period," Dale added.

Linda set her fork down on the edge of her plate. "Out of all the adults we know, Dale, do you think any of them would say 'period' at the dinner table?"

Dale shrugged at Philip as if to say, There she goes again.

"I'm not pregnant," Linda added, returning to her meal.

"Either way's fine with me."

"Noted, Dale."

Philip cleared his throat. "The duck's great, honey."

"Thanks," Marion responded distantly. "I hope our daughter eats some."

Kathryn stabbed at a piece of duck the size of her hand and bit it in half. Linda shook with silent laughter. "Cigarettes are an appetite suppressant," Marion said.

"*Cigarettes?*" Dale asked incredulously. He shook his head at

Kathryn, clicking his tongue against the roof of his mouth "I thought Atherton was a smart school."

When she leveled her gaze on her uncle, Kathryn was reminded of how, growing up, she had often tried to move objects with her mind. There were, after all, only five feet between Dale's chair and the plate glass window, and from there a thirty-foot drop down the hillside.

"It could be worse, I guess," Marion mumbled.

Kathryn felt her father bristle. Even Linda, the expert at ignoring her own husband, shifted in her seat uncomfortably. Dale was, of course, clueless. Marion attacked her duck with renewed vigor, feigning ignorance of the reverberations her flippant comment stirred in the others.

When she met her mother's stony eyes across the table, Kathryn felt removed from it, spun into a private place inhabited only by her mother, a place where the woman could finally ask the question that was hardening her face: How could you have been so stupid?

Maybe it would take a few more years before Marion would ask herself what lessons she had neglected to teach her daughter, what she could have done to keep her from a man like Jono, or at least wise her up to what he really was. But for now, Kathryn saw that Marion's attitude had not changed in almost six months. Kathryn could bathe in her pain and betrayal all she wanted, but Marion considered her daughter's self-pity to be a useless distraction from the more pressing question. How could you have let yourself come so close to death?

"Excuse me," Kathryn whispered as she rose from her chair.

Halfway to the stairs, Kathryn looked over her shoulder. Philip's eyes had followed her out of the room, but her mother had braced her forehead on her palm while Dale sympathetically held her other hand.

The sight of Marion accepting solace from a relative she despised was enough to tighten Kathryn's chest with anger. But the scene also forced her to reassess her real reason for not wanting to return home. At Atherton, she had enjoyed being something more than the survivor of a tragedy narrowly averted by a stroke of good luck that her own mother suspected she might not have deserved.

In her desk drawer, she found her old address book, the one she had left behind in hope that once she was swept up in her new life at

Atherton, she would never have cause to call any of the numbers in it. She could think of only one person in San Francisco who wouldn't treat her like a near miss.

Pier 39 was clogged with a jungle of late-afternoon tourists. Kathryn was early, so she walked slowly amid the din of shutter-clicks and the voices of parents urging their children out of one last gift shop. The Friday afternoon sunlight parted the clouds over the bay, revealing patches of blue that would soon be lost to night. Increasingly cold gusts of wind off the water hinted at the impending dusk.

She found an empty bench in front of a kite shop and took a seat, puffing on a Camel as she watched a group of Asian tourists have their pictures taken with a blonde, blue-eyed little boy who to them was an exotic, Aryan wonder. His mother stood close by, her fixed smile nervous and wary.

When they were little girls, Kerry's father, Ernest, had begrudgingly taken them to the pier every Saturday afternoon, all the while grumbling about the mini-conglomerate of tourist traps that made up a false city within a real one. She and Kerry usually managed to lose Ernest to an empty bench and a copy of the *Guardian* while they made their way down the pier to an old dress shop buried at the end. There they would nominate choices for their wedding gowns under the supervision of the elderly proprietor, who was thrilled to have two females in her store who hadn't yet lost their taste for marriage. Kathryn wondered if the shop was still there.

"Justice Parker?"

Trying not to seem startled, Kathryn turned and got up from the bench at the sound of a nickname she hadn't been called in almost a year. Kerry looked well—she acknowledged how freighted that phrase was even as she thought it. Her longtime friend resembled a 1950s Hollywood starlet on a photo shoot in the wilds of Africa. A barrette lifted her bangs off her forehead, and two flaps of platinum blonde hair fell to both shoulders. Her smile brightened her green eyes and widened to turn them into slits above her baby fat cheeks ("pouty," Kerry would have called them). Her alabaster skin was unblemished and without pallor. But her safari jacket was loose fitting and her

cargo pants sagged around the knees. Kathryn guessed the outfit had a
dual purpose; it concealed curves she no longer wanted to advertise as
well as the fanny pack on her waist, containing what Kathryn knew to
be her regimen of protease inhibitors.

They kept standing several feet apart, with tourists weaving around
them; Kerry smiling warmly and expectantly, and Kathryn so stricken
by Kerry's evident health she wasn't conscious of the emotions her
face betrayed. "Sorry," Kerry finally said. "I know you used to hate that
nickname, but the whole drive here I was thinking about that time
you walked out on Mr. Connors in the middle of history."

"Didn't he tell me to shut up?"

"'Cause you were totally mouthing off to him."

"Probably because he was going to test us on shit we hadn't
covered."

"See? Justice Parker!" Kerry gestured to Kathryn with one hand
that swept the length of her body, indicating that some things never
change, even though she was examining her old best friend as if they
hadn't seen each other in twenty years.

Kathryn was surprised by the lump in her throat. Kerry closed the
distance between them. Kathryn prepared herself for a hug that might
mist her vision, but instead Kerry just tugged one of her hands. "Let's
walk. Keep warm."

They started down the pier, slowly, as if each was afraid of knocking the other off balance.

"The number your mom gave me. I didn't recognize it."

"I moved," Kerry said with a faint, satisfied smile. "I got an apartment in the Richmond. It's closer to school."

"San Francisco State?"

"The one and only."

"You're not taking any of your dad's classes, are you?"

"Are you kidding? No. But it's tough going around campus as
Ernest Slater's daughter. People think I'm going to kick their ass if
they don't use the recycling bins."

After several years working as a freelance journalist, during which
time his pieces were slashed to death by editors reminding him that
the sixties were over, Kerry's father had returned to academic life as a
professor of environmental ethics, and had once again taken up the

task of turning young minds against every new real estate development from the Presidio to Palo Alto.

"Remember the aquarium they were going to put in here?" Kerry asked.

"Right. Those plastic tubes under the bay that people were going to walk through."

"And my dad got so pissed. Like the bay needs any more crap put in it."

They were almost to the end of the pier, where gift shops gave way to a few restaurants, the sun-streaked bay visible through their windows. Kathryn guessed that if the pier didn't end, they would have kept walking. It was easier than standing face to face.

"How's Atherton?"

"Great," Kathryn answered flatly.

Kerry would still know Kathryn well enough to know that she was bullshitting. But Kerry didn't press, and as they slowed their steps, their absence of conversation bloomed like fog between them.

"The other girls and I . . . we meet," Kerry finally began. "Actually, we're meeting tonight, if you want to come. If you hadn't called me, I was going to call you," she explained before she trailed off, staring down at her feet as she kicked the toe of one duck boot with the other.

"Other girls?" Kathryn asked tightly.

"Heather comes sometimes. And Callie  Do you remember her? She was Peter's girlfriend."

When Kerry finally met Kathryn's eyes, Kathryn realized the warmth of Kerry's greeting and the ease with which she had started the conversation arose from her sense of camaraderie. Shared victimhood.

"I'm negative," Kathryn told her as gently as she could

For a brief second, Kathryn saw the sting of her words in Kerry's eyes. Kerry managed to harden her ever-youthful face into an adult mask of resolve. She was nodding slightly to display her approval of this news.

"It was stupid of me anyway. Asking you to hang out with all the girls Jono was cheating on you with. I just thought . . ."

"It's okay," Kathryn said untruthfully, touching Kerry's shoulder weakly before letting her arm fall to her side. Kathryn looked back at the long route they had taken because it was easier than taking in the sight of Kerry, who was unable to hide the fact that this news had devastated her.

"You know about the window period?" Kerry asked.

"Six months."

"Well, that's like worst-case scenario. Usually, it's more like three."

"Kerry," Kathryn said. "Did the TV people call you?"

Kerry grunted. "TV people? What movie is that from?"

Kathryn said nothing.

"*Poltergeist*," Kerry answered herself with a smile, saw Kathryn didn't wear one and bowed her head. "Yeah. They did."

"And?"

"They're paying," Kerry said flatly. "I could use the money. I've got my parents paying my rent. And I'm on my father's health plan still. It makes me uncomfortable."

"How much?"

"Not a fortune, but I could use it for transition money while I try to get a night job."

Kerry's intention was obvious, to make herself as small a burden on her family as possible, in case illness made her an unavoidable one. "What about you?" she asked.

"I have the woman's number. . . ."

"Heidi?"

Bothered by the use of the producer's first name, Kathryn faltered. "Yeah. Her. What do they want?"

"A story. And I'm sure they're going to ask the same question everyone's asked."

Puzzled, Kathryn met Kerry's eyes again.

"Did he do it on purpose?" Kerry said.

Kathryn held her gaze for as long as she could before bracing her arms across her chest in a tardy attempt to suppress a shiver.

"Maxine's is still here," Kerry finally remarked, gesturing over Kathryn's shoulder with her chin.

"Really?"

"Yeah. Maxine is long gone, but the store's still right down there." Kerry pointed to the old vintage clothing store they had visited as children. "Want to check it out?"

Kathryn just nodded and followed Kerry to the entrance. She and

Kerry separated as if they were strangers who had passed through the front door at the same time.

The woman behind the counter couldn't have been much older than they. She didn't look up from her magazine as they hesitantly entered. The store was smaller and more cramped than Kathryn remembered. Classical music droned from hidden speakers; burgundy carpeting muffled their footfalls. The lamps resting on top of the overloaded racks were of every style that could be considered remotely antique. The place looked randomly put together, its stabs at elegance obvious and uncoordinated. The dresses swelling the racks weren't the fairy-tale gowns they had been to two seven-year-old girls.

Kerry was standing in front of a mannequin outfitted in a flowing taffeta gown that spilled off the platform, almost reaching the carpet. A plait of gold beads tapered from the breast down to the waist; patches of white indicated where a few had been stripped away by time or abuse. They caught the amber lamplight and sun slanting through the windows. Kerry fingered the hem of the dress in one hand, her lips slightly pursed and a furrow creasing the bridge of her nose.

Kathryn was struck by the weary resignation with which Kerry regarded the thing of beauty, one fistful of it held in her hand. Kerry's eyes traveled up the length of the dress. Her stooped posture beneath the baggy clothes made her seem like an old maid regarding a costume she could have donned in her youth.

Kathryn had to remind herself that disease had not added years to Kerry. If it had brought wisdom, that was only because it brought the prospect of death to her youth. It flattened the eagerness from her voice. Her eyes, still their startling shade of green, seemed to see less.

Kerry released the fistful of taffeta and backed up several steps, as if to take in the entire dress one last time, like a painting she was about to depart from in a museum.

Kathryn tried to pinpoint the expression on Kerry's face: she seemed wary and suspicious of the happiness the dress suggested. At eighteen, her expectations had become liabilities. When Kathryn's vision started to fog over with tears, she turned and left the store, the entry bells jarring in her wake.

Kathryn shuffled down a concrete extension of the pier that jutted like a finger into the bay. The winds assaulted her, bringing with them the sharp odor of salt water and the stench of sea death. She had won her battle against the first threat of tears by the time she heard Kerry's footsteps on the concrete behind her. Kerry took up a post right beside her, and they both stared out at the sun's last light falling on Alcatraz and the green humpback of Angel Island.

"Why'd you call me, Kathryn?"

Kathryn couldn't tell Kerry that one look from her mother across the dinner table had her feeling like a freak in her own home, that for some reason she had craved Kerry's companionship because Kerry had known Jono better than she had allowed her parents to.

"I didn't mean to say it like that," she finally said. "Back there, when I told you I was negative."

"What do you mean?"

"It was like I was distancing myself from you or something. I don't know."

"Maybe," Kerry said. She was leaning forward on the railing, hands clasped in front of her, narrowing her eyes against the windy bay. "That's your right, I guess."

"No. Kerry . . ."

"Kathryn, just because my immune system is *compromised* now doesn't mean I get to erase what I did."

"I didn't call you so I could hear you say this. It's not like you owe me an apology."

"That's fair, I guess," Kerry said. "Just so you know, that the worse things you could ever say to me—things you might have imagined saying to me a million times—I've already said them to myself. You know, the first thing my doctor said when my results came back was, 'This isn't the death warrant it used to be.' And you know what I thought? It should be. But as strange as it sounds, that would have been too easy for me. I could have just curled up in my room, never taken any of my medicines, and thought, 'Well this is what I get for doing eight balls every weekend and getting so high it didn't even matter to me that I was sleeping with my best friend's boyfriend.'"

Kerry's candor stung. "How is that easy?" Kathryn asked.

"It's harder to live every day with the knowledge of just how low you can go."

"You made a mistake."

"Kathryn, we never used to bullshit each other like this. That was like our claim to fame."

Kathryn met Kerry's eyes. "This is not how you should pay."

"This?" Kerry turned, resting her butt against the railing, her eyes moving past Kathryn to where the sun had almost completed its descent behind the Golden Gate. "This isn't as bad as you might think." Kerry's words didn't sound hollow, but her voice was tentative enough to suggest that she had forced herself to arrive at this conclusion recently and hadn't quite found her footing. "I'm not scared of dying. And I might not. Not 'cause of this anyway. I get scared when I think about what kind of person I'm going to be after so many days of being jealous of anyone who's well. Just looking at people on the street and trying not to hate them because their blood's cleaner than mine. That could end up being a much worse illness." Kerry's eyes centered on Kathryn's again. "Why'd you call me?"

"Because I wanted to know if you were okay."

Kerry nodded and bowed her head. Kathryn couldn't tell if she was disappointed with her answer, or content. She turned to the rail again. "I never said I was sorry, Kathryn."

"You don't have to."

"Yeah I do. If not for you, then for me. Part of not dying is calling in a bunch of favors I don't deserve. And also, it's being glad that your friends aren't sick."

When she got home, Kathryn poured herself a glass of red wine from the bottle she hadn't touched at Thanksgiving dinner. She made her way out onto the terrace that jutted over the hillside, its wooden patio furniture fenced in by sleek nautical rails. More often than not, her father had to scramble to remove the cushions before they could be torn free by fierce winds. This close to the ocean, sunbathing days were rare, and Kathryn saw that the cushions had been permanently removed, revealing blonde, salt-stained wood.

She and Kerry had promised to start "communicating again," whatever that meant. She sipped her wine, craving the drowsy buzz, as she watched the fog move in. Mist hugged the water under the bridge, and thick, gray tides sluggishly rolled in not far behind. Behind her, the big-screen television flickered in the living room, the rest of the house glowing with what Philip had dubbed "fog combat lighting."

She'd left the TV tuned to the Weather Channel and its endless footage of snow plows crawling down I–95, Boston seen through a white, hazy, swirl, weather maps showing what looked like a giant purple omelet lying across the Eastern seaboard. Her mother had been right. She'd made it out just in time. The Thanksgiving Blow was unseasonable and unpredicted. But the sight of it made her strangely homesick for Atherton, and conjured up images of Randall enduring Thanksgiving dinner in his parents' Park Avenue apartment. Making no effort to call her, just as she had made no effort to call him. With a jolt she realized she didn't have his phone number at home.

That can't be right, she thought. She was about to go check her address book when she was startled by her mother, removing plates of leftovers from the fridge. Kathryn stopped several steps inside the deck door, the empty wineglass in her hand making her feel caught. "You want something?" Kathryn didn't look at her.

Marion saw Kathryn's wineglass and arched an eyebrow before she went about preparing herself a plate. "How was she?" she finally asked.

"All right," Kathryn answered, trapped between her mother and the deck door. "It sounds like she's been to therapy."

"Poor baby," Marion said under her breath, with a tinge of disdain.

"Excuse me?"

Stony-faced but righteous, her mother set down her spoon, still filled with a clot of sweet potatoes. She braced herself against the kitchen counter.

"You think she deserves it, don't you?" Kathryn asked.

"No. But I don't think she's a victim either."

"What about me?"

Marion looked right at her daughter. "You're fine. Aren't you?"

"I may not be sick, but I'm not fine." Kathryn tightened her grip on the stem of her wineglass in hopes that it would keep her from hurling it to the floor. "Mom, have you ever stopped judging me long enough to ask yourself what I was feeling?"

Marion folded her arms against her chest, looking her daughter up and down as if to make sure she hadn't imagined the words she had just spoken.

"Are you serious?" she asked softly. "I asked myself all the questions that I needed to. I drove you to the doctor, I was there when the results came back, and every time I asked myself if I was capable of caring for you. If I was capable of losing you. And I'll be honest. I wasn't happy with the answer that I came up with."

"I can't listen to this," Kathryn said, one hand already on the deck door.

"Then you shouldn't have asked!" Marion retorted.

Kathryn turned. "It's not about your anger! It wasn't about you at all."

Marion's stare was fixed. "Exactly. I had to prepare myself to have my daughter's life cut short by someone I didn't even know existed. To a *murderer* who knew what he had. And now, what does it matter that this guy didn't get my daughter sick or addicted to drugs? Because he managed to take her away from me anyway. She has no interest in seeing me or her father, and suddenly everything I've ever done for her has been erased by a guy I never even knew. But you're *fine*, Kathryn. You're away at school and you don't ever want to look back. And quite frankly, after all the energy I spent, I just can't fight that son of a bitch any more."

Marion's eyes had welled and she let out an exhausted breath, bowing her head and shaking it slowly back and forth. "Judge you, Kathryn?" she said, sounding weaker. "How could you think that? I wanted to *save* you. And for the first time, I couldn't."

"You're right," Kathryn said, softly. "You couldn't."

Marion lifted her head, not in anger, but at the sound of apology in Kathryn's voice.

"You think I hold that against you?" Kathryn asked.

Slowly, as if summoning courage, Marion closed the distance between them. She cupped Kathryn's chin in one hand, as if she was debating whether or not to embrace her. "I don't ever want you to know how much I worry about you"

Hesitantly, Marion released her chin and returned to the counter. Kathryn waited—yearned—for her mother to say more, but Marion had returned to assembling her plate, sluggishly, as if the wind had been knocked out of her. Kathryn studied her for several more minutes, waiting for her mother to continue and push them a little bit further over the divide they had approached so quickly and unexpectedly. "I can make you a plate," Marion finally said.

Kathryn nodded before realizing her mother wasn't looking at her. "Sure," she said.


She managed to telnet into Atherton's network.

There was one message in her inbox, and it wasn't from Randall. She opened it.

> Kathryn,
>
>   I've found the image of you in fog-shrouded San Francisco to be increasingly troubling each time it pays a visit. This is obviously latent something or other on my part, and I'm sure with your keen insight, we could figure out just what. Let's make a start. Give me your flight number and the time you're returning on Sunday.
>
>                        Solicitously,
>                        Mitchell Seaver

She was halfway through typing her response when she realized she was grinning at the computer screen.

# CHAPTER TEN

By Friday afternoon, the nor'easter was moving inland. Frail flakes fell over the intersection of Victoria and Prospect, where a utility truck sent flashes of its yellow bridge lights over shuttered windows and snow-covered driveways. Randall slowed his steps, watching as a cherry picker rose with a metallic groan, carrying a utility worker bundled so tightly against the cold he looked like he was tending to a toxic spill instead of a tangle of frozen branches and coiled wire. The gray sky could pass easily for dawn or dusk. Without power, time had become relative.

For the first time, duty and not desire drove him to Eric's house. He yanked his scarf tight around his neck, then drove his hands into his jacket pockets. Snowdrifts covered the sidewalk, but the truck had cut a path up the center of the street. He followed it, his footsteps crunching the tread-packed snow, each step taking him closer to the mission that now offered only partial redemption, if not in Kathryn's eyes, than maybe his own, and further away from Jesse and his ludicrous but tempting invitation that had followed his successful quest to be the physical embodiment of Randall's weakness.

Randall eased open the back gate. On the back porch, Eric was squatting, struggling with something. Randall rounded the porch and mounted the first step silently. Eric still didn't notice him: he was too busy wrestling with a wooden case of wine bottles. He had the stem of one bottle gripped in both hands. As he yanked, his heavy coat slid farther down his back, revealing nothing more than a T-shirt underneath. It didn't take long to see why the wine bottle was stuck; its bottom had exploded and a blossom of urine-colored ice adhered to the bottom of the case.

"You should try the fridge."

Eric let out a grunt and jumped. The wine bottle shattered and he landed on his butt with a hollow thud, holding the top half of the bottle in one hand like a weapon. He tossed it aside and brought his forearm across his nose. "Where have you been?"

His eyes were bloodshot and his nose was running profusely. For a moment Randall wondered if he was sick. But he was just too drunk to have bundled up properly before going outside. He got up, dusting off his jeans with his gloved hands. "You missed the big feast."

"I should have called. I'm sorry."

"You coming in?" Eric kicked open the back door for Randall to enter. He left it open behind him.

The kitchen was dark, but candlelight from the dining room guided the way. Randall halted in the doorway, silently appalled at the sight that greeted him. Eric had assembled a Thanksgiving feast out of supermarket takeout cartons. A pre-sliced turkey took up the entire center of the table, fringed by cartons of yams, cranberry sauce and stuffing. He'd stuck tea candles into the fray and in the electrical outage their flames gave the illusion that the food was crawling with tiny insects. Aside from appearing revolting, the spread reminded Randall of too many jerrybuilt holidays he had endured, thrown together with only the decorative trappings that failed to force out the cheer.

"It's only been there a day." Eric moved past him into the living room, where he swiped an open bottle of wine off the mantel and upended it. The result was a weak splash that barely filled the glass halfway. Eric glowered at the empty bottle for a second before returning it to the mantel. He turned around to see Randall still frozen in the doorway to the dining room.

"I'm not hungry," Randall said.

"Something to drink? I managed to salvage another bottle. It's in the fridge."

"Something harder."

"Afraid I can't help you there." Randall's eyes shot to the liquor cabinet across the room. Eric took a seat at the head of the table. "You didn't expect me to keep that stuff forever, did you? Funny. In the beginning, I thought it would be childish to throw it all out. Yesterday I had plenty of time to myself to reconsider." Eric leveled his gaze on Randall, then he smiled tightly and lifted his glass in toast. "Valinger. A small vineyard outside Santa Barbara. I have to special order it, so needless to say, I'm not pleased about the accident on the back porch."

"Why do you keep it outside?"

"Habit."

"Bummer. I thought it was some kind of tradition."

To Randall's disgust, Eric picked up his empty plate and started shoveling day-old turkey onto it. "It started when I was a senior here. Our . . . my refrigerator broke while I was working on a paper and I didn't have time to get it fixed, so the . . . man I was living with, he and I started chilling our wine on the back porch. It just became habit."

"No time to buy a fridge, but you still had time to enjoy a good white," Randall commented. Eric's blank expression told Randall he was only going to laugh at jokes he'd made himself. Unsteadily, feeling derailed from his mission of finding the key to Lisa's storage locker, Randall sank down into the chair opposite Eric's.

"Where have you been?"

"You were worried?" Randall asked.

Eric shrugged.

"You thought I had wandered off into Elms like Pamela Milford?"

Eric's eyes flared slightly; Randall would have missed it if he hadn't been looking for it. He pushed his plate back without touching anything on it, proof that assembling it had just been an attempt to drive home the fact that Randall hadn't called.

"I was at the dorm," Randall finally said.

"Two days at the dorm without power. What did you do?"

Randall fought a vision of Jesse's hands pinning his wrists to the pillow on either side of his head. "Not much." He straightened in his chair. "Maintenance finally came by yesterday and opened all the doors. When the power went out, the ID readers got all fucked up, so I couldn't leave or else I wouldn't be able to get back in."

Eric's disbelief was evident in the three seconds he took to glare at

Randall across the table. He sat back in his chair and drank the last of his wine. "Did you call them? Tell them you weren't going to be able to make it?"

"My parents?" Randall asked, with sharp anger intended to warn Eric off the topic.

"They must be worried."

"They're not."

"Why not?"

"None of your goddamn business."

Eric smiled dryly, shook his head, and clucked his tongue. He sat forward propping both elbows on the table. Randall's hands gripped his knees hard enough to hurt. *The key*, he thought, *I'm here for the fucking key*. But first, Randall knew, he would have to endure another interrogation from a man who had lied to himself for the past twenty years.

"It's always what you're not, isn't it?" Eric asked.

"Excuse me?"

"Every time I raise the subject of who you are, or where you came from, all I get from you is a list of things you refuse to be." Eric stretched his arms out in front of him, cracked his knuckles and rose from the table. "I have something to show you," he said, moving into the living room.

Randall watched him root through a pile of papers on the table next to his reading chair. He returned carrying a piece of paper, which he dropped onto Randall's empty plate. For several seconds, Randall didn't touch it. He could read it from where he sat. Three terse sentences requesting a leave of absence at the end of the semester without stating a reason why. Eric settled back into his chair.

"Read it to me."

"Fuck you," Randall whispered.

"What was that?" Eric asked, cupping one ear. "You don't like it? You can always toss it into the fire."

"I didn't tell Kathryn anything, Eric!"

"Why do I find that next to impossible to believe?" Eric barked. "What are you going to say now, Randall? That I should be proud that I was such an accomplishment for you? That you just couldn't resist bragging to your friends that you'd managed to bed your married professor?"

"You are *nothing* to brag about. And I'm starting to feel just as ashamed of this as you are."

Eric looked briefly stung, but then he replaced the look with one of feigned concentration. "Finally. What *you* feel! Maybe the minute you start considering yourself something other than my mistake, you might realize that your lapses in character are just as bad as the ones you've accused me of."

Randall got up and turned from the table before anything about his failing composure would give Eric an idea of how deep a scar he was prodding at.

"Start with your parents!"

Randall hurried to the back door. He heard Eric knock his chair back onto the floor. He was almost out the back door when Eric grabbed his shoulder and spun him around. Randall batted at Eric's arm, but Eric managed to catch his wrist in a vise grip and Randall grimaced at Eric's alcoholic rasps. "Enlighten me! Why is it that they have no desire to see you on Thanksgiving?"

Randall groped for the doorknob with his free hand. Eric twisted Randall's wrist with drunken force, bending his arm against the joint. "Eric!"

"Come on, Randall! You're so *bright*! Can't you see how generous I'm being? I'm giving you a chance to convince me that you're something more than the rotten little shit I think you are. Rise to the occasion!"

Eric released him, and before Randall could catch his breath, Eric had him by both shoulders, shoving him against the back door with enough force to rattle the glass pane. "Argue with me! Show me the real you!"

Randall was intimate with this kind of fury, this rage that a self-hating man could summon in seconds. He twisted his head away, but Eric cupped his chin in one hand, fingers pulling at his lips.

"I think you didn't go home because your parents already know that you're the person I'm starting to see. A spoiled brat who learned how to be an adult from back issues of *Vanity Fair*! A stupid little boy with no idea of the damage he's capable of doing. You, Randall, can only charm someone for so long before he figures out what you really are. And imagine *my* disappointment to learn that you're not much better than a *whore*!"

Randall seized Eric's crotch and ground it in his fist. Eric's mouth opened in a silent O before Randall tightened his grip and shoved. Eric's feet stuttered over the linoleum before he keeled over backward, hitting the floor at the small of his back.

Randall bent down over him. "I've been up against a lot more frightening men then you in my life. Men who've done a lot more than slowly kill their own wives. If you ever touch me again, I'll show *exactly* what kind of damage I can do!"


By the time he made it to Overlook Park, the cold had dried out his eyes. Randall clawed snow from one of the benches and sat down. Night darkened the sky over the powerless city below, throwing the concrete edges of buildings into relief, turning the streets into rivers of shadow. The snow had let up and the wind had all but died. The aftershock of Eric's drunken violence had faded more quickly than the sting of his words, now amplified in Randall's head by the dark silence.

Before Atherton, Randall had cherished times of silence and solitude as opportunities to imagine a better self, down to enough detail that by the time something would pull him out of his daze, he would have managed to catch a brief glimpse of who he wanted to become. But in the past four months, this comforting exercise had been stolen from him by the first people he had cared for in years. His silences became crowded with their startling visions of who they thought he was. And as Randall realized how inaccurate those visions were, he was forced to question for the first time whether his own aspirations and ambitions were pathetic and unattainable dreams.

Eric was a murderer. With his own identity called into such serious question, Randall had to cling to that truth with all he had. If discovering the truth behind Lisa's death couldn't exonerate him in Kathryn's eyes, then proving Eric was a killer would help Randall deal with the burden of what had brought him to Atherton in the first place.

He was staring down at his boots when he noticed several frail bars of light stretching across the snow toward the fence. Surprised, he lifted his head. Electricity was returning to Atherton in a low symphony of metallic whines and groans; the sign on top of the Yankee

Savings & Trust Building winked on, a yellow halo through fog. He blinked against the amber light punching through shutters, the stark halos of street lights shining on piled snow. In his left eye, the light went blurred.

He reached up, delicately sliding the blue disc over his brown pupil with one gloved finger.

Voices were shouting at each other upstairs, muffled through the ceiling. Eric stopped halfway to the kitchen, still holding the platter of turkey in his hands.

For a second, it sounded like giant fingers were tapping against the walls of the house. Then he realized that the clicks and groans were the lights coming back to life. The voices upstairs came from the television he'd left on in the bedroom: two meteorologists discussing the nor'easter's dissolving strength as it swept inland. With power restored, harsh light fell unflatteringly across the ruined feast on the dining-room table. The house's sudden light made the past two days seem like a smeared, drunken unreality. The throbbing in his forehead came back to life as well. He numbly set the platter back down and sat in one of the dining-room chairs, wondering what he had hoped to accomplish with the words he'd hurled at Randall.

The mere mention of his parents dented the young man's composure; Eric was convinced that his parents were abusive, and that the burns on Randall's legs were the result of a deliberate act. Discovering whether or not that was true would have forced Randall to admit that he was something much worse than a thing of beauty who had bestowed upon Eric the gift of his body.

Rage. That's what he wanted from Randall. Some fissure down the center of the young man's demeanor that could reveal a fault line of guilt and remorse equal to what Eric felt. He was lying to himself if he believed he had simply wanted to punish Randall for letting their secret get out. He wanted to see the boy undone. His motive had been the same when he showed Randall Lisa's parting note.

But had it worked? Randall had shown rage, but no guilt, at least not regarding Lisa. It was almost as if Randall was too preoccupied by a larger evil, without the time or the energy to seek repentance for his affair with Eric. He couldn't begin to fathom what evil, but it didn't matter because he'd lost him for good. And it wasn't consolation to tell himself that keeping Randall at all was improbable, preposterous, and downright wrong.

Eric crossed to the front windows. Outside, the streetlights illuminated the snow-covered street with a surgical illumination that drained the scene of any winter romance. He hadn't sobered enough, because he was searching for Randall's shadow somewhere between the streetlights.

Gone. Never mind the ache, he told himself, just convince yourself that driving him away was the right thing to do. And given your history, is it any surprise that you've accomplished the right thing in the worst way possible?

Not this house, but another near it. Not this new decade, and not the one before it, but nineteen years before. Not Randall, but another young man, with the same startling blue eyes, and guided by a similar brutal passion.

If Eric didn't spend the money his mother left him, it would continue to drive home the suddenness of her death. Its presence in his bank account would summon and resummon the phone call from a breathless grocery clerk informing him that an ambulance had just carried her away after she fell down right in front of the store. The only way to make the money less haunting was to take the money and do something with it that was all his own.

It was August 1982, and Eric had no vision of life that extended beyond the campus of Atherton University. He had convinced himself that his transition into the Ph.D. program the following year would be simple; he had ingratiated himself with all the right professors. At night, he would lie awake debating whether he should move on, but he would fall asleep before answering. The perfect way to seal his fate was to use his mother's money to buy a house near campus.

The ad made it clear the place was a dump. Overgrown hedges concealed the brownstone's first-floor windows. A brick fence crowned with spikes lined the perimeter of the bush- and weed-ridden front yard. The view from this part of the hill was of industrial and unsightly

Atherton, with its smokestacks sending plumes of black smoke toward gray sky. Walking slowly up the front path, Eric, at twenty-two, saw the house as perfect for the contemplation, isolation, and brooding he now regarded as essential to the nourishment of his mind.

He stepped cautiously into the foyer, even though he was fairly certain he would be the only prospective buyer to show up at the minimally advertised open house. A staircase, bowed and warped, led to the second floor. Wires dangled from the ceiling, suggesting the foyer had once been lit by a chandelier. The house was decrepit without being haunted and he had already fallen in love with it.

But he was not alone. The man in the living room held one bent wrist against his waist, as he ran his other hand over a windowsill. The posture was oddly theatrical, but the man did not check his fingers for dust. Maybe he was just testing the quality of the wood. Only when he turned did Eric recognize him. The man's piercing blue eyes looked Eric up and down and his thin slash of a mouth bent into the best crooked smile it was capable of.

"We know each other," the man said.

"You're a sculptor," Eric answered.

Michael Price let out a grunt and shook his head as if he had been reminded of a memory too distant to remain unpleasant. "Kinetics of Form?" he asked, moving closer.

Eric nodded, noting that with Michael's much-talked-about change of majors had also come a change of appearance. The one time "artiste" had traded in his paint-splotched work clothes for yuppie tweeds. His black mop of hair had been cut almost militarily short. Everything about his appearance was more streamlined, more clipped, than that of the passionate duplicator of the human form who so ardently defended himself against accusations that he would never be an artist. Had Michael Price given in to the demands of a businesslike world, or did all architecture majors dress as if they had just come from a board meeting?

When he realized he had been staring at the man for more than a few seconds, Eric thrust his hand in front of him and Michael looked down at it, amused. At last he shook it without enthusiasm. "Nice place, isn't it?" he asked.

"I think so," Eric answered.

Michael moved through the room, hands clasped against the small of his back, surveying the house as if he already owned it. "It could use work, though. I wonder if the landlord's willing to put in the time. And the dough."

"The house isn't for rent. It's for sale."

Michael halted his proprietary stroll. "Really? Well, I just saw the realtor sign out front."

Eric shrugged as if forgiving Michael for having intruded, even though the house wasn't his yet.

"You're looking to buy?" Michael asked with a twinge of skepticism.

"Yes."

Michael stared at him as if waiting for him to contradict himself. Eric could think of nothing more to say. He sensed the sudden weight in the air between them. The odd, fluttery sensation in his chest he felt at being fixed in Michael Price's eyes—was it related to the fact that Eric had quietly managed to keep tabs on the guy ever since they were in class together? Only later would he realize how many decisions could be made in a deceptively brief moment.

"I'm sure I could use a tenant, though," Eric heard himself say.

"You haven't even bought it yet." Michael was obviously amused.

"You see anyone else here?"

Later he would tell himself that it was his only recourse. That if he wanted to be anywhere near Michael Price, he had to put himself in a position of power over this man who had such an inexplicable power over him. In return for a low rent, Michael agreed to help with the renovations, and during the following three months they shared less talk than effort and sweat as they painted, caulked, and refinished the time-beaten interior of the house. And as they worked, it became clear to both of them that regardless of paperwork, they would share the house equally. Michael allowed Eric his silences, but with the confidence of someone who didn't expect or need, but *knew* he would be gratified as soon as they were over. And through their minimal conversations during that time their attraction for each other built, until that sharp, late-fall day when they stood in the restored living room, the single piece of furniture a ratty sofa pushed to one freshly painted white wall, the only sound the click of the gas feeding the pilot flames of the newly installed gas space heaters, when

Michael removed a long, slender gift box from the inside pocket of his trench coat.

Michael extended it to him. Eric's hands were sweaty, shaking slightly as he opened the box; Michael chuckled when he noticed, and even though Eric found the laugh unsettling, maybe a bit malicious, he went about unfolding the tissue paper inside.

But then Michael reached in and tore the red cashmere scarf from the box, whipping it through the air like a triumphal banner, before hooking it around Eric's neck. "Something to keep you warm until you get back home," Michael said in a low, resonant voice.

Eric kept his neck bowed, his fists twisted in cashmere.

"It's beautiful," he whispered, before he realized Michael was still holding the scarf at both ends, tugging gently.

"Look what we made," Michael whispered before he pulled Eric's mouth to his.


Thanksgiving traffic turned I-95 into a river of brake lights, and twenty minutes after picking Kathryn up at Logan, Mitchell was forced to slow the Tercel to a crawl before they were stopped completely. The snow she'd missed out on was piled along the side of the freeway in melting slush piles. Kathryn was tempted to ask Mitchell if she could smoke. Then she noticed him peeking at her out of the corner of his eye.

"Stop that."

"What?" Mitchell asked innocently.

"Haven't you read *Ways of Seeing* by John Berger?"

Mitchell shook his head, amused.

"All women have a third eye. We use it to watch ourselves. So when a guy stares at us, it's basically another set of eyes we have to deal with. And some of us *can't* deal."

"If you weren't so self-conscious about being self-conscious, I might believe you were actually insecure," Mitchell said.

"Thanks, Dr. Seuss."

Mitchell grinned in satisfaction. He seemed unfazed by the gridlock traffic, but it was starting to get to Kathryn. She drummed her fingers on the door handle.

"Go ahead," Mitchell said.

"What?"

"Light up. I won't say anything."

Kathryn let out an exaggerated sigh of relief and promptly dug into her backpack for her cigarettes. She cracked the window and exhaled her first drag with dramatic slowness. The glare of headlights blotted out the landscape on either side of the freeway, aggravating her feeling that the last several hours had cut her tether from all that was familiar in her life.

"You know," Mitchell said, breaking the silence, "last time I checked, it was flying west that was getting you down."

Kathryn shrugged. "It was a good trip. I needed to see my parents."

"That act's not going to win you an Oscar."

Kathryn laughed and squinted at him, trying to ascertain if his persistent interest was for real. "It's nothing. I just . . . Randall and I had a fight before I left."

"What about?" Mitchell asked, his words short, sounding put off by the mention of Randall's name.

Kathryn clenched. Was it right, this urge to protect Randall, to keep a secret he had devoted so much time, energy, and deception to keeping from her?

"Randall's sleeping with one of his professors."

"I see."

"I mean, I didn't think anyone actually *did* that. I thought it was just a bad joke, you know? Like, screw your professor to get an A." She puffed at the cigarette. Up ahead, police lights marked the scene of the accident holding up traffic. The cars surrounding them began inching forward, and soon Mitchell was able to put his foot on the gas once again.

"Actually," Mitchell said, sounding as if he had needed the last minutes to formulate an appropriate response, "I think there are a lot more professor-student relationships out there than anyone would like to admit." He seemed put off by this fact and stared darkly ahead. "I take it you didn't know."

"No. I didn't."

"That's unfortunate. I hope you're the only one who does know. Otherwise this professor is in some serious danger."

"I don't know anything about this guy. I mean, I don't even know if Randall's in love with . . ."

A knot tightened in her stomach. Dr. Eberman. The professor Mitchell worked under, for the love of God. She turned her face to the window. The Tercel was gathering speed and the wind through the cracked window threatened to tear the tip from the Camel. She brought the cigarette to her mouth and took a long drag that burned.

"I doubt it's about love."

"Mitchell. I really shouldn't . . ."

"The only reason I asked is because . . . Well, let me put it this way. Newly uprooted freshman arrives at school, away from home for the first time  Freedom to spare, but without the experience or, forgive me, maturity to figure out just what to do with it. It's logical that he seeks out some sort of faux authority figure. An authority figure he can control."

"Control?" she asked, intrigued but skeptical.

"With sex," Mitchell answered.

"Keep going."

"I'm of the belief that these professor-student relationships are more about an exchange of power than they are about . . . love." He said the last word with evident disdain. "My working theory would be that Randall receives a kind of authority and direction from this professor. But it's on his terms. He can withdraw when he'd like to. Withhold sex if the professor gets too parental."

"What does the professor get?" she asked.

"A sexual partner he too can manipulate, until he decides to dispose of him in the name of decency."

Kathryn couldn't help a pained grunt. Thinking of Randall as a liar was a lot easier than viewing him as an easy mark for heartbreak.

"This doesn't bore you?" she asked

"What do you mean?"

"I don't know, I just feel like I keep dumping this shit on you every time we see each other. The petty intrigue of my little dorm unit."

"Well, yes  But it's your shit, Kathryn."

She had to laugh.

"I'm certainly not surprised," Mitchell went on. "I've taught freshmen in discussion sections for almost a good two years now. I happen to know they're the most self-analytical creatures on the planet.

They're on their own for the first time, so suddenly they're examining every minor decision they make as if each one was an embodiment of their true identity. And half the energy they should devote to feeding their minds they spend trying to create some sort of aura of identity out of their own verbiage."

"I'm praying you're not talking about me right now."

"Oh, no. Your powers of analysis seem to have been devoted entirely to someone else."

It bit hard and sank deep, but Mitchell had no way of knowing that—until he saw her glowering at the harsh light of the highway ahead. "Which might not have been such a bad thing. If Randall hadn't lied to you."

Kathryn kept silent until Mitchell hooked onto an off ramp she didn't recognize.

"Where are we going?"

"My place. Is that all right?"

Realizing he had never once mentioned where he lived, she was surprised. And excited. "Absolutely," she answered as calmly as possible.


Bayfront Storage had no sign. Behind a chain-link fence topped with battered coils of razor wire, two banks of single-story, garage-size lockers were laid out in an L shape. The neighborhood was mostly abandoned warehouses, their cargo doors left open or splintered, offering unwanted glimpses of shadowy possibilities inside.

With one hand on the steering wheel, Tim reached over and popped the glove compartment and dug inside, feeling for something Randall couldn't see. "What are you doing?"

"Checking something."

"Oh, for the love of God, Tim!"

"For your information"—Tim found some identifiable part of the gun Randall guessed he was looking for, withdrew his hand, and snapped the glove compartment shut—"once you leave the safety of our little hill behind, Atherton happens to be one of the most crime-ridden cities north of New York. Besides, it's only a .25 caliber semi. My mom used to keep it in her purse, till she did some research on my new place of residence."

The place was devoid of all life, like the neighborhood. "I thought they'd at least have a dog."

"Sixty bucks a month doesn't get you top-notch security."

"Pull up a little bit," Randall said.

"What do you mean he *attacked* you?"

"I mean, he threw me up against a wall and called me a whore. For the tenth time. Can you pull up, please?"

Tim shook his head and complied. They sat on a steel-girder bridge that crossed over a drainage canal. The canal's sloping concrete walls funneled ice-strewn debris toward the bay, several blocks to their left. Evenly surfaced maintenance walkways had been set in the walls in a steplike formation. The highest walkway was a five-foot drop from the bridge's rail.

Randall tapped the window. "See? The fence ends."

Tim bent forward over the armrest. The chain-link fence stopped perpendicular to a concrete wall that matched the fence in height, but, blessedly, was free of the razor wire. The wall ran twenty feet down the top of the canal. On the other side sat one bank of lockers. "Back up a little bit."

Tim let out an annoyed snort, but complied. "So, you didn't get a chance to look for the key?"

"No," Randall answered, eyes out the window.

"So what? He just flipped out?"

"He was drunk." Randall almost sighed when the lockers came into view again; the two banks didn't meet. "How high do you think that back wall is?"

"High."

Randall turned. "For two people?"

Tim grimaced as if in the throes of a migraine headache. "Come on, Randall!"

"Look, if we can get over the back wall and into that alley, we can just walk out into the middle of the parking lot. We'll be right in front of her locker."

"And then what?"

Randall examined the lockers nearest to the fence. Padlocks dangled from their garage style doors "It would be basically breaking and entering if we had the key or not, Tim. No one was going to give us permission," he said. Tim slumped against the driver's seat. "Tim," Randall said more carefully. "Look around. A woman coming down here by herself. This was a secret."

"One last time," Tim insisted. "What the hell did Eric do to you?"

"I showed up. He was drunk . . ." Randall stopped. How could he have forgotten? Eric's violent outburst had almost blotted out the memory, that was why. "He emptied out the goddamn liquor cabinet."

"You're just remembering this now?" Tim asked, urgently.

"Shit," Randall whispered.

"He knows you have the bottle, Randall. That's why he flipped out!"

"Maybe not. He was pissed because Kathryn knows."

"Kathryn. Murder weapon." Tim lifted his hands as if they were scales, and then dropped his right one hard. "You decide!"

Tim drove with the speed and quick thinking of a white boy trying to get out of the ghetto, and soon they were speeding through desolate downtown. "If he gets his leave of absence, when does it start?" he asked.

"End of the semester."

"That's barely four weeks from now."

"Not much time."

Tim didn't interrupt with a shrill plea for Randall to run to the authorities, and Randall was relieved. The reporter could finally see his big story taking shape. "I'm about to tell you something I probably shouldn't," Tim said.

"Why's that?"

"Because it violates a little pact I made with myself. You remember, the one about not getting involved in this just so you could sleep better?" Tim glanced at him sourly. "I talked to Richard."

"Goddammit, Tim!"

Tim held up one palm to quiet him. "I didn't tell him squat. And he didn't think it was unusual, considering we talked so much about Eberman when the accident happened. So chill and let me finish." Randall sat back, still steamed, still scared. "Do you remember what time you got to Eric's house that night?"

Randall thought for a second. "It had to be after eight, 'cause I called around seven thirty and Eric thought Lisa was already on her way to Paula's."

"She was," Tim answered. "Richard told me the 911 call reporting the accident was placed at seven thirty."

Something inside of Randall leaped, and he twisted against his seat belt. "You didn't know this before?" Randall almost shouted.

"I didn't ask before. And look, it doesn't mean Lisa didn't know about the two of you. The only reason I even bothered to check is because *Eric* has to know what time that call was placed. So he probably knows there's no possible way she was driving like a madwoman because she had just seen the two of you in bed together. But that's still what he wanted you to think"

Randall felt a surge of satisfaction. He spotted the bridge up ahead and expected Tim to make a left turn. "It's good to know you're still on my side," he said quietly. Any distance—of time or otherwise—between him and Lisa's death was a small relief. But that left the matter of her note. What did she know, and what did she see?

As the Jeep moved across the bridge, both of them noted wordlessly that it had been repaired, the barricade removed, the newly placed metal a polished blemish against the length of weathered rail.

Randall stepped out of Tim's Jeep amid returning students lugging their suitcases up the front walk of Stockton. He fell into step with them, then heard Tim call out to him, "Kathryn!"

Confused, Randall pivoted around to see that Tim had lowered the window.

"How did she find out?" Tim asked.

Randall searched for the best response as he approached the Jeep. When he saw Tim's arched eyebrows, he realized he was prepared for Randall to duck the question. So Randall answered as close to the truth as he could. "A little bird told her. But he's flown the coop."

"Anyone I know?"

"He barely knew anyone," Randall said, and walked away before Tim could ask him to elaborate.

# CHAPTER ELEVEN

ICE-LACED HEDGES CONCEALED THE FIRST-FLOOR WINDOWS OF THE brownstone. Mitchell held open the front gate and Kathryn passed through it, up the front walk through a generous front yard that had garden potential but was mostly snow-smothered grass and bushes. Two-thirty-one Slope Street sat behind a stone fence topped with cast-iron spikes. The shutters were drawn over all four windows in the house's stark brick facade.

For some reason, Kathryn had assumed Mitchell lived in one of the nicer row houses just east of campus, not far from his mentor, Dr. Eberman. She'd been surprised when he made a right several blocks short of the hill's crown, taking them into an unfamiliar neighborhood of low-end apartment complexes descending the hill's eastern slope. Compared to its neighbors, the brownstone seemed downright stately, a holdover from the neighborhood's better days.

"You live here?" she asked. Mitchell nodded, tugging his keys from his pocket as he moved past her.

He threw open the front door. She took a few hesitant steps into the darkened foyer. Mitchell flicked the switch and light from a brass chandelier fell on walls painted so white she almost squinted. She followed as Mitchell ducked into the living room. Another chandelier came on and she gasped.

Mitchell turned to see her reaction.

Kathryn held up both hands as if to shield her eyes.

"The Garden of Earthly Delights," Mitchell informed her proudly.

It took up the entire living-room wall, in vivid color and dizzying detail. She had glimpsed the painting before, but enlarged onto an entire wall its effect was overwhelming. The naked figures cavorting in a surreal garden of science-fiction–like fountains and gently rolling hills looked like pure anarchy. The scene showed pleasure taken to its most ghastly extreme. From where she stood in the doorway, the clusters of naked figures looked like swarming insects. The living room itself seemed designed not to distract from the reproduction. A faded Oriental rug covered the hardwood floor. The sofa and chairs were a muted beige. The other white walls suddenly made more sense; she guessed each one was a potential canvas.

As she approached the wall, she almost walked into the glass-topped coffee table; only its slight metal frame made it visible.

She felt Mitchell move next to her.

"It's . . ."

"Go ahead."

"It's too much."

"It should be," Mitchell answered, not offended.

"What's it supposed to be? Heaven?"

"Not even close. Earth."

"If you went to Woodstock, maybe."

Mitchell laughed. "Interesting you should say that. Hippies in the nineteen-sixties were all too eager to embrace the central panel as a glorification of their own beliefs about free love. Promiscuity. But of course, they conveniently forgot that this is only the central panel of a tripartite altar piece. Several inches to the left, Bosch punished these figures by piercing them with spears and feeding them to monsters." Mitchell sounded matter of fact, playing the museum director in his own home, but in his tone she could detect a hint of disdain for the naïve love children of the 1960s.

Kathryn backed up several steps, taking in the huge, colorful canvas, then turned to Mitchell, bringing their faces inches apart without meaning to. "Hell has no place in the living room, right?"

Mitchell met her gaze. "Not enough space."

"Well, it's kind of a dated idea anyway."

Mitchell backed away from her before sliding one arm out of his coat. "Dated? What do you mean?"

"The idea that we have to be shipped off someplace else to be punished for everything we've done. Aren't there enough punishments here on earth?"

Mitchell dropped his jacket on the sofa. "Exactly." His smile lifted his features so completely she felt a swell of pride. He gestured back to the wall. "Some scholars have nicknamed this Satan's garden. It's all the pleasures and temptations of the physical world. The evil influence of the flesh at its most beautiful."

Kathryn looked back at the wall. Memory struck: Folberg Library the night before break, Maria bent over a color photocopy of a painting—which, she now realized, must have been a Bosch—a grid designed for accurate enlargement. "I don't think it's that beautiful," she said.

"Something to drink?" Mitchell asked, surveying her.

"What do you have in the way of alcohol?" she asked with a grin.

"Wine?"

"White if you have it. Red will knock me on my ass."

"White's all I have, actually. From a special vineyard outside of Santa Barbara." Mitchell moved into the dining room, hitting the light switch as he went. Yet another chandelier threw light across a black wooden slab of a dining table fringed by six cream-colored upholstered chairs. Not the type of furniture you expected to find in a grad student's house. What she was seeing was a minimalist showroom. The muted colors and freshly painted walls suggested not only renovation, but almost an antiseptic cleanliness. It gradually occurred to her that there wasn't a single personal effect in the room. No photographs. Nothing on the walls beyond a mural so extravagant you could almost walk into its wild dream of a landscape.

She had picked up a candelabra from the mantel when Mitchell returned with her glass of wine. "These are nice," she said, turning it over in her hand. The candelabra were an identical pair in polished silver, but to each of their three candleholders someone had affixed a white pearl. "Did you make these yourself?"

"I did. Actually."

"Crafty," she said. Gay was what she meant.

Mitchell gently removed the candelabra from her hand and pointed her to the wall. "Bottom left. See the man bent over what looks like a giant fruit?" She did. The man's back was unnaturally, painfully arched as he bent over. The fruit—if you could call it that— opened like a blossom, spilling what looked like giant berries. "See the pearls?" Mitchell asked.

"That's what they are?" She asked, approaching the wall. Closer up they looked like marbles, but when she bent forward, she realized they had a sheen to them.

Mitchell was right behind her. "According to Catharism, the pearls represent the fallen souls of angels that have become trapped in the mud of the material and the physical. They are the souls of people still trapped within their physical shell, but spiritually alive. Cathars called them The Living Ones."

"Why six?" she asked.

"I'm sorry?"

"Is six some sort of significant number?"

Startled, he looked down at the candelabra in his hand and finally got the drift. "No. Three candleholders each. They had to match, didn't they?" He shrugged and returned it to the mantel. She nervously slugged her wine. Mitchell settled onto the couch, but she was too nervous to sit and continued looking at the Bosch, less to look at it then to have a safe place to rest her eyes.

"Are you renting this place?"

"No. I own it."

"Wow."

"I had a good lead. And you saw what the neighborhood is like."

She nodded, noticing that he had brought himself water back from the kitchen. "You're not going to join me?" she asked, lifting her glass.

"I drink only on special occasions."

"So I guess I'm not special, then?"

He smirked and met her eyes. "Annoying children are *special*."

Go for it, she told herself. "I think you know what I meant." She crossed to the couch, easing down next to him before she took another swallow of the wine. He watched her, his face tight, his eyes distant. "Thanks," she said softly.

"For what?"

"Picking me up at the airport. It meant a lot."

"It wasn't any trouble."

"Maybe not. But you were exactly who I wanted to see when I got off the plane."

His eyes narrowed and his wan smile tightened his jaw. At the sight of his discomfort, she downed the last of the glass and set it down on the coffee table with a hard click. "You've got to meet me halfway here, Mitchell."

"Maybe if I ask you how your trip went you could tell me the truth."

Kathryn felt abruptly abandoned. "Oh, I get it," she groaned. This wasn't Mitchell's regular reticence—this was about *her*. She got up from the sofa fast enough to quicken the wine's pulse in her temples. "Going on the way I did at dinner. About Jono. You think I'm damaged goods."

Mitchell folded his arms across his chest and cocked his head to one side in an exaggerated display of attentiveness as she continued. "Admit it. I scared you off. And let me tell you, you got the *Reader's Digest* version, buddy."

"I don't scare very easily," he said, his voice almost hard. "And if I did, why would I be asking you for the whole story?"

"Noblesse oblige. I learned that phrase from my roommate. Supposedly it means charity. But only if you're rich. And you"—she gestured to the surroundings—"are obviously rich."

Mitchell picked up her empty wineglass.

"Thank you. I'd love another."

He clucked his tongue against the roof of his mouth. Obviously, he'd intended to go and put her empty glass in the sink. But he got up from the sofa, bowed his head, and went to the kitchen. Part of her knew she might be blowing her chance with him, but another part thought his frigid response might be a sign of resistance going brittle and giving way. Yet another part of her already had a splitting headache, and behind all that churning lay the hard fact that if she didn't end up in Mitchell's bed, that meant going back to the dorm and encountering Randall.

Mitchell returned and she was touched to see he'd filled the glass all the way. She reached out to take it, but he didn't let go of the stem. "Go easy," he said.

"On what? You or the wine?"

From his blank expression, it looked like the line was a bomb. She gave the stem a tug, fingers wrapped around his, and he released the glass gently. "You don't want the whole story," she muttered before taking a slug. "He's dead anyway, so what does it matter?"

"Why don't you start by telling me how he died?"

"Why don't I start by moving on?" she snapped.

Mitchell didn't answer that and she let out a defeated breath. "Mitchell, I spent months listening to psychologists tell me how to make a chart of how angry I got and when. One of them told me that I might be able to deal with everything better if I cut caffeine out of my diet."

"They don't sound like very good psychologists. But it must have been traumatic if you decided to see them in the first place."

A question without a question mark on the end, she thought. Resting one hand on the mantel, she kept her back to him, hoping to conceal all evidence of her anger. "How did I get like this?"

"What do you mean?" Mitchell asked, his voice maddeningly even.

She swung around. "Here I am, with you, trying to find out if you're the least bit interested in me, and who do we end up talking about? Jono. And if not him, who else? Randall. When did I become reduced to nothing more than a product of other people's fuck-ups?"

"Betrayals."

"What?"

"Randall betrayed you. He lied to you. And it sounds like Jono might have done the same."

His face was as calm as a monk's, as if the truth of what he said was as self-evident as snowfall. She gauged his sincerity, searching for a hint of condescension, but she found none.

"If it's worth anything," he began carefully, "I don't think you're damaged goods."

"What do you think I am?"

"I think you're a young woman possessed of incredible convictions, and since you arrived here all your so-called friends have tried to convince you that your beliefs are wrong. As a result, you've learned how to laugh at yourself, set aside what you thought was true. Which might keep you relatively sane here at Atherton. But something happened with Jono, something that strikes you, a bright and articulate person, absolutely speechless. And the depth of that silence suggests that whatever you don't want to discuss has made you who you are right now."

"Jono killed himself." She took several seconds to summon her composure before lifting her glass as if to say, There you go. Mitchell's gaze remained fixed on her. The next logical question passed like a current between them: Why?

"Kathryn," Mitchell began, and she turned her back, expecting him to ask what she couldn't yet answer. "You may want a boyfriend. But I don't want to be something that temporary to you. I'd like to be the one who can listen to all the things you're afraid to say."

"He was sick."

No response came from behind her.

"He was HIV positive. And he knew. And he wasn't a drug dealer in the conventional sense. He never accepted cash."

"He knew. So you believe he was deliberately infecting . . ."

"I know he was." The words came out of her before she had time to realize it was the first time she had ever spoken them to anyone.

Mitchell let several seconds pass "But not you?"

"I dodged the bullet."

Finally, she turned around, having fought back tears and found anger. Mitchell hadn't moved from the couch. She met his eyes and he nodded slightly, as if a suspicion of his had been confirmed. "Is that what you wanted?" she asked.

"It's what you wanted. And you know it." His voice was gentle.

"It doesn't feel like something I would want."

"There's more, isn't there?"

"Mitchell, please."

"I'm not asking you to tell me now. I'm asking you to do something else."

She lifted her head from her wineglass.

"Write it," Mitchell told her.

"What? Like an essay?"

"Any way you like. Word it however you want. Just get it on paper. And get it out of you."

Stricken, she met his gaze and was frozen by its intensity.

A car engine sounded just outside the house. Mitchell shot up from the couch. "Excuse me."

Kathryn watched him duck into the kitchen. She downed all her wine and set the glass on the table.

In search of a bathroom, Kathryn mounted the stairs. She halted when she saw the giant harp leaning against the far wall of the landing. For a second she thought it might be a real instrument, but when she saw the giant mandolin—almost as tall as she was—leaning against the wall opposite, she realized they were some kind of sculptures. Even though they had been leaned against the wall, overhead tract lighting was positioned on them, suggesting that their placement was deliberate.

She ran her fingers over the top of the harp. Both pieces had been carved out of wood and painted meticulously to resemble real instruments. But something had abraded the paint from the top of the harp, revealing several thick swaths of raw wood.

No doubt both items had some sort of symbolic significance, but she hadn't gone to the bathroom since Chicago, and she didn't have time to ponder them. She looked around. The narrow hallway ran the length of the second floor. Three shut doors greeted her. She tried the knob on the one nearest her and it opened.

A single bedside lamp threw pale light across six single beds all crammed into one bedroom. Each bed had a frame of unfinished wood, with a matching nightstand and gooseneck lamp. Between the footboards, there was barely enough space to move through. As in the living room, she saw no personal belongings. Nothing distinguished one sleeping area from another. She thought of Stockton Hall, where everyone marked off personal space with a profusion of posters and framed photographs. In contrast, this room was downright eerie. Here the sterility she had first noticed downstairs had advanced absolutely. Even nuns' cells would at least have crucifixes and rosaries.

Outside, a car door slammed, startling her out of the room.

She shut the bedroom silently as she heard the sound of Mitchell's voice outside. She spotted a window at the far end of the hallway and moved to it. The slats on the shutters had been drawn shut, and she pushed the window upward with a minimum of noise. Her fingers pried at the shutter's clasp before she realized it had been painted shut. The best she could do was to pull the slats open. When she did, she saw the twin swaths of headlights in the house's driveway below. The metal gate hadn't been pulled shut behind the car.

Mitchell stood in the headlight's halos, speaking quietly to Maria, her arms folded over her chest in what had to be anger. Kathryn couldn't hear a word they said. Lauren Raines was strapped into the car's passenger seat. Maria turned from Mitchell, rounded the nose of the car, and bent forward through the open passenger window. Before she could finish whatever she was saying, Lauren unbuckled her seat belt and leaped from the car.

"She's here? Now?" Lauren cried. The words rose to her, sharp as smoke.

There was obvious excitement in her voice, but no sooner had she stepped from the car than Mitchell had her by both shoulders. Kathryn could make out Lauren's face as it fell—not only in disappointment, but in a sudden submission to authority. Mitchell's authority.

Maria took over the task of steering Lauren back into the passenger seat. That done, she rounded the nose of the car, whispering something fiercely to Mitchell as she went.

Unsure of what this exchange had meant, she knew that one thing was clear. Mitchell didn't live in this house alone, and when Lauren had told her she was "spending a lot of time off campus," this had to be the place she had been referring to. But why *wouldn't* Mitchell even mention his housemates in passing? Especially when she'd mentioned Maria and Lauren to him the night before break?

The car was backing out of the driveway and Mitchell was gone. She managed to shut the window silently and race back down the stairs. She arrived in the living room just as she heard the back door creak open.

By the time Mitchell returned, she was standing next to the mantel again.

"Who was that?"

"A housemate of mine."

"So you don't live here alone?"

"No." He answered flatly. His stretch and yawn seemed forced. "Would you like me to drive you back to Stockton?"

"We're done?" she asked.

"I've given you my thoughts. And you have my suggestion."

"An essay."

He nodded and dropped his arms to his sides. Part of her suspected that his suggestion was more for his sake than for hers. He obviously didn't have the stomach to listen to her discuss Jono at length.

"Sure. I'm ready," she said.

She lifted her eyes to the mantel where she saw the candelabra. Six pearls, she thought.

And six beds.

Mitchell's footsteps echoed in the foyer.

Randall sat cross-legged on his bed, Lauren Raines's essay on the comforter beside him, and *The Duality of Hieronymus Bosch* by Dr. Eric Eberman open before him to page 111, bookmarked with Lauren's STD results. When he'd first purchased the book, Randall had underlined scores of passages, all of them potential conversation topics he could use during his initial seduction. He had to use only two.

Even though Tim had dismissed Lauren's essay as irrelevant to Lisa's death, Lauren's words haunted Randall. Repeatedly he had been compelled to return to them late at night.

> How can I embrace my sexuality when all it does is try to sink its teeth into me?

Why the essay had been in Eric's house was still beyond him, and now that Eric had all but banished him from his home, the only place he might find answers would be in his sole published work.

He flipped pages until he came to a color plate of "Hell," the right wing of *The Garden of Earthly Delights* triptych. Anyone who refused to call Bosch a surrealist was an idiot; this depiction of damnation proved it. A giant knife blade extended from two severed human ears, carried by or crushing—it was impossible to tell—an army of the writhing and naked. Below what looked like the ruins of a city bombed out by the Nazis, brick-walled cavities emanating . . . a naked woman was lassoed to the spine of what looked like a giant mandolin. A naked man was strung up on the strings of a giant harp.

Randall found it all too absurd to be frightening, and it certainly didn't compel him to obey the dictates of an organized religion, which, he believed, did little more than indulge its members' fears. At the sight of the first bird-beaked man who arrived to deliver his punishment, outfitted in blue robes and wearing what looked like a mushroom on his head, Randall would laugh himself into oblivion before he could suffer for all eternity. He had glimpsed hell and this fanciful, fevered heretic's dream didn't even come close. Hell was the actual physical world you saw right in front of your eyes the minute you realized you no longer had a home, where every highway and street could swallow you up without delivering you anywhere. Hell was an open sky and flat plain. No monsters, and only a brief blast of fire now and then.

Yet it wasn't difficult to see why the images had such a hold on Eric. The man had nursed himself on such God-generated self-loathing there probably wasn't a doubt in his mind that he would end up in hell if he acted on his bodily desires. Of course, he would want it to be spectacular and theatrical.

Outside Stockton, Randall heard a car door slam, and got up to look out the window.

When Kathryn emerged from Mitchell Seavers's Tercel, jealousy and anger knotted his stomach. Was that prick his replacement? After she disappeared under the overhang of the entrance, Randall sat down on his bed, waiting endless minutes for the sound of her footsteps shuffling over the carpet in the hallway. To his surprise, he found himself staring longingly at Jesse's dark, empty side of the room. When he knew she was right outside, he wished for the first time in months that Jesse was right across from him, because now more than ever, he needed some comrade against Kathryn's iron judgment. But it was a futile wish and Randall found himself hoping that Jesse, wherever he was, was suffering.

He heard the door to Kathryn's room shut behind her; she didn't even pause outside her door.

After several long minutes, Randall got up, turned on his desk lamp, and returned his attention to Eric's book.

Twentieth-century viewers of Bosch's work have demonstrated a reluctance to view his *Garden of Earthly Delights* as a condemnation of human sexuality consonant with the established views of the medieval church. In particular, the central panel, with its deceptively beautiful depiction of a paradise earth, has been the subject of relentless speculation.

Wilhelm Frangier put forth a highly questionable but nonetheless wildly popular theory that the entire altar piece was commissioned by a secret heretical cult known as the Brethren of the Free Spirit, and that the central panel is actually a depiction of the cult's religious rites. Little is known about the Brethren of the Free Spirit beyond the fact that their practices included some form of ritual promiscuity, and that its members believed that unrestrained sexual activity was a method they could use to return themselves to the state of purity possessed by Adam before the fall. Consequently, its members were also known as Adamites

However, it is impossible to isolate the central panel from the altarpiece as a whole, and objective viewers must not forget that only several inches to the left, the same figures who take delight in the earth's fleshly pleasures are punished in hell for their joy.

*As if Eric would ever forget*, Randall thought.

Given the preponderance of evidence that Bosch may have been a mitigated Cathar who held the belief that the physical world was Satan's terrain, it is possible to speculate that the Brethren of the Free Spirit were not truly a sect of medieval "love children" reveling in the unbridled pleasures of the flesh, but rather a secret cult that used sexual promiscuity in a ritual fashion designed to help them escape the trappings of the flesh. *The Garden of Earthly Delights* might be a glorified depiction of one of their rites, which consisted of a single orgiastic burst of sensuality—in essence, an orgy designed to purge members of the day-to-

day temptations of the flesh. Perhaps for the Brethren of the
Free Spirit, freedom did not mean indulgence; it meant
purging.

He searched his memory for a clear recollection of the night when
he had discovered Lauren's essay. Eric and Mitchell had been arguing. But as he lurked in the driveway outside, Randall had barely been
able to make out their words. He'd heard Eric as he stood at the sink
in front of the kitchen window. Eric had asked to be kept in the dark.

Randall slid the book off his lap and picked up Lauren's essay.

At first reading, her words had seemed desperate to him. There
was little narrative in her essay; she opened with an overwrought para-
graph about *how* her uncle had poisoned her, and didn't reveal he had
even molested her until the second page. Whoever she had been writing to—Mitchell, Eric—Lauren had worked to detail the effects of
what had been done to her, not illuminate the events for an outside
reader who was unaware of her past. As a result, the entire essay had
almost a pleading tone to it.

Pleading for what? Randall asked.

After several minutes of staring out the window, an answer came to
him, striking in its simplicity.

Lauren Raines was asking for admission.

Randall tried to let this hypothesis take firmer shape in his brain.
But he was distracted by a clatter from across the hall, steady and constant. With growing certainty he opened the door and crossed the
hall. Kathryn's door was open and she was sitting intently at her desk,
her coat still on, and her flingers flying as if she were playing music.

Kathryn was typing.

# III

# The Garden
of Earthly
Delights

*Through shapes more sinuous than a sculptor's thought,*
*Tell of dull matter splendidly distraught,*
*Whisper of mutinies divinely quelled—*
*Weak indolence of flesh, that long rebelled,*
*The spirit's domination bravely taught.*

—EDWARD CRACROFT LEFROY,
"A Palaestral Study"

# CHAPTER TWELVE

"I'M STARTING TO WONDER ABOUT THIS MAN YOU LIVE WITH," SAID Pamela Milford one afternoon, when winter was still lingering, but slanting sunlight lanced the branches knobbed with new buds.

"What would you like to know?" Eric asked, unable to refer to him by name.

"What does he do?" she asked.

"He wants to be an architect. A great one."

"Will he? Be great, I mean."

Eric stopped walking, but Pamela did not release his hand. He stared off into space as if Michael's career ambitions required the deepest of thought. Truthfully, he was hesitant to look at her because he was terrified that although he had been seeing this woman for only three weeks, she would be able to read anything from the slightest tic in his face. How much longer before Pamela figured out that every night, after trying to infuse their requisite good-night kiss with more passion, and performing the obligatory running of hands around her body, he made the long walk back to 231 Slope Street to slip into his bed and wait for Michael's short knock on his bedroom door, praying that by the time Michael would have joined him beneath the covers his desire for the man's desperate kisses would evaporate?

"Eric?"

Finally, he looked at her. Her blonde hair had been blow-dried straight, brushed to her shoulders from a part in the center. On another girl, her slanted, pale blue eyes might have seemed too close together, but they were in proportion with her oval face and her tiny nose. The unseasonable cold had brought color to her otherwise pale skin. She was a small girl, but she looked perfect walking beside him.

She was his only escape, and he knew he had to chase this fixed and puzzled expression from her face.

"He might be. He has the ego."

"And it's just the two of you in that big house. How fun."

"We keep to ourselves."

"I'm sure he misses you. Since you've been spending so much time out of the house." She gave him a devilish smile, which appeared ludicrous because they had done little more than paw at each other's clothes in the shadow of the overhang above her dorm entrance. "We should all have dinner." It was a gentle command and she was waiting for him to agree.

But instead, he reached into his inside coat pocket. Now was as good a time as any to give it to her. He handed her the long gift box and she looked from it to him with a smile that indicated she had been successfully distracted.

She shook her head in pleasant disbelief as she opened the box, but when she finally saw the red cashmere scarf, she gasped.

"Eric! Where did you get it?"


"Dr. Eberman?"

Eric looked up to see Rhonda, the sweet-tempered, seventy-year-old departmental receptionist, standing in the half-open doorway to his office. "Someone's here?" he asked.

"Mitchell."

He nodded and moved to his desk chair. Only after his wife had died had Rhonda started showing up at his office to announce visitors. She must have thought that any unannounced visitor might provoke him into a nervous collapse.

Mitchell entered without looking at him or saying anything, casually closing the door behind him. No doubt the word of Eric's request for a leave had already permeated the department.

"I wanted to tell you first," Eric finally said.

"I found out from Maria. Dr. Moreau mentioned it to her this morning. She also managed to mention that you were next in line for department chair."

"I wasn't aware she was planning on stepping down."

"If you had been," Mitchell turned, "would that have affected your decision?"

Eric was surprised by the lack of anger on Mitchell's face. "I've asked for a leave of absence. I haven't resigned," he said.

"You can't blame any of us for thinking this is just the first step."

Eric shook his head in weak denial and lowered his eyes to his desk. Despite the violence that accompanied it, telling Randall about his departure was nothing compared to this. His commitment to Mitchell, while chaste, ran deeper. But in a way, it reduced him to the same feeling of helplessness. As with Randall, he had given in to too many of Mitchell's demands and then lacked the courage to put a stop to the young man's plans when he knew he should have. For a while, Eric had given Randall free rein over his body. But with Mitchell, Eric had given his intellectual blessing to a mission that was doomed from the very start. Eric realized the full scope of what his leave would allow him to escape, and sought for ways to soften the blow for the young man who had once been his star pupil before he became driven by the desire to convert others.

Back to business, Eric thought, and kill the guy with kindness while you're at it. "I'm assuming Phil Wick is going to take over the second semester of Foundations."

"Wick's a pompous ass. He'll hand over the course to us."

"Which might not be a bad thing."

Mitchell gave him a cool smile. "Maria's furious."

"That young woman was born furious. How the two of you managed to become compatriots is beyond me. You're a scholar and her only goal is to attack and deconstruct all the mechanisms she thinks are trying to oppress her." Eric met Mitchell's eyes. "Which might explain why you aren't furious."

"I share some of her questions."

"Ask them."

"What will it feel like to leave behind all that you've done here?"

"Are you referring to shepherding you, her, and all the other master's students toward predictable conclusions you can hammer out in your theses? Or maybe you're talking about how I teach a mass of nameless undergraduates I wouldn't recognize if I ran into them on the street? The ones who only realized I was their professor after Lisa's death was in the paper. Mitchell, if any of that sounds like a compelling reason not to spend some time away from a city where there's a memory of my wife around every corner, you'll have to point it out to me."

A bravura performance, he thought. But it had been completely lost on Mitchell. Eric had omitted one major commitment and he could sense Mitchell preparing to drive the blade in quick, or wait to find the softest spot to stab.

Mitchell slowly crossed to the chair in front of Eric's desk and took a seat. "Forgive me for what I'm about to say," Mitchell said flatly. "Lisa's death was tragic. But so was your marriage."

Eric felt anger rush into him like hot water, flushing out his careful plans to make this farewell an easy one. "I know you well enough to know how badly her death must have wounded you. But they don't, Eric. How can you expect them to believe that you're leaving them behind because of a wife you didn't even seem to care about?"

Eric sucked in a breath and leaned forward over his desk. "That house is yours. And the people who live in it are your priority. If any of them need a parent, they should look to you."

"That house exists because of what you wrote."

"My words put through the wringer of *your* vision."

"In your house!"

"Not anymore. It's yours now. We've been over that."

Mitchell considered this, crossing his hands on his lap. Eric realized the finality of his tone wouldn't be enough to close the topic, to forever break his tie to 231 Slope Street. And to Mitchell.

"It isn't that they need you, Eric. They looked up to you. I taught them to venerate you."

Mitchell's last words chilled Eric. He had inadvertently sanctioned not a meeting of minds under one roof but a cult. Eric rose from his chair and crossed to the window.

"I should have seen this coming," Mitchell said quietly. "Lauren Raines is our resident success story. You read her application and then you never even bothered to meet her."

"It sounds like you're doing fine work, then," Eric said to the window. "Without my involvement."

Several seconds passed before Eric turned to see Mitchell had pivoted in the chair to face him. "So this is a bona fide farewell, then?" Mitchell asked.

"As of now. Yes."

Mitchell nodded, seemingly unfazed. "Where are you going to go?"

"I haven't decided yet." He sat on the sill, feigning contemplation and trying to hide how much this exchange had rattled him. "I'm thinking about Livingston."

"The Writers Workshop?"

"In Montana. Yes."

"Sounds pretty isolated. I figured you might head to New York." Mitchell commented. Eric was confused by the false levity in his voice. "Are you going alone?"

"Of course," Eric answered.

Eric was so taken aback when Mitchell got up and extended his hand, it took him a few seconds to get up from the windowsill and shake it. "Now seems like the time to thank you for all you've done for us," Mitchell said.

"It was nothing."

Mitchell smiled and withdrew his hand. "There's no need to be humble," he said.

Mitchell turned and left the room, leaving Eric to ponder what response he could have used to shirk off his ownership of the House of Adam one last time.

Apple martini night at Madeline's was the restaurant's attempt to bring out a modest crowd on Monday evening. Randall rested his chin on his fist, gazing above the bar at the television that had first told him about Lisa Eberman's death two weeks earlier. A sitcom father tried to run across a stage-set living room with his children clinging to different parts of his body. Invisible people exploded into laughter. It was like nothing Randall could pretend existed.

He swallowed his drink, shocked to see the glass empty when he returned it to the bar. Randall's regular bartender since the start of the year was leaning toward him. Teddy had been hired for two reasons, his dimples and his ass; he was also one of those hopelessly straight guys who basked in the attention of gay men.

"Eight o'clock on a Monday night, Randall. This is a new record for you."

"Have I ever told you that you remind me of my roommate?"

"Is that a good thing?"

"In theory, maybe," Randall said, speech sluggish but not slurred. "Don't be that flattered. I'm seeing him everywhere right now." *Especially since he's not anywhere around*, Randall thought, *which is exactly where I'd like to be*. Before he could curse the decision he had made over Thanksgiving break, Randall summoned a grin and lifted his empty glass, and Teddy removed it from his hand and set it on top of the ice drawer.

"Well, in a few seconds you're not going to want to be complimenting me anyway." Teddy leaned farther over the bar and lowered his voice to a whisper. "I need to see some ID."

"Are you fucking kidding?" Randall whispered back.

Teddy grimaced and shook his head no. "Look, you know I don't give a shit."

"I know you love big tippers," Randall said in his singsong voice as he tugged his wallet from his jeans. He slapped it onto the bar and started going through the billfold when he noticed a slip of paper between the cash. He thought it was a receipt.

"Randall, look," Teddy continued. "My manager just asked who the twelve-year-old in the Versace was. She's been breathing down my neck tonight."

Randall was paying no attention. It wasn't a receipt. It was the slip of paper on which Jesse had left his cell phone number. And the paper had been left on Randall's desk as a bittersweet parting gift. He stuffed it back in with the bills.

"Randall," Teddy hissed through clenched teeth. "She's right over there."

Randall's eyes sluggishly followed Teddy's thumb to where a pinched-faced woman in a black satin pants suit had locked her sights on them.

"Okay, then . . . maybe a quick blow job will clear this up."

"Come on, Randall."

"Not you, Teddy. Your manager."

"You don't even have a fake ID?" Teddy asked incredulously.

Randall exploded with laughter. "I wouldn't know which name to use!"

Teddy grimaced and Randall followed his eyes to see Satin Pants rounding the corner of the bar in their direction. Teddy recoiled. Randall felt a hand tap his shoulder. "Move on, honey," Randall said. "The last time I was with a woman I was thirteen years old."

She reached around and pulled his wallet off the bar, and he swiveled to yank it out of her grip. "I don't think I gave you permission to go through my wallet," Randall slurred.

"ID. Now!" she barked.

"Say please."

Faster than he could process, she grabbed his wallet again, flipped it open and removed his Atherton ID. "Uhm, what did I just say?"

"Teddy, this guy doesn't have a license and you're serving him?" she shouted, pulling Randall off his stool by one shoulder. "You're out of here." She pressed his wallet to his chest.

Randall's feet crumpled against the floor before he could regain his balance, but the manager still held a grip on his shoulder.

"Get your hands off of me," he warned, but she refused, pulling him by one shoulder toward the door.

He slammed his arm up against hers. One of her ankles twisted and she toppled into a table of diners.

"Wha'd I jus' fucking saay, bitch?"

She managed to right herself, her eyes sharp with both anger and confusion. He stumbled out of the door and onto the sidewalk, bringing one hand to his mouth. He didn't regret his choice of words, but he was frightened by their unmistakably Texan drawl.


Kathryn had been back at school for twenty-four hours, and a good twelve of them had been spent at the computer. Nausea commanded her stomach, but she didn't know if the eight cups of coffee were to blame, or if the malady was caused by recognizing she was a bad writer.

> You want to believe that truly evil people are born with
> some sort of telltale birthmark or defining characteristic
> which makes it clear from the get-go that they're designed
> only to do harm.

When in her entire life had she used words like *get-go* and *telltale*? After all the shit she'd gone through with him, this was the best way she could describe Jono?

Her eyes were smarting from the flicker of the monitor. Microsoft Word informed her that she had six pages, but she informed herself that they were mostly crap. So far, her essay was rambling and barely comprehensible. Instead of putting down the raw events of her relationship with Jono on paper, she had written around them at every turn.

"Still working on your novel?" April asked as she tossed her book bag onto her bed.

Kathryn grunted.

"Did Tran talk to you?"

"No. Why?" she asked absently as she paged down

"The room was locked when you got back from the airport last night, right?"

"I think so."

"Well, nothing's missing."

Confused out of her daze, Kathryn swiveled toward April. "Huh?"

"The power went out over the break," April explained "And there were still people here, so maintenance had to prop all the doors open for a few hours 'cause the ID readers went on the fritz. Now some girl on the second floor says stuff was stolen out of her room and . . ." April stopped when she saw Kathryn's bloodshot eyes. "Have you eaten?"

"I'm vegan now."

"Vegans eat. Come on. Let's go." April extended a hand.

"I'm not hungry," Kathryn said.

When April approached, Kathryn felt a seizure of fear and rapidly closed the file before rising from her chair. "I'll be right back," she said, as she fished her coat out of the closet.

"Come back with any more coffee and I'll kick your ass. That shit's poison! It's worse than heroin!"

Because coffee was exactly what she needed, she waved April off as she left the room.

She hurried downstairs and out of the dorm. Crossing onto Brookline, she almost got herself run over. She hurried onto the sidewalk. The approach of finals had extended campus hours and large knots of students were moving down the sidewalks through narrow passages of shoveled snow.

"Kathryn!"

Another second, and she would have run right into him.

Randall's eyes lit up with drunken and sarcastic surprise as he held himself to a lamppost with one arm, extending the other like an airplane wing. One foot was sliding out from under him through the snow.

"Apple martini night?" she asked.

"Uh-huh."

Passersby weaved to avoid them. Several of them burst out laughing once they were a safe distance away from the Versace-clad drunken cliché. So what if she hadn't spoken to him for a week? If she didn't do something, he would get arrested for public drunkenness.

"I got thrown out!"

Randall's sliding foot passed the point of no return and he hit the thin covering of snow ass first. Kathryn winced at the impact. Randall's head fell forward, a grimace tightening his face, which he covered with both hands. After glancing around in embarrassment, Kathryn hooked an arm around his waist. "Work with me here," she muttered to him.

"I'm so . . . sorry, Kathryn."

"Not here, Randall. Just get up."

His drunken sobs sputtered against his palms. Another tug at his waist and she'd end up in the snow with him. She stood over him, unable to do little more than brace her hands against her hips and shoot withering looks at anyone gawking. She looked back at him and saw he had lowered his hands into weak fists in his lap. Tears swelled in his eyes, and his drunken lack of coordination made him look like a four-year-old.

"Just get up. Please."

"You know I've been thinking . . ."

"Think after you get up."

He looked pained at the bite in her voice before putting out his hand to her. She clasped it and weakly gave him a slight pull, amazed that he managed to right himself. But then he slumped against her, one arm sloppily landing around her shoulders.

As they made the slow, shuffling walk back to Stockton, his head found her shoulder and by the time they made it to the entrance she assumed he was about to pass out. But instead, he cried silently into her shoulder as she led him, as briskly as she could, up the stairs and down the hallway. At the door to his room, she turned him and propped him against the wall.

"I need your key."

Randall's chin met his chest, upper back sliding against the cinderblock.

She knocked on the shut door. "Jesse?" she called.

"Gone," Randall slurred.

"What?"

Across the hall, April cracked the door, read the scene instantly, and stepped across the threshold. "I've got it," Kathryn said sharply.

"Cozumel," Randall mumbled as he slid to a seated position on the floor. "The phone lines end . . . He went there when he was little . . . A hurricane destroyed one . . . one half of the island. The phone lines ended."

April shook her head and ducked back inside.

"I need your key, Randall."

He slapped a limp hand against his pants pocket. After she dug it out, she hoisted him to his feet, leaned him against her, and opened the door onto a pitch-dark room. After several seconds of blind shuffling, Randall's breath came out of him in a grunt, he collapsed, and she landed on top of him on the bed. She groped until she found the halogen lamp. Harsh light hit the ceiling, and Randall rolled over onto one side, bringing his forearm over his eyes.

Kathryn lifted his legs off the floor and dropped them onto the mattress before taking a seat at the foot of the bed and unlacing his boots. When she looked up, Randall's arm had gone to his side and he was staring at her through hooded, bloodshot eyes.

"It's perfectly all right for you to hate me," he slurred, his voice long and twangy, sounding almost Southern.

"I don't hate you," She slid one boot off his socked foot and dropped it to the floor.

"Liar." A woozy grin curled his cheeks. "Sorry. That's me." Laughter seized him, lifting his chest slightly off the mattress. "Do you think it's all just a bunch of . . . bullshit? Like college is supposed to be this great place where we find out who we really are . . . How is that great? If who we are sucks." His head fell back to the bed.

Drunken groveling might have inspired pity in her, but drunken self-pity just fueled her frustration. She yanked the second boot off his other foot and the sock caught, sliding down his ankle. She dropped the boot to the floor and tugged the sock all the way off.

The skin on his ankle was marred by a raised area of pinkish skin. She lifted his bare foot with both hands, examining it in bewilderment.

Bravely, she prodded the area—it didn't look like a bruise—with one finger.

Randall didn't stir.

She pushed up the cuff of his jeans and was shocked to see that the mark extended up his shin with the same consistency and color.

"Randall?"

But he was down for the count, his breaths slow and deep and his head tilted to one side against the pillow. She released his foot and rose from the mattress. April stood in the open door.

"He just needs to sleep it off. He'll be all right."

But April was staring past her. Kathryn followed her gaze.

Jesse's mattress was stripped, the wall above it a shock of white cinderblock. The surface of his desk was clear. The large desk calendar was missing.

Kathryn looked to April for confirmation that she wasn't hallucinating.

April just shook her head.

Kathryn went to his closet and pulled back the curtain. Even the hangers were gone. She let the curtain fall, turned to April, and lifted both arms in a gesture of silent belief.

Randall started to snore.

• • •

"I don't know," April said, more agitated this time. "Some people just flip out, Kathryn. One of my lab partners lost her shit over the break and told her parents she'd rather die than come back. I mean, think about it—it's not like Jesse had any friends here."

Kathryn watched April shove her arms hurriedly into an extra large T-shirt  By contrast, Kathryn was almost placid, sitting on the edge of her bed with her hands folded in her lap.

"Maybe he withdrew?" April asked.

"You're more upset than I am. I don't even like him."

April's face clouded. She sat down on the edge of her bed, maybe hoping to find Kathryn's calm by matching her pose.

"This might not have anything to do with anything. And I wasn't going to tell you."

"But you are. Right now."

April gave one last sigh. "The night I left, I ran into Randall standing outside the door, listening. Jesse was obviously with someone."

"You do realize that Randall, every time he wanted to go in his own room, he had to stop and figure out if Jesse was screwing someone?"

"Yeah, well. This time it was a guy."

Kathryn grunted and lowered her eyes from April's, afraid of where this was headed, even though she had suspected it for months now. "How do you know?"

"I heard. And so did Randall."

"Well, I always thought Jesse had it in him," she said wryly. "Is that all?"

"Randall went in the room."

Kathryn focused on April again, as if the sight of her was an anchor amid the swirl of her revelation. "How do you know?"

"Because I pretended to leave, but I waited down the hall, went back, and checked."

"Congratulations. You were right."

"That is not why I told you, Kathryn!"

"Why, then?"

"Because . . ." April paused, obviously thinking on her feet.

"Maybe it's poetic justice," Kathryn said brightly. "Jesse screws whoever he wants and gets rid of them whenever he wants. Maybe this time he picked someone he couldn't get rid of."

Kathryn raised her eyebrows. As the larger implications of her words settled over them both, April snapped her mouth shut. "That is *so* not what I meant. I'm not saying Randall *did*—"

"What are you saying?" Kathryn asked sharply.

"Maybe Jesse went home, Kathryn. Maybe once he got there—"

"He told me he wasn't going home."

"Maybe someone made him go home. Look, we might all waltz around here like we're independent adults, but we're not the ones writing the check for this place." It was a tempting theory. Maybe Jesse had simply feigned self-possession and independence, and maybe his father, who he had described to her with a strange detachment, had decided to yank the rug out from under Jesse's new life.

What exactly was it that Jesse had said? Kathryn tried to remember.

It was time for him to move on, but his father hadn't realized it yet.

*Cozumel*, Randall had slurred only a moment earlier.

Jesse went to Cozumel to escape his father?

Her head hurt.

April killed her desk lamp. "Just ask Randall in the morning. I'm sure he'll know." She buried herself in the comforter.

After several seconds of staring at the floor, Kathryn got up and went back to Randall's room.

Everything was as she had left it, including Randall, who was still stuporously asleep. She went to Jesse's desk and opened the middle drawer. Empty. So were the other three. She scanned the place again. Not one single shred of Jesse, and that was what bothered her. Whatever the reason for his departure, it had to have been hurried. Wasn't there one thing that would have been too heavy to pack? Moreover, if Jesse was leaving Atherton, why did he bother to take all his textbooks with him?

He didn't, moron, said a voice inside her head. He threw them in the trash.

Disgusted by her swelling suspicion, she sat down on the mattress. It didn't give the way she knew it should and she heard springs squeak, the sound slightly choked. Off. Down on all fours, she peered under the bed, scanning the underside of the bed frame through shadow. Finally, she saw what had caused the strange sound.

Something was wedged between the mattress and the springs, shoved back to the far left corner, almost to the headboard.

She got to her feet, glanced again at Randall to make sure he was still out, and then lifted the extra long twin with both hands. Hidden there was Jesse's laptop computer.

She held up the mattress with one arm and removed the laptop from the bed of coils.

Why would Jesse bother to get rid of his textbooks and leave behind a brand-new computer he could use anywhere? Considering the thoroughness of the job he'd done, she found it almost impossible to believe that he just forgot it.

There was only one logical answer, and even though she didn't like it, she had to be the one to ask the question.

Jesse wasn't the one who cleaned out his room.

# CHAPTER THIRTEEN

SECURITY LIGHTS THREW HALOS OUT FROM THE GARAGE DOORS ONTO the expansive parking lot between both banks of storage lockers. Randall crouched down over the padlock, working the bolt cutter with short punches. Behind him, Tim had moved in as close as he could get to Randall, safely out of the nearest corona of harsh, bluish light. Of all nights, this one was clear, windless, and, Randall thought, oppressively silent in a manner that only amplified the grating of the bolt cutter chewing against the padlock.

"Shit," Tim finally said in a panicked whisper.

"Calm down."

Tim stepped closer, adjusting the flashlight's beam. In his other hand, he held the new padlock they'd use to replace this one. If the son of a bitch ever came off. "So far this whole thing's been too easy. Our luck is bound to run out."

"Say that again and . . ." Randall clenched his teeth as if it would add torque There was a loud snap and before Randall knew it the lock clattered to the concrete.

"Inside!" Tim commanded.

Randall yanked the lever and held on to it as the garage door ascended. Tim ducked through and Randall followed into the darkness, groping to find the interior lock. He shoved the door down. It hit the concrete, bounced, and then settled an inch above the pavement

All Randall could see was the flashlight beam angled purposelessly toward the ceiling. He grabbed for it and Tim grunted as Randall pulled it from his grip. "We're safe," he assured Tim.

"Bullshit," Tim hissed. "I bet we're about to make a bunch of new four-legged friends."

"Any rat stupid enough to stick around here is frozen solid."

"I'd still fell better if I was . . . *Fuck!*"

Randall swung the beam just in time to catch Tim righting himself, his hands braced against something massive concealed by a canvas tarp.

"You all right?"

"It's a car," Tim said, catching his breath.

Tim remained hunched over in the beam's halo, but he wasn't injured. He drew the tarp up with both fists until a rear bumper and license plate came into a view.

"Make that a van. An *Aerostar*. Christ, my mom drove one in, like, 1983."

"The Volvo was new."

"You think this was Lisa's?"

"Maybe."

"The plates haven't expired. It can't be that old."

Randall swung the flashlight beam away from Tim, who let out a frightened, "Hey!"

In a slow, sweeping motion, Randall revealed empty pavement and a corrugated metal wall—and a pile of cardboard boxes that might contain everything Lisa wanted to keep a secret from her husband. Breathless, he approached them. They were all empty. He kicked one of them into the others and they toppled. "Dammit."

"Over here!" Tim ordered. The van was obviously the only thing inside the entire locker. Randall complied, angled the beam onto the Aerostar as Tim pulled back the tarp, yanking it from the van's roof before sending it sliding down the rear window.

"Fuck me," Tim whispered. "Give it over."

Randall did, and Tim aimed the flashlight through one of the van's side windows. The two backseats were filled with cardboard boxes, some taped securely, others spilling sleeves through their top flaps. More clothes than Randall had found in Paula Willis's guest bedroom, and personal belongings too, it looked like. Several open flaps revealed what looked like scrapbooks, as well as hardcover books left over from Lisa's brief postgraduate career. When they came to the driver's side door, Tim pulled the handle. The door popped open.

"Get in," Tim ordered, and Randall rounded the nose of the van before climbing into the passenger seat.

For a relative antique of a minivan that had spent extended time inside a locker, the Aerostar was surprisingly clean. The seats and carpet were vacuumed, and the flashlight beam glinted over a full, capped bottle of water wedged between the cup holders.

"She was on her way here," Randall said.

"What?" Tim jerked forward in the driver's seat, angling the beam toward the ceiling, which filled the van with diffuse light. The words had come out of Randall's mouth before he even had time to process the thought. "Keep going," Tim urged him.

"She doesn't want him to know she was leaving until he gets the note. This way it can be a big surprise. She rents the locker so she can take her sweet time packing up all her things. A couple boxes at a time, never so much that Eric gets suspicious. Then, when she's ready, she hops in the Volvo like she's going to her sister's, but instead she comes here. And Eric doesn't have a clue until he gets her little good-bye note. And it's the perfect revenge. Because he's ignored her for so long, just assumed she would always stick around. And she's gone before he even has the chance to know what hit him."

"If only she could have skipped the scotch," Tim muttered.

They sat thinking through this scenario for a few seconds before Tim began sweeping the flashlight across the rear of the van. "So what now? We go through her scrapbooks?"

Randall's eyes followed the beam.

"There's no way we can go through all of that back there. We have to unload it."

"Randall, this just looks like clothes and photographs. I mean . . ." Tim froze the beam in mid-scan, and Randall saw what had caught Tim's attention. The sealed manila envelope rested on the carpeted floor behind them between the two middle seats. Randall reached back and retrieved it. He turned it over on his lap as Tim shined the flashlight down on the address.

"David Handler?" Tim asked.

"No clue."

"Maybe Lisa had something on the side too."

Randall grimaced, tore the envelope open, and dumped the contents onto his lap: a cover letter clipped to what looked like some sort of lease. Randall took the letter and handed the document to Tim, who turned the beam back to the ceiling.

"Attorney at law!" Randall read off the address line at the top left corner of the page.

"This is . . . Wait a minute . . ."

Randall began reading the letter aloud. "Dear Mr. Handler, my apologies for the delay in getting back to you, but since our phone conversation last month, I have gone on a sort of fact-finding mission that will hopefully make my case somewhat stronger than you considered it to be last month."

Wordy, Randall thought. Like the way her sister Paula Willis had tried to get everything out before her time was up. But Paula Willis was cancer-free, and Lisa probably had no idea that her own days were numbered.

"This is a deed. Or something," Tim said without looking up from the paper he'd flattened against the steering wheel.

"I recently discovered that my husband is the owner of a property not far from our own home. He has, according to county records, owned this property since his senior year at Atherton, and has never seen fit to make me aware of it. This is probably because without my consent, or even advice, he decided to hand this peace of real estate over to one of his graduate students."

"Mitchell-fucking-Seaver?" Tim cried out. Randall looked up before realizing that Tim had read the name right off the deed, which he held up in one hand for Randall to examine. "He gave that loser a house?"

Randall examined the real estate deed. It handed over ownership of 231 Slope Street to one Mitchell Clarence Seaver on the second day of October, the previous year. "The Adamites," Randall whispered as he saw Kathryn emerging from Mitchell's car, then typing furiously on the computer.

Tim hadn't heard. "All right, so this David Handler guy is obviously a divorce attorney. And if Lisa was jumping all over some real estate transaction, then I doubt she knew about you and Eric. So I guess we did what we came to . . ."

But Randall wasn't listening. What had Eric told him when he asked about Mitchell? Not only is Mitchell not even homosexual, he's barely what you'd call sexual, he said. He'd bristled at the mention of his name, turned his back on Randall in the kitchen, and accused Randall of not being able to understand an academic type like Mitchell. And he'd showed Randall the note when he knew what time the accident had happened, knew that Lisa hadn't seen them in bed together that night.

Randall slammed one fist against the closed glove compartment, an intoxicating blend of rage and relief running through his veins. Tim jerked in the driver's seat. "Jesus! What?"

"The file on Lauren Raines. Remember? The one you thought had nothing to do with this. It was an application, Tim."

"For what?"

"Two-thirty-one Slope Street isn't just a house. It's some kind of cult!"

"Oh, come on, Randall! It was a girl feeling sorry for herself."

"Yeah, and test results for every venereal disease under the sun. Listen to me, Eric talks about this heretical sect in his book. They're called the Brethren of the Free Spirit—"

"Randall!"

"Shut up, Tim. I'm serious. Supposedly, they were this group of people that believed if they held orgies they could cleanse themselves, or purge themselves, I don't know but—"

"Get out of the car, Randall!" Panic sharpened Tim's words.

Randall turned to see the air drifting in front of the windshield had a strange substance to it, parting and shifting in tendrils, driven by invisible currents through the darkness.

Smoke.

Without warning, his chest tightened and his throat began to close up, turning his breaths into stabbing gasps. The flashlight beam angled at the van's ceiling revealed a thickening cloud, and when he heard a series of popping and ticking sounds, Tim pivoted against the driver's seat and Randall, unable to breathe, saw flickering firelight silhouetting his profile from beyond the glass.

"Tim . . ." But it came out in a breathy whisper.

"All right. All right. Wait a minute." Tim hadn't heard him and was talking to himself. "Just get out and we'll see. . . ."

"No!"

A strange stench filled the van—the burning of pure fumes. A raw chemical smell that summoned images of twisted tracks, overturned fuel cars, and a wall of flame—specters that plunged Randall into a paralytic panic. Tim was tugging on his shoulder.

"Randall. The whole place is metal. Calm down! We'll just get out—"

With a sound like muted thunder, the garage door flew open and suddenly a curtain of fire blossomed behind the van.

"Tim!"

Tim's gaze shot from the flame-fringed doorway to Randall, his eyes widening when he saw his friend pitched forward, both hands braced against the glove compartment. Randall could hear Tim's breaths whistling through his nose, and Tim now seemed more alarmed by Randall's panic than by the flame-filled exit behind them. Randall felt himself shaking his head in denial, and then saw Tim turn forward, hands tearing at the visor overhead before he scanned the steering wheel in front of him.

"Son of a bitch!" Tim cried.

When Randall saw him grasp the keys dangling from the ignition, he shouted, "No. Tim!"

"There's only one way out of here, Randall!"

Randall just groaned. If he had been able to breathe, it might have been a scream. The van's engine sputtered to life and Tim's foot hit the gas. Randall fell backward against the seat and his hands flew to his face as orange light filtered in at the edges of his vision. As Tim backed out of the locker, Randall's ears filled with a roar that had previously been confined to the nightmares of his past. His heart stopped hammering in his chest and his vision returned to total black.


On the second floor of Folberg, Kathryn found an individual study carrel bare of books on its single shelf. She glanced up and down the long aisle before hefting her backpack onto the desk. For the entire day, she had walked from class to class with half her mind focused on her imminent exams, and the other half focused on Jesse's laptop shifting around at the bottom of her book bag.

Now she sat staring at the bag. With a deep breath she summoned her nerve and removed Jesse's computer, along with April's power cord, which she had taken without asking because she couldn't bring herself to tell April what she had found. She hooked the cord into the carrel's power outlet and popped the monitor open.

Unlike most students she knew, Jesse had not chosen to personalize his computer's wallpaper; icons for only the essential programs stood out against a light blue background. April had been the one to tell Kathryn how to password-protect her computer. No one had done Jesse the favor, which probably explained his bizarre choice of hiding place.

Upon their arrival, Atherton students were assigned E-mail accounts on campus, after which they could download the Eudora E-mail program from the campus network free of charge. The program had a feature that automatically saved all sent and received messages until the user instructed it to delete them, after which it transferred them to a folder aptly named "Deleted Messages." Jesse had now missed two full days of class and she hoped to at least find some inquiries into his absence from professors or teaching assistants. But she knew from glances at his bookshelves—before they had been cleaned out—that Jesse's schedule consisted of mostly basic lecture courses, and the reality of the situation was that no one would notice he was missing until some adept TA figured out he hadn't signed in for at least two or three discussion sections, which itself was hardly a rare occurrence among freshmen. But maybe she would discover some E-mail transaction documenting an official break from Atherton. Or maybe she should fess up to herself and admit that it was a morbid curiosity that had led her to power up the computer.

At first, she had trouble with the touch-sensitive mouse; one press of her finger against the pad would send the cursor sliding across the screen. Her sweaty fingers aggravated the problem. She managed to position the cursor over the Eudora icon and clicked. A logo indicated that the computer was trying to log on to the Internet with a connection it didn't have. A password might be required to connect, but she knew from experience that sent and received messages could be accessed without it.

Several more maneuverings of the mouse, and she was looking at an

entire record of Jesse's E-mail activities since he had arrived at Atherton
University. She felt a wave of disappointment; Jesse was not an avid cor-
respondent. The majority of it was obvious cyber junk, the rest bearing
the addresses of academic departments—none of them queries into his
absence—most of them reminders of imminent paper deadlines and
last-minute schedule changes. Only a small smattering of student E-mail
addresses appeared—full names divided by an underscored space and
followed by @Atherton.edu.

One of those names was Lauren Raines. Kathryn shivered and
clicked the file open.

> Jesse,
>     Is that how you spell it? I have a cousin whose name is
> Jessie, so I wanted to be sure. : ) Thanks so much for the feed-
> back on my story. It meant a lot So I hope this doesn't sound
> too forward, but were you serious about dinner? Let me know.
>                                                   Lauren

Kathryn closed it, returned to the list. Shocked to find a guy's
name—Taylor Barnes—she opened the E-mail.

> Wassup?
>     I've been giving your "suggestion" some thought. After
> you mentioned it, I think I remember meeting your room-
> mate. Tim introduced us once. (Do you know Tim? He's
> really cool. Helped me out a lot.) Anyway, I've been think-
> ing about your "idea" a lot and . . . .I'm totally into it. Let
> me know what your roommate says.
>                                                   Taylor

Kathryn puzzled over it for a second before determining that Taylor
was male, and probably the guy Jesse was having sex with on the other
side of the door while Randall listened. She made a mental note of his
name, considering he was probably one of the last people to have seen
Jesse at Atherton.

Finally she spotted a non-Atherton address: *bcolby@wilkescolby-
law.com*

When she opened it, she was surprised by its length.

J Man,

Hope you're doing well after the uproar of our phone conversation last night. Without rehashing it too much, I just wanted to clarify some of the details of what your father and I have managed to work out. Keep in mind, the consensus is this is a bogus charge While it helped that your father was honest about how intoxicated he was when the police arrived, the judge handling the case is known for being media sensitive. Due to the recent spate of celebrity-related drug arrests, I think his sentence was deliberately, and unfairly, harsh.

In lieu of facing a trespassing charge, your father will be spending the next twenty-eight days at Bright Hill, a highly reputable rehabilitation center in Pacific Palisades. Terms of his stay are that his contact with the outside world will be limited, and he won't be allowed to leave the facility for the duration. I accompanied him yesterday evening when he checked himself in, and I can assure you he's in good spirits. He asked me to let you know that finances and the like are all in order, and he expressed regret that all of this might have distracted from your new life up at college. However—and I have to stress this—he would very much like you to visit, and he suggested Thanksgiving.

Jesse, I might be crossing the line here, but your father's feeling a great deal of shame right now and while I know things between the two of you can get volatile, I've been around you two long enough to know you guys share a pretty deep bond. I think he feels he's failed his only son. He's getting some real good help now, and I know your support would help him even more. There. End of sermon.

Please feel free to call the office if you need any more information, and I wish you every success at Atherton.

Best,<br>Bill

Had Jesse gone home to visit his father in rehab?

She checked the date on the E-mail.

November 17. Almost a week before he told her point-blank he had no plans to go home for Thanksgiving.

Was Jesse called home to take care of his father's affairs? Nothing in the E-mail indicated such a demand. The lawyer seemed a pretty smooth character. He was also a family friend, and he had highlighted the fact that the finances were all in order, encouraging Jesse to go about his new life at college.

This shot April's theory dead. No one made Jesse go home. Worse, whoever had cleaned out his room in a hurry and left the computer behind wasn't a parent. His father was basically being held prisoner and his mother had died.

Having an alcohol-addicted father shined a harsh light into who Jesse was, but that knowledge gave her nothing close to an answer. She gave up on his E-mail and went into Microsoft Word. His files were as meticulously organized as he'd kept his own desk. Each of his four courses was assigned its own folder and a quick check revealed first and second drafts of papers.

A fifth file was titled "Journal." A diary? Her breath caught at the thought, but when she clicked on it she was greeted with twelve files, all bearing other people's names. It couldn't be possible. Was this a cold chronicle of Jesse's sexual conquests? Why else would Lauren Raines's name be close to the top of the list? She let out a disgusted breath, feeling no triumph in having the worse things she had suspected about the guy laid out on the monitor before her.

She opened Lauren's file before she could lose her nerve.

> 10–2 I knew Shifty Eyes was holding a clamped lid down on something that was about to burst. Today in class, she read a story about a girl who gets fucked by her uncle. How stupid does she think we are? She read it with such forced solemnity that it was obviously true, and it was also obvious that she enjoyed doing it with him. Of course there was lots of head-nodding when I talked to her about it after class. Turns out she's an engineering major. Fitting. Designing bridges, control.

Kathryn was quietly horrified, but what struck her above all else was the evident anger in Jesse's words. He was riled by the idea that Lauren would try to pull one over on the class masquerading fact as fiction. She forced herself to keep reading, finding more dated entries. More brutal dissections of Lauren's superficial behaviors, and Jesse's attempt to read psychological motivations into them. By the time she came to the final entry and read what Jesse had done to Lauren for the big finish, she fell against the back of the chair, her face tightening into a grimace.

*This* is what Lauren wouldn't tell? No wonder.

She gathered her composure and browsed files bearing names of people she didn't know—all of them Jesse's sexual prey. Jesse took pride in getting a girl to abandon her feminist film theory analysis of Alfred Hitchcock's *Vertigo* even as he went down on her. A lacrosse player had needed only a few beers before he was asking Jesse to call him his bitch. There were even fewer laws involved in Jesse's games than she had imagined. But *bisexual* was a term she was hesitant to apply to him. Jesse used his body to force someone into exposing her, or his, innermost secrets. What better target than a closet homosexual? (But where did Randall fit in?)

"Make sure they aren't afraid to ask for what they want, at the same time you're making them feel as good as you can. You'll be shocked what you find out." Those had been his parting woods to her after the only conversation they'd ever had alone.

As she continued to read, she realized none of his other conquests inspired the same anger and determination as Lauren Raines. Her secret had gotten to him the most of all, and there was pure venom in what he had done and how he had described it.

Her powers of analysis were clouded by her visceral reaction to Jesse's conquests laid bare. Jesse's life at Atherton was a barren, lonely place, sparsely populated by the secret sexual desires of strangers. His diary was a fitting addition to the portrait of a guy who rarely left his room, who had led a pathetic and empty existence amid throngs of freshmen embracing their new independence. How much of her own imagination had transformed Jesse into a monster?

Of course, there was one file she hadn't read yet. Unlike the others, it bore only a first name.

Randall.

These entries weren't dated. With his roommate, Jesse didn't seem to follow a ticking clock that wound down to an eventual bedding. The entries were also longer.

> His art history professor gives him a hard on. (Eberling? Edmund?) This is probably the first honest thing he's said to me since we moved in together. Should I feel honored? For the first three weeks, the guy could barely look my way, afraid he'd get wood, and now he's telling me he wants to sleep with a married guy? I wonder what the chipmunk across the hall would think if she found out.
>
> Weird. Last week his parents lived on Park Avenue. Last night they moved to Soho.
>
> Tried to get him to talk about his parents last night. Same ol' shit. They're rich, they're assholes. Wah wah wah, Poor Randall! It's like he's rehearsed this stuff. And how many times does he have to mention his mother's drinking? He's never even told me her full name, but I know she's always about to "drown in a bathtub of Glenlivet." Cute? What novel did he steal that from? He's just trying to get me to stop asking.

Kathryn felt hollow. Jesse was right.

The details of Randall's home life did always seem woefully thin and rehearsed, and moreover, sharpened in such a way as to throw down a roadblock. She recalled their conversation in the men's bathroom, when her flip comment about his parents' wealth had resulted in a monologue from Randall about escaping their evil influence. He'd sidelined her inquiry about their trip to Boston with a comment about how his mother had hit the sauce when his father went out of town on business.

> Last night he was banging away at the computer. I asked him if he decided to actually start doing some work. He

said he was working on something for Kathryn. I didn't
bother asking what, since I knew he wouldn't tell me, just
waited until he went to the bathroom and checked his most
recently viewed files  Are these two morons writing stories
to each other?

Tonight. Found Randall passed out in front of our dorm.
He'd been at one of those gay and lesbian alliance dances
and was totally plastered. I had to carry him up to the
room. He was babbling like he was in the midst of some
kind of fever dream. Kept bitching about how hot he was.
Fire this, fire that. Finally, I realized he wanted me to take
his clothes off. That's when I thought maybe the whole
thing was just a big ploy .  . Well, shit! Fire is right. The
guy's got like second degree burns over both his legs. But
I've got a pretty good guess where he got them

Drywater, Texas.


Kathryn stopped to breathe, guarding herself as best she could
before she leaned forward again toward the screen.

Found the article today. Kathryn came up to me in the
library right after and I thought about showing her. But I
think I'm going to sit on this one until the time comes. What
this guy has done is fucking awe-inspiring! Running away is
one thing. Reinventing yourself is another  He had to have
gotten some help along the way. I can only dream . . . and ask
him once the time comes.

Kathryn stared at the monitor for a second before she tried to page
down.
That was it.
She rubbed the heel of one hand against her forehead, trying to
force blood back to her brain.

Found the article today.

She scanned the journal folder again; it didn't reveal anything close to an article. She closed Word and opened a full file search of the entire computer. Trying to numb herself as best as she could, she brought her fingers to the keyboard and typed "Texas" She hesitated before adding "article," and then finally "train derailment."

The search turned up an .html file. She clicked on it.

## DEATH TOLL AT 40, ONE MISSING
## AFTER FIERY TRAIN DERAILMENT

The headline ran above a black-and-white photograph, an aerial view of railroad tracks, flame-devoured train cars, and scorched earth. Part of the train was still intact, each car leaning more than the last before they disappeared into a blackened nightmare of metal marking the fiery eruption that had spread outward from the tracks, turning trees into spindly skeletons and reducing trailers to their charred roofs.

Alongside this photograph was an even more striking one, shot at night from a great distance and obviously not long after the derailment. Even though it was black-and-white, fire lit up the night sky on the open Texas plain with an almost heavenly glow.

Jesse had found an archived edition of the *Dallas Morning News* and this article had been on the front page on July 17, 1997.

Melinda Cruz is still trying to find the words to describe the catastrophic derailment of the Dallas-bound Southern Union train that unleashed a burning tide of diesel fuel and propane, reduced her home to smoldering rubble and killed her neighbors. Cruz, 51, her husband, Marvin, and her two young daughters are the only surviving residents of the Valley Vista Mobile Home Park, five miles outside the small town of Credence. "We're used to the sound of the trains going by," Cruz said. "But that night it was just like this roar that kept getting louder and louder, and then suddenly the bedroom window just went orange."

A week after the accident, there is still no word from the National Transportation Safety Board on the cause of the disaster that left the Cruz family homeless and spread sorrow throughout Henrick County. Red Cross workers spent the last seven days combing through rubble and identifying the dead. Most victims were asleep in their beds when the train came off its track at a little past one in the morning. All the victims have been accounted for except for fifteen-year-old Benjamin Collins. The body of his father, William, was recovered earlier this week from the ruins of the mobile home he shared with his only son. Investigations have been careful to point out that at some locations close to the tracks, fire burned at temperatures hot enough to reduce steel to gas.

Some locals believe that Valley Vista Mobile Home Park has been cursed from the time of its beginnings. Certainly the community of modest dwellings has been no stranger to tragedy. For years, Credence city planners refused to grant residential zoning to the tract of land the development occupies because it was located next to an unmarked intersection of highway and railroad track where eight auto fatalities had occurred. In what now seems like bitter irony for Melinda Cruz and the relatives of the victims of Valley Vista, the last auto fatality—which resulted in the installation of warning lights and crossbars and in the subsequent residential zoning of the adjacent tract of land—claimed the life of Mary Anne Collins, the twenty-eight-year-old mother of the boy whose body has yet to be recovered from Valley Vista's ruins.

Before memory devolved into nightmare, the flames chased him through scrub. Pure fear propelled him past the trailers, their windows reflecting the advancing fire. But there was no time to stop and warn, no time to do anything other than run from the roar that was collapsing into a symphony of metal shrieking against metal. The singing of his own joints was not a result of exertion. His legs were on fire. He was fifteen again, running stupidly from the fire he carried with him.

But in a moment of dreaming self-awareness, Randall could tell that the flames were too high, that they chased him with nightmare speed. Now, the hushed voices conversing above him pulled him back to consciousness, along with the cold weight pressing against his forehead.

"Did you or didn't you see a car?"

"No car. I pulled out of the locker and I saw the gate to the facility had been opened, but I just kept driving. We had broken in. It's not like I was going to wait around for the fire department."

"A puddle of kerosene. Doesn't sound like you guys are being tailed by a trained assassin."

He opened his eyes and saw Tim sitting on the bed beside him. When he saw Randall's eyes open, he removed the wet rag and either grinned or grimaced at him, or both.

Randall's eyes went to the window: an unfamiliar view of sloping rooftops and the black water of the bay beyond. Overstuffed book-shelves lined the walls. Then he saw the man in the doorway, his wiry, gray hair haphazardly brushed back from a high forehead, his pin-point eyes behind glasses over the bridge of a prominent nose. He held a steaming cup of coffee close to his chest and examined the young man lying on his bed without alarm or surprise.

Randall knew exactly who he was. Richard Miller, the reporter. He reared up off the bed in anger. Tim pushed him back with the heel of his palm. "Where the hell else was I supposed to go, Randall? You were out cold and I was driving a dead woman's van," Tim pleaded.

"I'll let you two handle this." The reedy voice belonged to the reporter, who left the doorway and pushed the door shut behind him. Randall rolled over onto one side away from Tim. "I told you not until I was ready," Randall managed, breath weak.

"Eric Eberman tried to kill us tonight. And you're still not ready?" Tim stood up.

"Is that what you told him? That Eric followed us down there and tried to burn us alive?"

Tim's answer was his silence. Randall rolled over onto his back. Tim stood at the window, back to him. "Who else?" Tim asked.

*Mitchell Seaver*, Randall thought, but there was no way in hell he was going to tell Tim now that Tim had brought him to a reporter's apartment against his will. "You wanted to prove whether or not Eric was a murderer. Well, guess what—tonight he tried to murder the two of us. How much more proof do you need?"

"Bullshit, Tim! If he didn't know about the goddamn storage facility, how the hell could he have followed us there?"

"He knows we have the bottle. He attacked you, threw you out of the house. Maybe he's been following you since then. Seeing how close you are to the truth."

"What's the truth? That he killed his wife because of a *house*?"

"Pettier things have led to murder."

"Give me a break. She *saw* something. She *knew* something."

Tim struggled for a response and failed to find one. His face fell with a mixture of fatigue and disappointment. "Right. Your cult. I forgot. Give me a break. How much longer are you going to ignore the obvious just because no matter how much you try you can't bring yourself to face the fact that Eric killed his wife?"

"Because of a house!" Randall repeated, propping himself on both elbows.

"Because she was going to divorce him. And it wasn't going to be easy or pretty. She was hiring an attorney—she went to county records and found out about 231 Slope Street. And if she really started digging she might have found out that he was screwing one of his male students. How much more would she have needed to ruin him?" Tim poked a finger in his chest. "Tell me, Randall, are you really so in love with this son of a bitch that you can't face the truth—or are you maybe a little bit moved at the lengths he would go to protect your little secret?"

"Where's the letter?"

Tim was silent. Randall swung his legs to the floor.

"Tim! Where's the letter?"

Tim turned to face the window again. "It's over, Randall."

Randall tried to control his anger as he realized that Tim was giving him an order. "You gave it to Richard, didn't you?" Again, Tim was silent. "I still have the bottle," Randall barked.

"Newsflash. Richard says it isn't worth shit. We shuffled it back and forth across campus and at the end of the day there's no way to prove it was ever even in Eric's house. It's not like we can just waltz into a police station and say, *Voilà! Here's the murder weapon!*"

"So I have to do what you say?"

"Basically. Yes."

"How dare you," Randall whispered.

"How dare *you!*" Tim shouted. "I'm walking around right now with the knowledge that a woman was murdered and I've got a pretty good explanation why! And you are asking me to keep playing these stupid cloak-and-dagger games. Well, I can't anymore. Especially when they end the way they did tonight. I've given you what you wanted. You've got the best mouthpiece available to you waiting in the other room, and I gave him to you."

"And if I don't tell him anything? What? He's going to run a story about the letter you and I stole from a burned-out storage locker?"

"No. He's going to call the lawyer who found a letter from a dead woman on his doorstep."

Anger gave way to a feeling of pure helplessness, and Randall felt his mouth open before he could find any more words to protest. "After all we tried to do, this is it?"

"She didn't know. And she didn't see you two. Isn't that enough?"

"It's not enough." The threat of tears quavered in Randall's voice, and Tim recoiled slightly at the sound, confused disgust replacing anger on his face. "I've spent weeks trying to find out why that woman is dead. And I would spend months if I had to. And now all I'm going to be is the guy he was sleeping with the night she died."

"Maybe that's all you are."

Tim left the room.

Randall couldn't get up. What shred of redemption he had hoped to gain from this investigation had just slipped out of his grasp, and as a result, he was back to being what everyone saw when they looked at Randall Stone. Eric's practiced whore, Jesse's skilled liar, and Kathryn's fallen friend. Briefly, he had enjoyed a new identity created in the eyes of others, but all of them had seen through their own creations. As far as he had tried to run from it, Randall Stone had been returned to the young man he was when he first arrived at Atherton: an orphan, whose new freedom came with a simple price.

Randall rose from the bed and moved to the doorway.

In the living room, Richard swiveled his chair away from his desk, piled with papers surrounding a circa 1983 word processor, to eye him. Tim looked up from the beer he held in his lap, hope and fear meeting on his face.

He had told Eric he was perfectly aware of the damage he was capable of doing, and the rage of that proclamation had flooded him with adrenaline. But when the words had left his mouth, he had believed that the damage he could inflict could bring about some truth amid the tangle of lies that had brought him to Atherton University. Now, all he was capable of doing was casting renewed suspicion on Lisa's death in hope that someone more powerful than he would follow the trail to 231 Slope Street.

"Are you going to record this?" he asked.

Home at last at 231 Slope Street, Eric was about to hang up his coat when he heard Pamela's laughter. It went through his nerves like a raw, electric wire. Down the front hallway, the kitchen spilled light across the hardwood floor he and Michael had so lovingly refinished that summer. He went to the kitchen doorway. When she saw him, Pamela, her face already glowing with whatever was in the glass she was drinking from, lit up with pleasant surprise. Across from her, Michael smiled, his expression a bitter parody of Pamela's. His robe was sliding off his back, his hair was slightly tousled, and his eyes did not possess the same alcohol sheen as Pamela's.

"He lives!" Michael announced.

"Play with us!" Pamela urged; she had gotten his arm and was pulling him down into a chair.

"What . . . are you playing?" he managed.

"She's lovely," Michael said under his breath, too low for Pamela to catch.

"You're not allowed to make fun of me!" Pamela said, her back to them as she uncapped the bottle of Tanqueray on the counter.

Beneath her playfulness, a spark of fear electrified her every motion. What had Michael done to unnerve her?

He turned to Michael. "When did she . . ."

"An hour ago." Michael's eyes were on Pamela. "Did you two have a date tonight?" he asked her.

"Did we?" Pamela sank down into her chair, staring at Eric over the top of her glass.

"I guess this is it," Eric answered. When his eyes met Michael's, he saw that he was smoldering with a rage that in a man with less ego might have been just simple pain. Eric was unable to look away until Pamela broke the silence.

"Believe me. I'm not one for drinking games. But this is the simplest one I know. No flipping quarters or anything like that."

"Well, that's no fun, is it, . . ." Michael trailed off, groping for what to call her.

"Pamela!" She finished for him. "How many times do I have to tell you, Michael?" She laughed and shook her head. "You're just mad because Eric's already told me all about you, but he hasn't told you a thing about me."

Sarcasm and irony were not in Pamela's nature, and Eric eyed her for signs of them.

"It's called I Never."

"That's the game?" Michael asked.

"Aren't we a little old for drinking games?" Eric asked.

Pamela ignored him, and this above all else told him something was wrong. "We go around the table and each of us has to call out something we've never done. But if you've done it, you have to drink."

"I'm game," Michael said, his voice brittle with false enthusiasm.

Eric got up from the table and Pamela grabbed his wrist, pulling him back down into the chair as she perfected her pleading baby face, her bottom lip jutting out, her eyebrows meeting above her nose. "It's fun."

"You two play. I'll watch," Eric said.

"Eric hates games he can't win," Michael remarked.

Pamela released his wrist. "There's no winner, Michael."

"Then it isn't really a game, is it?" Michael asked.

But Eric was at the sink, turning on the faucet and running water over the two dirty dishes. "I'm first," Pamela said behind him. "I've never had sex while someone else watched."

Silence. Eric turned around to see Michael sipping primly from his glass. Pamela braced herself against the edge of the table and laughed too hard.

Michael swabbed at his lips with one hand.

"Your turn," Pamela said to him.

"I've never purchased illegal drugs."

Pamela leaned back in her chair, not drinking. Michael nodded his approval at her.

"Has coke been legalized?" Eric asked.

His eyes on Pamela, Michael answered, "No. But I have very generous friends."

Eric went back to staring down into the sink, praying that both players would lose interest in their game in a few minutes. When he saw his knuckles had gone white against the edge of the counter, he withdrew his hands. "All right, let me think." Pamela giggled, and then took a breath. "I've never slept with Eric!"

Eric could not turn around. Pamela's laughter was cut short by the sound of Michael slamming down his empty glass and leaving the room.


Without warning, the cork snapped in two, sending the corkscrew spinning across the counter. Eric cursed before pulling the bread knife out from the cutlery set, stabbing at the mangled bottom half of the cork with the blade until it split into two chunks that slid down into the wine.

Lauren Raines.

The name came to him suddenly, almost as if someone had whispered it into his ear. Earlier that day, he had been so desperate to give some finality to his meeting with Mitchell that he had forgotten Mitchell's reference to the application completely. Only now did Eric realize he had never laid eyes on it.

He pulled a wineglass from the cabinet, checked to make sure it was clean, and poured himself some wine. He debated whether or not to try to fish the chunks of cork out of it. Or he could go upstairs to his second-floor office, which he rarely used, and search through the file drawer where he had stashed the other applications for the six residents of the House of Adam after reading them.

He sipped the wine; no pieces of cork stuck to his tongue when he swallowed.

Had Mitchell given him the girl's application and he'd simply forgotten? The combined effects of fatigue, the trauma of Lisa's death, and a growing nightly allotment of wine had ripped holes in his memory.

But what did it matter now? In three weeks, Mitchell would have all the freedom he wanted because Eric would no longer be around to point out how far Mitchell had strayed from the original philosophy he had gleaned from Eric's book—that humans could set aside their desires, but without pledging allegiance to a higher power other than their own minds.

In the living room, he'd left the stereo turned to the campus station's late-night classical program, the volume so low that the flutter of flutes sounded like rain against the windows. He settled into his reading chair and picked up the brochure about Montana he'd gotten from a travel agent. Nothing about Livingston. Maybe the slightly scatterbrained woman thought he just wanted to look at pictures of the Grand Tetons, which to his surprise, he did. Flipping through the glossy pages, he felt a strange stirring in his gut at the sight of endless, open plains, sunlight lancing the towering cloud formations. Some people felt horror at the sight of open spaces. Eric suspected they feared feeling anonymous, unrecognized by a landscape they could never mark or alter with their mere presence.

He ignored the sound of the car engine until headlights bounced over the living-room windows and the engine died.

He checked his watch. It was almost one thirty. He moved quickly into the foyer and opened the front door.

Lisa's old Aerostar was parked in the driveway, right behind his Camry.

Eric staggered to the edge of the porch.

It looked as if someone had aimed a flamethrower at its back end; boluses of charcoal soot had rained down the side windows, and one corner of the rear bumper was a carbuncle of black, molten rubber. A car his wife had sold months earlier was sitting in his driveway, looking as if it had been towed out of hell.

How drunk was he?

He turned back to the door. It stood open, and the sight of the darkened downstairs hallway raised the hairs on the back of his neck.

He went in and slammed the door behind him. Not thinking, he made a beeline for the kitchen and the phone. He managed to dial only nine by the time he realized there was no way to articulate his fear to the dispatcher. This was some kind of sick prank, and it made so little sense that his fear dissolved into confusion.

He returned to the living room and retrieved his wineglass, standing where he had a view of the van through the front windows. No, he wasn't hallucinating.

He took a slug from the glass.

The liquid instantly set fire to his throat, and in his rush to get both hands to his mouth he dropped the glass. It shattered, sending a spill of auburn liquid rolling across the hardwood until it met the tassels on the edge of the Persian rug.

"She was divorcing you."

His eyes still smarting from smoke and fumes, Randall stood in the dining-room doorway, tightening his grip around the bottle of Chivas Regal. Eric whirled around, his eyes wide above the forearm he held against his mouth.

"Did you know?" Randall asked.

Eric lowered his arm, gasped, and winced. He pointed weakly toward the windows and the van outside.

"That was her getaway car," Randall told him. "She was keeping it in storage."

Eric shook his head, and Randall could see he was trying to summon anger, but instead his fingers went to his throat, massaging the skin there.

"Sit down, Eric. This is going to take a minute."

Randall examined the bottle he held in both hands as Eric slumped into his reading chair, hunched over and struggling to breathe. The scotch shouldn't have been affecting him this quickly. Randall wondered if his pained grimace was due to the fact that he knew what he had just swallowed.

"You gave Mitchell Seaver a house. And she wanted to know why."

"I don't know what you're—"

"She didn't even know you owned it. She had to go to the county records to find out. And when she did, she wanted to know why you would just hand over a piece of property to one of your grad students.

So she went there. What did she *see*, Eric?" Randall crossed in front of the reading chair. Eric's eyes followed him behind his glasses. "What did she really know?"

"Why don't you tell me? It sounds like you know more than I do"

Randall wasn't going to give him such an easy out. "Paula's been in remission for over six months. Lisa wasn't going to take care of her every weekend. She was moving out, slowly, but she was doing it. And she was going to divorce you."

"She never said anything to me."

"Just like you never told her about two-thirty-one Slope Street?"

"That house was mine to sell."

"You didn't sell it. You gave it to him."

"It was a ruin. I couldn't rent it out anymore."

"So you make up for the loss by giving it away, not even charging Mitchell a dollar?"

"What I did with that house is my business. W*hat* are you trying to tell me?"

"You killed her to protect your cult," Randall said. Maybe he couldn't live the truth, but he could sure as hell find it. "She went to that house and she saw your little cult freaks fucking each other, and you killed her before she could use it against you in a divorce. That's what your little Adamites do, don't they? It's right there in your book. The Brethren of the Free Spirit, who try to free themselves from the day-to-day temptations of the flesh with one single burst of sensuality. A flattering term for an orgy."

Eric had grown stiff and remote and Randall waited for him to deny everything, or try to talk him down with cold reason, or maybe even seduce him. But instead, Eric let a silence pass through the room. His voice came out breathy and distant. "It was an accident, Randall I never meant to imply that we . . . killed her."

"You showed me her note because you wanted to make me feel responsible. But you knew the entire time that there's no way she could have seen us together that night." Randall's voice quavered and he tried to slow his words to keep his breath between them and his anger at bay. "She never even knew about us. You made sure of that. We were beyond cautious."

Eric's frame sagged with defeat—and even though Randall didn't want to admit it—dumb shock. Eric didn't look caught or guilty. He looked sidelined by some sudden realization. His eyes had drifted past Randall, but then he met Randall's stony gaze with a weak and shell-shocked one of his own. "They weren't my secret. You were."

Randall set the bottle down on the coffee table, his angry resolve fading. The man sitting in front of him was not acting like a cornered murderer.

"I never blamed you for her death," Eric continued. "I showed you that note because I blamed myself so much that I couldn't stand the solitude of it. I wanted a partner in crime, just because my burden was so big I had to share it. It was wrong of me, Randall, I know that. If anyone killed her, it was me, because I let her kill herself. Because when she started drinking and going to the doctor for more and more drugs, I wasn't the enemy anymore. She was trying to fight her own mind."

Randall couldn't bring himself to look at Eric. The quiet sincerity of Eric's sorrow blurred the portrait of Dr. Eberman as monster that Randall had clung to so desperately during the past two weeks. It stirred the fire of feelings Randall had vowed not to let burn for the man he was supposed to destroy.

"And then it was easy for me to forget that I ruined her life. That I promised to love her even when I knew I never could. And I asked her to give up her own life for the sake of mine, even though I knew I couldn't share it with her. Yes, Randall, I killed her. You didn't. And if I had known I was going to end up driving you this crazy with guilt, I never would have shown you the note. Never."

Randall stared down at the scotch bottle.

"I'm sorry, Randall."

"Don't say that to me. . . ."

"I have to. I made a horrible mistake with you. But I never thought I was capable of hurting you. I thought you were the one that had all the power over me. I was greedy. I took more from you than I ever should have, and I justified it by lying to myself and saying you were strong enough."

"Stop, Eric."

To Randall's surprise, Eric obeyed.

"What do they do?" Randall asked once he found his breath.

"Mitchell calls them purgings. They were supposed to stop after the first year," Eric muttered. "They were supposed to isolate their sexual desire, and then wean themselves from it gradually. But they never did. And now what I thought was a wonderfully insane experiment is nothing more than your bargain-basement cult. Maybe I should have seen Mitchell's arrogance. I should have realized he didn't want anything more than a band of disciples "

Randall watched the moist sheen on Eric's eyes as the man's jaw tightened to suppress the first quaver of tears. "There are few things I find more frightening than a college student who believes every single one of his convictions," he finished.

When Randall looked at Eric, he didn't see a murderer. He saw the man who would wake up tomorrow morning to find his life ruined in the *Atherton Daily Journal*. For the first time since arriving at Atherton, Randall spoke without measuring his words first and gauging how they would shape someone's perception of him. "I wanted to be who I was with you."

Eric's eyes shot to his and held his gaze, until Randall picked up the scotch bottle and pressed it against Eric's chest. "Your wife was murdered."

Eric held the bottle to his chest when Randall released. He narrowed his eyes on Randall. He seemed mildly puzzled but little else. "Good-bye, Eric."

Randall stopped on the front porch, waiting for Eric to call after him. But when he looked down he saw that one of his blue contacts had adhered to the palm of his hand. Eric had been staring at his fake blue eye and his revealed brown one. Randall stared out at the desolate street, closing his hand over the contact lens, searching for someone who might see him emerging from Eric's house for the last time. The street was empty.

The scarf was balled up inside his jacket pocket. He had kept it hidden for the past two months and had never looked at it. And he barely did now as he wedged it inside the mailbox, positioning one hem of red tassels so they spilled over the top, visible after he dropped the lid.

• • •

Even though Kathryn had been typing furiously for the last two hours, April had drifted off to sleep.

> After the article ran in the *San Francisco Chronicle*, Jono was nowhere to be found. I went so far as to call his mother, and even she had no idea where he was. I didn't know what I was going to say to him. All ten girls who had tested positive had come forward by then, and I thought I was going to be the eleventh, so maybe I just needed to hear him deny it

At first, she didn't hear the light knock on the door, so familiar that it paned her: Randall April let out a groggy groan. Kathryn stopped typing.

"Kathryn?" Randall called through the door.

She opened her desk drawer. She had already folded the printout of the *Dallas Morning News* article down the center. Randall knocked again

"Kathryn?" This time it was April stirring.

"I've got it," Kathryn whispered, rising from the chair.

Kathryn could see the shadows of Randall's feet at the bottom of the door on the other side.

"Kathryn?" he whispered against the door.

She crouched down and slid the article under the door with a flick of her wrist. As she took a step backward, she could see a shift in shadow though the crack at the bottom of the door as Randall bent down to pick it up. There was a rustling of paper and then silence. Behind her, April shifted in bed.

The door heaved, straining against its hinges, doorknob rattling. Randall had either kicked it or punched it, it was impossible to tell.

"Huh?" April grunted, sitting up behind her.

Kathryn held her ground, surprised that she hadn't even jumped.

"What the hell?" April asked behind her.

"It's all right. Go to sleep," she whispered.

She waited to hear Randall's door shut across the hall, but instead all she heard were his rough footsteps, gaining speed as they moved down the hallway.

# CHAPTER FOURTEEN

DAWN PEERED AROUND THE EDGES OF THE WINDOW SHADE.

Her vision blurring, Kathryn clicked on the print icon and sat still in her chair as the pages came humming out of the laser printer. She was done, but the realization didn't fill her with satisfaction. She felt weak, exhausted. Not proud, but emptier. Cleansed? She wasn't sure.

Milky light rose over the rooftops as she made the long walk to 231 Slope Street.

The front gate was locked so she slid the ten stapled pages inside the mailbox.

Eric's eyes drifted open to see the expanse of hardwood floor stretching out from under his nose. Gray morning light glinted off it. His forehead throbbed, but it was footsteps that had awakened him. He blinked, and could make out a set of boots standing inches from his face.

It took most of his strength to roll over, and when he did he saw Mitchell standing over him. Before Eric had time to make out the mask of silent outrage on his face, Mitchell lifted his arm. The newspaper slapped against Eric's face and fluttered open as Mitchell's footsteps retreated into the foyer and across the porch outside.

Struggling for breath, Eric managed to lift himself up onto his elbows.

The bottle of Chivas Regal still sat open on the dining-room table, right next to the still half-full glass he poured himself after Randall had left.

Trying to numb himself, Eric rolled over, spreading out the mess of newspaper pages. But he had covered up the front page, and realized that his thumb and forefingers were hiding his own forehead. He withdrew his hand and saw a black-and-white picture of himself next to the headline: **STUDENT'S ALLEGATIONS RAISE NEW QUESTIONS IN DEATH OF PROFESSOR'S WIFE.**


"Kathryn. Get up!" April was tugging on her shoulder. Kathryn weakly batted at her, but April didn't let go.

"No."

"It's Randall!"

"*What* is Randall?"

April responded by pulling her out of bed by one arm and leading her into the hallway. Thank God she was wearing a T-shirt and pajama bottoms. Halfway down the hall, they stopped in the doorway to an open room. Kathryn didn't recognize any of the students sitting cross-legged on the floor, staring rapt at the miniature television in the far corner. She was distracted from the screen — outside the window, a satellite dish extended above the tree-line of leafless branches, and the clamor outside the dorm seemed louder than the usual Wednesday morning exodus from Stockton.

"Is this local?" April asked.

"Uh-uh," one of the TV watchers answered without looking away from the set. "This is a Boston station."

On television, the news footage cut from a shot of students walking to class on McKinley Quad to a bleach-blonde reporter standing outside the Quad's front gates, a banner at her waist announcing that she was broadcasting live.

"But this morning's revelations have been greeted with a mixture of reactions. Here on the Atherton University campus, students and faculty alike are skeptical of the timing of Randall Stone's allegations that he was in bed with Eric Eberman on the night of his wife's fatal accident. Some are asking why the eighteen-year-old student waited

so long to come forward and, even more important, why did he never
go to the police? These sentiments were summed up in a terse statement issued late this morning by Atherton's vice president of public
affairs, John Hawthorne."

"What the hell is he doing, Kathryn?" April whispered. Kathryn
just shook her head.

"Hawthorne says, quote, 'The university remains highly skeptical
of Mr. Stone's allegations in light of the fact that he chose to voice
them to a news source. It remains to be seen whether this young man
has any basis for these very serious charges. If so, Atherton University
will deal with them appropriately.' "

The news footage cut to file shots of Lisa Eberman's mauled Volvo
station wagon being hauled from the river. The same footage Kathryn
had watched from behind the bar at Madeline's with Randall the night
of the accident, without a clue why Randall had gone so white and distant when he heard.

". . . and of course one of the most pressing questions here in this
small college town, rocked by scandal, is what exactly do the police
think of this young man's claim that he carried on a month-long
sexual affair with Dr. Eric Eberman? What possible bearing might
this new information have on the death of forty-one-year-old Lisa
Eberman just three short weeks ago? So far, the answer from the
police has been a resounding, 'No Comment!' "

Kathryn turned to April. "Where is he?"

"Gone," she answered, her voice hushed. "Either that, or he's bar-
ricaded himself in his room. Some reporters got into the dorm this
morning. They were pounding on his door when I woke up. Tran and
I called campus security."

"You didn't talk to them, did you?"

"Of course not. But now they're parked up and down the block.
Just about everyone in Stockton's had a chance to say, 'Get that goddamn microphone out of my face.' Kathryn, did you *know* about
this?"

Kathryn just stared down the length of the hallway to where the door
to Randall's room still bore the construction-paper signs announcing the
room's occupants, both of whom had now disappeared.

"This is fucking huge, all right, Kathryn," April continued. "His story's on the front page of the paper, and now reporters from up and down the eastern seaboard are crawling all over campus."

"Do they know I'm his friend?"

"Maybe. I don't know. I didn't tell them anything. Did you know he was going to—"

"No." Kathryn shook her head violently.

April shut her eyes and bowed her head. "Look, I don't even really know what's going on, but I know that this Eberman guy's life has just been ruined. Are you saying you don't have any idea why Randall would want to do something like that?"

When April saw Kathryn's expression she let out a short hiss of breath. "I know who might have a clue," she said.


Tim answered on the third ring.

"Have you seen it?" Kathryn asked.

"Yeah."

Kathryn waited for him to continue, but he did not. "Nice work," she said finally.

"Hey! Wait a minute! How much has he told you?"

"Nothing. I figured most of it out on my own." *With a little help from Jesse Lowry*, she thought wryly.

"Then I don't feel comfortable—"

"Oh, spare me, Tim!" she barked. "You practically accused Eberman of murder in the *Herald* and then three weeks later Randall outs him in the *Atherton Journal*. This has got your name written all over it."

"As I just said, I don't feel comfortable—"

"Randall's *gone*, Tim. He dropped his bomb and then ran for cover. Was that part of your plan?"

His shocked silence indicated she'd just scored a point. "We didn't have a plan."

"You helped him, though?"

"Yes."

"Tim, you didn't have the first clue who you were helping."

"*What?*"

"Just get over here. I have something to show you."

She hung up before Tim could respond.

• • •

It had only taken Tim a few minutes to read "Drywater, Texas," by Randall Stone. Once he was finished, Kathryn handed him the print-out of the article on the catastrophic derailment of a Dallas-bound Southern Union train that destroyed the Valley Vista Mobile Home Park. When she knew he was finished, she waited for him to look up from the paper he held in both hands. He didn't.

"How could a dead runaway get admitted to this school?" he finally asked.

"I don't know."

"So? What?" Tim tossed the paper back at her. She didn't make a move to catch it and it fluttered to the floor.

"How did Randall get you to go along with this?"

"He had proof that Eberman murdered his wife."

"What proof?" Kathryn barked.

"He said . . ."

"Oh, he *said*!"

"What are you trying to get at here?"

"Everything Randall has said since he got here has been a lie, Tim. He's not from New York and his parents aren't even alive, much less living in some apartment on Park Avenue. And his name isn't even Randall Stone. And maybe we can add in everything he said to get you into bed with him so that you could help him do what he did this morning. Which was ruin a man's life."

Tim swallowed his anger and kept his voice steady. "You think he's lying about Eberman?"

"I don't know where it ends with him, Tim. And you don't either."

"Kathryn, for two people with no investigative experience, we turned up some evidence—"

"Really?" She picked up her copy of the *Atherton Journal*. "Why isn't any of it in here? We've got Randall in bed with Eberman. We've even got Randall going down on Eberman in his friggin' office. But nothing about murder."

Tim rose from the chair as if it would be easier to speak to the vanity. "Because I fucked up. Look . . ." He turned as if he was arguing his case before a judge. "We found a letter that Lisa had written to a divorce attorney. Something about a property dispute. Anyway, the important thing was that it proved she was planning on getting a divorce. But Randall was still too chicken to come forward. I mean, some of the shit he was saying . . . It was crazy. Anyway, last night, I delivered the letter to the attorney it was addressed to, thinking that even if Randall didn't talk, a letter from a dead woman would be enough to reopen the case. Well, it turns out I put our most important piece of evidence behind the iron wall of attorney-client privilege."

"The lawyer won't talk?"

"Not to us. He'll talk to the police, who don't even know what he has. Richard couldn't mention the letter without a quote."

"Because you stole it," Kathryn answered, unable to keep the reproach out of her voice.

"Look, I don't know what you want!"

"Take a look outside, Tim. Look at what you and Randall have done. Don't you think that if Randall's allowed to slaughter Dr. Eberman's reputation just by talking to a reporter, it's only fair that the reporters crawling all over this campus know exactly who's making these accusations?"

"It's not an accusation, Kathryn. They were fucking."

"Tim!"

"All right. So Randall lied about his past. Maybe he was ashamed of being an orphan. Maybe he grew up in foster homes. That doesn't change the fact that together he and I found compelling evidence that Eric Eberman murdered his wife! And considering that this porno article in the *Journal* is the best we could do, I'm not going to jeopardize any chance of getting the police to look at this again!"

Kathryn shook her head at Tim's resistance. "He changed his name, Tim. He came here with a fake identity prepared. He wasn't just ashamed of his past. He's eighteen and he *erased* it. He's not just an orphan who grew up in foster homes. He's a con artist, Tim, and he pulled one over on you, me, and maybe even Eric Eberman."

"Kind of stupid for a *con artist* to write down his big secret and just give it to you, isn't it?"

"He told me it was just a story."

"Still, he gave it to you." Tim sounded happy to have a new battleground to stand on. "You want to know what he told me about you?"

"I probably won't believe it."

"He thought he was Eric's motive for killing his wife. And part of him liked that. But another part of him stayed awake nights just thinking about what *you* would think if you knew what he had done. Sleeping with a married man. He thought if he found out the truth it would make it all easier for you to accept in the end."

Kathryn looked away, shaking her head free of Tim's words and the memory that after giving her the story, Randall had pleaded with her not to show it to anyone else. And she had agreed.

"You're probably the only one here he holds himself accountable to."

"He's not here anymore," she muttered.

Nor was Jesse. And what had he written on Randall when he discovered that Randall's entire identity was fabricated, that Randall was a runaway believed dead? Jesse had called it awe-inspiring.

"The fact that Randall just decided to leave town fucks with his whole credibility," Tim said. "Since I honestly believe that the strength of his accusations are the only thing that's going to help get at the truth here, I'll do something that should satisfy you."

Kathryn felt something go soft inside her chest. "What?"

" 'Who is Randall Stone?' That'll be the headline."

"In the *Herald*?"

"Yeah. It'll have to be subtle, and it'll have to be mainly about the fact that he's skipped town. The *Herald* will make it clear that in its attempt to write a fair and balanced piece it was unable to find any way to contact Randall Stone. Which will put the university on the spot, since they're the only ones who have any concrete documentation on him. And if his identity is really as fake as you think it is, Atherton will figure out they've been conned too. Although how the twelfth-ranked school in the nation doesn't already know is beyond me."

Kathryn nodded. "You just want to force him to come back and defend himself."

"Yeah, I do," Tim answered sharply. "And maybe when you get over how much he betrayed you, you'll remember there's a dead woman at the middle of this."

Chastened, she took a breath before responding. "Fine. But he ran away before. Maybe he's done it again."

Tim rolled his eyes and moved for the door.

"Tim?"

He stopped without turning.

"You really believe she was murdered."

"Yes."

"You believe everything Randall told you?"

Tim turned. "I don't have to. The letter we found made it clear that Lisa knew her husband handed over an entire house to one of his grad students for free. Randall thinks they were some kind of cult, but that just sounds crazy. . . ."

"Who?" Kathryn asked. Her blood had gone cold.

"What?"

"A grad student?"

"Some guy named Mitchell Seaver. Total prick. Anyway, Randall thinks Mitchell used it to start some whacked-out cult that holds orgies or something. He found this weird essay in Eric's house, obviously written to Mitchell, from this girl who'd been molested by her uncle. He tried to tell me it was some kind of application. The point is he was grabbing at straws, trying to delay the inevitable."

*Cult.* The word burned across her mind, stopped her breath in her throat.

Tim continued, "Lisa was divorcing Eric and it wasn't going to be pretty. Given his extracurricular activities, I think Eric would have liked to see that not happen."

She couldn't bring herself to look up from the floor as Tim left the room. She was thinking of the essay she had slid into the mailbox at 231 Slope Street. Her stomach turned at the thought of six people reading it.

As Kathryn approached 231 Slope Street, the brownstone rose out of what looked like an erupting cotton field; snowflakes were camouflaged by the milky white sky and visible only where they skittered across the house's facade. With gloved fingers she dug into the mailbox slot, hoping to feel the slip of her essay against the metal, but the box had been emptied, her essay presumably taken in with the mail. The house's gate was locked.

Behind her an engine groaned up the hill. Kathryn saw a Honda Civic round the far corner—Maria's car. She crammed her back against one of the stone posts, listening as the Civic slowed to a halt. The driveway gate clanged open and the Civic's tires crunched gravel.

Kathryn stepped out from her cover to see the gate make its slow swing shut. She ducked through it, as close to the hedge line as possible.

At the end of the driveway, Maria popped the Civic's trunk. She and Lauren dug inside and backed up, carrying opposite ends of something large and heavy. They squeezed between the car and the house's side wall. Whatever they were holding responded with a clinking of glass.

Kathryn waited until Maria and Lauren had disappeared behind the house. Then she moved quickly down the driveway and along the wall. At the back corner of the house, she could hear the girls grunting as they moved up the back steps. "Why don't we take some of them out?" Lauren asked.

"Just keep moving. Please." Maria's voice was tight.

Kathryn dared to peer around the corner. They were inside, Maria's butt still propping the back door open. Kathryn reached out and caught the edge of the door, letting it close on her gloved hand.

Footsteps scraped across the kitchen floor, followed by the thuds of glass bottles hitting the countertop. Kathryn kept her hand wedged in the door. Snow dusted her face.

"All right. What first?" Lauren's voice asked.

"Start by opening them."

"Yeah. I figured."

"This isn't calculus, Lauren. You've seen Mitchell do it a hundred times."

"Stop it, already!" Lauren snapped. "I barely even know the guy and you're treating me like I was his best friend. I understand you're upset but—"

"That's *all* you understand," Maria barked. Where was the delicate, doe-eyed girl Kathryn had been introduced to at the library? After a tense silence, Maria continued, tone steady, "Grind them until there aren't any lumps. Use the funnel to get them in the bottle and try to make sure it doesn't stick to the side. Then put them back in the case . . ."

"I can't believe you're blaming me for this!" Lauren cut her off.

"It was a stupid idea, Lauren!"

"Why? If Mitchell wanted to know so badly, who better to tell him than that . . . *faggot's* best friend? You should have seen them at the beginning of the year, they were like—"

"I don't care what they we're like!" Maria shouted, sounding nothing like an angry girlfriend, and too much like a mentor whose patience had been tested to its limit. "Unlike Mitchell, I didn't care what Eric was doing in bed with anyone. But—"

"I told him to *talk* to her."

Maria continued over her, "But now she's just a step away from living in this house. Can you not see why that bothers me?"

Kathryn heard rapid footsteps leaving the kitchen and assumed that Lauren had exited in a huff. But it was Lauren's voice that shouted, "How the hell was I supposed to know her boyfriend almost gave her AIDS?"

Kathryn's hand blocking the door tensed around its edge. The first sting of betrayal gave way to a cold fury that fueled her courage. She peered through the cracked door. Lauren stood with her hands on her hips, glaring at four bottles of white wine on the counter in front of her. She turned to one of the cabinets, reached in, and removed something. Kathryn saw her prying at the childproof lock on a bottle of prescription medication.

Lauren uncapped the bottle and emptied pills into a ceramic mortar on the counter. She picked up the pestle lying next to it and angrily ground the pills into a powder.

Previously, Lauren's transformation had seemed cosmetic to Kathryn. But watching her now, Kathryn saw dark circles under her eyes that dramatized the pallor of her skin, which itself seemed more drawn. She'd lost weight, and the simple task of grinding the pills left her breathless. Then her attention began to wander from her repetitive work. Her eyes drifted to Kathryn's unwavering gaze.

Lauren cried out and leaped back from the counter, tipping the mortar and sending a shower of blue powder onto the floor. She lost her balance and hit the floor butt first. Kathryn kicked the door open, strode across the kitchen, shut the door to the dining room, and threw her back against it.

"What are you doing?" Lauren gasped.

"I ask the questions right now."

"Kathryn, any questions you have, you have to ask Mitchell. I'm sure he's told you—"

"He hasn't told me *shit*! He pretended to be interested in me, he asked me out on a date and the whole time I was pledging your fucked-up fraternity. What the hell is this, Lauren?"

Lauren just sat there, her hands pressed to the floor alongside her thighs, seemingly so unthreatened by Kathryn that she wasn't going to cry out. Kathryn stepped away from the kitchen door. "All right, fine, how about your question then? It's a good one. You couldn't have possibly known that my ex-boyfriend almost gave me AIDS. So how the fuck do you know now?"

Lauren lifted her head, expression blank. "Mitchell said it was the perfect lesson."

"What do you mean?"

"Kathryn, I'm not going to talk to you when you're—"

Kathryn wrenched the collar of Lauren's shirt into one fist and yanked her off the floor. "Get off me!" Lauren cried, grabbing at Kathryn's wrist, and Kathryn shoved her, sending her into the side of the counter. She cast a nervous glance toward the door, but no footsteps came echoing through the house in response.

Despite Kathryn's display of force, Lauren remained unnervingly composed, staring blankly at Kathryn as if just biding the time it would take for her to leave. Lauren's complacency was adding fuel to her already smoldering anger; Mitchell had shared everything she had told him with strangers, and she wasn't about to be stonewalled by someone who seemed to be filled with the unquestioning resolve of a . . . she couldn't think of a better term than cult member.

"I know you were molested, Lauren. And I know Jesse knew too."

Nothing. Not a blip. Maybe false pity would do the trick. "And I'm very sorry."

Lauren straightened herself, raking her blackened hair back into place with one hand. "You think that's why I'm here? I don't need you or anyone else to feel sorry for me. And I don't live here now because I need pity. We don't deal in pity. And Kathryn, no one here's going to hold your hand because you were so hot for your badass boyfriend that you turned the other cheek when he infected all your friends with AIDS. We're not going to feel sorry for you because your sex drive almost killed you."

Kathryn was too stunned to interrupt. Lauren's composure was giving way to anger that forced breath between each of her words.

"This house is for people who are fed up with being told that their bodies are something to be obeyed. They're not. They're something to be overcome. How many more false costumes will lust have to wear before everyone else figures out what we have?" Her words sounded rehearsed but urgent, and Kathryn had no doubt that Lauren believed them, with a little help from what she'd been grinding into a fine powder. "Our sex drives promise everything and deliver nothing. It offers only the briefest of pleasures and gives the most lasting of pain. And human beings are so weak that they endow this meaningless physical act with all the emotional qualities of fulfillment and purpose that can be found in every other aspect of daily life."

"Mitchell and Maria, they taught you this?" Kathryn asked.

"My uncle taught me. And Jono Morton taught you."

Kathryn started to lunge at her and was happy to see Lauren shrink back against the counter.

"Jono taught me that it was entirely too easy to live my life as nothing more than a product of what someone else did to me." Kathryn's voice was hard, the words of her reply becoming true and apparent to her even as she said them. "If he taught me anything, it was just how easy it is to consider yourself nothing more than the disease you might have, or what someone else did to you. The only thing you've been *taught*, Lauren, is how to make wallowing in your own self-pity sound like an intellectual pursuit."

Kathryn turned for the door. "I told him you weren't ready," Lauren called after her.

"Yeah, well, maybe he just wanted to fuck me," she answered without stopping.


"Is Mitchell Seaver here?"

The receptionist looked up from her magazine, startled to see Kathryn standing in front of her desk. Almost all the office doors on the first floor of the art history department were shut, and Kathryn guessed that emergency meetings were being held in hushed tones on the other side about the fresh disgrace Eric Eberman was bringing to their department.

"You're a student?" the receptionist asked, still holding her magazine open.

"Yes. Not a reporter," Kathryn answered with as gracious a smile as she could muster.

The old woman chucked. "Mitchell should be in Adamson right now. Filling in for Dr. Eberman."

Adamson Hall was one of the oldest buildings on McKinley Quad. Gothic in form, it held only two lecture halls, and when Kathryn stepped into the foyer she could hear Mitchell's amplified voice coming from behind the swinging doors directly ahead. She stepped through the doors, surveying the darkened two-hundred-seat auditorium in front of her. Most of the seats were filled with students hunched over their notebooks. On stage, Mitchell lectured from the podium in a halo of light. The authoritative sound of his voice, rising and falling in pitch so as to avoid a boring monotone, recalled all the nicely packaged lectures he had used to calm her into letting down her guard and sharing her personal trauma.

Before her renewed fury could paralyze her, she began walking down the aisle. A few students stirred in their seats, but when Kathryn glanced in their direction she saw that they weren't students at all. The rear rows of the auditorium were filled with reporters, bored, some checking their watches or consulting notepads on their knees that were half the size of the ones the students were using.

Despite the presence of the journalists who had come to document his mentor's downfall, Mitchell Seaver was giving a command performance.

She was halfway down the aisle when he spotted her, but he didn't stop lecturing until she ascended the steps to the stage.

"Kathryn," he muttered as she approached the podium.

When he saw the expression on her face, realization flickered in his eyes before it was replaced by a look of bewildered indignation. The star had been interrupted.

Slapping a man was a revenge reserved for soap opera heroines; it was a desperate, usually hysterical attempt to show strength, and in her experience it usually failed miserably at making a woman feel better or a man chastened. Instead, Kathryn grabbed Mitchell by one shoulder to steady herself.

"The answer's no," she whispered, before she rammed her knee into his groin.

Shocked gasps turned to laughter, and as she left the hall, flash-bulbs lit up the back rows.

Eric held the front door open, expecting John Hawthorne to duck through it quickly as if seeking cover. When Hawthorne stepped formally across the threshold, Eric guessed that this meant the reporters outside had abandoned their vigil. By five o'clock, all three local television stations had already called the house, and Hawthorne had been lucky to get hold of Eric before he had disconnected the phone.

Without a word of greeting, Hawthorne moved into the living room, eyes darting to the shutters that had been drawn over the windows. He scanned the room, maybe in search of the wrench used to kill Lisa in the library, Eric thought bitterly.

"My office faxed a preliminary response to the *Journal* this morning, and then we put out a general press release." Hawthorne tossed his coat onto the arm of the sofa and backed up to the gas fire, warming himself with his hands crossed behind his back. His eyes met Eric's without warmth or sympathy. "The university is, of course, puzzled by these allegations and highly suspicious of the source."

"Something to drink?'

"Talk to me like I'm a student, Eric. What's going on here?"

Eric gave him a dry smile and saw Hawthorne regretted his word choice. All he wanted with Hawthorne was to convey his unwillingness to fight. There was no lawyer present, and Eric didn't plan on hiring one.

"I didn't kill my wife. Can you fax that to the *Atherton Journal*?"

"That isn't my concern," Hawthorne said. Clearly he didn't appreciate Eric's candor. He surveyed Eric with disdain, as if he wanted to make sure Eric didn't have any more barbs up his sleeve. "I am the first in a long line of visitors. None of whom you will want to welcome into your living room. I also happen to be the friendliest one of the bunch."

Eric managed a nod. "Are you sure I can't get you something to drink?"

"Is this humor that I'm being deflected with?"

"Yes."

"I admire your levity given the circumstances."

"And I admire the fact that the university I've worked at for over a decade has sent the campus publicist as its emissary," Eric retorted. Hawthorne raised his eyebrows, indicating he was little more than impressed that Eric could attempt to be the angry one in the room. "Atherton will be rid of me soon enough. I'd like the remaining time I spend here in my own home not to be wasted."

"What do you have?" Hawthorne asked. Eric looked at him finally, puzzled. "To drink. What do you have?"

"Wine. White."

"I'll take it," Hawthorne answered.

In the kitchen, Eric poured Hawthorne a glass from one of the bottles he had stolen from the House of Adam.

Hawthorne accepted it with a wan smile and took a tiny sip. "Do you even know Randall Stone?" he asked after a heavy silence.

Eric nodded at the fire. Hawthorne didn't press any further.

"The fact that Randall Stone made these claims to a newspaper has the administration viewing him with more dubiousness than it's viewing you right now. He doesn't have a prayer if he ever plans to file a complaint against you with the disciplinary council. Also, I'm not sure if you're aware, but it turns out that Mr. Stone is currently nowhere to be found. All that being said, I was allowed to take a rather extraordinary step."

Eric, who had barely been listening, his mind on the purging that would take place that night, turned at Hawthorne's final sentence.

"I secured a copy of his application. Under the condition that I keep it to myself, of course."

Eric had to stop himself from asking Hawthorne if he had brought it with him. Even now, the idea of being given a glimpse into Randall's past, a past the young man had ferociously guarded, lit a hot flicker of excitement in him. He managed to quell it with sarcasm. "That's pretty impressive, John. If some students run for president, Atherton doesn't want anyone finding out they were admitted with a two point zero high-school GPA and two parents who donated a new dorm."

Hawthorne blanched and stared at the floor. "Are you familiar with this young man's background?"

"He's from New York," Eric answered weakly. *Also his legs are covered with burns and I never once believed his explanation for them.*

"I'll get to the point. What I discovered in his application could end up being a double-edged sword."

"I'm not following."

"The registrar's office swears they know nothing about it and just by asking I've become rather unpopular all of a sudden. But Randall Stone is probably the first student Atherton has ever admitted who was homeschooled for his entire high-school career. Never mind that his birth certificate's missing."

"I thought we had a rather thorough admissions committee."

"They believe they're thorough, which might explain why they haven't returned my calls."

"What are you saying, John?" Eric asked, genuinely confused.

Hawthorne met his eyes. "Randall Stone is engaged in a media battle and nothing more. If I had the full faith and confidence that you did not have a sexual relationship with this young man, I could find a way to let this information slip regarding his application. And the next time this young man tried to talk to a reporter, first he would have to explain just why he was admitted to Atherton without a basic high-school education and proof of his own birth."

Eric was struck silent. *Proof of his own birth?* What was Hawthorne saying? But the man mistook Eric's silence for indecision. "I imagine it's a tough decision. Asking the university to go to the barricades for you. And to be quite frank, the resulting explosion might be something even I couldn't manage."

Eric remained mute. Hawthorne took his second swallow of wine since sitting down. "Pretend I'm not who I am. Pretend I don't work for Atherton. How well do you know this young man?"

"Well."

"Then it should be no mystery to you why anything regarding Mr. Stone might merit my attentions first? Why the university sent me as its emissary, as you said."

Eric said nothing.

"Can you imagine the story? A complete refurbishment of the Sciences Library, a brand-new Technology Center at half the original estimate. Three more projects in the works. And what did Atherton have to do to get its discount? Admit a young man who probably didn't have the credentials to be accepted to your average junior college."

Eric's breath left him and a sudden chill told him that blood was leaving his face. Hawthorne noticed. "Eric, you didn't know?"

Eric gripped the mantel to hold his balance as the past sank its teeth into the present.

"Michael Price is listed as Randall Stone's legal guardian."

# CHAPTER FIFTEEN

APRIL WAS SLIDING HANGERS ON THE ROD AND TOSSING CANDIDATES for the evening's outfit onto her mattress. Kathryn lazily flipped through the pages of Randall's story. "Come on, Kathryn. You can laugh about it a little! Aren't you the least bit excited you got on the news?"

"Enough, April."

A television cameraman had been taking his break inside Adamson Hall that afternoon, and as a result the sound bite of Mitchell doubling over against Kathryn's knee had run at the tail end of the local Channel 2 News as comic relief, the anchors speculating on whether or not it was the final scene in a college romance gone wrong.

"Well, Karen was totally psyched. She had that prick as a TA last year and all he did on her papers was correct her grammar."

On the back of her neck, Kathryn could feel April approaching the chair. She felt an urge to hide the story. Fuck it. Randall was long gone anyway.

"Did he cheat on you or something?"

Kathryn's laugh felt like a cough.

"Kathryn." April's tone was grave, so Kathryn turned, resting the story on her lap. "Talk to me."

Kathryn sank her teeth into her lower lip and lowered her eyes from April in a gesture that must have looked like shame. "Where are you off to?"

"The library. With Karen."

"Can you be late?"

"I guess."

Kathryn got up, squatted, and removed Jesse's laptop from under her bed. April's expression remained fixed and expectant right up until Kathryn handed her the laptop. She took it reluctantly, looking from the computer to Kathryn. "It's Jesse's," Kathryn answered before she could ask. "I found it under his bed."

"You should have shown it to me earlier."

"April, don't start in on me, all right? It—"

"No. I just mean you don't know crap about computers."

April took a seat on her bed, crossing her legs and popping the computer open in front of her. The phone rang and Kathryn grabbed for it, trying to ignore the small voice inside that shouted *It's Randall! Answer it quick!*

"Hello?"

"Did you kick some guy in the balls on TV?"

"What?"

"Carol just called me. She said she saw you on the six o'clock news . . ." And her father, who had no way of knowing all that had happened to her in the past forty-eight hours, broke down into half-choked laughter.

April was deftly working her way through Jesse's files. Kathryn clamped her hand over the mouthpiece. "Journal. It's a Word file."

"You're a star, Kathryn," her father said when he caught his breath.

"Does Carol still live in Minneapolis?" Kathryn asked.

"Yep. She said they ran it on the local six o'clock news there. At the end, though. Like those stories about little dogs that can howl the 'Battle Hymn of the Republic.' No luck here though, but your mother and I are staying up past eleven just in case."

"Great."

"Violent outbursts aside, are you all right?"

"Uh-huh," she answered without pretense of happiness. She could see that April was reading the file because her expression was tight, her eyes locked on the screen as her hand clicked the mouse to page down every few seconds.

"So what did this jerk do, anyway?"

"He wanted me to join a cult."

Her father started laughing again, and repeated her answer to her mother. "Is she kidding?" she heard her mother ask from the other room.

"Yes. I'm kidding. I gotta go, Dad."

"Do you think I can see a tape?"

"Good-bye." She hung up. "Which one are you reading?"

"Guess," April answered without looking up.

Kathryn slid open her desk drawer and removed the printout of the article. She dropped it next to April and went back to her own bed. April finished reading the file and then picked up the article. She finished reading that too without flinching, without even shaking her head at what she'd just discovered. Instead, she turned her attention back to the computer.

"So?"

"Disgusting."

"Which one?"

"Jesse."

Kathryn waited for her to continue. She didn't. "And Randall?" she asked impatiently.

April glanced up at her, as if debating whether to give her input. "Sad. But I'm not surprised."

"Excuse me?" Kathryn asked incredulously.

"All right. Let me be fair. *This* I never could have predicted, but if you had ever asked me if I really thought he was some sort of Park Avenue prince, well . . ."

Her attention was back on the screen.

"What are you looking for?"

"His cache."

Kathryn got up and went over to April's side of the room. On the screen, April had opened a folder labeled "Temporary Internet Files."

"He never cleared it," April said.

"What is it?"

"Every time you go on the Net and download a web page, your computer automatically saves a copy in your hard drive so it can load it faster the next time you visit the site. Unless you tell it not to, which Jesse didn't. Look at this . . ." April paged down. The list was endless. "This is like a record of everything he's ever looked at on line."

"Great. Porn."

"No, actually. Either Jesse was planning on writing a history of the passport, or he was interested in getting out of the country." April kept looking at the computer. "He checked out passport and visa requirements for Canada and three countries in South America. And he visited just about every website he could find with general travel information for . . ." She clicked. "Boy was a world traveler—it looks like—islands in the Caribbean, Brazil, Nova Scotia. He also visited three travel agency websites on a regular basis. Bestrip dot com. Rates Etcetera dot com."

Kathryn remembered a drunken Randall, collapsed outside the door to his room. His babble jibed with what April was discovering. "Cozumel," he had slurred. Followed by "The phone lines end."

"What are you saying?" Kathryn asked.

"I'm just saying what's right here. And maybe he could pay for it too. The guy sure never wasted a dime shopping on line."

Kathryn shook her head.

"What else did you look at in here?" April asked.

"His E-mail. There was a message from his dad's lawyer. A couple weeks ago his dad went to rehab. Got sent to rehab, actually."

"What for?"

"It didn't say."

"For how long?"

"Twenty-eight days."

"Starting three weeks ago. I'd say that gives Jesse plenty of time to get out of town."

"Oh, come on, April!"

"Kathryn, what do you want me to say?" April slid the computer aside and stretched her legs. "The guy never put down a single root here. He didn't even make any friends. Reading those entries, it was like the only people Jesse ever came into contact with at this school were people he despised, that he thought were weak. And if his father is such a fucking nightmare that he got *sent* to rehab, maybe the only reason Jesse came to Atherton in the first place was to get as far away from him as possible. Now his dad's in some clinic, and Jesse has the chance to get even farther away, and by the time his dad finds out it'll be too late."

"So you think he just hopped on a jet to Brazil?" Kathryn asked sarcastically. "He just ran away like a little kid?"

"Considering how awestruck he was when he found out Randall did the same thing, maybe he got inspired." April rose and slid one arm through her coat.

"And he just leaves his computer?"

"A small oversight considering what he was planning on doing."

"How small? It's got all the evidence of what he was planning to do. Not to mention concrete proof that he was an unforgivable asshole."

April stared hard at her. "Randall may be a professional liar, Kathryn. But that doesn't mean he did something unthinkable to Jesse when he figured out who Randall really was." Kathryn lowered her eyes as April centered a searchlight on the suspicions that had been plaguing her for the past three days. "Here you've got a sociopath with a drug-addict father who, if he doesn't long to get away, sure has an obsession with faraway places. And then he figures out he's living with someone who managed not only to run away from home, but come up with an entirely new identity. He called it 'awe-inspiring,' Kathryn."

April stopped, but from her face it didn't look like she was finished, just afraid to keep going. She began buttoning her jacket.

"You think Randall went to meet him, don't you?"

The thrill of deduction vanished from April's face. "Why not? What's keeping him here? He got his revenge against Eberman. And he's lost you as a friend."

When April laid a sympathetic hand on Kathryn's shoulder, Kathryn stepped out from under it and moved to her desk chair, but April didn't leave.

"Kathryn, I love you. But you like drama. Epic, who-shot-JR drama. And I hate to be the one to tell you that maybe you and Jesse weren't really engaged in some immortal battle for Randall's soul. Maybe Jesse just needed Randall to show him how to do what he'd wanted to do for a long time now. And when Jesse asked, Randall listened to his balls instead of his brain."

April waited for Kathryn to say something, and when she didn't, April withdrew from the room.

Once she was gone, Kathryn picked up Randall's story and read.

Outside the principal's office, Mrs. Warrington waited, sitting next to Ricky and fearing another outburst like the one he'd had in class. During their silence, the entire waiting room began to rattle, chair legs knocking against the linoleum floor. Ricky was silent and sullen, unresponsive to the shaking caused by the passing locomotive.

"Sometimes I think that sound will drive me crazy," she said with a smile.

Ricky turned his head and stared at her blankly. "It's the only reason we're here," the boy said.

Suddenly, she remembered Ricky's poor mother. The boy leaned forward, his hands gripping the arm of the chair, the only thing that separated them. He spoke through clenched teeth. "We are here because my mother was killed by a train!"

She jumped when the phone rang.

"Hello?"

"Kathryn Parker?"

She didn't recognize the man's voice and didn't answer.

"Kathryn. This is Eric Eberman."

"I don't know where he is."

Silence came from the other end, and Kathryn rose from her chair slowly, as if to protect herself from someone who might enter the room. "Kathryn, I've finished reading your essay and I'd like to discuss it with you."

Her mouth opened even though she had no clue what to say.

But he had already hung up.

"Meeting him. It kind of put you in perspective," said Pamela Milford.

Eric had drawn her coat around her shoulders and her sticky fingers were attempting to button it, to no avail, so he took over. She reached past his shoulder for the red scarf dangling from a hook on the coat rack. She was still drunk, but her words came out with almost subversive coherence.

"What do you mean?" he asked, not wanting to, after he'd finished buttoning her coat.

"Like I said, I bet a lot of people don't get his sense of humor. Don't get *him*, really. But I bet you spend a lot of your time sticking up for Michael, explaining Michael. Maybe you've taken the time to understand him in a way that nobody else in his life has. And to me, that says you have a lot of character." She pulled one end of the scarf over the other and wedged both between her sweater and the collar of her jacket. "It's a compliment, Eric. Are you going to fight me on it?"

Was she pretending for him? Did she really think Michael was just joking, or had alcohol clouded her judgment?

Eric cupped her cheek with one hand, leaned in, and kissed her gently on the lips. When he withdrew he saw her eyes were still slitted, her lips still slightly puckered, as if still savoring the taste of his lips, testing the sincerity of it.

She reached up and patted his jaw. His head was swimming and part of him didn't want to her to leave him there, with Michael's rage quietly and patiently awaiting him upstairs, but if she didn't go he was sure Michael would come downstairs.

"I'll call you."

She nodded. "Good."

But what she meant was, "You'd better." What she meant was *I know, and have known for a while, a lot more than you think I do*.

After she passed through the door, he held it open for several moments, taking the time to watch her pass through the front gate and cross the street, all without glancing at the house.

Only when she was gone did he realize.

She was wearing the scarf.

When he turned around, Michael was at the top of the stairs, his hip resting against the newel post. He was backlit by a lamp, but Eric himself was harshly illuminated by the chandelier overhead; he knew his every move was readable, while he could discern only Michael's silhouette.

Michael spoke first. "I want the scarf. Then I'll leave."

Low, driving winds parted the clouds that had sent down snow that afternoon, shadowing the thumbnail moon over the roof of Eric Eberman's house. Kathryn hesitated at the bottom of the front steps, one hand on the rail. The shutters were drawn over the living-room windows, an eerie reminder of 231 Slope Street. Flickering firelight danced in the narrow spaces between the slats.

As she went up the steps, she noticed the sedan parked halfway up the block; the shadows of wind-jerked tree branches played across its solid, polished black paint and tinted windows. Its front tires seemed too far apart and the top of a thick radio antenna stuck up over the back of the roof. Trademarks of an unmarked cop car. Jono had once run them all off for her in a casual display of his bad-boy knowhow Of course, she'd had no idea at the time why Jono had cause to fear undercover cops.

Eric Eberman was under surveillance. The shadow behind the steering wheel had gone still as Kathryn stared straight back at the car.

When the front door of the house opened, Kathryn just watched as a beam of firelight stretched across the front porch almost to where she stood on the top step. Eric Eberman was just a shadow

"You can come in." His voice sounded measured and calm.

"I already told Mitchell Seaver I don't want to live in his house."

"Yes, I saw the local news. Although there wasn't much *telling* involved, was there?"

There was a wry note of admiration in his voice, and if she could see his face, she wouldn't have been surprised to see him smiling.

He withdrew and left the door open.

Before entering the foyer, she gave a last glance at the shadow cop, wondering whether or not entering the house would somehow incriminate her, associate her with a suspected murderer. She followed the light of the fire into the living room. Eric had settled into a reading chair. Her essay was folded across his lap. He licked a thumb and flipped pages as she hovered.

This was the house in which Randall had spent most of his time when he wasn't with her. Burgundy-painted walls, dark, varnished bookshelves lining them, slightly worn but inviting furniture. An atmosphere of scholarly meditation in which one woman drank herself to death, and the man sitting in front of her received sexual pleasure from an eighteen-year-old. Like the room, Eric Eberman's appearance ran contrary to his actions.

"What do you want?" she asked, anger meeting fear in her voice.

"I want to know why you hold yourself responsible for Jono's death."

She shook her head slightly, not as defiantly as she had intended to, and looked to the shuttered windows as she heard Eric rustling pages.

"This young man set about getting your friends addicted to cocaine so that he could infect them with HIV. Unless that, of course, is just an assumption on your part."

"It isn't. He told me."

"But he spared you. On purpose. In here" — he held up the essay as evidence — "you detail that he was insistent about contraception with you. In fact, you say that at times you thought he was being over-cautious. Condoms even for oral sex, you wrote."

"I know what I wrote," she said tightly.

Eric paused, and she summoned up nerve. "Did Mitchell give this to you?" she asked.

"Mitchell never saw this." He saw how puzzled she was and added, "Yes, I stole it from the mailbox. Because I would not stand back and watch Mitchell pry his way into another person's pain in the name of acquiring another adherent."

Struck by his seeming sincerity, Kathryn sat down on the sofa at the end farthest from his chair. Eric rested his chin in one hand, his elbow propped on the chair's arm. "Why did he spare you? You don't say."

Her father had told her that some day she would have to talk about it to someone. Her psychotherapy had been a failure, her resistance manifesting itself in a thousand criticisms of her psychologist's tech-niques, all cavils that simply allowed her to keep the lock on her pain in place. She had been too afraid to discuss it with the people she con-sidered her friends, because the telling of it might reveal the depth of her anger or, even worse, give those she loved a dismissible explana-tion for all of her attitudes and fears. With Mitchell, she had come close to revealing almost every detail to a man who was only using her secrets to seduce her into sexual sobriety. Maybe Eric Eberman, his life ripped out from under him and seemingly free of judgment, was the only listener she had left.

"Jono wasn't afraid to die." She felt as if a knife blade has just been removed from her throat. "He was afraid of being alone. Whenever we were together, it was rarely just the two of us. He always made sure we traveled in a pack, if we were going to dinner or if we were going out. He was always the leader. When he found out he was sick, his biggest fear was being alone with his disease. Deep down, I believe that he wanted to infect most of our circle of friends so that he wouldn't be . . . alone."

"You just surmise this?"

"No," she answered without a pause. "He told me as much the day he died."

Somehow, she had stumbled several steps forward into the most disturbing part of the story, the part she had only sketched in her essay. "In his world, I was supposed to be the one who would take care of him. That's why he *spared* me."

"And the ones he infected on purpose?"

"He told me they had to pay. That he had sold them pure joy in bags and vials, unlike any they had ever known. He called them rats. Because if you put a cocaine drip into a rat's cage, the rat will kill itself rather than stop drinking from it. His *rats*, he said, had to pay by sharing his fate."

"How was it his fate? It's treatable."

"Not if you never take your medicine. Not if you spend every weekend living like it's your last. Living like you're not sick. If he had ever stopped to take a pill around me, if I had ever found any medicines in his bathroom, then I would have known. I never did. HIV may not be a death sentence. For Jono, it was. Why live at all when you have to live like you've always got one broken leg? He said that to me once."

Eric sat still, seeming to absorb this, and as she stared down at her clasped hands, she realized that despite what she had told Lauren Raines earlier that day, maybe Jono had taught her a more important lesson. Back then, if she had loved anything about him the most, it was his indefatigable courage and confidence. She'd envied it and aspired to it before realizing it had been nothing more than armor Jono had placed over the soft tissue of his disease; he lived life at a peerlessly fast pace because it helped him run full tilt from a death he thought was always right at his heels.

Bullshit, she thought, Bullshit, she said to his ghost. You always ran because you thought the other leg would break at any moment.

It was Jono who had led her to despise Jesse Lowry so much, a man who had been so bold as to follow no laws or rules.

And it was Jono who had led her to love Randall so much. Because Randall seemed to have Jono's same fearlessness, tempered by a sincere love for her that Jono had lacked. Randall had the same enviable self-confidence but—she had thought—no disease or secret lurking behind it.

When Eric spoke, his voice was respectful of the thoughts he knew were running through her head. "And when Jono was exposed, he chose to take his own life. Yet the last line of your essay is—"

"I wonder what solace I can take in knowing I was responsible for his death." Kathryn was unable to keep the quaver from her voice, blinking back tears only to force them down her cheeks She swabbed them with the back of her hand.

"I couldn't find him. The day the article ran was the first time I ever knew how many others there had been. I even went so far as to call his mother and she didn't know where he was. Hours later, he called me. He was at his apartment and . . . he said he had the gun in his hand and he was going to do it. And I said, 'Go ahead.' And he did."

"Kathryn, surely you don't think that just because—"

"He bled to death." She met Eric's eyes for the first time since she had sat down. "I heard the gunshot and I hung up and I didn't call anyone. His mother went to his apartment and found him three hours later. The kickback from the gun had knocked his aim off. The police said he'd aimed for his heart and the bullet ended up in his throat."

Eric's eyes had widened slightly, not with exaggerated sympathy, or disgust, just simple recognition of what she had been through, an acknowledgment of what had plagued her.

"He bled to death. And I didn't call anyone."

Her final words left her feeling empty, the way she had felt when she finished the essay, even though these final details hadn't made it onto paper. They said nothing, listening to the steady hiss of the gas fireplace and the occasional scrape of branches against the house.

"A man I used to live with once told me that the truth lurks in everything we don't say," Eric said, more to himself than her. "Or everything we don't write. For a long time, I believed him. But I know he's wrong now. Our silences contain only what we fear the truth to be. What you didn't write was that you killed Jono. And that's not true. He killed himself."

Eric pushed himself out of the chair and disappeared into the dark dining room. When he returned, he set a glass of white wine in front of Kathryn.

"Courtesy of Mitchell Seaver," he said

Jolted, she looked up, seeing Lauren grinding some kind of medication with a mortar and pestle. Eric returned to his chair before he saw that Kathryn hadn't touched the glass. "Don't worry. That didn't come from the bottles they drank from tonight."

"I don't understand."

"I mean you can drink it. There's nothing in it except wine."

He was gently challenging her, so she picked up the glass and took a tiny sip, anticipating the sting of something other than alcohol. Nothing.

"What do they do at that house?"

"Tonight, they're holding what Mitchell calls a purging. Once a week the members gather to satisfy their most base physical desires in hopes of cleansing their bodies of carnal temptation, in the name of accessing a more superior intellectual terrain in the morning. In other words, Mitchell has gathered all five of his pledges together. He's plied them with wine tainted with some tranquilizer or painkillers pilfered from my wife's medicine cabinet. And now he's encouraging them to copulate like animals."

"Why does he drug the wine?"

"He claims it's to lower their inhibitions. Open up the senses for a brief, controlled period. He's experimented with different combinations. Trying to find just the right amount."

Kathryn saw Lauren again; the dark circles under her eyes, the pallor of her skin and obvious weight loss. "He's getting them addicted."

Eric's eyes met hers with surprise and it took him a second to swallow this idea. "That would make sense, wouldn't it?" he finally said, defeat in his voice.

"Why . . ." she trailed off.

"Because I believed him. I had spent years suppressing what I really wanted, and I was intoxicated by the idea that sexual desire could be expunged from our bodies. I wanted him to succeed, to find a way."

"And he didn't?"

"No. He's no different from the scores of college students before him who have all tried to imagine their own utopia. Somewhere along the way, they become convinced that their own fears should dictate how everyone around them lives, and their vision ends up being little more than an excuse to try to destroy those who refuse to agree with them."

"You thought I was going tonight, didn't you?"

Eric nodded. "And tonight, Mitchell didn't pick the drug."

Her hands tightened around the stem of her wine glass, and when Eric noticed that she had gone rigid, he rose from the chair and crossed to the dining table, where he picked up a half-empty bottle of some liquor.

"What did you . . ." Her voice caught in her throat. "You poisoned . . ."

"Nothing fatal," Eric answered. "Just a little something to let them know that . . . I know." The last two words brought a bitter laugh out of him.

"Know what?"

Eric set the bottle down and turned to face her. "Mitchell murdered my wife when she found out what he was doing in that house."

Kathryn went cold. Mitchell murdered. "How do you know?"

"Your good friend Randall figured it out for me."

At the mention of his name, Kathryn couldn't suppress a tremor of pain. She took a slug of wine.

"He mentioned you often."

"Please," Kathryn protested.

"I know he lied about where he came from. But I suspect that you and I might know different halves of him. I thought we might be able to put them together. Make some sense of who he was."

"He's gone."

"I guessed," Eric said. "But I know where he went."

Before Kathryn could react, Eric bent down over the coffee table in front of her. He pulled a thick magazine from a stack of alumni newsletters and began flipping through the pages. He set it in front of her, splayed open. She bent over and saw color photographs of what looked like a massive but sterile penthouse with sweeping views of downtown Manhattan.

Baffled, she looked at Eric for an explanation.

"If Randall had come to me weeks ago with the fact that my wife had been poisoned, I could have figured out who had done it in a second. But he didn't. He couldn't. Because someone else had already convinced him I was a murderer."

"Someone's late!" Pamela cried out to him.

Her foot slid off the top step, but she caught the banister just in time. Behind her, the windows of the Chi Kap house were shadowed by drunken partygoers. Her eyes were drifting lazily as she righted herself, several locks of blonde hair threaded by sweat across her forehead.

"Have you been dancing?" he asked, mounting the steps and putting his arm around her waist. He glanced back at the house. To his relief, the front porch was empty. Ahead of them, Fraternity Green was blanketed in a darkness deepened by a fine sheen of late snow.

"Well, after an hour I just said . . . fuck it . . . and I danced alone, but not for long. Please." She squeezed his hand hard at her waist, almost twisted the wrist. "Tell me it makes you jealous."

"It does. Come on. Let's go home."

"No. Let's go to your place."

"No. No . . ."

She pulled herself free from his grip and stumbled backward off the sidewalk and onto the ice-patched lawn. "I asked around about him."

"Michael?"

"Have you heard of the Catch House? Down by the wharf. He goes there, Eric—"

"He's moving out."

She straightened herself up, struggling for some dignity, whipping at her stray hairs with the back of a hand, but only managing to plaster them vertically across her forehead. Later, he would try to find the right words to describe her laugh, because it was her laugh that caused everything that followed.

It was a short laugh, satisfied, one that lifted her shoulders, and it was followed by a slight nod. It was both knowing and dismissive. It said that no matter what she had suspected, she had never truly believed that another man could possibly be a genuine opponent in her fight for Eric's affection. The abruptness of it tugged at some lingering attachment Eric held to the separate realm of passion he and Michael had managed to create at 231 Slope Street.

That was how it ended. With one woman's knowing smirk, a pat on the hand, and a mild compliment for returning to real life, where two men were never supposed to find the magnetic rightness he believed he had found with Michael. Instead, he was meant to walk hand in hand with her, a woman just tall enough to fit her head on his shoulder, for his entire life.

"The scarf, Pamela. I need it."

"You gave it to me."

"I made a mistake."

"What mistake . . ." She frowned, trying to wriggle into reason from her smug alcohol haze.

"When I bought it from the store—"

She backed away, both hands protectively going to the scarf at her neck. "What store?"

"It wasn't mine to give you." He didn't rush her, but it only took him a few steps to close the distance between them, and his hand was reaching for her neck when she batted it away with one of her own.

"How stupid do you think I am?"

"Pamela, you're being ridiculous. Come on—"

"Ridiculous? I'll tell you what's ridiculous. All my friends in there telling me that I'm your beard. Do you know what a beard is? Because I didn't. I had to ask."

She backed away and he was afraid her feet would slip out from under her on the icy grass.

"I made a mistake." His voice sounded pathetic and weak. Pamela's face fell with more pain than anger, and for one brief second, he thought they might resolve this amicably, find a quiet resolution, two articulate people muffling the betrayal between them.

"If that faggot wants his scarf back, *I'll* give it to him!"

She turned and ran.

• • •

"She vanished." Eric stared down into the fire.

Inverness Creek. Kathryn had seen it only once, when she and Randall had tried their snowy shortcut through the Elms. Floating patches of ice and pools of black water. And a five-foot drop from the top of the bank to the water below. Randall had stopped her from sliding down. She had noticed how captivated Randall had been by the steep drop at their feet. And when she had recounted what April had told her about Pamela Milford, Randall had responded with, "*Maybe* she drowned."

Eric continued, "All I could hear was running water, so I followed the sound. When I got there, she had landed facedown on the ice. The creek was entirely frozen over and one of her legs . . . it was bent. Not just broken. Bent at an angle that looked . . . impossible. By the time I made it down to the edge of the ice I could tell she was unconscious. And then I saw the toe of one of her boots had punched through the ice and the water was coming up in a thin geyser around her foot.

"That's when I realized how thin the ice was. I tried to get to her anyway, but I had barely taken my first step when the ice rose and fell. And I knew if I put any more weight on it, it would break and she would get sucked under and I wouldn't be able to get to her. So I left."

Eric turned from the fireplace and locked eyes with her. Somehow, over the time it had taken to tell the entire story of him and Michael Price, she had become his judge and jury.

"I went to get help. I thought if the ice didn't give way when she hit it, then maybe I had time to go back and get somebody. And I did. I went back to the party. I could barely speak, I was in a panic, but I found some guys and I told them Pamela had run into the Elms. And they came with me. And we got to the creek and I even pointed to where she was but . . . she was gone."

"The ice broke?"

"It didn't just break. In her place, there was a hole twice the size of her body."

Kathryn shivered. "Michael?"

Eric just looked at the flames. "I told myself I was wrong. That Michael didn't have anything to do with it. And I told the police that she just got away from me. But when they finally found her body, the scarf was gone."

Everything in Kathryn wanted to dig her heels in, to stop them from continuing in the direction Eric had headed in. "It could have drifted away."

But Eric turned into the dining room and returned with a red, moth-eaten scarf. He extended it to her, and she took it. The cashmere fibers, once soft, had frayed and coarsened with age.

"He left it for me."

Fearing it was the incorrect answer, Kathryn said, "Michael."

"Randall," Eric corrected her.

Eric returned to his chair, and she stared down at the scarf. Part of her brain had yearned to fill in the picture of Randall Stone left incomplete by his sudden departure. But never, after all she had discovered, would she have guessed that the real nature of his arrival at Atherton had such a diabolical purpose. The explanation she had craved couldn't be swallowed without pain

"His real name is Benjamin Collins. He's from Texas," she said finally, lifting her eyes from the scarf. "When he was young, there was an accident."

"A fire?" Eric asked.

She nodded. He had seen Randall's scars long before she had. "A train wreck. I'm not sure, but Ran . . . *Ben* might have caused it. It destroyed the trailer park where he lived . . ."

But even as she filled in the other half, where Randall came from, more questions arose than answers. How had he made it from Texas to New York, and how on earth did he come into contact with Michael Price? She returned her attention to Eric. He was at least present, concrete. "Are you saying that Michael Price *sent* Randall here?"

"Randall's application to this school was a mess. But with Michael Price listed as his legal guardian—well, I'm sure some oversights on his part were also overlooked by the admissions committee."

"Why though?"

Eric shrugged. "Maybe so Randall could do exactly what he's done"

"It doesn't make any sense."

"Ask him," Eric said, gesturing to the magazine spread open on the coffee table in front of her.

Realization tightened a fist of anger inside her chest. Eric had lured her to his house only to make a simple demand of her. "That's the only reason you told me any of this? So I can . . . what? Go rescue him?"

"He doesn't have the first clue what his *legal guardian* is capable of."

Kathryn stood up. "It sounds like they were made for each other."

"Randall is not a murderer. But Michael created him, and now he's served his purpose."

"If Michael sent Randall here to destroy your career, he can't go and harm the person making the accusations!"

"They've already been made, Kathryn. And do you honestly think that a man of Michael's stature, a man with his career, is going to allow a paper trail of scandal to lead back to him?"

"He's listed as Randall's legal guardian—"

"On an application so filled with holes that the vice president of public affairs for the university told me that if it was ever made public the university might not recover from the scandal. There's a reason Michael didn't put Randall here with the perfect application. With an obvious forgery, it's Michael's way out!"

Eric stood, eye to eye with her, almost pleading. "Maybe we don't know who he really was, Kathryn. But the young man I knew was too arrogant and too selfish to obey the wishes of a man like Michael. All your friend has to do now is make one mistake, and Randall Stone will cease to exist as quickly as he came to be."

*One mistake*, Kathryn repeated to herself.

Did Jesse Lowry qualify?

Her eyes fell to the magazine, the ostentatious chandelier with its ceramic tentacles. The cold white walls and marble floors. The place that had engendered the young man she may or may not have known. Desperate curiosity fought with her wounded pride. "After all the lies he's told, I'm supposed to rescue Randall?"

"No. You're supposed to decide whether Michael Price should be the one to punish him."

"Why not you?" she snapped.

Eric went silent, as if ashamed of his own fear. "I wouldn't have asked you here if I didn't believe that you are the one Randall wants to see. That you could get him away from Michael before anyone else could."

"What about the police?"

"What would we tell them? The twenty-year-old story of a man now suspected of killing his wife. They would want to know why I waited so long. And I don't even know the answer to that."

Kathryn tucked the magazine under one arm and turned, giving Eric the illusion that she had come to a decision. Truly she hadn't. In the doorway, she stopped and turned and saw that Eric was watching her departure intently.

"If I go to 231 Slope Street right now, what will I find?" she asked.

Eric drained the last of his wine. "Good-bye, Kathryn."

As she descended the front steps, Eric's words echoed in her. One mistake and Randall Stone will cease to exist. She thought of Jesse's empty side of the room.

Lauren Raines had thrown herself against the front door of 231 Slope Street and was pounding it with both fists. Kathryn pushed the front gate open and rushed up the walk. As she approached, Lauren whirled around, her eyes wild and tear-stained. She lunged at Kathryn and swung. The sharp punch caught her under the jaw and sent her toppling into the icy hedge beside the front steps.

"They locked me out!" Lauren screamed. Kathryn tried to scramble out of the bushes and shield herself from another blow. "Maria heard us! She heard everything we said, and they locked me out of the fucking house. You stupid—"

Lauren hurled herself at her and Kathryn caught both of her clenched fists. Lauren bent at the knees, bucking and twisting to get free of Kathryn's grip. "We need to get inside!" she hissed at Lauren.

"We can't!" Lauren wailed. "They lock the whole house down during a—"

"Purging. I know."

She released Lauren's wrists with a shove that sent her stumbling backward until she tripped over the first step and landed ass first on the third, her breath going out of her in a pained grunt.

Kathryn ran down the driveway.

Oddly, the back door stood open, and without thinking she raced inside.

The only light in the living room came from the six candles on the mantel, mounted in the silver candelabra. In the foyer, she hit the switch and the chandelier flooded the staircase with light.

The giant harp and mandolin were missing from the upstairs landing. The bedroom door stood open and a girl, not much older than herself, lay facedown in the hallway as if she had been struck dead in the middle of a sidestroke into the hallway. Her matted red hair fanned out on the carpet around her downturned head; her emaciated, naked back rose and fell with labored breaths, her spine visible with each inhalation.

In the bedroom, Kathryn saw that the six single beds had been pushed together into one. Candlelight danced across the still, naked flesh and twisted, sweat-soaked sheets. The bodies were strewn in various positions of thrall. Whatever drug Eric had slipped them had acted slowly, not taking effect until they had thrown themselves into their orgy. And once it became clear that they had been drugged beyond what they had done before, only one of them had managed to try to escape the bedroom. The giant harp leaned against the left wall, its bottom resting against the edge of the mattresses. Her eyes swept to the other wall. Maria had been lassoed to the giant mandolin, her wrists secured above her head. Her head rolled forward and the sounds of vomit and air rasped in her throat.

Kathryn crawled across the beds, ignoring the weak groans of protest as her knees dug into a stomach, an arm, or a breast. She pried at the hemp rope securing Maria's wrists until it came free, and caught the girl around the waist before she could crumple onto the other bodies. She managed to turn her over, and Maria opened hooded eyes to try to focus on her, her mouth a half grimace.

She saw Lauren standing in the doorway.

"Call 911!"

Lauren just lifted one arm. She was holding a kitchen knife with a trembling wrist. Candlelight danced off the blade.

"Lauren!" Kathryn roared. "Call 911!"

Lauren violently shook her head no, and Kathryn slid out from under Maria's weight, crawling through the tangle of limbs. Her feet hit the floor and she approached Lauren without fear, even as Lauren raised the knife in front of her. Agony was stitched across her face. Her resolve was gone. Instead, her jaw trembled and her eyes were smarting with tears.

Kathryn gripped Lauren's wrist and squeezed. Lauren dropped the knife to the floor. Her knees buckled. Kathryn could hear the desperation in Lauren's sobs, the frustration of someone who had looked endlessly for an opiate to her pain, only to have the cure end up being worse than the disease. She looked like a little girl, desperate not to accept a crushingly inevitable conclusion.

When Kathryn sank down next to Lauren and enfolded her in her arms, the girl didn't protest, but fell weakly against Kathryn's chest and sobbed into her jacket. Kathryn couldn't manage any words of sympathy or pity. Still, Eric's justice seemed like pure cruelty.

Maria had managed to bring one forearm to her forehead. Breaths whistled down her throat. Kathryn focused, seeing two other bodies—male or female, she couldn't tell—lying facedown, pressed to the mattress by Maria's weight. The young girl who had been lying across the doorway had managed to crawl to the top of the stairs. One arm weakly clawed the top step.

Five. Including Lauren.

Kathryn's eyes shot to the giant harp. Frayed tassels of hemp rope dangled from the top of its spine.

She shot to her feet when she remembered the open back door to the kitchen.

"Where's Mitchell?"

Maria answered with a racked breath and another sob. She had rolled onto one side. It took all the strength she had to lift her head.

"*Where's Mitchell?*"

Maria lifted her arm limply from her side and for a second Kathryn thought she was reaching out for help. Kathryn almost took her hand before Maria managed to extend her middle finger.

Eric stared down at the bottle of Vicodin in his hand.

Half a bottle remained.

But who exactly was he doing this for? For Pamela and Lisa, casualties of his lies? For Michael, who had finally punished him to his own satisfaction? For himself, a man who could no longer live with the reality that while he had never murdered anyone, he had engendered more than his fair share of death?

He had already taken five, and would down the rest, pill by pill, once those made him good and numb.

In the living room, he turned out all the other lights, but let the gas fire glow. He refilled his wineglass and sat down in his reading chair, waiting for the pills to sand the edges off the memories he assumed would loom inside him before death settled in.

Outside, the wind knocked branches. But another sound, clearer and closer, distracted him. A metallic creak with a slow, swinging rhythm to it.

Pain thundered against his skull, sending his body forward as the sound of shattering glass filled both his ears. He hit the floor knees first, his vision spinning. Glass sprayed against the hardwood all around him. He lifted his head. The back door was swinging in the wind.

He fought to stay conscious, more out of curiosity than a desire to live. The pills seemed to cushion the pain. He rolled over onto his back.

Mitchell rounded his reading chair, gripping the stem of the wine bottle he had just shattered over the back of his head. His overcoat slid off one shoulder, flaps parting, revealing bare chest beneath. His lower jaw hung open as if the bone had been torn free from the socket. His eyes were wide with the exertion to keep them open, and his pupils danced on Eric like flickering flames.

"You . . . punish . . . us?" Mitchell rasped.

Eric didn't move as Mitchell stared down at him.

"You fuck . . . your little boy . . . and you punish . . . us?"

"You murdered Lisa. I don't think I could ever punish you enough," Eric whispered.

Mitchell groaned and lifted his arm, swinging the shattered wine bottle over his head. Eric crumbled to protect his head, then felt needles of pain stab the back of his neck. Mitchell retracted the shattered bottle with drugged slowness, and Eric's face smacked against the floor. Blood, pleasantly warm, rushed down his back.

Mitchell gripped the collar of Eric's shirt, tugging and dragging him until he was on all fours. Searing pain spread out across his upper back.

"Tr-traitor!" Mitchell howled.

Jerking like a puppet in Mitchell's grip, Eric pawed at the floor beneath him, but when he managed to look up the gas fireplace filled his vision. Mitchell crouched down next to him, still gripping the collar of his shirt, the other hand pulling on the waistband of his pants, sliding him across the hardwood floor toward the flames.

"Chapter Five . . . Errric . . . What h-happens to th-those . . . who can never escape their . . . own b-bodies . . ."

Heat flushed Eric's cheeks and he flailed at Mitchell with one arm. He felt his fingers land on the hot metal grating, then slide free. Mitchell would not punish him. He would punish them both. His hand gripped the gas lever before Mitchell seized his wrist and pulled, but Eric held on. When he whipped his other arm out to grab at the edge of the fireplace, his weight shifted and he hit the floor face first. His other hand gave one final, desperate tug.

The lever broke free, and gas hissed from the new opening. In a second, Mitchell had pinned his clenched fist to the small of his back, his other hand grasping Eric's neck as he lifted him toward the fire.

"Those souls . . . who never escape . . . are doomed to spend eternity in a lake of fire!"

Eric opened his eyes. The flames were only inches from his nose, and in the hand Mitchell held to his back he gripped the metal lever. Could Mitchell smell it? The fumes suddenly outmatched the heat in intensity.

"*Hey!*"

It was another man's voice.

Mitchell didn't release his dual grip.

"*Let him go! Now!*" shouted the strange voice.

Mitchell's mouth was at his ear. "Your wife would have k-killed her . . . self . . . anyway. But I couldn't resist having your little whore t-try . . . to pin it on *you*!"

"*I said let him go, asshole!*"

Eric screwed his eyes shut. He saw water and ice, Pamela and Lisa. He made their fates his.

· · ·

When she heard the gunshot, Kathryn didn't stop running.

A second later the front windows of the Eberman house exploded outward with enough force to split the porch rail down the center.

Kathryn hit the sidewalk on her knees, her head tucked to her chest, arms raised above her head. The thunder echoed shatteringly among the houses, followed by the squeal of car alarms down Victoria Street.

When she lowered her arms, she saw twin tongues of fire curling up the front of the house from the shattered cavities of the front windows. In the middle of the street, half of the porch rail sat upended on a bed of blackened glass. The other half dangled from the front porch for several seconds before its thin tether of splintered wood gave way and it fell to the seared lawn with a thud.

She got to her feet and saw she was standing next to the unmarked police car. Its windshield was a spider web. The driver's seat was empty.

She made it to the foot of the steps of the house and stopped. The front door was still shut on its hinges but the bottom half had been blown halfway down the steps. Through the splintered hole she could see a curtain of fire filling the foyer.

With one hand on the rail, she closed her eyes and tried to force breath back into her lungs. Then she heard the plaintive mourning of sirens carrying across the hill.

# CHAPTER SIXTEEN

TWENTY-FIVE STORIES OVER SECOND AVENUE, THE BOWERY TOWER sent a halo of weak, golden light into the low, fast-moving cloud cover. Frosted green plate-glass windows, held together with exposed metal cladding, punched squares of light through the snowy fog. The taxi pulled away slowly from the curb, the driver carefully navigating through fast-accumulating drifts of snow spilling from the gutters. Randall crossed the street, bound for the massive stainless steel canopy that arched over the building's entrance.

His heart had stopped racing, and he moved down the sidewalks with a numbness that a stranger could have mistaken for determination. This visit to the birthplace of his new self would be his last, that was the thought he clung to as he visualized Jesse's cell phone number, wedged in his wallet. But at some point, just not now, Randall would have to face the reality that Jesse might have either discarded the cell phone by now, or that it was too late for Randall to take Jesse up on an invitation he had already refused. For all he knew, Jesse was already in Cozumel by now, bound for the side of the island that had been destroyed by a hurricane years ago, where the telephone lines vanished midway across the island, leaving the poles empty.

It didn't matter, Randall told himself, he would find Jesse. He had no one else to run to.

Mahogany-framed panels of frosted glass formed the lobby's walls. Pin lights from the ceiling outlined a path on the marble floor, leading to the bank of elevators with their gold-plated doors. Behind his convex stainless-steel desk, the doorman lifted his head from a copy of the *New York Post*.

"Welcome back, Mr. Stone."

Randall managed a strained smile. "Merry Christmas."

The doorman nodded and returned his attention to the paper. He was one of the four building employees who knew that Michael Price didn't live alone.

In the elevator, Randall inserted his key above the button marked PH, turned it once, for what he hoped was the last time, and removed it. The button illuminated under his fingertip. As the elevator rose, he fished a copy of the *Atherton Journal* out of his Prada satchel. By the eighteenth floor, Randall's heart was a steady hammer in his chest.

He had weathered Michael's volcanic mood swings for two years before leaving for Atherton. Had the past three months left him so out of practice that the sweat lacing his back was a sign of fear? The doors slid open, revealing a sweep of white marble and plate-glass windows lit by the flickering light of a television. He muffled fear with anger, cursing himself for hesitating to take the first step out of the elevator.

Randall announced his presence only with the echo of his footsteps on the marble floor. Above the fireplace separating the great room from the master bedroom, the flat-screen television displayed a silent barrage of flaring police lights and fire trucks to the empty assemblage of living-room furniture: a white leather sofa, a glass coffee table with a metal frame so spare that the table top seemed to float above the zebra-skin rug, and three empty chairs with steel frames and cow-skin upholstery intended to be beautiful and painful to occupy.

Randall dropped the newspaper on the dining table. Looking beyond the fireplace, he could see Michael's bed was made, the room dark. Beside him, the double doors to Michael's studio were drawn shut, a sliver of light in the middle. Michael was not to be disturbed when he was working, but maybe tonight was an exception. Randall had done what he promised, even if he did have to force Michael into admitting it—that Eric's downfall was what he secretly wanted before he'd even considered placing Randall at Atherton.

"Michael?"

No response from beyond the double doors.

Downtown was almost invisible beyond the far rail of the terrace, which took up the remainder of the rooftop. New figures had been added to Michael's cadre of wax sculptures, all of them apparitions emerging out of the blanketing snow. Beyond, spotlights angled up onto each piece had been partially covered, and the result threw chiaroscuro across their featureless white faces and extended limbs.

He had loved this view once; it had elevated him above the streets where he had struggled to survive. Living here had once seemed like an accomplishment. Before the walls of Michael's penthouse had begun to shrink inward, and Randall could taste his desire for renewed freedom and the hope of something close to a normal, autonomous life. But he had failed at that miserably, and now the view welcomed him back like a parent satisfied to see his dire predictions come true.

Randall crossed to the terrace door, his eyes catching a view of the new sculpture. Male and muscled, it stood on a stone platform, its arms outstretched in an embrace of the driving snow. The perfectly proportioned body was evidence of Michael's constantly improving technique, and Randall was surprised to see the skin textured with the accurate folds of muscle groups. But the accomplishment ended abruptly at the neckline; as with all of Michael's sculptures, the face was a blank mask of dry, clotted wax.

"Michael?" he called out as he turned from the glass.

He noticed that the much-talked about chandelier had finally been installed, and the result was just as hideous as the sketches Michael had proudly shown him back in July. "It'll bring life to the apartment, don't you think?"

"I think it's scary," Randall had told him, meaning hideous.

"I didn't ask you what you thought."

"Yes, you did."

It was suspended from a gathering of wires that extended down through the raftered ceiling. Massive ceramic tentacles curled inward, all of them patterned with a Gaudí-inspired mosaic of tiles. Light bulbs were concealed in the cavities of each one, emitting an amber glow onto the black lacquer dining table. The whole thing looked like a giant octopus preparing to rest on the ocean floor. Randall assumed that Michael had loved the impossibility of it, for the electrical company had moaned about how impossible it was to wire, and after that it would be flat-out impossible to install the proper electrical lift system.

Michael had shrugged off the advice, opting for an antiquated rotary crank system and vowing he would find some way to hang this insanely heavy monstrosity from his ceiling.

The double doors to the studio slid open. Randall straightened up against the glass. He felt his best attempt at a smile tug at his mouth, but Michael simply met his eyes briefly and strode to the dining table. Fear forced its way up from Randall's stomach, tightening his chest. Feeling suddenly powerless, Randall was reminded of the quiet, visceral terror he had felt the first time he saw the man who would end up being his last customer.

Michael had not changed much in the last three months. If anything, he had grown larger, his body encroaching even more onto the particularities of his form and face. His pinpoint black eyes had been forced into recession by his prominent brow and high, etched cheekbones. His thatch of salt and pepper hair looked too small for the crown of his head, which seemed to have grown, his skull spreading its plates to enclose a brain flexing ever outward with visions so large they threatened to consume him. His hands, planted on either side of the newspaper, were bloated paws with swollen knuckles.

Michael Price's bulk was a product of the anabolic steroids and human growth hormone he injected and swallowed; they threw his hormones violently out of balance. Living here, Randall had learned to both weather and mitigate his drastic mood swings, but now he felt like a child thrown back into the water without a float to hold on to. Michael's sullen and unreadable silences frightened Randall the most.

Michael gave a slight nod, and brushed the paper aside. "Old news!" he announced.

"What?" Randall asked.

Randall watched as Michael crossed to the living area, picked up the remote and unmuted the television. Randall realized that the fire trucks he had glimpsed on the screen just seconds earlier sat outside the smoldering remains of Eric Eberman's house.

Randall sucked in a shocked breath and hoped Michael hadn't heard him. Michael threw himself onto the sofa, its leather squeaking under his weight, intent on the television.

". . . Neighbors report hearing a gunshot followed by a short, loud boom. While there's already little doubt that tonight will go down in history for the prestigious university, it seems that the strange twists in tonight's story won't stop coming."

Two thirty-one Slope Street emerged under the glare of police lights. Gurneys were being whisked down the front walk, their occupants clutching weakly at blankets, poor attempts to conceal the nudity made obvious by their bare shoulders.

"Police are refusing to address rumors that Professor Eric Eberman, believed dead in the fire that consumed his home, was the former owner of the very house where several members of an off-campus fraternity engaged in a failed mass suicide attempt."

Randall groped for a seat on the sofa, knocked breathless by the sudden, violent flow of images and information. He reached over, picked up the remote, and hit MUTE before Michael could protest. Eric and Lisa's wedding photo filled the screen. He turned to find Michael's eyes on him, his hands folded behind his neck. Suddenly, the only sound in the apartment was the whistle of the wind around the twenty-fifth floor.

"Grieve. I'll allow it," Michael finally said. "After all you've done, I guess it's impossible for you not to walk away with a small shred of affection for him. But just remember, I wanted him fired. Not dead."

Randall dropped the remote on the coffee table.

"Something to drink?"

Randall didn't answer, fearing his voice would release the tide of confused grief he was holding barely at bay. Michael heaved himself up from the sofa anyway.

"I assume you've lost your taste for scotch."

Randall shook his head before realizing Michael had his back to him. He swallowed a breath. "Anything. I don't care."

For several seconds there was only the clink of ice cubes against glass, and Randall stared at the rug, keeping his eyes averted from the devastation the television offered. "I guess your wish has been granted," Michael said. "Considering that you've set fire to the place, I won't force you to go back there and voice your complaints to a disciplinary committee. As you promised to do." Michael turned. "I doubt they would conduct a post-mortem investigation of Eric's actions anyway."

Because he couldn't help it, Randall looked at the television again.

A stern-faced policewoman shepherded Kathryn past the glare of the news cameras. Kathryn walked with her eyes on the pavement in front of her, not bothering to brush away the bangs drifting onto her face. Randall told himself to be strong, forced himself to watch, even though this image was the worst. The news of Eric's death seemed unreal. But seeing Kathryn, one of the only women he had ever loved, reminded him of all he had failed to be. Looking shellshocked as she was led away from the scene, Kathryn was the embodiment of all the great promise he had seen in Atherton, all of it now turned sour and deadly.

Beneath her image, a news ticker announced sports scores and counted off the hour in four different time zones.

Randall looked up to see Michael pushing a drink into his face. Who cared how many times he'd told the man he couldn't stand bourbon?

"Headline News picked it up about an hour ago. I've watched it twice already." Michael toasted the television and swallowed half his drink.

"Congratulations," Randall said to his drink.

"You make it sound like this was all my doing."

"It isn't?"

"If I remember our original agreement correctly, you had four years to expose Eric for what he really is. Excuse me. *Was.* Four years for you to have your little dream of a college life and put Ben Collins that many more miles behind you in the process. And all I asked for in return was one little scandal. That's all. *This* is all your doing."

"Can you blame me?" Randall tried to chase the anger from his voice. "After everything you told me about him, can you blame me for thinking he murdered her?"

"I'm sure he murdered her. But face it, Randall. Your talent is for making older men believe they need *you*, when the truth is just the opposite. You obviously have no knack for exposing murderers."

Surprisingly calm given Randall's backtalk, Michael took a seat next to him. Randall kept his gaze fixed on the television, his drink cradled in both hands.

"And besides, my concern was for you. You managed to carve out an admirable little niche for yourself there, and if you'd just left this half-assed attempt at a murder investigation alone, who knows? You might have been able to get your degree "

"And then what?" Randall took his first sip of bourbon.

Michael fixed him with the kind of stare he'd use on a guest who had just cracked a tasteless joke in the middle of a formal dinner party. "I'm sure we would have reached a mutually beneficial agreement. We used to excel at those." He bent forward, elbows resting on his knees. "After all, look where you are. Here. I've given you a name you can actually keep longer than one night. And who knows? If you had bored another one of your johns with that ridiculous story about killing your entire hometown with a train, well, they might have expressed their disbelief with something sharp."

Michael grazed Randall's Adam's apple with three fat fingers before Randall reached up and clasped them with one hand.

Their eyes met. Randall swallowed the pride he had managed to accumulate during his period of independence, tried to recall the docile whore he had been for so long. "We both know that there's no way I could ever repay you for what you've given me."

"Maybe. But that says more about you than it does me, *Ben*. Don't just try to thank me for all you've been given. Give some thought to everything you've taken."

Randall released Michael's fingers and got up to walk toward the windows.

Behind him, Michael continued. "You have a tendency to over-compensate. We both know that. At one time, it served you well. Hitchhiking your way across the country, telling every truck driver a different story that brought you that much closer to New York. But you're here. And you don't have to lie to *me* to survive, do you? Still, it wasn't enough to out Eric. You had to turn him into a murderer. . . ."

"He was, wasn't he?" Randall turned.

Michael seemed puzzled.

"He did kill Pamela Milford didn't he?"

Michael's face hardened again. "In many ways. Yes."

"Just checking," Randall muttered, muting his disbelief so Michael couldn't hear it.

"Given your past, I can understand why you would feel the need to overcompensate. Go beyond the call of duty, if you will. I had hoped your stay at Atherton might help that. But there are only so many times I can assure you that little Ben Collins is dead and buried."

Randall tightened his grip on the glass.

"I'm not quite sure how I can teach you to be content with who you are. But I do know this. You're talented. This"—he gestured to the television—"took talent. Lies of course, but at least your lies brought about some justice. Eric's lies brought only death. And still, I sense there's a part of you that just can't stop running."

"What would I run to?"

It took several seconds for Michael's lipless mouth to curl into a thin smile. "Exactly."

Randall took another drink, went to the sofa, and set his glass down. He bent down and kissed Michael's forehead. "Good night," he whispered.

But when he straightened, Michael held his wrist. Fear crept at the back of Randall's neck as he looked down into Michael's eyes. Michael's gaze-and-grip didn't waver.

"Thank you," he said finally, soft enough to indicate that he had struggled to get the words out. His eyes and fingers lingering, he finally released Randall's wrist. "It's good to see your brown eyes again."

Randall nodded nervously and backed away from the sofa. His steps quickened as he headed for the spiral staircase leading to the second floor.

Randall's former room was located at the end of a long, carpeted hallway at the rear of the penthouse. The intended maid's quarters for the apartment, it was the only room on the second floor. In the two years since he had first visited Michael's apartment, the man had never ordered or invited him into his bed. Michael groomed him, dressed him, and fed him, but the man had never touched him in a manner that couldn't be considered paternal. The bedroom's single window looked out on Manhattan's eastward landscape, and at any hour of the night the room was filled the city's persistent, gray light. Randall stood at the window. The trilevel Christmas lighting atop the Empire State Building had gone out, followed by the red GE sign atop Rockefeller

Center. Now, he was waiting for the Chrysler Building's white curves to go dark. Michael had decided not to bless the bedroom with a phone or a clock, so this had been Randall's old method of marking the night's progress when he couldn't sleep.

His grief for Eric remained tearless. Despite the fact he now held many of his own images of the man, the one he now recalled most vividly was the photograph of Eric and Michael that he had first laid eyes on a year ago. The pair stood on the front steps of 231 Slope Street, but the house was unidentifiable behind them. Randall was shocked by a slimmer, prettier Michael, but his attention had been instantly drawn to his companion. Randall was moved by the image of Eric's large, generous eyes, betraying their discomfort with Michael's arm clamped around his broad shoulders. As Michael's penthouse began to grow more oppressive, Randall found himself creating an imaginary life for Eric Eberman, becoming more and more infatuated with the mysterious old friend Michael had refused to talk about. Finally, Randall had hatched a plan that he phrased in the coldest of details, but which was secretly loaded with the promise of escape. I'll ruin Eric's life, if you let me have mine, was what he meant but never said.

Atherton hadn't offered him the escape he craved, and that left Jesse Lowry to be his deliverer.

In the less than three months he had spent at Atherton University, Jesse Lowry had made regular cash withdrawals from his credit card each week, none of them in excess of what he convinced his father was needed to cover general expenses. The catch was that Jesse didn't have any expenses. The meal plan fed him, and only rarely was he required to actually buy dinner for a potential sexual conquest. His only indulgence had been the navy pea coat he wore everywhere. For Randall, Atherton was a golden opportunity. For Jesse, it was little more than a train platform where he could switch cars and ride beyond the reach of his father. His father, who used to get high and visit Jesse's bedroom when there weren't any women in the house. Jesse planned to run away from school and make himself over, to become a Randall Stone, who did not bear the guilt of Benjamin Collins.

On the night before Thanksgiving, after pressing himself inside of

Randall and whispering Randall's real name, Jesse had revealed his one weakness: Even though he had planned his escape for months, he was afraid to do it alone. And who better to guide him and show him how than Randall?

Randall told him to go by himself. Randall might have earned the burden of yet another murder on his back, but he still had one shot at redemption And despite all that Jesse had managed to figure out about him, he still had no idea who had financed Randall's new identity and given him his college life. Jesse foolishly and arrogantly believed that by destroying Randall's friendship with Kathryn, he had severed Randall's only tie to Atherton.

After returning from Eric's house, Randall had found Jesse's side of the room cleaned out, and on his desk a bittersweet parting gift: the number to Jesse's cell phone. A bullying assertion that Randall would eventually give in, or a last desperate plea? Randall had warmed himself by considering it the latter.

At the top of the staircase, Randall paused. Darkness concealed the bottom half of the steps, the great room plated in shadows. He reached up and searched the wall, checking to see if the new chandelier had a dimmer switch. Instead, his fingers grazed the metal door of an electrical box. He popped it open and saw the rotary crank for the chandelier. The switch had to be downstairs.

Beyond the soaring fireplace, the master bedroom was dark. But if Randall used the phone in the kitchen, Michael could sit up in bed at the smallest sound, peer through the fireplace, and spot him directly across the apartment. For a second, he pondered throwing on some clothes and hitting the streets in search of a pay phone. But calling the elevator would result in a soft chime followed by a sudden spill of light across the living room, which would stir Michael, who slept like a great cat.

The studio. He descended the stairs carefully, trying not to rattle the staircase. Michael kept an answering machine hooked up to the phone there so that he could hear who was calling without stopping his work. It was also one of the only rooms in the apartment that had a door—big double doors that Randall had to wedge his fingers in between and open only several inches for fear of scraping them in their tracks.

Once inside, Randall slowly slid them shut again. When he turned, he saw the towering metal armature in the center of the room and almost screamed. The giant stick figure sat on a rolling platform, almost six feet tall with a spine, two curled arms without hands, and thin, slightly spread legs. In winter, Michael rolled his just-finished pieces out onto the terrace where the frigid winds gradually solidified the wax. Randall realized why its shadow had seemed substantial and frightening. It was metal. Michael's confidence must have improved with his technique. Randall had only seen him work with wax armatures, so he could reheat and remold a portion of the figure's skeleton before he built the body up around the bones. Metal required a firm commitment from the start.

He slumped back against the doors and caught his breath, scanning the darkness of the studio for the answering machine's blinking red light. Just inside the door, blocks of microcrystalline wax stood in stacks. Michael worked in wax because it was cohesive and lightweight, and most important, it didn't produce any dust. But even a small splash of water, less dense than the wax, could permeate the block's surface and result in an explosive eruption of wax and steam, which is why all the sculptures required a protective coating after they dried, and also explained why Michael had stacked the blocks in the opposite corner from the utility sink.

Randall spotted the machine's blinking red light on the worktable. He bent forward over the table and the thick fabric of what had to be Michael's smock brushed his head from where it hung from its hook. He pushed the number pad sticky, under his fingers. He almost let out a sigh of relief when he heard the first ring.

And then it was matched by a high-pitched chirping sound directly outside the studio doors.

Randall leapt back, almost pulling the phone out of its socket. When he knocked the smock from its hook, navy blue buttons hit the floor at his feet. He stared down at Jesse's pea coat as the double doors slid open.

Kathryn bent forward over the desk, which made the doorman recoil, one hand clamped to the phone. Since he had already refused to call up to the penthouse, she guessed he was going to call the police.

"How many times do I have to say it's an emergency?" she asked.

"It's also two in the morning," the doorman sputtered.

Kathryn shot a glance out the lobby windows. Behind the wheel of his Jeep, Tim watched the proceedings with an arm bent on top of the steering wheel, gnawing at a thumbnail, probably ready to flip out and insist for the hundredth time that they should go to One Police Plaza.

"Is there any reason this can't wait until morning?" the doorman asked.

Fighting panic, Kathryn grasped at the hard lump of Tim's .25-caliber semi-automatic pistol in her inside jacket pocket. Tim must have seen her touch it, because she heard the Jeep's door pop open.

"Does that go to his phone?" Kathryn demanded.

"I'm sorry."

"When you call his apartment, does it go through his phone line?"

The doorman nodded.

"If he's asleep, I can just leave a message."

"Ma'am . . ."

Tim threw the lobby doors open, but when he saw Kathryn didn't have the gun in her hand, he stopped in mid-step. "Who's he?" the doorman asked. Tim approached the desk and extended three crumpled twenties in one fist.

After barely a second's pause, the doormen took them and dialed. "Who should I say you are?" he asked pleasantly.

Kathryn told him what to say and the doorman held the phone between his ear and his shoulder as he waited. "He's not answering," the doorman said, then abruptly went stiff and gripped the phone harder. "I'm sorry to bother you, Mr. Price, but there's a young woman down here and she claims it's an emergency." He shot her one final reproachful look before continuing. "Her name is Pamela Milford and apparently she has your scarf."

The doorman hung up.

"Wait!" Kathryn protested.

"It was his machine." He folded his arms over his chest. "If either of you has an American Express you're willing to let go of, maybe I'll consider going up there."

"Come on, Kathryn." Tim's hand gripped her shoulder, and she shrugged it off. The phone behind the desk rang.

"Yes . . . I'm so sorry . . . I see. Will do. Thank you so much, Mr. Price." He hung up, face furled with anger. "Go on up, Miss Milford."

Kathryn moved for the elevators. Tim called, "If you're not down in fifteen minutes, I'm calling the cops."

"Fuck that. Just pull the goddamn fire alarm."

She pulled herself free from his grip and headed for the elevators.

# CHAPTER SEVENTEEN

"You must be Kathryn."

"Who else?"

"Someone with a rather cruel sense of humor."

Without leaving the elevator, Kathryn cocked her head at Michael Price, puffed her cheeks and stuck out her bottom lip. The guy was a bloated horror. Worse, it looked as if his muscles had been pumped up with hot air. When he saw the sarcastic sympathy on her face, Skeletor backed up several steps, gesturing for her to enter.

With one hand against her jacket pocket, she stepped out of the elevator, moving quickly into center of the vast, loftlike space without allowing the man out of her line of sight. Michael's expression was fixed. "Nice place," she said.

Michael nodded as he sized Kathryn up, as if she were there for a job interview. "You're looking for Randall," he said.

"Is he around?"

"No."

"Any idea where he might be?"

"Unfortunately, no."

Kathryn lifted her eyebrows to indicate she was listening. Michael dug his hands into both pockets of his smock, bowing his head as he moved between her and the open elevator doors. She felt a surge of relief when he stepped out of the only path between her and the exit.

"Apparently, his roommate managed to save up a good bit of cash while he was up at school. And extended an offer that Randall couldn't refuse. It seems this young man has Randall in quite a thrall. Well, you probably know him." He turned. "Jesse?"

She met his gaze. "I do. He's gorgeous. Beautiful, really."

Michael heard the venom in her words and his eyes flickered.

"Where did they run off to?" she asked.

"According to the caller ID, Randall made the call from the Boston airport."

Kathryn managed a smile, which she felt turn into a snarl. "Nice of him to tell you about the money Jesse saved up. Just in case you were worried about his financial situation."

Michael looked at her hard. "I don't follow . . ."

"It's all very confusing, isn't it? But I'm relieved. You see, Jesse just vanished without a trace right after the break. And I had all sorts of horrible possibilities running through my head. And then I remembered the power went out for a whole day. I mean, *who knows* who could have just waltzed right into the dorm?" Kathryn shook her head theatrically at the implied horror of it all. One arm drifted to her side, the other inside the flap of her jacket. She heard her pulse in her ears. "Oh, and the other thing about the cash. I guess that explains why Jesse left behind a thousand-dollar laptop."

Michael's brow creased, but she continued.

"I guess you figured that because Randall was good at lying to everyone else, why couldn't he have just fibbed to you? It would have come naturally, wouldn't it? Now that he was so far away from you. So you didn't believe him when he said he was spending Thanksgiving at Eberman's house, did you? You went to Atherton, waited outside the dorm. And then the power went out and you figured out you could just go right inside. And when you actually laid eyes on Randall's roommate—God, I'll bet jealousy wasn't even the word, was it? And Randall had never mentioned him once, had he?"

Her words were arrows, but she bet they were piercing his pride and not his heart. Michael had slowly begun to close the distance between them, so she removed the pistol from her pocket and leveled it on him. He stopped and eyed the gun in her hand.

"You know about the money Jesse saved up because you threw it away. And you left the computer behind because you didn't know it was there. And when you came up with your big plan to ruin Eric Eberman's life, you made one mistake."

"I didn't come up with the plan on my own, but go ahead."

Sarcasm had left her and she was forced to draw a breath, seeing that her previously steady grip on the pistol had started to tremble. She tensed her arm.

"You didn't expect anyone to love him. And you didn't expect anyone to miss him."

"Who is it that you love?" Michael asked with unnerving calm.

"The man he became when he got away from you."

"In the three years before I saved him from the streets, he was a male prostitute," Michael remarked. "And the only way he could live was by being anything to anyone. I would hate to think you were just another customer."

"The major difference would be that I never had to buy him."

Michael rolled his eyes. "Pseudo-intellectual fortune-cookie wisdom. Is this the kind of psychobabble Atherton is filling its students' heads with these days? You were *new*, Kathryn. Fresh meat. What few friends the boy actually had he killed when he decided to toss debris from a junkyard across the railroad tracks next to his house. Don't kid yourself. Once the novelty of having a friend wore off, he would have run through you as quickly as he ran through me. And don't ruin your own life for him. Put that little toy away before I have to point out how absurd you look."

Behind her, metal slammed against metal, followed by a resonant crash. She jerked, but didn't turn. Michael jumped, and his eyes darted over her shoulder to the sound's source. As if he'd been caught stealing, he hardened his pose and returned his gaze to her. "Randall spoke highly of you. Don't ruin that."

"Get Randall now."

"Guests don't give orders."

"Now! If I'm not out of here in ten minutes with *him*, there's a guy downstairs whose going to call the cops."

"And what is he going to tell them?"

"He'll them anything he feels like!" Kathryn shouted.

Michael's eyes bolted down to her foot. She managed a quick glance without moving her head. Water ran in a thin rivulet between the marble tiles. Michael's face whitened at the sight of it. She gripped the gun harder.

"And if they don't show up fast enough he'll pull the goddamn fire alarm. And once they get here, I'll tell them about how you murdered Pamela Milford for a fucking scarf!"

Michael's veneer of composure vanished. But it wasn't the mention of murder that caused it. He was horrorstruck by something behind her. When she glanced down she saw that the water had spilled out of the grouting, sliding in a thin, advancing sheet toward Michael's planted feet.

Breathing rapidly, Michael lifted his eyes to hers. All pretense had been replaced by cold hatred.

"Is he dead?"

"Careful," Michael whispered.

"*Is he dead?*" she screamed.

But Michael just shook his head, his face like that of a tired, swollen little boy, as if waiting for her to fire the first bullet, which in her building rage she felt like doing. She was startled by the sudden cold tongues of water she felt leaking through the toes of her boots. Everything in her wanted to turn around, but she didn't dare.

"Water and wax don't mix."

"*What?*"

Michael vaulted to her, seizing her gun hand by the wrist.

She pulled the trigger, saw the bullet tear into his thigh, shred his blue jeans, and emit a red tuft. He hit the wet marble knees first, and suddenly Kathryn's entire world tilted. She heard what sounded like the explosion of a giant balloon, followed by a blast of air in the seconds before splintered-wood-turned-to-shrapnel tore a strip from the sleeve of her coat. Michael wouldn't release her wrist, so she fired again. The bullet hit marble and a geyser of white dust shot up between them.

His hands crossed over his face, he fell over backward, and she managed to right herself, finding her aim. Dizzy, she glanced toward the explosion's source. It had punched through a set of double doors, leaving splintered holes in the darkness. Water gushed from underneath the doors. Before she had time to focus on Michael, there was a second, larger explosion that sent her flying sideways over one leg. Plate glass shattered.

She hit the floor on her back, blinking madly and holding the gun to her chest. Flying plywood slammed into the chandelier overhead. Chunks of ceramic punched her chest. Dust clouded her vision, coating her lips even as she spit. Her hands were clasped, but they were lighter. She'd lost the gun.

Behind and above her, she heard a hollow impact. She barely had time to figure out that it didn't sound right. She propped herself up, eyes scanning the floor. Michael was nowhere in sight. She turned her head, about to call out for Randall, when she saw the dining table tilting like a scale as a massive chunk of tiled ceramic slid down its length. She fell into a half crouch as the chunk hit the marble in front of her, but before she could stand, the tabletop flipped and slammed into her back, driving her face into the marble and drawing in blackness at the edges of her vision.

Her head spun as she fought for consciousness. She hadn't felt her legs go lax, but now they were limp and pressed to the floor. Spitting water from her nostrils, she arched her back; the table slid several inches down and stopped. She let out a groan that was both rage and fear, but it forced her mouth back to the marble. Michael could kill her at any second and she wouldn't be able to fight. Trying to calm herself, she took several, slow deep breaths, gathering strength in the pit of her stomach. She gnashed her teeth, tensed both fists, and threw herself upward.

The table slid to the right, its edge digging into her shoulder before it tipped, flattening her right arm against the floor. Pain burned through her. She pulled her arm out, tearing her sleeve, and rolled over onto her back, drawing one bloody wrist to her chest and clamping the flowing wound with the other hand.

Overhead, the chandelier swayed gently. One shattered tentacle dangled its broken light bulbs. She got to her knees, shooting panicked glances in every direction.

No gun. No Michael.

On her feet, she sloshed through the water toward the shattered double doors. Snow drifted through the broken plate-glass windows, landing on the flotsam covering the floor.

At the double doors, she was stunned by what she saw. A giant metal stick figure had toppled, catching the basin of a utility sink on its descent, pulling pipes free from the wall and sending jets of water across the floor. Tool racks had been torn free and a barrage of sculpting tools bobbed toward her on the weakening currents flecked with melting wax. Water and wax don't mix, he'd said, and when she saw the smoldery cavities of the giant wax blocks, she realized what he'd meant. She bent down and grabbed the sharpest thing she could find, a pathetically small putty knife. Level with the overturned armature, she glimpsed the spools of bent and torn chicken wire dangling from the figure's arms. If Randall had been attached to it, he was gone now.

She spun around, the knife in front of her, but no one charged her.

Had Michael chosen to escape as well?

The apartment seemed empty and silent except for the whistle of wind through the shattered glass and the incessant gurgle of water fighting its way out. Obvious signs to get the hell out now. She backed up to the elevator doors, reaching behind her to stab the button. Then her eyes landed on the terrace. Spotlights on the sculptures chased away any shadows. She whirled, slammed one fist against the elevator doors, stabbed the button with several more punches of her trembling fingers, and turned again.

Jesse's face stared back at her.

His waxed mask had been striated by flying wood, revealing purple lips and closed eyes, the lids pale blue. Wax had been torn free, revealing several curled fingers. His dead form was elevated on a stone platform, his arms extended in what looked like a waxen embrace of the wind whipping across the terrace.

In her chest, she felt the beginning of a scream. Choked by panic and deprived of the breath it needed to get past her throat. She let out only an asthmatic wheeze. She pounded against the elevator doors. With a chime, they parted.

Michael took one step forward from the elevator and drove his fist into her stomach with enough force to send her skidding across the floor. She reared her head up off the wet marble. Fiery pain radiated out from her belly. Then she saw the syringe he held clamped in his fist.

"Come see!" He wrapped her soaked hair around one fist and tugged. She slid with him, legs kicking in protest, howling sounds that fought to be screams. Just beyond her feet, the elevator doors glided shut with a soft thud  Even as her hands clawed at the fist entangled in her hair, her fingers went sticky with blood, numbness tingling at her fingertips.

"Fast acting, isn't it? Unfortunately, its longevity leaves something to be desired. Randall's little fuck buddy out here woke up before the wax even dried. Not pleasant!"

When her head slammed into the deck door, the impact resonated through her skull without pain and she fought to keep her eyes open.

Michael squatted down gingerly next to her, slid one bulky arm under her back, and lifted her. Her vision went askew and the shattered, swaying chandelier was suddenly replaced by the sight of wind-driven clouds  Wind hit her, but no chill ran through her body.

Michael lowered her onto her knees to the snow. When her head fell forward, he righted it with a pull of her hair, and she looked up to see Jesse.

"Lend me some of your insight, Kathryn!" Michael whispered into her ear. "Just what is it about those perfectly formed pecs and that rounded bubble butt that is capable of reducing so many poor fools to their basest desires? I put my very own hands on those body parts, even enhanced them a little bit as you can see, and I still don't have the slightest clue."

Jesse's face tilted down at her placidly through her smarting tears. More wax had been torn free from his chest, and she was barely able to focus on the portion of rotted skin that revealed a glistening rib.

"You see, it's somewhat important that I find out. Because I like to familiarize myself with just why it is that those I've given so much to feel the need to betray me! This happens to be the second time I've handed over everything I've had to someone I've loved, only to find out they were going to *steal* it! Take what I gave them and run off with it."

A faint echo blurred the edges of his words and her head rolled forward. He kept his grip, but where he ripped at her hair, she felt only slight tugs that sent diffuse tickles through her scalp.

"Arrogant little fuck. Can you imagine his surprise when I told him I was Randall's father? He laughed. He laughed and he told me Randall didn't have *anyone*. I knew what he meant. Anyone but *him*. If only he hadn't been packing, I might have never been so brave!"

He dropped her. Wet snow clogged her nose. He rolled her over onto her back. Her eyes wanted to fall closed, but she managed to focus on him as he crouched over her, one hand cupping the back of her head. She tried to scream, but could only curl her mouth. Life had gone from her limbs. She didn't realize Michael was stroking her bangs from her forehead until his fingers passed over her right eye.

"Do you really think I killed Pamela Milford for a scarf? Or does that trite summation make it easier to ignore how badly Eric betrayed me? You know, he wrote me a letter afterward. Do you want to know what he told me? It was so poetic."

Her lips drifted shut.

"Of course he didn't have the courage to just ask me to forget him. He had to rely on some sloppy metaphor. The snow garden. That's what he called it. A place for people incapable of moving forward, incapable of letting go of their pain. He said it was the snow-blanketed lawn you get stuck in when you decide not to use the sidewalk. And once you're there, such memories freeze you, keeping you from the present and the future. How's that for poetry?"

His laugh sounded distant.

"*This* is my snow garden! I *make* something of my memories."

Blackness fell over the terrace.

For a brief, panicked second, Kathryn thought she had lost consciousness. Then, next to her, she saw the snow crunch under Michael's shoes as he leaped to his feet.


Downtown Manhattan turned Michael into a silhouette as he stepped through the deck door, drawing Kathryn's pistol from his pocket. With his other hand, he slid the deck door shut behind him and threw the lock. Behind him, Kathryn lay prone across the snow.

Michael walked around in the disorienting darkness, his feet splashing several steps across the floor, making sweeps with the pistol. Finally, he caught sight of Randall watching him, standing in shadow at the top of the spiral staircase, next to the fuse box he now controlled. Randall tightened his grip on the chandelier's rotary crank, but Michael stood still.

"Is she dead?" Randall called, his voice echoing on the vaulted ceiling. He didn't want to hear, but knowing the truth, if Michael told it, would make this even easier. It would be fueled less by self-preservation than the hot fire of revenge.

"Come down here and see for yourself."

Closer, you fuck, he thought. Three steps closer. "Jesse was running away," he shouted down the stairs. "And me, I don't really exist. Not on paper, at least. But what about her?"

Michael kept still, the gun aimed at Randall's shadow. "Do we really have to do this in the dark?"

"Answer me and I'll turn the fucking lights back on!" Randall roared.

There was a flash of muzzle flare. Randall threw himself against the wall, slamming the fuse box shut with his back. The bullet hit the spiral staircase with a hollow ring. His hand still held the crank, and he peeled himself off the wall just in time to see Michael charging across the dining room toward the stairs.

He yanked the crank forward with all his strength, tensed his arm, and drove it through its rotation. The chandelier twisted, bobbed, and then plummeted silently. Ceramic met marble in a bone-rattling crash. Michael's arms flew out in front of him. A shattered tentacle pinned his legs to the floor.

The resounding crash was followed by a silence punctuated by whistling wind.

"Michael?"

He was answered by throaty laughter. And a muzzle flare that lit the rafter and whistled into his chest.

He hit the wall and then carpet.

"I'm still here, Randall!" Michael howled.

Randall brought one hand to the second heartbeat of throbbing blood in his chest. He pulled himself to his feet by the rail. The pain was too unreal to care about.

"I'll be right down!" he shouted. "Just let me turn the lights on first."

Randall flipped open the box and threw every fuse with the side of his palm.

Spotlights shot to life on the terrace.

Electricity hummed and then spat as it fought its way down to the chandelier, erupting in sparks from the tattered wire.

Blue strobes lit Michael's body—his chest reared up off the floor, fell, and jerked again. One arm shot out from under his body, the other jerked and splashed against the marble. Strands of lightbulbs flickered inside the shattered ceramic cavities.

Randall watched. Michael's body gave up before the chandelier did, and after several more minutes of surging, misdirected power, the penthouse returned to darkness.

Sirens wailed in the street below.

Randall sat cross-legged in the snow, holding Kathryn's head to his bleeding chest. Light flakes filled the distance between him and Jesse's blue-veined face peering out from his tomb of wax. Kathryn gave a pained groan, managing to gather a fistful of his crimson-stained T-shirt. He released the back of her neck and her face tilted toward his.

"Kathryn?"

Her lips parted, puffed, but nothing came out other than breath. He lifted one hand from under her to smooth the damp hair from her face, and lowered his mouth to hers.

"You knew me, Kathryn," he whispered.

When their lips met, hers gave beneath the press of his, and the tip of her tongue slipped briefly inside his mouth. He held his mouth to hers for several seconds, wondering if it was the loss of blood that made his head spin and his vision blur. Slowly, he withdrew. It took him awhile to find the strength to let go of her, and when he did he took care to lay her on her back.

At the edge of the terrace sat an empty stone platform exactly like the one on which Jesse had been mounted.

Randall stepped up onto it and stared down at the view Michael had selected for him. Twenty-five stories below, fire trucks formed a parade down Second Avenue, police cars emerging from the side streets to fill the gaps between them. Tim Mathis's Jeep Cherokee was stuck in the middle of the fray. For a brief, dizzying moment, Randall pondered staying, but then the wound in his chest came back to life, pulling him out of his daze and forcing him down off the platform where he would have met his death if Kathryn hadn't come.

Back inside, he risked one last glance over his back and saw the dance of blue and red lights crawling up the walls of the surrounding buildings, and Kathryn, sleeping in the snow with Jesse standing over her, his arms extended as if at any moment he might leap down from his perch to rescue her.

# The Living Ones

## May 2005

"KATHRYN?"

Her eyes opened and shot to the clock on the nightstand, then to the sun beating against the window shade. Around its edges, slivers of light fell across the cardboard boxes alongside the bed. She groaned in protest and rolled over, her breasts pressing against the soft sweep of his chest. In response, his fingers did a cakewalk down her spine, igniting gooseflesh as they went.

"Coffee," he whispered into her ear. "And then you've got lunch in an hour."

Giving up on sleep, she lifted her head, staring up into his blue eyes, still hooded with sleep, laughing, she saw his peaked blond shock of pillow hair. She smoothed the Mohawk with one hand. He leaned over, lips grazing her cheek, nibbling a bit before he withdrew. "I don't want to make you late for your date."

"It's not a date."

"Who is it then?"

"Old friend."

"How old?" he asked, trying not to sound curious Trying to maintain his respect for the spaces in her life she silently designated as blank. She folded her arms around his back, pressing her head against his chest, trying in vain to pull his weight onto hers. He gently slid free from her embrace and she shut her eyes against the pillow, listening to him get up, lightening the bed. His bare feet padded across the carpet, knee colliding with box. He cursed and she laughed.

When she rolled onto her back, he was at the door to a walk-in closet, pulling on a T-shirt. "Black or with something?" he asked. "I know you need it. You and April set a new world record last night."

"With tears or vodka tonics?"

"Both." He turned around and raised his eyebrows to ask what she wanted.

Short and stocky, with his round, boyish face and soft features, Ken Farlan was the kind of man she never thought she would end up living with. But they had been together for the last two years of her college career. A New England boarding-school boy who'd ridden the silver chute of money and connections into Atherton, he gave frat boys a good name, and he had enough innocence not to know what he did to her when he wore nothing but a T-shirt.

Tim returned his attention to the closet. "That's what the Commencement Ball's for, I guess. Crying and vodka."

"What else was I supposed to do?" Kathryn said. "You and your Neanderthal friends were too busy staging a Macarena revival."

"It's called the chicken dance, but I'll forgive you."

"Don't you always."

Ken rounded the bed and bent down to kiss her on the cheek. She reached up to stroke his back, but before she could pull him down to the bed, he planted his palms firmly on the mattress on either side of her chest. "You and April were off in your own world. I didn't want to interrupt." He kissed her forehead. "I didn't mean to neglect you."

She smiled and cupped his chin.

The night before, with the McKinley Ballroom packed with graduates in evening gown, and black ties that loosened with each drink, April got up enough drunken courage to take Kathryn by the arm and lead her out onto the mostly empty terrace to give her a graduation gift. April watched intently as Kathryn tore open the manila envelope and tipped it: Sliding into her hand were two construction paper signs bearing the names of Randall Stone and Jesse Lowry. When Kathryn looked up, April's eyes were bloodshot.

"It's stupid, I know. It was just right after I went out and took their signs 'cause I couldn't stand the thought of some RA just coming and ripping them down, you know?" Once she noticed that Kathryn had been struck dumb, she added quickly, "I'm sorry. I mean . . . I didn't even think I was going to give them to you. Unless I got really drunk . . ."

April's alcohol-loosened sobs left her trembling. Kathryn needed several seconds before she got her wits about her and managed to hug April.

For Kathryn, the solitude that followed that night in the Bowery Tower, of holding in all the horror she had witnessed, had forced her to forget that Randall and Jesse had been known and grieved for by others.

Once she found her breath, April managed, "It's not like I was even their best friend. And it pissed me off afterward when everyone was pretending like they knew them just 'cause they'd been on the news. I didn't know either of them as well as you did. But it's like now that we're all leaving, we're leaving *them* forever. You know?"

As he stood over the bed, Ken stared down at her, curious, absently brushing hair back from her forehead with one hand "You gonna miss it?"

"Atherton?" Kathryn asked. "Hell, no. We'll be back here in a year anyway. Swigging weak drinks at some reunion while the Alumni Association tries to milk us for half our paychecks. Five whole dollars. Wow."

"That would be your paycheck, Ms. Guidance Counselor."

"That's social worker to you, asshole," she retorted with a drowsy smile.

"I meant this place," he said softly, shrugging at the room around them. "This was our first place. We have to tell our kids about it, right?"

"Don't worry. We'll find someplace worse in Seattle "

He laughed.

She swung her legs to the floor and located her bra, dangling from the bedside lamp. "Nice aim," she remarked.

"We're meeting your parents at eight."

In the closet, Ken pulled a pair of jeans up over his bare ass. "Ken!" she barked.

"What?"

"We graduated already! Enough free-balling."

"Most of the guys are doing it till the end of the week," he whined.

She rolled her eyes and shook her head.

"You spoil all my fun," he muttered as he left the room.

She snapped the hook of her bra, started scanning the debri yet-to-be-packed possessions on the floor. Dishes clattered in kitchen. "Ken?"

"Yeah?"

He was back in the doorway.

"It's Tim Mathis. The guy I'm meeting for lunch. That's who it is."

Ken nodded. "The guy who drove you that night?"

"Yeah."

She could sense his gratitude at being told and included. But the small moment allowed her to recognize how much she had left to tell him.

"Coffee," he repeated, shuffling into the kitchen.


Jean Pierre's was packed with recent graduates and their proud families. Parents debated ordering lunchtime bottles of champagne; younger siblings fidgeted and slid out of their chairs. Kathryn followed the hostess toward the wall of plate-glass windows. Sailboats cut white trails through the sun-speckled whitecaps. Across the bay, the shore was dotted with Tudor-style cottages, their windows revealed in anticipation of summer.

Tim Mathis scrambled up from his chair when he saw her, pulling his napkin off his lap at the last moment. She slowed her steps, noticing the brown leather portfolio resting against the leg of his chair. Gone was the bicycle chain he always used to wear around his neck. His peroxide hair was now a dull shade of red-brown, brushed forward and free of gelled spikes. A rumpled oxford puffed beneath a lightweight blue blazer. Almost as formal as her pleated skirt and short-sleeved top.

He took a step toward her, then stopped when he saw her extended hand, the only gesture she could offer to bridge the three years since they had last spoken to each other. "Congratulations," he said with a too-broad smile, taking her palm.

"Did you go to the ceremony yesterday?"

"I took the train up just this morning."

As she sat down across from him, focusing all of her attention on her napkin, smoothing it over her lap with too much care. "You look great," he said, his words finally drawing her eyes to his.

She nodded as if she wasn't so sure, and smiled.

"So what's next for you?"

"Seattle. My boyfriend got a job there."

Tim arched his eyebrows "What?" she asked "You thought I'd never find one?"

He forced a smile. The slight edge to her voice betrayed her suspicion that this was anything but a meeting of old friends. Tim, ever the reporter, had a mission, and when he didn't rush to fill the gap in conversation, her suspicion was confirmed.

"What does your boyfriend do?"

"Investment analysis. I know. Don't leap out of your chair."

"No. I remember. Those companies come on campus a couple months before graduation and recruit like hell."

"Not you, though," she cut in. "I've been following you. I read your piece on New York's Civil Union Law. Good stuff."

"I'll be sure to tell my editors They'd be happy to know we've expanded our demographic. Christ, take one look at our ad pages and you'd think the only ones who pick up a copy of *Ideal* are gay bon vivants with swollen bank accounts and no dependents."

She laughed appropriately and looked to the window. She was blinded by the sun. A good enough excuse to take her sunglasses out of her purse and hide her eyes from him. He clasped his water glass with both hands as she slid on her shades. "Sorry," she said. "It's bright . . ."

Now a light shade of sepia, Tim nodded. When he bent back in his chair and reached for the portfolio, she spoke. "Don't bother, Tim. I've seen it. It's not him."

Halfway to the portfolio, his arm stopped. It took him a second to settle back into his chair. "Maybe you could use a closer look."

"He had five minutes to get out of the building before it was flooded with firemen and half the NYPD. And he did. You don't really think he stopped to change his outfit and dye his hair, do you?"

"It was a big building," Tim answered, his smile bright. "The surveillance camera image was taken three days later."

"Yeah, after half the country saw his picture on TV, you expect me to believe he waltzed into the middle of a bank, in full view of the camera, and no one spotted him. I don't think so."

"Point taken," Tim said to the tablecloth.

The surrounding laughter seemed suddenly distant, and she shifted her gaze back to the window and the blue green expanse of the Atlantic visible at the mouth of the bay.

"Listen," Tim began. "I thought maybe we could talk about that night."

"You're late," she said as gently as she could. "It's been over three years. Not to mention the fact that the police held me in New York for three weeks and I never heard a peep from you. Never mind when we're both still students. Why now?"

Absorbing her challenge, he sat back in his chair as he pondered whether or not to meet it.

"You were copping to the murder of a homicidal maniac. Considering that the court of public opinion was in your favor, I didn't think you were hurting for my moral support. But let me propose a toast. To Kathryn, who had the dubious distinction of adding death-by-chandelier to the roster of murders committed in self-defense."

When she laughed, his face told her it wasn't the reaction he desired. He set his water glass back down onto the table and bent forward. "Come on, Kathryn." His voice was soft but insistent. "Ben Collins, a.k.a. Randall Stone, is still at large. And thanks to you, he isn't wanted for anything more than leaving the scene of a crime. You were the last person to see him. I thought after this long you might stop covering for him."

She kept her gaze out the window. "What are you going to call it?"

"Excuse me?"

"Your *book*, Tim. What's the title?"

"I don't know what you're—"

"Peter Lowry called me."

Tim's eyes went wide at this news: a lapse of professionalism on the part of his newfound benefactor. She looked straight at him now, fighting to keep her tone steady.

"When he stopped just short of threatening me, I told him what I'm going to tell you right now. I don't know where Randall is. And you're not going to find out. Peter Lowry can play the grieving father all he wants now that his son is dead. But something tells me that he's not throwing money at this little project of yours just because he wants the world to forget that he was a drug addict who drove his only son away."

Tim ducked the implication. "In all fairness, Peter Lowry should have a chance to set the record straight. He got raked over hotter coals than you did. His son gets butchered and the press has a field day with the drug-addict dad. And all those rumors about him molesting Jesse! Come on! The guy deserves to have his side of the story told."

"And you?"

Tim shook his head at the supposed irrelevance of the question.

"I know Randall used you the worst, Tim He slept with you because you were a reporter with access to the local paper. But you're not going to get payback. Just let it go."

The waitress arrived and Kathryn rose from her chair. "I'm not hungry. Thank you."

"Kathryn?"

"Write your book, Tim. See if he comes back to reclaim the life he left. He's free now. This is what he does best, remember?"

She slid her purse off the back of the chair. Tim glared at her. "Jesus. What is this? Friends till the bitter end? You want *me* to give up? Take your own advice."

His words sliced at the correct nerve, and she paused for a moment, holding her purse to her chest and staring down at him through her sunglasses. The phrase that visited her often before sleep, in a voice that sounded like her own but wasn't, escaped her before she could stop it.

"I knew him," she whispered

Tim furrowed his brow. Stirring to keep her composure, she turned away from the table.

"*What?*" Tim barked after her.

She waved good-bye over one shoulder.


As she turned Ken's Mercury Mountaineer onto Victoria Street, the branches shed their spring blossoms onto the windy sidewalks. She eased her foot off the gas and watched the slow passage of Eric Eberman's former house; the resurrected front lawn was lined with store-bought flowers, the windows clean sweeps of plate glass without flanking shutters.

The Elms rose in a green canopy at the end of the street.

She parked the car and fished the envelope out of the glove compartment. No return address Her name and home address in San Francisco typed across the front. Her father had given it to her at graduation the day before, and she had forced herself to wait for some compromise between the right moment and the most private one to open it.

The Elms was harder to navigate when the trees weren't stripped of their leaves by winter. She made her way to the sound of water splashing against rock, and came to the small, stone bridge passing over the drainpipe. Elm leaves caught the sunlight as she moved carefully along the bank. Inverness Creek flowed generously in eddies of black water funneled by its muddy walls. She found no spot in particular and took a seat, letting her legs dangle over the five-foot drop as she tore the envelope open.

A pearl had been affixed to an index-size note card with three strands of Scotch tape laid out in a protective cross. Glued right below was a white slip of paper cut from the page of a book, each sentence meticulously highlighted in yellow.

> The pearl is the symbol of those souls who remain
> trapped within the mud of the material world. Imprisoned
> by their bodies and their flesh, they somehow manage to
> remain spiritually alive. Cathars referred to those souls as
> the living ones.

She read the words written in ink below.

Happy Graduation

Love, Randall
(because he's the one
who learned how)

After several minutes, she brought the card to her chest and held it to the place where the ache Randall had left behind throbbed most acutely—when she paused too long at a stoplight, or searched for sleep. She held it there until she was no longer stanching an open wound, just protecting a gift from the sudden gusts of wind that drove life skyward to the branches overhead.

# Acknowledgments

Two opposing texts on the work of Hieronymus Bosch proved critical in informing the fictional speculations of Dr. Eric Eberman. In *Hieronymus Bosch: Between Heaven and Hell* (Benedikt Taschen Verlag, 1987), art history professor Walter Bosing makes a brief and compelling argument against the popular twentieth-century tendency to interpret Bosch's work with modern-day psychology, which could not possibly have informed the painter's medieval mindset. In *The Secret Heresy of Hieronymus Bosch* (Floris Books, 1995), Lynda Harris lays out an exhaustively researched argument that Bosch's work was truly laced with codings of heresy that strongly indicate an artist who was influenced by heretical, primarily Catharistic, beliefs.

Eric Eberman's speculations regarding the true nature of the Brethren of the Free Spirit are an imaginative leap on my part. The true origins of Bosch's inspiration are subject to a seemingly endless debate. So far the debate has proved only that lovers of Bosch's work are desperate to find some scholarly basis to their own, often visceral, reactions to it. As a result, many conclusions are informed as much by psychological longing as by hard research. This strange marriage informs the sometimes irresponsible interpretations of both Eric Eberman and Mitchell Seaver.

I am indebted to my father, Stan Rice, for helping to reacquaint me with the administrative mechanisms of a large university campus, and Dr. Mark Lerner, for assisting me in accurately representing Boston's suburbs. Any errors are mine and not theirs.

Jonathan Burnham and David Groff shined light into the dark portions of my first draft. The entire team at Talk Miramax Books continues to astound me with their focus, accessibility and compassion; special thanks to Kristin Powers, Kathy Schneider, and Hilary "Fierce" Bass. My agent, Lynn Nesbit, deserves too many thanks for one page. Because *The Snow Garden* was written during a period of personal transition, I'm compelled to thank a special group of people who might not know how invaluable their support was: Brandy Pigeon, Sid Montz, Jeff Morrone, Brian Sibberell, Spencer Doody, Jay Marose and Julia DiGiovanni.

# CHRISTOPHER RICE

## A Density of Souls

PAN BOOKS £6.99

In the brooding milieu of New Orleans, four friends are about to discover the fragile boundaries between loyalty and betrayal. Once inseparable, Meredith, Brandon, Stephen and Greg enter high school only to learn that their friendship cannot withstand the envy and rage of adolescence. Their individual struggles are fuelled by the generations of family feuds and furtive passions hoarded within their opulent Garden District homes, and soon two violent deaths disrupt the core of this closeted society.

Five years later, the former friends are drawn back together as new facts about their mutual history are revealed and what was once held to be a tragic accident is discovered to be murder. As the true story emerges, long-kept secrets begin to unravel and the casual cruelties of high school develop into acts of violence that threaten to destroy an entire community.

*A Density of Souls* marks a stunning debut and its series of shocking twists will leave you reeling. Bold, compelling and haunting, this is American Gothic in a new and intriguing guise.

'*Less than Zero* meets Donna Tartt spiced with Stephen King'
**New York Magazine**

# ANDREW PYPER

## Lost Girls

PAN BOOKS  £6.99

Criminal defence lawyer Bartholomew Crane is despatched to a small lakeside town in northern Ontario with a brief to defend a schoolteacher accused of murdering two teenaged girls. He assumes it will be an open and shut case and that he'll be back carousing in Toronto before the month is out, because the girls' bodies have never been found and the Crown's evidence against the teacher is scant. But the deeper Barth digs into the teacher's – and the town's – past, the more unnerved he becomes.

Peculiar visions haunt his imagination: telephones ring ceaselessly in the dead of night; the gargoyles above his hotel's entrance seem to be watching him; and sometimes, out of the furthest corner of his eye, he can see two identically dressed girls following him wherever he goes . . . Is his mind playing tricks on him? Has Barth been dragged into the town's collective hysteria? Or is there something altogether more sinister at play?

'Think *The Shining* mixed with *The Sixth Sense.*
A truly scary ghost story that will have you turning
the pages late into the night.'
***Maxim***

## OTHER BOOKS

## AVAILABLE FROM PAN MACMILLAN

**CHRISTOPHER RICE**
A DENSITY OF SOULS          0 330 48933 X          £6.99

**ANDREW PYPER**
LOST GIRLS                  0 330 39040 6          £5.99
THE TRADE MISSION           0 330 39041 4          £6.99

**CHRIS NILES**
HELL'S KITCHEN              0 330 48292 0          £5.99

All Pan Macmillan titles can be ordered from our website,
www.panmacmillan.com, or from your local bookshop
and are also available by post from:

**Bookpost, PO Box 29, Douglas, Isle of Man IM99 1BQ**
Credit cards accepted. For details:
Telephone: 01624 836000
Fax: 01624 670923
E-mail: bookpost@enterprise.net
www.bookpost.co.uk

*Free postage and packing in the United Kingdom*

Prices shown above were correct at the time of going to press.
Pan Macmillan reserve the right to show new retail prices on covers
which may differ from those previously advertised in the text
or elsewhere.